Long Gone, Come Home

"...nce, family, and ambition... In Birdie, Chenault-Kilgore has created an unforgettable heroine whose resilience and determination will resonate long after you finish reading."

—**Bryn Turnbull, internationally bestselling author of** *The Last Grand Duchess*

"A heart-filled tale about a young woman willing to sacrifice it all for love and family. Set against the background of the Great Depression and Jim Crow, Chenault-Kilgore's debut tugs every emotion as Birdie fights to make a way out of no way."

—**Kaia Alderson, author of** *Sisters in Arms*

"A poignant and powerful debut novel... Monica Chenault-Kilgore has penned a sweeping, poetic story of love and family told through the eyes of a courageous and unforgettable heroine."

—**Chanel Cleeton,** *New York Times* **and** *USA TODAY* **bestselling author of** *Our Last Days in Barcelona*

"An extraordinary tale of resilience and determination... *Long Gone, Come Home* takes us on a journey of the 1930s jazz era and civil rights movement through the eyes of a tenacious and unforgettable heroine. Birdie's enduring story is one of love, loss, family and survival... I was blown away by this powerful, heart-wrenching and ultimately hopeful debut!"

—**Eliza Knight,** *USA TODAY* **bestselling author of** *The Mayfair Bookshop*

"Nuanced and atmospheric, this is a story of people pursuing big dreams amid great injustice, and ultimately realizing the value of family and the enduring power of love."

—**Kristin Beck, author of** *The Winter Orphans*

"A remarkable story wonderfully told...with a wealth of captivating characters in a story about relationships, identity, struggles, and the heartbreak and joys of a Black woman and her family... Birdie is unforgettable—from page one, this complicated young woman grabs hold and doesn't let go until the last sentence."

—**Denny S. Bryce, bestselling author of** *Wild Women and the Blues*

LONG GONE, COME HOME

MONICA CHENAULT-KILGORE

GRAYDON
HOUSE

GRAYDON
HOUSE®

Recycling programs
for this product may
not exist in your area.

ISBN-13: 978-1-525-80476-2

Long Gone, Come Home

Graydon House
22 Adelaide St. West, 41st Floor
Toronto, Ontario M5H 4E3, Canada
www.GraydonHouseBooks.com
www.BookClubbish.com

Printed in U.S.A.

For my mother, Olivia

I love you

LONG GONE, COME HOME

WE ALL FLY HOME

A wonderful plan
Taking the road through tall trees
To the scarlet sun

Worries tossed aside
Twisting and floating on air
Dancing in the wind

The path is littered
Seasons gather at our feet
Courageously ours

Passing through water
Seeking the deepest river
Beyond its riches

I'll swim up to you
Your arms encircle my waist
Dripping wet we kiss

We travel away
Over dry stones in the road
Losing each other

Then we all fly home
Where alone and together
Our love lingers still

More often than not, life whisked men away from my family. Life was war in far-off lands or murderous mobs with rifles and rope riding up to a front door. Life was easy money from criminal acts which always ended badly. Life even snatched away those men who, with the best intentions, left Kentucky farm towns for better paying work up north or out west. They rarely came back.

My sisters' father died when I was too young to remember. All that was left to remember him was a faded picture of a tall, slender, shiny black man dressed in uniform and a medal of ribbon and bronze with something written in French. Mama kept them in her drawer under English linen. She told us he fought with France during the Great War and when he returned home, the church folks hoisted him up with pride.

Within two years of coming home, his body was found hanging from a tree down by the Kentucky River Lock and Dam. Ghosts must've risen from the water to hang him because no one was ever convicted of his murder.

When we spoke of him, which wasn't often, I would call him Daddy. Eventually I learned he was not my real father. Ghosts must've got my father too. No matter who I asked, I never received an explanation of where my father came from or where he went. Mama would just say my father was pretty, followed by a "just like you." After a while, I stopped asking.

PART ONE

The road through tall trees

To the scarlet sun

CHAPTER ONE

Mt. Sterling, Kentucky

1936

Broken bits of sunlight pierced through the high-arching trees forming a patchwork carpet along the dirt road. In the distance, an amazingly old wagon was being pulled by a horse that was just as ancient. Birdie Autumn Jennings watched the slow-moving horse and wagon while shielding her eyes against the sudden burst of sun that pushed its way through tree branches. Yellow clouds of dust rose each time the horse's hooves hit the dirt. The air filled with the scent of moist clay and fresh grass which grew stronger as the wagon approached.

Is that Bucky? How can that old horse still be alive?

As a little girl Birdie would ride in the back of that very same wagon to and from a one-room schoolhouse. It was the sole mode of transportation for her, her two sisters and every other brown child in the farming community on the outskirts of Mt. Sterling. The families who were determined their children get a proper education paid a nickel for them to ride the wagon to and from the school that stayed open throughout most of the year, unlike the nearby state school that only had classes around crop schedules.

Watching the plodding horse and wagon draw near, sensations of her childhood returned. Birdie could almost feel the sudden fits and jerks of the wagon as it moved over the undisciplined road. She remembered how the motion and the heaviness of the heat in the early summer lulled her and the other children into dreamland. She could almost see bobbing heads, tight curly hair covered with a dusting of fine yellow dirt and crisp white ribbons tied around thick braids. She could feel the tips of her eyelashes, sparkling with silt, brushing against shiny, sunburned cheeks and the warmth of her best friend curled up beside her.

As the wagon passed, there were no children riding in the back. Bucky, with his massive gray head swinging low, hauled what looked like high piles of burley tobacco and a few overflowing sacks of new soybeans.

"Ugh… I hate this place. It's so damn countryfied," she whispered with a whiff of superiority. "That poor, old horse. You'd think they'd have a truck by now."

A sharp stone cut through the sole of her shoe and abruptly reminded her of the fact that she had to get to work.

"Damn, maybe I should have taken the bus to Wrights."

At sixteen, Birdie had to put school behind her, at least for the season. For many of the families in the small farming community on the outskirts of Mt. Sterling, Kentucky, things had gone from bad to worse to unstable financially. Everyone who could work took jobs at larger farms, factories or wherever they could to help keep a roof over their heads. The Jennings household, consisting of Birdie, her mother and two sisters was no different. To do their part, Birdie and her older sisters, Chicky and Bessa, worked full-time tying tobacco at Wrights Tobacco Company. Her mother promised the three girls that they would return to their education by the following year and ultimately be college bound.

Birdie's mother, whom everyone called Mama, came from a long line of lone women who took no tea for the fever. When circumstances dictated, problems were faced head-on, without tears or hesitation. Slightly disappointed about the detour from her academic studies, Birdie took it in stride knowing without question that Mama's directive, along with her promise, would be the path the family needed to tread until they got back on their feet.

The unfinished end of the alley behind Birdie's house led directly to Wrights. With a brisk pace, it was the cheapest and fastest way to get there outside of a bus ride which required a transfer to a crosstown line. Now, despite the pain in her foot, Birdie had to walk with a real purpose to get to work on time. She couldn't be late again. They would absolutely fire her if she came in a minute after the shift started. She pulled her purse and rumpled lunch bag closer to her and picked up the pace.

Every day the supervisor made it plain that she, along with just about any other woman working there, wasn't wanted. It was a miracle she was even able to get this job. There was always a threat the boss would give her job away to a man. Every day she'd hear the supervisor's backhanded threat, "You doing good, gal, but I just can't rectify in my mind us paying you gals to do this work. Too many of you women out here taking these jobs away from hardworking men who got to feed their families. Pretty or not, all you gals are nothing but distractions. Y'all keeping our men from doing their work an' lowering productivity."

He never missed an opportunity to lean in close to Birdie and say in the slowest countrified drawl imaginable, "If it wasn't for them carpetbaggers and troublemakers threatening to march on Washington, you gals, 'specially you colored ones, wouldn't even be here. They were watching out for you alright. You better be glad of it."

Birdie did her best to stay as far away from him as possible but for the most part didn't think anything of his comments. He said something nasty like that to all the women, black or white, who worked just as hard as the men stemming, rolling and tying tobacco leaves. Whenever the supervisor came around to supposedly inspect their work, Birdie kept her head down, eyes on her apron, and kept pulling tobacco leaves away from their stems. She was careful not to lose count of her stems to make sure at the end of any given day no one could argue whether or not she earned her pay.

When Birdie started at Wrights, the office manager sternly told her that they would be keeping an eye on her and if she wanted to stay at Wrights, she'd have to meet production standards each and every day. As the new girl she would only be paid by the amount of leaves she could process instead of earning an hourly wage like the other workers. Birdie brought home ten dollars and eighty cents a week. Somehow the local businesses were able to skirt the federal laws and pay whatever they wanted.

Mildred, one of the few other colored women who worked in the finishing and packaging room, made twenty-seven cents an hour for her swollen, aching hands and stinging nostrils— even though some colored men who worked alongside her made thirty-three cents and it was said that most of the white men in the same room made thirty-eight cents an hour. A small price to pay for the opportunity to work ten hours a day and bring in a paycheck, no matter how unbalanced the scale, for bread and milk. Waves of workers came from as far as three counties over for a chance to work the early harvests of burley and bright tobacco despite being underpaid for the dizziness and vomiting that so many suffered after only a few days on the job. Most were only a generation removed from being nurtured from the land as farmers and had learned to work for today while keeping fervent hope for a better future. The tobacco business was booming and there should have been jobs for a lot more men and women in the area. But too many times there was a sign tacked on the doors of factories and plants all over Kentucky and beyond that read "Help Wanted. White Only."

However, despite the daily bruising, today the threats, monotony and drudgery didn't matter. Birdie ignored all the nuisances of the day because tonight held the promise of fun and excitement. She just wanted to get through the day so she could clock out, go home and get ready for her long-awaited night. Tonight was to be a monumental event for all of Mt. Sterling. A grand music concert led by one of the most popular big band leaders on the hit parade was performing at the Paramount Theater. Birdie hummed throughout the day to keep her mind off her pacing supervisor and on the fun time ahead.

Mama had given the rarest of blessings that Birdie could go to the concert with her sister Chicky. Mama, a staunch member of Second Christian Church, allowed her girls to go unescorted despite knowing that talk from neighbors would focus on Birdie, just shy of seventeen and considered too young to attend any music concert outside church—it could lead to unchristian-like behavior. So, Mama's blessing came with the strictest warning of time and correctness. Chicky was to keep an eagle eye on her little sister at all times and there was a promise of hellfire-to-come if they didn't get home at the exact tick of the tock as instructed.

Mama recognized that her daughters worked hard to contribute to the family income. She probably thought they earned the treat. This was a once-in-a-lifetime concert that was as close to a big-city event as many folks in Mt. Sterling would ever see. Birdie saved as much as she could to buy something to wear and pay the fifty-cent admission, a feat that certainly contributed to charming Mama into letting her go. She couldn't wait to show up at the Paramount in her new rose-red dress, accented with cute shirred sleeves and a flared hem that gave it the ability to swing along with the jazzy sounds. By the end of day, Birdie practically ran home on the tips of her toes.

Although they could have walked into town, Birdie and Chicky took the bus so as not to sweat out their freshly pressed hair and clothes or muddy up their shoes. From a block away, the Paramount Theatre was transformed, with its old ornate marquee shining like a beacon among a dull string of buildings. The theater was magnetic, attracting practically everyone from the four corners of the tri-county. Mama and their older sister, Bessa, who chose to stay home with her nose in a book, must have been the only Mt. Sterling residents not swirling around the theater.

By the time the girls entered the theater the band was in full swing. Only a few were sitting in the fancy red velour seats. Young people packed the front of the stage as many more wriggled their way from the lobby doors down the aisles hoping to squeeze into a space in the crowd. The front of the balcony was no different. There was a line of daring people leaning dangerously over the rail without a care of potential jeopardy.

"Oooo..." Birdie squeezed her excitement through her teeth. She stood in front of her seat and spun around, taking in the vibrant colors of the band and audience against the cavernous movie house's gold and red velvet grandeur. She closed her eyes and inhaled a mixture of perfume and rose water, face powder, sweet hair pomade and a trace of freshly pressed hair. Birdie let the scent and the music fill her up. The music was electrifying, and her body couldn't help but bounce along with the syncopated beat. This was supposed to be a dignified sit-down concert, but the crowd wanted no parts of a refined affair. They were behaving like the Paramount was a rowdy night club. A gyrating jitterbugging crew broke out in front of the stage and in the aisles. Arms and legs were flying everywhere as the growing throng of dancers swung about without a care of the proximity of any other humans. Even the roped-off "whites only" section rippled in response to the thumping jazz music. The section's patrons bounced along without any regard to the color line.

Edward Kennedy "The Duke" Ellington and his Washingtonians were here for a rare stop this side of Louisville. The concert was billed as his all-star traveling orchestra, a smaller band than the original, but the sound was bigger than Birdie could ever have imagined. The band started out playing "It Don't Mean a Thing," then a new tune called "Caravan," where every instrument cried out with a sound that wound around the hall with hypnotic snakelike charm. The Maestro exuded immense charm as he nodded to band members to pluck them out for solos while smiling at the crowd.

It would be an insult not to show the fine tan king of jazz her appreciation by swinging to every note, chord and lyric he created. Sitting was impossible. If you wanted to catch sight of the smiling Duke and, particularly, if you wanted to be seen by him, as Birdie hoped, you had to stand, tippy toe hop and crane your neck to see above the crowd. Everyone in front was up on their toes trying to get a good view of the Duke and his musicians.

Birdie scanned the theater. Chicky had disappeared from

her side and was nowhere in sight. A half hour ago, Chicky said she was going to the ladies' room, but she hadn't returned. Without her sister's threats of reporting her every movement, Birdie felt free to move from her seat and stretch out in the aisle with the rest of the bopping dance rebels. Her heart was jumping out of her chest, ready to take its own spin on the dance floor.

Watching couples in the aisle, Birdie looked for a dance partner. She wasn't brave or bold enough to join the writhing group gathered at the band's feet alone. She was taught at home and in church that the proper thing to do would be to wait until she was asked to dance, but these boys were taking way too long!

Through the fog of excitement, she heard a deep voice from behind. "Hey, lil' suga', you look like you wanna dance."

She turned to see the tobacco-tarnished palm of a large, knobby hand. It led up to a thin-faced man with sparkling clear brown eyes and a smile that stretched across his face. His slicked-back hair glistened in the light. Birdie had never seen him before, but it really didn't matter who he was. She jumped into motion. She had to dance and didn't want to waste one minute.

Birdie followed her new dance partner down the aisle to the one open space close to the elevated stage. They squeezed in to join the other unrestrained couples dancing the jitterbug, the shag, a loosely formed big apple and a few truly liberated folks doing the Lindy hop. In the seats, she could see heads leaning together, eyes darting back and forth and lips flapping. Birdie knew somebody was going to say something to some other old biddy and word would get back to Mama that she was making a fool of herself for the whole world to see. She could hear it now: *Who would let that young girl dance like that with that old man?* Both she and Chicky, most likely, would get an earful as soon as they hit the door. She didn't care and allowed herself to be spun around to the blare of the horns and hopping rhythm. Besides, everything and everyone from the rafters to the floor was swinging.

Whoever this man was, he was good. The wide smile never left his face as they danced in the narrow spot. As the music peaked, he jumped high in the air and the tail of his jacket flew up even higher. Birdie couldn't help but follow. Jumping up, her skirt took flight, rising to reveal the tan skin of her thighs above her stockings. He reached for her hand at just the right time to spin her forward, then back and then under his arm where they stepped side by side. He swung his hand around, guiding her to dip, twirl and take two steps backward so smoothly they looked as though they rehearsed the entire routine. He gently placed a hand at her back then around her waist to pull her closer to him. Birdie let out an *"Oooh yeah"* and matched his steady smile. He didn't even break a sweat while she and the whole theater caught fire. Once the band blasted the final chord, all souls within the vicinity slowed down to take a breath.

Still holding on to her hand, he said, "Hey, little mama, I'm Jimmy. What's your name?"

A little out of breath and suddenly shy, Birdie pulled her hand back. "They call me Birdie."

"They? Who's they? Can I call you that?" His smile broadened. Without waiting for a response, he added, "Well, lil' Bird, I can see you know what you're doing on the dance floor, and you look good doing it too. Would you like something to cool you down?"

Birdie nodded and fanned her face with her hand as she moved toward the back of the theater. She could feel the eyes that followed her down the aisle had multiplied and now followed her up the aisle. Even though her head was still in the clouds, she could almost hear her name bubbling up from the mouths of the straight-backed spectators. Some folks had no shame staring directly at her with *I'm going to tell* or *Girl, I know your mama* looks. Some even snickered, covered their mouths with their hands or waved pointed fingers in the air to mark their words. Birdie knew what their stories were going to be as soon as she began dancing with the strange man.

"Them mad old ruffled hens need to mind their own business," she thought aloud.

She returned her focus to her dance partner who was only two feet ahead of her. There was something about his back and shoulders, and the cool, commanding stride that held her gaze. Mesmerized, she followed. He held his head high and only once did he turn to see if she was still behind him. It was as though he knew she would be there.

In the lobby, Jimmy bought two Coca-Colas from the concession stand and handed her one.

"Dancing as hard as you do, I thought you might need this. You sure you're old enough to be out here with me?"

Birdie took the drink and immediately started sipping.

"You're welcome, Miss Birdie," he said in a singsong voice. "You're a miss right? You're a little too young for anything else. Am I right?"

"Oh. Thank you. So, Jimmy, I've never seen you around here before. Where are you from?"

"I'm from all over the place, darlin'. But you could say I grew up in Louisville. I'm staying out this way with a friend of mine while working over here at Wrights."

"Really? Wrights? I work there too. How come I've never seen you before?"

"I've been working there a little over two months. You probably haven't seen me 'cause I'm generally in the grading room working alongside the supervisor. Sometimes I'm on the truck going out to the farms. But I've seen you. Who's that always with you, that skinny dark-skinned girl who's always talking with her nose in the air? She your sister?"

Birdie, suddenly annoyed at the mention of her sister, thought, *Who is he, this backwoods hick, to be talkin' about my sister like that?*

She finished her cola in one long sip. From behind the doors of the auditorium, muted music rose to a crescendo and taunted her to return to the safety of her seat. Out of the corner of her eye she saw Chicky marching toward her. Chicky's eyes shifted from Birdie to Jimmy. Without even saying hello to Jimmy, Chicky grabbed Birdie's arm and jerked her back toward the theater.

Birdie mechanically followed her sister and turned back to see Jimmy leaning against the wall laughing.

"Chicky, get off of me! Where you been all this time? I've been looking all over for you."

Chicky shot back, "Naw, girl, you ain't been looking for me. I already heard you were showing your ass in front of everyone with that man. Girl, if Mama catches a word of what happened here, we're gonna get it—especially you, Miss Fast-tail!"

Chicky leaned in and whispered loudly, "Do you know that man? You know how those church hens love to talk and you just gave them some gristle to gnaw on. Lord knows they'll twist it around just to hide the fact they were bouncing their ungodly fat asses off them seats. Those hypocrites will be chewing on your foolishness for a long, long time. You betta know it, girl."

When the sisters burst through the doors of the auditorium, no one showed them the least bit of interest. The captivated audience had all eyes on the smiling Duke and the swinging Washingtonians. The band was on a smooth, melodic hit called

"Cotton." A few showboating big spenders took their time snaking their way up to the stage to shower heavy half dollar coins at the feet of the Maestro and his musicians. As each coin hit the wooden floor, the crowd clapped and cheered. It was obvious the crowd was entranced by the ebb and flow of the melody and more interested in paying homage to the jazz Adonis than gossiping about Birdie's exposed underwear.

Birdie smoothed down her hair, faced her sister and spoke calmly. "First of all, Chicky, you ain't saying nothing or doing anything. Now, fix your blouse because you got it buttoned up all kinds of crazy. I didn't see you anywhere around, so you must have been out with your boyfriend, Clarence, that Mama knows nothing about. And what happened to your hair, sis? That wasn't the style you came out the house with. I'll just have to tell Mama that instead of you watching me, like you were supposed to do, you were somewhere with that one stocking rolling down your leg and nowhere to be found."

"Why do you always have to be such a little bitch!" Chicky said as she stomped off. Birdie guessed her sister was actually going to the ladies' room this time to fix her appearance.

After leaving Jimmy unceremoniously in the theater lobby Birdie never saw her only dance partner for the rest of the evening. When the last note trailed off, the sweat-drenched, high-swinging dancers spun around for the very last time, and the fine band leader waved his hand to motion the musicians to take their last bows, Birdie and Chicky hightailed it out of the Paramount to make sure they reached home at the exact promised moment.

They ran home in fear and anticipation of hearing some backlash from Mama and were relieved when they managed to get through the door without interrogation—but they knew nothing stayed hidden for long in Mt. Sterling. Some twisted version of whatever was done in the dark would come to light in record-breaking speed. Stories grew as fast as tobacco and were carried with the same lingering stink. Tales of impropriety regularly fell out of the mouths of the most respectable town members while sitting in the pews of the A.M.E., First or Second Baptist, Methodist, Pentecostal, or whatever churches in the town. Both Birdie and Chicky knew they were in for a night of restless sleep because the silence that met them at the door tonight only meant their behavior would surely be the topic of conversation over cereal and coffee the next morning.

CHAPTER TWO

As usual, Saturday started early. Bessa left just as the sun was rising to get to work at her part-time job at the pharmacy and would be home before Birdie's cereal went cold. Mama had baking orders to fill. Mama baked and cooked for families in and around Mt. Sterling. It was her pride and joy to have a hand in nourishing just about everyone around. The girls sat quietly at the table while Mama buzzed about cracking eggs and creaming together butter and sugar.

"Well? You two are too quiet for having gone out on the town last night."

Mama plowed on. "Well, how was it? Did you like it? I would've thought both of you would be over the moon excited about the show. It must have been something spectacular. Most folks around here don't get an opportunity to go to a big event like this so young. To see a famous, big-named musician like that and all y'all can do is stare into your Cream of Wheat?"

Chicky spoke first. "Mama, the Duke and his musicians were so handsome. Every single one of them was clean and fine, and dressed to the nines. Some of the young folks were jumping up like crazy. It was as if we were at a dance hall contest."

Birdie shot Chicky a sideways glance. Mama raised an eyebrow. "People were dancing? What kind of dancing? Were they hopping around crazy like some kinda fool or something?"

This was what both Chicky and Birdie were trying to avoid, but it was too late. No stopping it now. Birdie could tell they were on the verge of getting a boring lecture or something worse. While attacking the poor ingredients in her bowl, Mama asked, "And you, Miss Bird...did you like the music too? Were you out in that theater concert jitterbugging or whatever they call it with Eh-Verr-Re-Body?"

Up to this point, Birdie had made no eye contact with her mother. She kept her head down pretending to examine each kernel of her breakfast cereal. To avoid having her mother ask a second time, and she didn't want her to ask a second time, Birdie peeked up from her bowl.

"Mama, it was so hot in that theater. People were all dressed in the latest but were drenched in sweat. Mr. Ellington was good but he's no Fletcher Henderson."

Birdie tried her best to divert her mother's focus. Old-timey piano player Fletcher Henderson was Mama's favorite. She wanted to get her mother talking about him and away from digging for last night's news.

"The music was a little too slow for me. Oh, I saw Mr. and Mrs. Brown. Mrs. Brown looked so nice. They told me to tell you hello," Birdie added.

Chicky saw this exchange as an opportunity to jump ship. When Mama turned her back to fill cake pans, Chicky quietly pushed back her chair, and announced in a loud whisper that she had to go get her hair done. Without anyone to help deflect, Birdie continued, "Mama, let me help you with those cakes."

Mama paused. "Hmmm…yes, little girl. I think you're going to have to help me all day today…maybe for the rest of the week."

There was no way out. Birdie resigned herself to being stuck at her mother's side for the rest of the day. She was given the chores of making dressed eggs for the church dinner and getting rolls started for Miss Pam, one of Mama's oldest customers. While scooping yellow egg yolks into a bowl, her mind ventured back to last night's music and her only turn on the dance floor. She thought about her dance partner, the back of his neck and the way his jacket moved over his body as he glided in front of her.

He was kinda nice and handsome. He really could dance. Where did he say he was from? Was it Louisville or Lexington? I never got his last name. I could ask my aunts in the Russell section of Louisville but without his last name… I'll ask the cousins instead. They might be able to shed some light on him with just a description…

"Girl, watch what you're doing!" Mama's voice cut through Birdie's thoughts. "You're pushing too much filling in those eggs. You got that paprika all over the place. I gotta take some of those eggs over to Miss Pam and you know she'll work to find fault with everything so she don't have to pay me.

"Bird, please pay attention! Don't think you gonna get out of this kitchen by purposely trying to be messy. That music you heard last night is going to be your last for a while, so you better get used to looking at this kitchen. I heard that brand-new little red skirt of yours was swinging all over the place. You ain't too cute today, missy."

Birdie sighed. This was going to be torture! Generally, she

didn't mind being Mama's main helper. She loved watching and helping her mother cook, bake and prepare for parties. Preparing food for an event always created a sense of excitement. Birdie admired her mother's precision in everything she did. When she shouted out instructions for shaping chicken salad tea sandwiches, fixing the spoonbread, or adding a gloss to pie crusts or cobblers it was all to make things just right. Today, however, all Birdie wanted to do was be alone in the room she shared with her sisters, reading about space aliens in *Amazing Stories* magazine or adventuresome and witty detectives in *Ten Detective Aces* magazine. She wanted to drift away with scandalous stories about movie stars in the *Photoplay* and *Movie Life* magazines she borrowed from one of the girls from Wrights and had hidden under her bed. The beautiful actresses that graced the covers were magical in her mind. The starlets looked out from the page, some demurely, others with rouged red lips slightly parted, and alluring eyes promising a view to unapproachable femininity.

Birdie was enchanted by them and spent countless hours imagining she was living their glamorous lives with rhinestone hair clips matching the diamonds and rubies gracing her décolletage. She would love nothing more than the luxury of lying on her bed, examining each page of the magazine hoping for a photograph or a piece of gossip about the beautiful Oscar Micheaux race movie starlets like Nina Mae McKinney, Freddie Washington or Dorothy Van Engle who were just as big to her as the milky white actresses she saw on every page.

A sudden knock on the front door was the rescue Birdie was looking for. A man and woman appeared at the screen door. They were a mismatched couple. The man was fair complexioned and as round as he was tall. The woman was deep brown, tall and skinny. A huge pocketbook dangled from her wrist as she cradled a stack of papers in her arms. Her face was serious and stern where his was comically full of big white teeth. As Mama approached the door, he spoke first. "Good morning, ma'am. Is there a man of the house?"

Mama responded curtly, "No. No need for one at the moment. May I help you, sir?"

The round man blushed. "Do you have a minute, sister? We're from the Good Neighbor League and would like to leave you with information about the beneficial New Deal programs our president Franklin Delano Roosevelt has provided to elevate us black people over the last four years. I don't know if you're Republican or Democrat but we hope that you can see the benefits of voting, and voting Democrat this election."

Mama sighed, wiped her hands on her apron and opened the screen door to let them in. Once seated, Mama ordered Birdie to fetch coffee for the visitors. In the small house whatever anyone said or did in the front of the house could be heard and seen in the back. Birdie listened from the kitchen as the woman spelled out in a slow country drawl that twenty-five thousand young colored men had found jobs through the National Youth Administration and the Civilian Conservation Corps. Also, the Works Progress Administration provided earnings for over one million colored families. The fat man chimed in, "Yes, that's right! Let Jesus lead you and Roosevelt feed you!"

Birdie continued listening in until their words disintegrated to a monotonous hum. Mama was sitting politely, leaning slightly toward the unexpected guests. Political talk was boring, and Birdie couldn't wait until either Landon or President Roosevelt was elected so both parties would stop bothering everybody by making promises. It didn't matter much to her. Mama had an opinion and spoke firmly on the subject.

Birdie could just about hear her mother's eyes rolling in

her head before she said, "I was there. I saw some of them so-called Democrats ride through towns with white sheets covering their heads. I've seen those Klan boys setting fires and wreaking havoc on families all through here. We need to do everything we can to stand up to them. But also, what have the Republicans done for us lately? They're always quick to tell us that they are the party of Lincoln, like he was our white savior dropped down from heaven. Of course, we are all better for it and appreciate what that Republican president did, but black folks have had to work extra hard to get where we are today. I know old folks with scars on their backs that still ache from whips. I also know some folks who don't have any physical scars from those times. They are scarred nonetheless from not being able to work and eat just because they skin is black. We've done good things, thank you Jesus, despite our men, and women too, being hung from a tree. Where are the Republicans on that? And where were they when they hung that Rainey fellow in front of thousands of smiling, happy white folks right here over in Owensboro? They didn't give his black attorneys no help. If they would have given him some backin' maybe that boy wouldn't have been hung like that."

The tall woman quickly interjected, "Yes, sister, that's why we're here today as representatives of the Colored Voters Division and the Women's Committee of the Democratic Party. We're here to tell you that the Democrats today are doing all they can to let you know all the good things Roosevelt continues to do for us and our country."

"I do like what President FDR has done so far," Mama continued, "and I really like that wife of his, First Lady Eleanor. I just don't know what to do. But you know something? It ain't nobody's business who I'm voting for and, no offense to you, I guess I'm gonna keep it that way."

While they continued to talk in the front room, Birdie

stared out the back door. She closed her eyes while the hum of the conversation floated out and evaporated into the heavy air. She lifted her head to the sun and pushed open the screeching screen door, stepping out onto the small porch that overlooked a patch of backyard and beyond, a dirt alleyway. Birdie walked past the garden where a few collards were unleashing new leaves. She stopped at the fence, where two scrawny dogs were in the alleyway, circling the ground, sniffing at the dirt.

A group of men strolled down the alley. They were probably going off to work at Wrights. The men were loud, speaking in bursts of short sentences of no more than three or four words. She heard another group of men farther down that were either shooting dice or playing three card tricks on the side of a garage. The climbing scale of their voices made her think about the music, dancing and wild crowd at the Paramount. Mostly, they reminded her of Jimmy and the image of his coattails flying high in the air.

Maybe he's down there. Was that his voice mixed in with the voices just now? The far-fetched idea grabbed hold of Birdie's curiosity and led her out the gate toward the intensified cursing and whoops and hollers.

Four men standing in a half circle were looking down at a man who was bouncing on his knees and shaking a fisted hand. The bouncy man whipped his hand open and tap-dancing dice rolled and hit the side of the garage. All the gamblers sung out when the dice landed, revealing each man's fate. Birdie kept her distance while they cracked jokes, one-upped each other and discussed who they thought would be Joe Louis's next opponent.

Birdie loved conversations about the exploits of the handsome "Brown Bomber" and she hung on to every word. One man animatedly told of witnessing the champion mercilessly beat down one of his opponents. The men conversed about the Negro boxer's challengers and career like a Sunday church sermon—with emotion, hope and promise, ending in hymn-like agreement that he was an absolute credit to his race.

Drawn closer to the edge of the garage, she was within a few feet of the circle of men. They threw crumpled dollar after dollar into a pile and suspended their tale-telling as the high-arching dice ricocheted off the garage wall and rolled to a complete stop. Although she wanted to, she didn't dare move any closer. One step further and Mama would justifiably whoop her ass. Her mother's advice bound her to her spot: *"Flying around some worthless man ain't gonna get you nowhere but burned. You need to stay a little bird for as long as you can till you learn to take care of yourself."*

As loud as Mama's words were in her head, Birdie stayed put, acting on faith that Mama was still in the living room entertaining guests and not peering out the back door looking for her.

"I've got a few more dollahs and a real good feelin' man."

A new and familiar voice joined the group. Although it was a bit brighter than she remembered, it was the same voice that whispered in her ear at last night's dance. She envisioned a smile that curled at the ends and turned around to see Jimmy standing close beside her. She caught a sharp scent of home-grown liquor, dry tobacco and Kentucky dirt that permeated the clothes, skin and sweat of every man who worked at the plant. She stepped back to move out of his range.

Jimmy waved a hand, signaling the men to pause their game. They complied politely, looking sheepish and a bit astonished to see the young female observer for the first time. Jimmy then placed a hand on her shoulder and guided her away from the group. His fingers were stained yellowish- green and brown. She knew the rim of dirt under his nails and around his cuticles would never go away as long as he kept working in the tobacco trade. It was known that a man with clean hands couldn't be trusted. A clean-handed man meant he was either a liar, a cheat, or both, couldn't fight, wasn't from around here, just got back from college, or never knew a good day of real hard work. It was obvious that none of these things applied to Jimmy No-Last-Name who stood beside her.

He leaned down close and whispered, "Hey, little bird. Why'd you fly away from me last night?"

"Wha…?" Birdie stopped short. Over Jimmy's shoulder she saw a gaped-mouth stare from Bessa, who had returned from work and was now leaning out over the porch rail. Pressed against her shoulder was Chicky with a head full of fresh pin curls shooting dagger eyes from behind the open screen door. Birdie's heart jumped because, rest assured, the next face to appear would be Mama's. The thought of her mother making an embarrassing scene sent a chill up and down the back of her neck and spine. It was hot as all get out in the afternoon sun and Birdie stood shivering in the heat waiting any minute to be chastised. For her sisters' benefits, she wanted to shake Jimmy's hand off her shoulder and jerk away. But for some reason she couldn't.

"I said, where'd you go, Miss Birdie? I been looking for you ever since that last dance we had."

"You sure I flew away, or maybe I just had somewhere more important to be?"

He chuckled. "Oh, so you had to go to high tea or somethin'? Or maybe your sister dragged you off last night because you had to go home before your mama came looking for you… you being too young to be out that late and all."

Birdie's eyes shifted from him to her back porch where Bessa and Chicky stood with their arms folded against their chests. Before she could respond he backed away and bowed his head slightly.

"I'm so sorry if I offended you, lil' miss. That was just plain rude. Please, please accept my apologies. I looked for you after the show and was just plain disappointed." He let out a big laugh. "Girl, you sure can move. I just wanted to get to know the person I enjoyed dancing with so much. Please, little lady, Miss Bird, I would like to talk with you for a moment if you wouldn't mind."

Birdie hesitated and shifted her eyes to her back porch. Both sisters were now at the gate shaking their heads and furiously waving their hands, motioning for her to come back. Birdie shrugged, turned back around then took a few short steps in his direction. Since Mama hadn't made an appearance, Birdie assumed she was still tied up with the Good Neighbor League folks. Knowing her mother, Mama would have fixed the guests a bite to eat. That also meant she would have time to take a walk with Jimmy and get back before being missed. Besides, Birdie knew her sisters would cover for her, follow her or straight up run down the alley to get her if it looked like trouble. She turned back to Jimmy and gave him a small nod.

They walked until they reached a section where the dirt alley intersected with a main street. Turning onto the street, they continued walking, following the sidewalk heading toward a small park called the Owl's Nest. The park was an unspoken demarcation line that separated the wealthy white neighborhood from the community of working-class black people that, more than likely, worked for the white families who lived on the other side of the park.

Owl's Nest Park had two entrances. One was a secluded path covered by an archway of overhanging bushes and vines that grew tall and twisted through an age-old fence. This entrance provided access to the park from neat rows of modest houses in the black neighborhood. The path opened to a worn baseball diamond where patches of grass barely covered dry yellow dirt. The other entrance, on the opposite side of the park, was bordered by large statuesque, plantation-like homes of long-established families. It had a wrought iron and red brick archway that welcomed visitors into a well-groomed grassy area with neat crisscross walking paths dotted with benches and gas lights. Smaller sycamore and birch trees shaded pathways and park benches. Tall, expansive oak trees stretched out around the outer rim of the park provided shade, respite and exclusivity.

They entered the park through the covered archway. The path, with its natural canopy, looked like a secret. No respectful young woman should be seen casually walking with a man down this path unless they were up to no good. But Birdie suddenly felt rebellious and free. She didn't care what anyone thought. Fragrant yellow honeysuckle blossoms dotted twisting, creeping bushes along the path. Birdie snapped off a singular blossom and pinched the bottom to pull out the stem. She placed the delicate flower to her tongue to taste its tiny drop of sweet nectar.

They walked deeper into the middle of the park to a red-brick shelter house which lorded over both sides of the Owl's Nest and served as the park's physical dividing point. From the shelter's small balconies there was a panoramic view of the pool and the playing field where a group of boisterous kids were choosing sides for softball. Jimmy leaned against the rail and gave Birdie a slow, uninhibited once-over.

"Well, what do you know, lil' Bird?" His voice slipped to just slightly above a whisper.

Having settled herself at a safe distance from him, Birdie moved closer to hear.

"First of all…" Her voice echoed in the quiet of the park, sounding loud and harsh in comparison. "I'm not little and I know all I need to know. Thank you very much."

"All you need to know, huh," Jimmy repeated even softer than before, almost soundlessly mouthing the words.

A slight buzz filled Birdie's ears. She wasn't sure if it was the fluttering of an insect or simply the sound of grass growing in the heat of the early afternoon sun. She only saw Jimmy's eyes, twinkling even brighter as his smile widened.

"Hmmm…what do you know about the world, Miss Birdie?" He took great pains to draw out her name and made a point to emphasize his omission of lil'.

She wasn't sure if he was making fun of her but decided to make light of his comments. "You know, you act like you know everything about everything. I get that you've been around, I guess."

Birdie felt she needed to say something to strengthen her position.

"I'm not some dumb little hick girl working on an assembly line you know. I know a little something about how the world works and I've got my own plans."

She really hadn't any plans until now. Not sure what else to say, she paused slightly, giving Jimmy time to jump in. When he didn't say a word, she proceeded.

"I'm gonna own my own restaurant."

"Own your own restaurant, huh? I can see that. That takes a lot of money. Where you plan to get that?"

"Well, I'll have an investor, or once I get married my husband and I will have the means to open a restaurant. Not here, of course. Not in this sad little town. I don't want to just be feedin' a bunch of church folks every Sunday. But a nice sit-down place somewhere like Cincinnati or maybe as far away as Chicago. Yes, my man will manage the restaurant and I'll do all the cooking."

Through a lighthearted chuckle, Jimmy quipped, "Oh, so you plan on marrying a rich man of means. So where do you plan on finding this Prince Charming? I don't see anyone like that in these circles."

"Well, that's not for you to worry about. It'll happen just like that…just like I said. I won't have to worry about a thing because the man I marry will—"

"Look." Jimmy held up his hands. "I don't mean to cut you off. Well, yes, I did. I just think you're too smart for that."

"Too smart for what?"

"Putting yourself in the back, hidden away in some old greasy kitchen at a stove cooking. Look at you, girl, if anything, you need to be out front for everyone to see. I'm sure people would come to your restaurant just to see you. You shouldn't be in the back working like a plantation slave."

Birdie wasn't quite sure how to react. Should she be flattered by his compliment on her looks or insulted by the slave reference? She had been helping to prepare food for others since she could hold a spoon. Feeding black and white folks put food in her family's mouth and clothes on their backs.

"Wait a minute…you like to eat, don't you? Well wouldn't you pay good money to get a good, belly-rubbing home-cooked meal when you really wanted it? You know, like after you worked hard all day or took some girl out on a date or something." She leaned forward. "Wanting to be a good cook and appreciated for your cooking is good business and can be a good living."

Jimmy held up his palms. "Okay…okay. I see you getting all riled up. But I'm telling you that dream of yours has one big fly in the ointment because I believe you don't need no husband to do anything that you put in your mind to get. But, if it makes you happy, you go on and dream about some man buying you a fancy restaurant."

There was a breath of silence between them. All that could

be heard was the sun bearing down on blades of grass wilting under the heat.

Jimmy shook his head and let out a laugh. "You mentioned Chicago as a place for this big swanky restaurant. Ever been there? It's one of my favorite places."

Birdie gave him a side glance. She hoped he didn't ask her too much more about dreams, wishes, hopes and desires because honestly, she didn't think she could defend them much longer.

"So what about you?" It was her turn to investigate. "What do you plan to do with your life? Or do you just plan to float around the country from factory to factory?"

"Float? Nah, girl. I must admit—and I don't admit this to too many folks, particularly pretty girls like you that I just met—I've done my fair share of what some say is questionable work." He paused to frame his answer to her raised eyebrow. "I'm just a man trying to survive. That's all. Just trying to find a place where I fit in. Where I can make a little money to live right and be my own man. Not sure where that is at the moment."

With a slow smile, he added, "But if I met the right woman, I'm sure, whenever and wherever that happens, that will be where I'll fit right nicely. We'd have us a bunch of boys and I'll teach 'em to be men the world would fear."

"Oh, so you're looking to get married so you can raise some troublemakers?" Birdie asked sarcastically.

"I don't mean like they'll be going around beating up folks. I mean the kind of fear that makes people feel safe enough to trust them. Safe enough to know they speak the truth. My children will be leaders. Doing things and changing things like we can't even imagine today. My children will guide those slave-thinking Negros back to the greatness we once were. Creating a world where we don't have to ask them, them crackers, for nothing. You know they ain't nothing but afraid of us. All of us with dark skin."

Birdie could see this was important to him but didn't want to pursue a deep conversation on race relations or politics. She just fled from that only a moment ago.

"That sounds noble. I think all our children, no matter what shade they are, should aspire to be the best."

Jimmy continued, "I'll teach my children to farm, and to fish, but they'll also help feed minds. They'll open their own banks and libraries. That's what my children will do. With the right woman I'll plant seeds that will grow into warriors. Not fighting no white man's war, but ours."

Birdie was surprised that he spoke so openly about having children. From the time she followed Jimmy up the aisle at the Paramount Theater, she knew he wasn't at all like the men who visited the house or hung out in the alley or chummed around at work for that matter. She half expected to hear the usual talk she heard from men when they didn't know she was around. She thought he would draw attention to himself and talk mostly about himself. Although he did a lot of the talking, he asked about her first and listened intently when she spoke. She felt so comfortable with him, she admitted to him that her mother was holding her captive because of her behavior at the concert and that she had to get back to help cook for church and some white family's party tonight.

"I'm only out now because we were ambushed by political workers."

"Them Good Neighbor Democrats? Yeah, they're working hard now to convince all of us to bring President FDR back in. I never thought I'd see them trying to stir up something down here though. They generally stay safe north of the Mason-Dixon line. There's a bunch of workers from the party's colored division all over New York."

Birdie interjected, "Really? You've been to New York? I've always wanted to see the Statue of Liberty, the big wide streets, *The Swing Mikado*—you know that musical show First Lady Roosevelt went to see—and all the other shows in Harlem. New York City just sounds so glamorous."

"You know about Harlem? I was just up in New York City. That place was all in a frenzy talking about Democrats this and Republicans that."

Jimmy stood up in front of her and continued as if giving a lecture. "When I was up there, they were having this big convention rally. It was nothin' but a sea of black people all around this big convention hall. I'd never seen that many black folks all together. They had so many speakers and lots of music to get everyone stirred up and excited about voting. Cab Calloway and his orchestra was there and some huge church choirs. When everyone began acting like the Lord was actually in the house, they dropped down these huge banners from the ceiling like they were falling from the sky. One was a picture of Jesus and another was Lincoln. And then one big banner right in the middle was of President Roosevelt. People were clapping and cheering up a storm. The speaker was saying, just as each of the banners rolled down, *Jesus emancipated man from sin; Lincoln emancipated you from slavery and Roosevelt emancipated you from social and economic abuse.*

"Now excuse me, Miss Birdie, I was happy to be in the midst of my people in that big city but that was more malarkey than I could take. Here we are, thousands of black folks, all together in one place talking about the betterment of our race and here are these three banners over our heads of white men smiling down on us."

Birdie leaned back. "Okay. Okay. That sounds like a sight to see. But do you mind if we talk about something else?"

Like a freshly tapped faucet, Jimmy kept going. He went

on about places he'd been like Detroit, St. Louis and Chicago and places he wanted to go, such as Puerto Rico, Cuba or out west to California. He wanted to hop on a ship and go sailing off to destinations on the continent of Africa. He spoke of how he loved the poet Langston Hughes, admired activist Marcus Garvey and revered saxophonist Coleman Hawkins—they made him courageous. He named people he wanted to know more about, like actor Paul Robeson, and others who created art, music and controversy. She listened and was enraptured.

Birdie asked question after question just to keep Jimmy talking about his world. *Who is that? Where is that? What did he say to you? How did you do that?* For every answer Jimmy provided, he would end by asking what her thoughts were on the subject. "Can you image that? Have you ever heard anything like that? That's something ain't it?"

Birdie was fascinated by it all. She was especially transfixed by the musical notes of his voice. As Jimmy spoke, the pacing and timbre of his words drew her in. His hands moved magically through the air, orchestrating images of his travels. At times, he seemed to be speaking to the sky and trees. Frequently, in midsentence, he'd fasten his eyes on hers and all she could hear was an intimate trail of music.

At times during their conversation, Birdie felt simple, small and even childish. She had never been anywhere outside of Mt. Sterling and had done nothing but go to school, church and work with Mama. What she knew about life, up to this point, was what she learned from *Photoplay* and detective magazines. Birdie wished she'd done something more because after several vivid stories of Jimmy's travels, she thirsted for something new.

Jimmy moved forward and gently swatted away a gnat flying dangerously close to her cheek. Silence amplified the sound of birds flitting through the leaves and branches.

Birdie suddenly jumped up. "Man oh man, I gotta go! My mother is going to kill me!"

"I'm sorry, lil' Bird. Let me walk you back. And on the way I'm going to tell you why you should meet me back here tomorrow."

"I can't do that," she said breathlessly. By now they were both walking swiftly up the street toward the alley. Birdie wanted to break out and run but was too embarrassed.

"Please. Come on, pretty lady. Meet me back here tomorrow afternoon for only a few minutes. I promise I won't keep you, so you won't get in trouble. I've got something to show you."

Birdie crept in the back door, making sure to open the screen door slowly so as not to make a sound. The house was quiet, too quiet. On the table were several cakes cooling on racks. In the icebox was a beautiful array of dressed eggs. *God bless Chicky and Bessa!* She said a prayer for her older sisters and promised to pay back the favor.

Birdie went upstairs. Bessa was lying on her bed reading some worn book which she did so often. Bessa was only three years older but Birdie thought her big sister acted as if she was as old as Mama. Birdie loved her sister, but it was hard to find any personality at all in Bessa. She operated like a well-wound clock. She did everything Mama said to the letter. Clothes were pressed and expertly folded. Beds were made with razor-sharp corners. Floors were swept and furniture was dusted. She never spoke out of turn and she never, ever yelled. Birdie thought that it was because Bessa's mouth was way too small. Nothing bad, dishonest or rude could ever escape from her little mouth. Sometimes Birdie didn't even know Bessa was there. When Bessa did speak in that slow monotonous drawl she had, you were so surprised that you'd stop what you were doing and listen.

Bessa looked up from her book. She propped herself up by her elbows and pushed her glasses up on her nose. "Mama stepped out to get a few things from the store. Chicky ran out of here to go somewhere, so Mama will want *you* to help her frost those cakes. I told Mama that old Mrs. Prather was in her backyard and you went to help her up the stairs. I knew that would give you some time because we all know how that old woman loves to talk and how long it takes her to say anything."

Bessa sat upright. "You know I don't like lying to Mama, but if I didn't, she'd be out for your behind right now. Birdie, you need to be careful. Don't be wandering all around creation with these good-for-nothings around here. It ain't going to get you nowhere. And the one you wandered off with just now is a perfect example of what I'm talking about."

"Bessa, I wasn't doing anything. He just asked me to take a walk with him and I did. Nothing happened." Birdie realized that after all the time they just spent together she still didn't know his last name. "Beessssah, please, he's just someone I met last night at the concert. I don't even know his last name."

Bessa rolled her eyes. "Girl, you better not have done anything stupid. You don't know that man. You don't know anything about him. You think you being cute, girl. What you need to do, instead of following behind some man, is get back to school and learn a trade. Learning a trade will give you something to better yourself so you can get away from here and out from underneath Mama's thumb. C'mon, girl, go with me to the vocational school and see how you like it. Being a pharmacist is good money and they need colored pharmacists just about anywhere."

"Sure. Sure, Bessa, I'll go with you sometime. Trust me, I ain't done anything stupid."

Both girls jumped at the sudden slam of the back screen door. Birdie looked at Bessa, posted up a fake broad smile and flounced downstairs before she was called to avoid questions. "Hey, Mama, you need help with those cakes? I'll do it!"

Mama was already tying on her apron while analyzing the cakes cooling on the rack. Scraping the softened butter into a pillow of confectioners' sugar, Birdie couldn't think of anything else but meeting Jimmy at Owl's Nest Park the next day. Now she could finally find out his last name.

CHAPTER THREE

Sunday church service labored on. Birdie stared down at her hymnal for what felt like four Sundays. The adult choir marched in. The children's choir followed. The senior choir sang hymn after hymn, each one having a minimum of four verses along with breakout solos. The pastor, coaxed on by an extremely higher than usual amount of "Amens" from his flock, stretched out his sermon while the same characters caught the Holy Spirit as they did every Sunday. Birdie thought it would never end.

Sitting on the edge of the pew, she could think of nothing but how to slip out unnoticed. She told no one about her plans. Not even her sisters. Mama generally stayed after service to put out tea, coffee and desserts for fellowship hour—that would be the best time to duck out and head for the park. The pit of Birdie's stomach bobbed and weaved when she thought about meeting him. She didn't know what to expect. *Would Jimmy even show up?*

When the service finally ended, Birdie dodged churchgo-
ers and briskly walked through the back alleyway, and then
four street blocks over to the park. She adjusted her pace and
demeanor on the street so as not to raise suspicions. Nosey
neighbors might wonder why she was entering the Owl's Nest
all alone on a Sunday afternoon. She ducked into the shaded
entrance and reached up to brush the soft trumpet flowers
of the honeysuckle vines with her fingertips, showering herself with sparkling wet droplets from the morning rain. The
baseball diamond was empty and the park quiet. She was relieved when she spotted Jimmy at the shelter, leaning against
an archway column. He was looking down, as if he was reading something. As she approached, he looked up and smiled.

"I wasn't sure you were going to make it, lil' Bird."

"Really? I wasn't sure that I would either."

Birdie sat a few feet away from him on the opposite side of
the column. She didn't dare move any closer to him.

"But I had to come. I was curious about something. Jimmy,
what is your last name?"

"Didn't I tell you? Well, I know yours. It's Jennings, right?
I know all about you. You have two sisters. Both work at
Wrights. One hangs around some brother named Clarence and
the other also works at the pharmacy downtown. She's going
to go to school to be something like a doctor. Your mother
belongs to the church over the way and makes the best cakes
and pies than anyone around. That's what I heard. I swear!
And you gonna be a movie star or marry some rich man who's
going to give you a restaurant on your honeymoon or something like that, right?"

"Stop teasing. Who in the world have you been talking to
and what is your last name?"

"Why? Are you the FBI or somethin'? You gonna investigate?"

"I'm leaving unless you tell me."

"It's Walker. Just for you, madam investigator, my full name is James Bryant Walker. You got any more personal questions I can answer for you?"

"James Bryant Walker," she repeated slowly. "I'm going to have to ask my spies about you."

"No need. I'll tell you whatever you want to know."

They moved over to a park bench shaded by a wide oak tree. By this time, Birdie felt courageous. "Okay, Mr. James Bryant 'Jimmy' Walker, now tell me more about you."

He was born in Alabama. His parents died in a house fire when he was very young. He and his younger brother were raised by his sister, Pearline, who wasn't much older than he, with the help of an aunt who relocated him and his siblings to Louisville, Kentucky.

"I was too young to remember, but the story goes that my sister was only six years old when she saved us. My brother was only a toddler at the time. She wrapped my brother in a wet blanket and pulled me from under the bed. She got us out of the house before the roof collapsed. We lived so far away from most folks that it was days before someone found us in the woods eating wild berries, garden vegetables and dirt. The doctors thought that I wouldn't survive because I had breathed in so much smoke that my lungs were burned. My baby brother was the one that didn't survive. And this I do remember. He died not from the fire but from some berries we were eating.

"Yeah, I was burned on the insides, but here I am. Now every time it gets cold or rainy my lungs have to work overtime trying to catch air. I don't mind. In fact, the struggle I have sometimes just to breathe actually makes me feel kinda peaceful. The scars in my lungs, even though I can't see them, make me think about my mama and daddy who I never knew. It reminds me that there was a time when we were a family."

Birdie was touched by his story and learning that he experienced such pain at a young age. She never knew her own father but the thought of growing up without a mother was unfathomable to her. She reached out and patted his hand, letting her touch linger longer than necessary. Jimmy flipped his hand over to interlace their fingers. They held hands for only seconds until Birdie, suddenly aware of their closeness, blushed and pulled away. He cocked his head to the side and gave her a wide grin to break the silence.

Birdie felt a warm blush rise to her cheeks. "I saw you were reading something as I came up. What do you have there?"

Jimmy pulled out a ragged pamphlet and a newspaper that was neatly folded under his arm. He shook out the pamphlet which displayed an illustrated picture of actor and singer Paul Robeson.

"This is the man," he said, rapping a knuckle against the picture.

"He is so handsome." Birdie leaned in closer. "He looks like he's a big ole country fire and brimstone preacher."

Jimmy rubbed his chin. "He does look like just about every preacher I know. But he's far from some Bible thumper. He's trying to baptize our brothers and sisters with some knowledge. He's talking about a need for a different kind of government, one that benefits all Americans—not just a few."

Wide-eyed, Birdie looked up at Jimmy. "Really, I thought he was just in movies and sung in plays and stuff."

"Nah, he's much more than that. We need more people like him in the public eye. Look at this…"

He unfolded an old, yellowed copy of the *Chicago Defender* newspaper with a bold headline that read "Snatched from Angry Mob."

"This is why we need folks with courage to speak up and confront those demons."

Birdie nodded. Every black household in Mt. Sterling held a similar story. She had heard ghastly accounts of a father, brother, uncle or cousin since she could understand words. So many families spoke of kinfolks who had been killed by mobs or had died outside hospitals from untreated wounds or ailments because doctors refused to treat a brown-skinned human in pain. She nodded silently because she knew it was an unjust world. But for now, she wanted that growling dog of atrocities to stay in its cage. Birdie searched for a way to change the subject because she hadn't slipped out of Mama's sights to be mad or sad today.

"The *Chicago Defender* newspaper, huh? I've got family in Chicago. One of my cousins just picked up and moved there. I hope to get up there and see it one day."

"Yeah, Chicago is the place to be right now. This paper here is always telling black southerners to come on up to Chicago to make a better life. I do a bit of work there sometimes to make some extra money. I picked this up in my travels a ways back."

He pointed out a few articles boldly calling out injustice, not just against black Americans, but to the poor of all races. Birdie stayed silent, listening to the cadence of his words. He seemed to take her silence as waning interest and changed the subject. From then on, they talked about movies, travel, sports and, what Birdie found most exciting, seeing each other again.

"Hey, do you like to fish? Wanna go with me sometimes?"

"Sure." She was already thinking up excuses to give Mama in order to pull off a full day getaway. Birdie knew she'd probably have to enlist Chicky as cover.

"Come with me on Thursday. We have to leave early. Can you do that?"

★ ★ ★

Birdie left the house as the early morning sky began to brighten. Her story was she was going to work an early shift at Wrights, then to a matinee movie with Chicky and some other girls. Chicky was happy to be part of the scheme. It gave her something to hold over her baby sister when she wanted to be with her boyfriend, Clarence. Luckily, Mama, along with Sister Shirleen from church, would be busy on the other side of town making deliveries of baked goods and ironing. That made it easy for Birdie to slip out and back without too much notice.

Jimmy and Birdie spent the humid morning and hotter afternoon on the banks of a little tributary off the Kentucky River. Birdie didn't know much about fishing but the sweet quiet, the shade from the trees governing the bank and the cool breeze off the river was delicious enough to take her mind off any trouble. It was the perfect spot.

"Don't worry, lil' Bird, I've been doing this for as long as I can remember. When I was a youngster, whatever we caught was all we had to eat."

Jimmy kicked off his work boots, rolled up his pant legs and waded out into the river until the brown water swirled around his knees.

"I know fishin' might be a little dirty for you, queenie, but these waters are clean. The river cleans itself twice a day… when the tide comes in and when the tide goes out. The rainwater off those Ohio and Kentucky hills makes the water look muddy. That's why them catfish and crappie aren't bitin' yet. They can't see or smell the bait. But I can feel it… We're going to get something that you can fry up for dinner. Just watch and see."

A boat labored slowly up the river cutting through the quiet currents causing water to slap against his thighs. Birdie laughed as the cold spray of water caught Jimmy by surprise. Jimmy was right. They caught ten fish, none of which she could bring home. Birdie wanted to take some home to show off but couldn't quite fit their presence into her story. All in all, it had been a beautiful day.

From this point forward, Birdie became an expert at sneaking out of the house and skipping work to be with Jimmy. She regularly fibbed to Mama about her whereabouts. It was easy up until the time Jimmy invited her to come along with his friends to see a baseball game in Pittsburgh. Birdie knew this trip would take all her newfound creative talents.

Jimmy loved baseball. He would talk on and on about Negro National League teams and his champion, Satchel Paige. Jimmy worshipped Satchel Paige. He planned to ride over to see him and his team, the Pittsburgh Crawfords, play for the championship. Even though it was early in the season, he knew the "Craws" were going to be this year's champions despite the New York Cubans breathing down their necks.

Pittsburgh was over three hundred miles away and going that far would require a real big, coordinated whopper of a lie to avoid getting caught. Birdie would need to enlist both Chicky and Bessa to pull such a trip off. Bessa couldn't be trusted. Her sister couldn't hold such a secret from Mama, so ultimately Mama would figure it out. Mama made it clear that there were to be no boyfriends until her girls went back to finish school. If Bessa blurted anything out about Jimmy, Birdie was afraid Mama would actually send her youngest daughter feet first to the grave.

Pittsburgh was out of the question, but Cincinnati was just a hop and a skip away. She really wanted to go with Jimmy to a ball game. The Negro League's Cincinnati Tigers were playing the Cincinnati Clowns in an exhibition game at Crosley Field. They could go and easily get back without being detected. With Chicky on board to cover, instead of going to Wrights, Birdie piled in a car with two other couples to see the Clowns' entertaining crazy pitches, catches and other antics on the field. Jimmy made a bet that the Clowns, who were playing it straight that day, had the power and skill to beat the professional Tigers in a real game. Jimmy lost the bet. Ultimately the Tigers proved too much for the Clowns.

On the way home they stopped for a bite at Maybelle Blue's. Maybelle's was a little shanty of a restaurant located off the highway on a dirt road in the woods where the city of Covington ceased and a spot nobody officially cared to claim began. The restaurant was listed in the Green Book, a directory of establishments that catered to black travelers where they could find places to safely eat, drink, sleep, fill up their car or just relieve themselves—which couldn't be done freely without the threat of trouble due to Jim Crow segregation. But Green Book listing or not, everybody knew about Maybelle's because she had a reputation for the best sweet potato pie this side of the River.

The crew, high and giddy from the game and satisfying meal, took over the open field next to the restaurant and played their own version of baseball. It started out as a game of catch because they had a ball and no bat. Then someone found what they thought was the perfect branch to act as a bat. That only lasted as long as the branch held out. The failed attempt at a real game gave way to the guys telling boisterous tales, fibs of professional prowess and the just-so-razor-close opportunities of what could've been their shot at playing ball in the major leagues.

"You saw how I hit that, right, Bird?" Jimmy chuckled. "Now you know I can play. I can play ball with just about anything. I could be in the leagues right now, makin' big money… Right?" He whispered in her ear, "Just say 'right' real loud to let my boys know who I am. Okay?"

Birdie followed with a loud and resounding, "Right! Satchel Paige could learn a thing or two from you."

They laughed and cracked jokes all the way back to Mt. Sterling. Jimmy and Birdie were still laughing after dropping off his friends, savoring a few moments alone before Birdie had to be taken home.

"You're not going to get in any trouble, are you?"

Birdie shook her head. "Chicky covered for me at work and if Mama asks, I will just say I worked late."

Jimmy's smile faded. "You know, I really don't like this lying stuff. Maybe I should go talk to her so we don't have to go through this. I care too much about you to have you lying to your family."

"No, Jimmy, no…at least, not yet. My mama is not going to be very accepting of me going out with you. Let alone learning about what we've been doing behind her back. Once she's alerted, she'll send out scouts and bloodhounds. She'll find out everything about you, where we met and where we've been. I'm surprised she hasn't said anything by now. You know folks in this town have nothing else to do but talk. I'm an adult since I'm working and all, but my mama won't see it that way. And what you don't know about her is that she can be mean. I mean really, really mean. And it ain't just me saying this. Ask anybody. Once she gets a whiff of you, well, I do believe she'll spit fire. Let's wait a little bit. Okay?"

"Alright then. I'll follow your lead for now."

They sat in the parked car listening to chirping crickets heralding in the evening. They followed the luminous dots of yellow lights from early lightning bugs as they rose from the wild grass and mysteriously blinked through the nearby trees. He leaned back in his seat and lazily smiled back at her.

"It's been a few minutes. I think that counts as a little bit. Now, can I ask her?"

"No, Jimmy!" Birdie laughed out loud.

"Well can I kiss you?"

She smiled and nodded shyly. Jimmy leaned toward her. When he was close enough to take in the misty moist air between them that mingled with each breath, he paused before politely pressing his lips against hers. It was the first time anyone kissed her on the lips for that long and it felt like something she had been waiting for all her life.

Jimmy pulled back. "I've got to get this car back to my cousin. I guess we should get going."

He started up the car and drove a block away from Birdie's house as she had instructed him to do. The air was light and scented with sweet summer fragrance. "Let me walk you up to the corner at least."

"Nooo, you can't, not yet. Soon, I promise."

As Birdie reached for the door, Jimmy placed his hand on hers. She turned toward him and they kissed again, this time longer than before. Birdie had spent a lot of time thinking about kissing Jimmy. In fact, she thought of little else.

He started up the car again, turned it off and pulled her toward him to kiss her for a third time. "Birdie, I want you to be with me. I want you to be my girl."

"I want to be with you too," she whispered before scooting out of the car.

Their trip went undetected by Mama. Chicky, on the other hand, held a raised eyebrow and smirking smile so Birdie had to do just about everything Chicky said without a smart response. Mama should have suspected something right then as Chicky barked out orders and Birdie jumped to follow.

Jimmy and Birdie found pieces of time to be together. They met often at Owl's Nest Park, took walks along the riverbank and tried their best to stay out of sight to avoid any chance of gossip trickling back to Mama. Every time they met, Jimmy would share a book, a poem, a news article or a picture of some strange artwork from a postcard or magazine that inspired him. He said he felt comfortable sharing his thoughts and interests with Birdie because most folks would just laugh at the things that caught his attention. He appreciated her listening to him and showing an interest. Birdie liked that Jimmy was different from everyone else she knew.

When the weather was too wet or cold, they'd find their way over to Jimmy's cousin's basement apartment on the other side of town. The apartment had small high windows that viewed the tips of grass and, farther across the street, the wheels of a train as they barreled down the tracks. When his cousin was at work, they would sit together on the shabby couch, playing cards and drinking cold colas. A winning hand warranted a kiss, until breathlessly they lost interest in the game.

On one fresh, cool night, he lay on top of her. *"Oh, Jimmy,"* Birdie whispered out from between clenched teeth. His name escaped from her lips as the warmth of his kisses and caresses covered her. Warnings from Mama and her sisters lost all meaning as Birdie inhaled Jimmy's enticing smell of rich, newly turned black earth, honeysuckle, forsythia and early jasmine. The scent and taste of his body aroused her every sense and drew her closer to him. While she called on a higher power, he whispered, "Birdie…my pretty little bird, you are so beautiful."

Jimmy gently loosened the pins that held Birdie's hair and its thickness blossomed and fell like a crown around the pillow. He held her head in both of his hands. The tips of his fingers pressed lightly into her scalp. Rough and sensational palms cupped her cheeks and guided her face up to his to receive more of his kisses. She parted her lips and tasted his salty skin. The flavor was as intoxicating as sweet honey and she was ravenous for more.

It was easier than she thought it would be. She blushed at her nakedness as his hands ran down her body. There was only a second or two when she wanted to lift herself up on her elbows, scoot out from beneath him and run away. But pulling her body away from his gave way to the desire to pull him as close to her as possible. She wanted nothing more than to drape herself against him. It was too easy to hold on to his arms and accept his hips pressing against hers. She pushed her nipples against his chest and her stomach against his moist skin.

Jimmy's fingers entwined Birdie's and she held on tight. She knew nothing would ever be the same again.

CHAPTER FOUR

Mama unflinchingly walked toward Jimmy before anchoring her small frame in front of him, leaving almost no breathing room between them. The difference in their height and stature under any other circumstance would be laughable. Mama's stance, however, gave the illusion they met face-to-face.

She stared him in the eye and in a measured tone Mama spat out, "Mr. Walker, you only need to know one thing about me and that is, for over eleven years I worked for Mr. Hoffman. You might know or have heard of the Hoffman family. They're the big Germans who own the butcher shop downtown. I helped all of them boys slaughter everything on four legs. They taught me how to do it quickly without leaving any meat on the bone behind. You see, I know my way around every rib, neck and backbone. I can just about do it in the dark with my eyes closed."

She stepped back slowly, suddenly shifting to a lilting tone. "Yes, Mr. Walker, now you know why I'm such a good cook."

Birdie's heart had stopped when she and Jimmy stepped into the kitchen. She held her breath when she introduced Jimmy and he reached out to shake Mama's hand. She almost fainted from lack of oxygen when Jimmy, after withdrawing from an unreturned handshake, blurted out, "I'd like to marry your beautiful daughter, Mrs. Jennings."

Silence traveled between the three of them. Birdie thought, *Maybe having this discussion in the kitchen wasn't a good idea.* Her eyes darted from one side of the room to the other, searching for any sharp objects in her line of sight. At this point, the only movement in the room came from the undulating fire beneath a large pot on the stove. A yellow flame curled around the pot's edges, tapping out a cautionary warning. Mama visibly relaxed as she walked over to the ice box. Jimmy, speechless and frozen to his spot, resigned from posing any other questions or comments to watch Mama's next movements.

He finally opened his mouth wide. "I'm so sorry, ma'am… I… I—"

Mama cut him off. "I've got some ham, cornbread and a few vegetables here. You gonna sit here now and tell me how you plan to support my daughter."

Birdie thought, *Is she planning to poison him?* She knew there was rat poison somewhere in the house. It was either in the basement or maybe it was under the sink. That was too close for comfort. Birdie's eyes shifted between Jimmy and the back of Mama's head as her mother lit the oven and flipped the other burners on the stove. Birdie instinctively moved to get plates to set the table for the three of them. She watched her mother's every move. *I don't see her reaching for anything other than a bit of bacon drippings, so I guess we'll have to wait and see if poison is on the menu.*

Birdie wasn't sure where her sisters had gone, but she prayed Chicky would stay away. The thought of Chicky popping in and adding another voice to this choir of misfortune made Birdie more nervous than she already was. Chicky's untamed mouth would stir things up even more and be the death of everybody in the room.

The meal tasted like straw in Birdie's mouth. They sat in silence, slowly shifting food from one side of their plates to another. Jimmy broke the ice first.

"Mrs. Jennings, I… I…really love your daughter. I know she's young. I tried to fight against how I feel. I can't help it. I wanted to wait till she got older. I will if I have to, but with this world about to explode and, you know, with that big war coming and all…and us black men having to go fight and die for America so that we can exist like slaves on this land we built…

"Mrs. Jennings, the way I see it, this world ain't changing overnight into something better. So why wait? For what? I just want us to be together, to be married to one another. I'll take good care of her. I promise you that."

Mama's hands, stationed on both sides of her plate, were balled into fists. "How you gonna do that? How are you going to take care of her? What do you have?"

Mama waved a hand in front of her face as she mimicked his words. "The world's about to explode. What are you talking about? You just drifted into town, caught a fly-by-night, shit job without a pot to piss in and now you come to me asking… No, telling me, you want to take my baby bird away from me? She could do so much better! My girl deserves so much better!"

Birdie had never seen her mother so animated and did another sweep around the room for anything that could be used as a weapon.

"Yes, ma'am," Jimmy said quietly. "You're right. I know what it looks like. I came from absolutely nothing. Yes, I've been around. I've seen what life is like outside of this city, this state and so many places around the country. I know what it's like to live knowing that there are people out there that would rather hang or bury me and everyone like me rather than give me what's fair. But I work hard. I always have. I can protect her. I want to do that for her."

His voice became steadier. "I don't have much, but I do love your girl. And I'm here, now, out of the utmost respect, Mrs. Jennings. I'll do right by her. Ma'am, I ain't ever going to be no doctor or lawyer or no college fraternity man or professor but I can protect and provide for her."

Birdie sniffed loudly, trying hard not to cry. In a trembling voice, she begged, "Mama, please. We're in love. I'm working. He's working... Mommy, please."

Mama slammed down her fists so hard food rolled off her plate and onto the table. "You pregnant, girl?"

Birdie's face turned beet red. Mama stood over Birdie and grabbed her by the chin, forcing her daughter to look up into her eyes. "Are. You. Pregnant?"

Birdie's eyes widened. "No, ma'am. No, Mama, I'm not." She couldn't bring herself to say that her period was due a few weeks back.

Mama snapped her focus back on to Jimmy. *"Get out!"* she snarled at him.

Jimmy looked at Birdie and slowly rose from the table. "I'll come by for you tomorrow."

Speaking directly to Mama, Jimmy stated, "Mrs. Jennings, I may not have much, but I am a man of my word."

Birdie lowered her head. Through the fringe of her lashes, Jimmy's stiff back shrank from sight as he walked toward the door. She saw the heels of his worn shoes leaving her behind.

As he disappeared, she imagined his naked dimples and valleys where she could hide herself and the nape of his neck dotted with curly naps of hair. The screen door slammed behind him and the air left the room. She was sealed in a stifling house alone with a mother who was about to kill her last born.

Mama turned to her daughter and snapped. "You know what? I'm going to give you exactly what you want, lil' girl." She gave Birdie a once-over. "I suspect I have to. You're grown now, right? You're an adult. Yes, ma'am, *you* are so grown now."

She sucked air through her teeth. "Mark my words, girl. You gonna regret this move. He is nothing but a lifetime of trouble. You don't even know his family, do you? Think I don't know? I've known for a while now. I usually don't give two hoots for gossip, but your Auntie Sis said that clan of his in Louisville runs around like a pack of untethered wild animals, and she knows everything and everybody in that town. That woman who raised him was a drunk and her husband, their so-called uncle, nothing but a womanizer."

She pointed in the direction of the front door that was still singing with the vibration from hitting the door frame.

"He's probably just like him. Sis said that the drunken woman's husband has a whole 'nother secret family in Cincinnati. Another family! I'm sure he's just waiting for his wife to die of liver cirrhosis so he can go live with them. That's what you'll be running off—excuse me—marrying into. You little fool!"

Birdie flinched, thinking Mama was about to whip out her hand to strike her. Mama's words had already left her skin red and stinging. This was not the time to talk back to Mama. Instead, with her head down and hands knitted together, Birdie stood up from the table.

"*Sit down!*" Mama yelled. "Sit down and listen. Birdie Autumn Jennings, this is all I'm going to say on this subject. I'm going to give you what you asked for. I'll sign the papers so you can marry him. But whatever happens, don't you come crawling back here for me to help you. And you gonna need some help, little girl, probably sooner than later."

The wedding ceremony took place in the living room at Birdie's home. From the time the sun rose, the house was packed with guests. All four of Mama's sisters came, along with their unruly young minions who ran roughshod all over the house and yard. Bessa nicknamed their aunts "the Amazons" because of their physical and vocal ferociousness. The Amazons were loud. They spoke plain and direct on whatever topic flew out of their heads whenever they felt an opinion or two had to be unleashed. From the time the clan poured through the front door, the tiny house shook from opinions and advice on all things. Each one of the Amazons found someone to boss around. From what to wear, to what to eat and how to act, instructions could be heard shouted out from every corner of the small house. Birdie thought Mama must've sprouted up from the ground because she was so unlike her sisters. Compared to them, Mama was a quiet, refined, and genteel creature.

Mama, the Amazons, Bessa and Chicky did their best to make the house beautiful and festive for the occasion. To cool the house down, every window was thrown wide open, allowing the sheer curtains to be carelessly carried away by a calming breeze. Every stick of furniture was polished, and the dining room table was set with Great-Granny's lace tablecloth and every piece of silver they owned. A huge turkey waited on the stove to be spread across the table along with collard greens, yams, peas with baby onions, biscuits, a red and pink Jell-O ring, scalloped potatoes and green beans with tomatoes. There was a chess pie, sweet potato pie and a syrupy sweet punch with orange sherbet floating in the center. Mama's signature was a tall luminously white wedding cake with curled roses on each of the layers.

Every chance they got the aunts pulled Birdie aside to give advice on how to be a good wife. Even though only a few had any practice at it, absolutely none of them ever had much success at it. There were no steady husbands or play uncles around for any length of time. The Amazons adapted like seasons to the nests of short-lived disturbances men caused in their lives. They were either widowed, divorced or in a constant state of in-between. However, there were always men buzzing around. Birdie learned early on that the women in her family, whip-smart and unafraid to tread through any challenge, constantly attracted men as evidenced by the additional place settings, chairs around the table and shoes by the door.

An Amazon or two, in constant rotation, flitted and fussed over Birdie while she waited upstairs for her entrance. As a wedding present, Chicky made Birdie a beautifully hand-stitched pale blue dress with a sheer organdy overlay. It was made from what was left of McCall pattern #7711 that had been pinned down on assorted fabrics, adjusted for every shape and size, and embellished for a number of special occasions for a number of close friends and relatives. Chicky had to improvise areas of the pattern by tracing Birdie's measurements on a brown paper bag. The overall effect was a perfect fit. The tug at the seams around Birdie's midsection was only slightly noticeable.

Chicky popped her head in the door several times to inspect her handiwork and give accounts on the festivities downstairs. She reported Jimmy looked very handsome even though he was shiny from a layer of perspiration. It wasn't just the heat, it was that he was clearly nervous. He was quieter than she

life. Maybe he was shaken by The Most Reverend Thomas's words, spoken with just a side of fire to make sure no one forgot God was present during their wedding ceremony. Or maybe he was spooked by the way Mama ignored him most of the time and at other times aimed the sharp words of sly references, abrupt announcements and singing prayers directly at his back. Or maybe it was nothing at all, just the official-ness of the ceremony and his way of showing how he would cherish and protect her now that she was his wife. Whatever the mild disturbance, Birdie dismissed it. The thought evap-orated completely as family members slapped Jimmy on the back and pulled her in for a congratulatory kiss on the cheek.

Jimmy's sister, Pearline, and his cousin, Jessie, were the only members of his family in attendance. Birdie knew Mama took note of the absence of Jimmy's family. She probably saw it as a sign the union was destined for shame, embarrassment or something catastrophic. But true to her word, she said nothing.

This was the first time Birdie met Jimmy's older sister. Pearline and Jimmy shared the same narrow face, slanted eyes and thin lips. The only exception, besides being a few shades lighter, was that her face looked as though she had never ex-perienced anything close to a smile. She appeared stern and re-served. When there were bursts of laughter, she simply nodded as to acknowledge humor but preferred to save her laughter for later. Birdie thought that maybe in private Pearline would burst out laughing to something she heard earlier in the day.

Jimmy and his cousin, Jessie, could almost be mistaken for twins. He had the same build as Jimmy and constantly smiled. It took little effort to get him to bust out in a big belly laugh. And like Jimmy, Jessie charmed everyone he met with ease. He worked the room to his advantage like a big-city politician, leaving everyone he spoke to in good humor. He was so charismatic that in only a few hours he was able to make a slight crack in Mama's armor. Mama actually giggled at something Jessie said when he went up to shake her hand.

The oddity of Jessie and Mama chuckling together was a sight that didn't go unnoticed by Jimmy. When he asked Jessie what he did to get "that woman" to not only crack a smile but laugh, Jessie replied Mama told him the story about the various vases that decorated the house. Mama told him that the vases contained the ashes of her daddy, her husband, a few uncles and some of her girls' unfortunate boyfriends. She pulled him close to tell him so he would know that all the family's beloveds from as far back as she could remember were still around to kick Jimmy's ass if he hurt her daughter.

Jessie patted Jimmy on the back stating, "That woman, your mother-in-law, is a hoot! I like that one. Good luck, brother!"

Jimmy started searching for and counting the number of vases that were scattered around the rooms.

CHAPTER FIVE

Birdie and Jimmy rented the bottom floor of a house across town, close to the busy downtown area. Never in her life had Birdie been away from home without her family. Even though she was only across town, Birdie felt hundreds of country miles away from her previous circle of life. Except for Mama, assorted family members found their way to the couple's doorsteps with containers of preserves, vegetables, fresh herbs or smoked meats. She put on a staged show of domestic charm just like the starlets in the movie magazines. With a perfectly starched apron tied in a neat bow around her waist, she welcomed her guests. It was an exhausting maneuver, but necessary. She knew they stopped by to be nosey and to gather information to carry back to Mama.

From the time she stepped out of her wedding dress, Birdie occupied herself with creating a picture-perfect home. She filled the small apartment with a hodgepodge of donated furniture, curtains and dishes. In the empty spaces, Birdie placed pots filled with plants and herbs from Mama's garden: sharp-pointed mother-in-law's tongue, climbing philodendron and big, wide green-leafed plants that carried the hope of blossoms in the spring. She made curtains from remnants of lace to let in the warmth of sunlight and left a window open, just a crack, to bring a cleansing breath of good luck.

As days progressed, an oasis filled with as much green inside as outside took shape. And in their fresh, lush space Jimmy held Birdie as if he needed nothing else to be happy. Every morning she awoke in the shelter of his arms, one circled her pillow and the other held her to his chest. Bright, smiling eyes greeted hers and she couldn't help but kiss his lips to start her day. She looked forward to hearing, Good morning, Mrs. Walker or good morning, my sweet bird. I'm a lucky man to have such a sweet, sweet bird in the palm of my hand.

Within a month, it was evident an additional family member would be joining them. Jimmy tickled and teased Birdie as she got bigger and rubbed her belly, back and feet. She was most content when, curled up together in their small junior bed, he'd read aloud to her. He read whatever he collected, no matter if it was magazine or newspaper articles, a recounting of history or a piece of whimsical fantasy or fiction. Even the most sober information became intoxicating poetry as he read the words aloud. With the baby growing inside her and Jimmy's sweet romantic expressions, Birdie's life unfolded into beautiful moments that filled up her days. She couldn't have been happier.

Carmen, born in the early spring, was plump, round and toasty brown with dainty pink lips shaped like Cupid's bow. Birdie wrapped the baby tightly in a faded yellow blanket that had been passed down for generations. Grammy insisted every child in her line should feel the embrace and protection of those that came before them as soon as they came into the world. Jimmy kissed both mother and daughter on the forehead and broadcasted to the empty hospital room, and all in the hallway within earshot, "My beautiful queen and princess!" With a booming voice to a whisper in Birdie's ear, he repeated it over and over again. Baby Carmen, eyes wide, bright and alert, followed each twist and turn of Jimmy's animated face as he rocked her in his arms.

The magic of the moment swiftly ended when Bessa, Chicky, two Amazons and their brood burst into the room. Jimmy's voice, along with the new family's sweet moment of knitted intimacy, was drowned out by loud, raucous, celebratory sounds of women cooing over the baby and new mother. It wasn't every day one of their own gave birth in a hospital. There had always been someone in the family who had the gift of guiding new life into the world and would regularly do so at the mother's home. Dr. Wolfgang would routinely visit the house afterward to give the mother and baby a once-over. But Jimmy insisted on paying for a hospital delivery which only added to the deep set of lines in Mama's face.

True to her word, Mama had gone through the days up to and after Birdie and Jimmy's wedding without uttering a single word to the couple. She became even more withdrawn as Birdie's pregnancy advanced. She delivered her displeasure by acting as though her daughter ceased to be important. She volunteered no information or advice to anyone to carry to her daughter. Her mother's buttoned silence landed like painful punches square on their mark, leaving Birdie hurt, bruised and in tears. Bessa and Chicky did their best to massage Birdie's wounds by lavishing Birdie with the extra attention she needed in her mother's absence.

Mama wasn't in the group of hospital visitors, although

Birdie held out hope her mother might make an appearance. When Bessa entered the room, she immediately kissed her baby sister on the cheek and fanned out a quilt across her hospital bed.

Bessa whispered in Birdie's ear, "You can stop looking. Mama's not coming. You know Mama. She invented the word stubborn. You know she loves you. She practically broke our arms, giving me and Chicky this quilt and a bunch of other stuff to give you. And you know she told us to give you a list of strict instructions to follow so you can heal."

Between the crowd of women surrounding her bed, Birdie caught glimpses of Jimmy, standing alone against the opposite wall. His fingertips were pressed together before his face as if in prayer. His eyes, as bright as the new baby's, were fixed on the flurry of female energy. He looked so happy her heart became filled with his happiness.

In the empty spaces between the crooks of women's arms and petting hands, Jimmy's eyes found Birdie's gaze. He let out a loud whoop and mouthed the words, "My queen" for her eyes only. The cluster of women stopped in their tracks, turned and stared at him as if he was a stranger who just happened to stumble into the wrong room. Breaking the silence, Jimmy announced he was going to go pass around cigars and celebrate being a proud papa with his boys. Without any acknowledgment, the women returned their attention to mother and baby. Only Bessa's and Chicky's eyes followed Jimmy as he inched his way toward the doorway.

In those few seconds before Jimmy left the room, Birdie closed her eyes, hoping for a moment of quiet. Despite being surrounded by sisters and aunts, she wanted and needed her husband close, at least for a little while longer. But he left before she could gather up the energy to protest.

Oh well, it's better I didn't get a chance to say anything to him. Somebody here is only too willing to pounce on any words between us and carry a tale back to Mama, Birdie thought to herself.

Bessa and Chicky hovered protectively near, pressing Birdie to sip red raspberry tea that Mama sent over, as they'd been instructed. Birdie finally began to relax. For now, the soothing tea and her family were all she needed to take her mind off her absent husband.

When the last of the women left, the air hung heavy with a hum of silence along with a sweet trace of jasmine, lavender and roses. A smiling light-skinned nurse, who knew Bessa from pharmacy classes, took Carmen down the hallway to the colored-only nursery. Stillness nestled into the room and its weight disturbed Birdie's attempts to rest. Fits of sleep brought dreams of stirring a black and caramel roux in Mama's large cast iron skillet. Between sleep and wake, she saw her mother's full face. Mama's eyebrows knitted together as she spoke slowly and forcefully.

"Open your eyes, girl. It only works if you can see. Open your eyes. Give your life some new breath. Open them. Use that new energy in your veins…in your life blood to cover you and your baby. I didn't bring you into this world. That hand you feel, that's God, not him. That man ain't here to save you, chile."

Birdie woke in a sweaty panic feeling her heart in her throat. She whipped her head from one side of the room to the other. Mama was not standing over her bed. Nobody was. Only harsh white light from the slightly opened door stretched across the floor and fell over her bed. She pressed her fingers against the sides of her forehead to soothe the band of pain pressing against her temples. It didn't help. Sound banged against the walls of her head and made her head throb.

Where is my husband? Where is my baby? Pain circled Birdie's head, triggering an alarm of helplessness. Suddenly, she felt as drained as if she were the last drops of water being twisted from wet rags. She pulled her knees up to her chest and knotted her fingers tightly together to keep herself and her thoughts still. She had no idea what time it was, but she knew Jimmy had been gone for hours. Since then, shards of uneasiness sliced their way into her head and wouldn't relent.

Jimmy will come back. He needs to be here. He needs to be here with me and the baby.

The next few hours were spent worrying about where Jimmy could be, who he was with, when he would return, or if he would return. The nurse brought Carmen to Birdie, and Birdie held her breath while the baby latched onto her breast. Even then, Birdie vacated the moment of warm intimacy to dwell on Jimmy's whereabouts.

Damn you, girl! Get a damn hold of yourself! She heard both her own voice and Mama's loudly in unison from somewhere deep inside her head.

Birdie tightened her arms around Carmen. The baby's warmth radiated against her skin and the fragrant air surrounding the infant poured through her like warm golden liquid filling her up from her toes. The sensation gave her what she needed to divert her worries. Birdie looked down at Carmen's cheeks, the delicate fringe of long eyelashes and the swirl of black curls that covered her head. She held her daughter's tiny hand, checking the tiny fingernails and dark skin around her knuckles. Each petite finger moved as if it was charged with searching for something to clasp onto. Mama's words came back to her. *That hand you feel, that's God, not him. That man ain't here to save you, chile.*

From this point forward both she and baby Carmen would be safe. Birdie would make sure of that.

★ ★ ★

Over the next few weeks, again there were covered plates and baskets of dried and smoked meats, casseroles, jars of summer vegetables and fruits, homemade jelly, fresh bread and cakes at Birdie's front door. Sometimes people would stop by to chat and take a look at the baby. Birdie welcomed the company. Birdie thought about Mama and her sisters often. She desperately wanted to visit just to chat and feel the warmth of the kitchen when something sweet was baking or cooling. It would take two buses and a bit of a walk to get to Mama's house. But Birdie couldn't afford the bus fare and carrying a squirming baby for the last few blocks would be more than a challenge.

Jimmy insisted she stay at home with the baby. He promised he would take care of everything. Birdie, coming from a long line of self-sufficient women who always worked, offered no protest to his request, but reminded him that she was quite capable of doing something that could bring in a little extra money to put into savings. During their most intimate nighttime conversations, while sharing dreams and kisses, they'd laugh and lovingly negotiate the size of the house they'd buy or how they would strike out on their own to open some sort of business. With that, Jimmy was gone all day, working at Wrights as much as he could and regularly doing overtime. But as the day's early morning frost loitered into the afternoon, he was turned away from the factory more days than not due to lack of work. Soon there wasn't enough to cover the twenty-six-dollars-a-month rent and the rest of the household necessities for the small family. Mt. Sterling, like the rest of the country, was still trying to get back on its feet since the Depression. Help-wanted signs popping up hinted that recovery was making its way through the town. More and more tobacco- and farm-related factories started retooling to manufacture a variety of products from airplane engines to bullets. Yet most openings posted stated "whites only."

Jimmy told Birdie that one company supervisor, a white man he had once worked shoulder to shoulder with on a small piece of sharecropper land outside of Louisville, told him that as a new supervisor he couldn't hire any black men. It wasn't because they didn't have work, it was that they didn't have Negro water fountains or toilets.

"Bird, some men carry around a jar in case they can't leave the line to find a place to pee. Where's the dignity? That ain't right for any honest working man to have to carry around their own urine…not living in today's world."

When he spoke out angrily about his encounters, she caught the arc of his neck, the rigidness in his spine and the stretch and bend of his fingers as they curled into fists. It broke her heart to see the change in his posture. The dwindling width of his shoulders spoke until he eventually would say nothing to her. Birdie found ways to get some groceries and coffee, establishing credit where she could, all over the town. She baked fruit cobblers and brewed extra strong coffee just the way Jimmy loved it to make sure his face carried the smile and sparkling eyes that had first captured her. She'd reach for a book or magazine and jokingly say, "Sit and relax, babe, I'm going to read to you like you've never been read to before." She would do so in the most animated fashion to get him to laugh.

When he was quiet and distant, she'd make sure to touch him. She'd brush against him, lightly place a hand on his chest or rub his back to remind him she was beside him. Once, when Jimmy was sitting by the window deep in thought, Birdie leaned over and whispered in his ear, "Let me be your poem, Jimmy. I'll be your Langston Hughes."

He kept his eyes on some imaginary point on the horizon and returned a slow smile.

She gently passed her palm over his cheek to caress the prickly growth of new beard at his chin. "Let me be the soft music whose notes won't leave your head. Let me be all that is shaped by your hands as you go through your day, as you slide your fingers over objects to smooth the rough and straighten the crooked."

His smile broadened and he reached up to fold his hands over her arms that were wrapped around his shoulders.

"Jimmy, let me be the curve of your Js, long dips of your Gs and every defining cross of Ts in the words that meet your eyes. My dear husband, I am your woman."

"Yes, you are my wife, baby bird," he whispered back. "How did I get so lucky?"

One lazy Sunday morning, Jimmy blurted out, "How would you like to move to Chicago?"

Bright white sunlight was shining through lopsided leaves of the plants Birdie had posted guard at their bedroom windows. Birdie, having just finished nursing Carmen, shielded her eyes from the morning light when she looked up at him.

"You want us to move to Chicago?" She patted the baby softly on the back awaiting a big "urp" from the little girl.

Jimmy didn't answer. It wasn't long ago when Birdie dreamed about living in a big city where she could roll up in a fancy car to parties and clubs like the movie stars in the magazines. Chicago was just the place for that. But now with Carmen, it was just a childhood dream.

"You want us to move to Chicago?" She repeated it slowly in case he didn't hear her the first time. "Jimmy, with the baby and all, I don't know."

He gave her a swift peck on the cheek before bounding out of bed. Standing over her, he extended his arms signaling

Birdie to give him the baby. Carmen's little feet pedaled the air as Jimmy lifted her up and held her high above his head. His bright, shining, laughing eyes met Carmen's as they exchanged matching smiles. Slowly, he brought her down close to his face and kissed his daughter repeatedly on the nose.

"Baby, just forget about what I said. Don't worry yourself about it. It was just a thought."

Jimmy left early every morning in search of steady work and when he returned Birdie watched for the bend in his posture, the tight line of his lips and a dulled luster of his eyes. It had been a month without any jobs or prospects. There was nothing left of the neighborly contributions of food, household items or baby clothes. No knocks on the door from visitors with a covered dish. They couldn't ask Mr. Johnny, the last-resort grocer who sold old food way above price, for an extension of their account. People patronized Mr. Johnny despite the ancient conditions of canned foods and dry goods and even after witnessing a roach or two skitter across the counter as they paid for their groceries. He was one of the few grocers in the black neighborhood that would allow you to run an account. The last bits of aged meat Birdie got from Mr. Johnny's had already overextended their account.

But an empty pantry didn't worry her as much as watching her husband. Like everything else, Jimmy began to diminish too. More and more, throughout the cold winter months, he stayed out late. The first time, it was after midnight when the door took a long creaking breath into the silent house only lit by starlight. Birdie tossed around the bed heated by anger and worry, jumped up repeatedly to check the baby and fretted something might have happened to Jimmy. It was cool relief to finally hear the door open and the familiar footsteps that followed. She chalked up his lateness to a need to relax, drink a bit or play cards. Of course, he needed to blow off steam from time to time. At least that's what she told herself each time she went to bed without him.

Never in her life had she slept alone. Growing up, Birdie and Chicky always shared a bed. It became more and more difficult to fall asleep by herself. She started wandering through the apartment late into the night. She missed Jimmy's arm around her, and his voice languishing words over her as he read. When he came home, no matter how late, he'd slide into bed next to her and kiss her shoulder, arm, or the valley of her back. It was always a soft and lingering kiss that grazed the fine hairs on her skin. Birdie kept her eyes closed tight to block in her worry and anger. Until she just couldn't take it anymore.

She whipped around, startling him. "Where have you been, Jimmy? Where have you been going off to and staying out late so many nights?"

Jimmy held his hands midair, surprised to see her wide awake. He quickly reclaimed his composure. "I've been here and there, baby bird...just trying to get a foothold."

Birdie raised herself up on her elbows. Her eyes shifted to the crib and she lowered her voice to a whisper. "Foothold? Hmmm, what—"

Jimmy abruptly cut her off. "Yeah, yeah, yeah, woman...a foothold. I'm trying to make some things happen."

"Jimmy, we need..."

"I know. I know. I'm working on it." He turned away from her and pulled the blanket over his shoulder.

Birdie listened for deep breaths of sleep but heard none. Heat radiated from Jimmy's side of the bed, and she kept what little distance there was between them. She stayed awake on her side of the small, pitiful island for the rest of the night. A voice crept into her head. The voice, indecipherable at first, grew and nagged at her. It whispered, *You and your new little baby girl are not enough for him.* She had heard it before. Most times she shook it off and distracted herself with taking care of Carmen. Birdie kept silent in an attempt to heal the wounds they left. To repeat the words, to say them aloud to anybody, would give them the strength she wanted to deny. So Jimmy's frequent late returns home from seeking steady work went unchallenged. But the voice that grew louder in the dark would spill over into the light. The words started to slice deeper and deeper.

In the morning, Jimmy's long body lay still, in the same position their feeble attempt at arguing left him. Birdie fed the baby, started a pot of coffee and began preparing the last bits of bacon and oatmeal. When Jimmy arose, he dressed and ate the breakfast she prepared. While she gathered and cleaned the dishes, he walked behind her, squeezed her shoulders and kissed her neck. No words were exchanged between them before he shut the door behind him.

It was a day when those who knew the life of working around fields began to anticipate the promise of spring. The crisp layer of lingering snow had retreated revealing slips of wet and well-nourished earth. Water dripped and trickled everywhere forming flowing pools, passages and trails. The rhythmic sound of unrestrained water was a reminder that deep beneath the surface was restless energy. It wouldn't be long before Mother Nature's internal handiwork, the fresh new shoots of vegetation, would begin peeking through the earth.

For those that knew, this meant there would soon be opportunities to put money into empty winter pockets. The surrounding farms, both large and small, would need field workers. That meant the long drought of piecing together

CHAPTER SIX

Birdie looked over at the unwrinkled sheets on Jimmy's side of the bed. Carmen, awake in her crib, elevated soft wanting cries to screams for immediate attention. Birdie pulled the chubby infant up and gave her a breast. She found comfort in having her baby so warm and close to her skin. Like Carmen, Birdie needed someone who wanted her right now. Carmen stopped crying and suckled softly, eyes closed, little fists toying with Birdie's hair.

Birdie paced the room with the baby clinging to her breast wondering what she should do. She told herself worrying couldn't be good for her milk and she didn't want to pass along her agitation to the baby. Still, her panic gave way to chilling fears. *Is Jimmy dead? Is he lying in a ditch somewhere drunk, beat up or something? Should I run down to the drug store and call someone? Who can I call? Mama? No…uh-uh. I can't give her any reason to say something nasty. Maybe his cousin, Jessie, would know something.*

Birdie didn't want to raise any false alarm. Or look like

some scared little girl. *The best thing to do is to say nothing, do nothing and wait. Just wait it out.* Once he stepped through the door, she'd scream holy terror.

For two whole days Birdie hid herself in the house. Fortunately, no one came by. She sipped day-old coffee and ate only bits of bread and cheese while observing a dark brown outline from a small leak advance across the ceiling. When Carmen napped, Birdie wandered through the apartment picking through scraps of paper, flipping through books with hopes of finding something that would give her a clue to Jimmy's whereabouts. On the third day, she moved from fearing he was dead to fuming at the thought he might be crawling up under another woman. Jimmy cheating on her was just one of the stories that played in her head. She sniffed and examined every inch of his clothes for lipstick, face makeup or the scent of perfume.

The angrier Birdie got, the colder the little apartment felt. Cold air swirled around her ankles. She wondered if there was either a window open or door ajar in the basement that invited frigid air to wind its way up through the floorboards. Shivering, Birdie reached into the crib to pull up the blanket covering the baby. She touched Carmen's forehead to get a precautionary sign. She couldn't have Carmen catching cold. They didn't have any money for a doctor. Birdie turned on the oven to warm up the small apartment.

She sat down at the kitchen table to wait for the heat to kick in. Speaking out to the cold, empty apartment, Birdie decided, "I can't stay holed up in this apartment waiting for that damn man to return. Jessie knows something. I'll go see just what he knows tomorrow."

She went over to the cabinets and pantry, opening every door to inspect the contents. She already knew what little was there. "Now, I need to get something for us to eat. There's nothing left in this house. I'll go crosstown to Betterens grocery store and see if I can get some milk, bacon and eggs, and maybe a few other things on account. Mr. Betterens has always been nice to Mama and me. He might extend me this small bit of kindness for a few groceries."

With her plan in place, Birdie wandered back to the bed and fell into a deep sleep.

She awoke in a haze of heat. Sweat trickled down her forehead, under her breasts and down her back. Birdie pulled herself up onto her elbows and listened for Carmen. Her night gown clung to her body, stained from sweat and leaking breast milk. She heard no light breathing or movement coming from the crib. She moved forward to get a look beyond the foot of the bed over to the crib. Her mouth dropped open and she scrambled out of bed to make sure her eyes weren't deceiving her. The crib was empty.

Screaming as Birdie spun herself around frantically, she called out to her daughter, "Carmen! Carmen!"

"Whoa, whoa, whoa... Girl, why all this noise in the middle of the night? And why you got this stove on? It's hot as hades in here!"

Jimmy stood in the middle of the kitchen with a drooling Carmen cradled in his arms. She contentedly sucked on two fingers while her sleepy eyes focused on her father's face. Jimmy chuckled while patting the baby.

"Bird, what you try'n to do? You put food *in* the oven to cook, not the other way around."

Birdie squinted to make sure she could believe the image standing in front of her. She wasn't sure if it was the heat, the sudden overwhelming sense of fear or the bright kitchen light that made the room spin. She wobbled on her bare feet, struggling to get her balance. Leaning against a chair, she stretched out her arms.

"Give her to me. I need to feed her now."

"No, no, no," Jimmy said softly. "See, she's sleeping now. Let me put her in her crib. Go back to bed, Bird. You need to get your sleep."

He brushed past her. His proximity jolted her back to clarity. It was like jump-starting a car battery. Birdie shifted from one foot to the other.

"No, Jimmy. Give her to me." Damp strands of hair were plastered to her face while others were electrified tentacles reaching out in every direction.

Jimmy gently unfolded Carmen from his arms and walked calmly to the bedroom to place her in her crib. He then turned and began smoothing and pulling up the sheets and blanket on the bed.

"Here, woman, lay down. I'm gonna run you some bath water. I brought us some steaks. I got some eggs too. I'll make us some breakfast. Is there coffee in this house? Oh, and I brought you something. I want to give it to you nice and proper like."

He continued brushing his hands over the bed. He reached for her hand. "C'mon, lil' Bird, rest a bit while I run you a bath."

Where the hell did he get steaks and eggs at two o'clock in the morning? Birdie wondered.

She had only enough energy to roll her eyes. Birdie could see Jimmy was trying every trick to bring the temperature down in the room. Giving in, Birdie got in bed as instructed, promising herself to have a real serious conversation with her husband about his whereabouts later. For now, calmed by the fact that he was alive and here, she let herself relax in anticipation of having his warm body next to her.

She woke from a deep sleep to his strokes on her cheek. Birdie felt as though she had slept for centuries. Except for light wisps of Carmen's breathing, the world around them was quiet. Jimmy led Birdie by the hand to the bathroom where curling steam arose from the tub. The only light was from the waning moonlight shining through the bathroom's frosted paned glass window. Jimmy unbuttoned Birdie's nightgown, lifted it over her head and helped her get in. The hot water surrounding her body was sublime. She lay back, closed her eyes and sighed. Jimmy said nothing. Birdie didn't want to break the spell, so she kept silent also.

He left and returned with the tortoise shell comb she always kept by the bed. Sitting on the edge of the tub, Jimmy ran the comb through her wet strands pausing to carefully undo the tangled ends. He softly parted her hair down the middle of her head and smoothed it down with flat palms. Birdie shivered. He paused. Holding her head in both hands, Jimmy leaned over and blew warm breath down the newly formed part. All the while Birdie kept her eyes closed. Her eyelids fluttered with the touch of Jimmy's breath on her bare skin. He hovered above her then, leaned down and kissed her eyelids. It was a brave gesture on his part. This was the first time they touched intimately since his unexplained absence. He continued in his bravery. Leaning further over, he kissed her full on the lips. Birdie responded to the warm, relaxing water, the heat from Jimmy's palms touching the sides of her face and his intoxicating scent. She couldn't help herself.

When they were wrapped closely together among cool sheets, Jimmy told her he had met up with an old friend, a man who needed something and would pay big money if he could get it quick. Jimmy apologized over and over for not telling her, but he had to leave on the spot and never thought he would be gone so long. In the calm of the moment, Birdie decided to drop her questions and protests. And over the next ninety-two days, it felt like true bliss. For three months after

Jimmy mysteriously reappeared, they were everything Birdie imagined a happy family could be.

Jimmy borrowed a car and took her and Carmen to Cincinnati to see the lights around Fountain Square. They walked through the art museum and nature conservatory in Eden Park where Birdie laid out a blanket and had sandwiches and cake at the hilltop park overlooking blossoming trees along the Ohio River Valley. Jimmy also made time to do what Birdie loved most, go to the movies. They saw the Bronze Bogart, Ralph Cooper, in the gangster films *Dark Manhattan* and *Bargain with Bullets*. They saw *Harlem on the Prairie*, the all-black Western musical with the singing cowboy, Herbert Jeffrey. Birdie loved the Western most of all for its adventure and fast-paced fun.

Jimmy returned to reading aloud to Birdie at night. There was always something with words and imagery that sparked her imagination of the world she had never seen. Birdie fell asleep listening to Jimmy's voice as he recited and read Langston Hughes's poems and essays. When she asked why he liked to read Langston Hughes so much, he responded, "Langston writes about all the people I know. Everything he puts down on paper is about someone or something I've experienced. And he's bold enough to say what he thinks outright—damn, what any black man thinks about, Bird."

He paused and gave her a long look. "This is you, Bird, right there in these passages. You see, you are this kind of poetry to me. If I could phrase it like Langston, I'd make a million dollars just writing poetry about you."

As the spring weather unfolded, so did steady work. Jimmy went back to work at Wrights. He brought home enough money to pay down accounts they'd built all over town. Because of his years of farming knowledge Jimmy became known as an authority on picking the right quality crop. Buyers fought for him to accompany them to area farms to help determine if the farmer's tobacco leaves could produce a superior product. Of course, company supervisors never acknowledged they depended on him, a black man. Supervisors just said they needed him to drive the truck and when they got to the farms, he was sent ahead to test the leaves. Jimmy's evaluation made him a friend or enemy of tenant farmers in the area. The heaviness of a farmer's pockets and ability to feed their families depended on Jimmy's assessment of their crop. Jimmy tried to get the best deal for black farmers. He knew a deal with the tobacco company was, for many, their only source of income. He knew they were undercut and paid next to nothing for tobacco that was free and clear of infestation. For the most part he held firm to this internal bargain to support the black farmers who struggled to make ends meet.

On the ninety-third day after Jimmy's return, the neat threads that held together the seams of their lives began, once again, to unravel. Birdie, startled awake in the dark night, heard scratching sounds on the front window. *Was someone trying to break into the house?* The old wood along the window frame groaned and cracked. Birdie's heart banged loudly against her rib cage. She snapped her neck over to the other side of the bed in hopes that she was mistaken about going to sleep alone. No Jimmy. Only Carmen spread-eagle, sleeping peacefully. The scratching continued, this time more pronounced and deliberate, at the back door. It couldn't be Jimmy. He had a key and would not have had to jiggle and scratch at the window or door lock. Still slightly confused from being yanked from sleep, Birdie squinted to focus and get her bearings. She eased herself out of the bed just as she heard the back door break free of its lock and creak open.

Jimmy, holding himself up only by a knuckled grip on the wobbly doorknob, tripped over his feet and dropped to his knees. His body slumped forward and his head fell back, letting loose the acidic smell of whiskey from a gaping mouth. Birdie stepped back, letting his body spill onto the cold linoleum floor. She observed him as if a specimen in a science project. He mumbled something and within seconds, sprawled out on the floor, he was snoring. She blew out an air of disgust before kneeling over him.

"Where the hell have you been and who have you been with?" Birdie tore through Jimmy's pockets in hopes of finding something, anything that would give her a clue. He didn't resist even when she began pulling off his boots and socks. She found matches, a cigar, a broken-tooth comb, a tarnished gold coin which she knew had no value, and a folded piece of yellowed, dog-eared paper.

"Damn you, Jimmy. So some little whore wrote you a love note. You better not be spending any money on that wench."

She quickly unfolded the paper. Neatly typed, it read:

```
PROMISSORY NOTE
April 22, 1939


To my family, I promise to give James Bryant
Walker one hundred dollars and the deed to
my house located at 1859 Erkenbrecher Avenue,
Cincinnati, Ohio, should I die.


Signed,
Archibald Inskeep
```

Birdie read it again, refolded the note and tossed it on the table with the other useless items. Jimmy might not have been keeping some other woman, but he was surely keeping secrets. Not finding a drop of the promised one hundred dollars on him meant nobody died and Jimmy was drinking just to be drinking. Birdie left him on the floor, turned out the kitchen light and went back to bed.

In the morning Jimmy never said a word about his comings and goings the night before, or any other night. He got up, ate breakfast, pulled at Birdie to give her a light kiss on the cheek and went to work.

Again, his silence began to grow. Birdie wasn't sure what else to do to bring him back. This time she began to withdraw too. It was in her resentful silence that she couldn't find the right time to tell Jimmy she was pregnant. Her waistline forced her to tell him.

"Why didn't you tell me before, Bird?" Jimmy held her hands tightly in his. "Why would you keep this a secret from me?"

"You've plenty of secrets of your own, Jimmy. I didn't think…"

"Secrets of my own? What are you talking about?" He was smiling but his voice carried a thread of anger. "I said what are you talking about, girl?"

"Oh, I'm some little girl now, am I?"

She no longer cared about his feelings. In fact, her anger drove her to poke at him even more. Besides, anger was more emotion than she had gotten from him in a while. She let her anger flare.

"Well, this *girl*, the girl you said you wanted to marry so badly, wants to know what nasty woman you been with lately…'cause you certainly haven't been spending time with me!"

Jimmy looked at her quizzically. "Oh, that's it. You think I've been seein' someone else…that I been cheatin' on you? Yeah, Bird, you're being a little girl right now. I ain't got no one on my mind but you, Carmen and now that baby in your belly. It is mine, right? Or is that why you been keepin' it a secret?"

Jimmy's words punched Birdie in the stomach. How could a man she loved so much, a man who claimed to love her back, say something like that to her face? She contorted with the pain of his words. Grabbing her stomach, Birdie twisted around to find the nearest thing to lean on. Jimmy lunged forward to catch her. Before he could reach her, she grabbed the closest thing to her, flinging the cup filled with the last bit of Jimmy's morning coffee along with the saucer directly at his head. Jimmy ducked. The cup hit the wall behind him but the saucer broke against his shoulder. Jagged shards of porcelain china printed with dainty pink roses fell to the floor at his feet. Cold coffee trickled down Jimmy's face creating brown stains around his shirt collar and trails down the front of his shirt.

Jimmy was as surprised as Birdie was to see her display that much anger. Speechless, chests heaving, they both stood facing each other.

"How dare you, Jimmy," she said in a slow growl. "How dare you say that to me?" Birdie's words were the only stones, rocks and bricks she had to hurl at him for all the times he strayed away from her. All the times he did not live up to the promises he made to her when they sat under the trees at Owl's Nest Park or lay in the sunshine on the riverbank, or after every intimate passage he read where some poet painted a picture of forever.

"Baby, baby, baby... I'm sorry. I'm so sorry." He backed up, bumping into the table behind him. He held up his hands as if she had a gun pointed at him. "I didn't mean it, really I didn't. I was just mad you didn't trust me...that you didn't think to tell me about the baby before now."

Birdie, slow to recover from her outburst, traced the trajectory of the flying cup and saucer. "Damn, that was one of my favorites too." She scooted past him to pick up the large pieces, holding them together to see if anything was salvageable. She looked up at him.

"Get out, Jimmy. Go on and go wherever you go. Leave. I really don't care where you go right now. But I'll tell you one thing: your ass better be back here tonight with your family. If you can't do that then don't bother coming back at all."

Jimmy looked as if to say something, then turned and walked toward the door. The flare of their first real argument splayed out in the raw light of day awakened a memory of the first time she followed him up the aisle of the Paramount Theater over two years ago. As she had done before, Birdie watched the wrinkles and folds of the back of his shirt, the slope of his shoulders and the curve of the fabric of his pants as they lay against his buttocks. She fought a desire to cry or call him back. Instead, she waved her hand in the air as if to break the spell and picked up the remaining pieces of her formerly fine china.

Birdie had James Michael Walker, Junior at home. The small apartment was filled with busy females just like the hospital room when Carmen was born. But this time, Mama was in attendance. Holding her head high, Mama breezed in as if nothing ever happened. In a rare show of affection, she kissed Birdie on the forehead as if to tell her daughter there was no need to grace the day with any discussion of anger, disappointment and absence. Mama, Chicky, Bessa and two Amazons laid hands, prayed, cooked and clean around Birdie throughout her contractions. It was an easy birth. After only a few hours, it was obvious mother and baby couldn't wait any longer. Birdie bore down and pulled him out with her own hands. She hugged the fresh newborn close to her chest, sighing with relief that her son was finally born.

Mama immediately yanked him away and began to pat the baby's chest. The baby's blue-and-purple coloring signaled trouble. His tight fists bobbed in the air as he struggled to catch a breath. Mama rubbed his arms and legs. It was then he began to take in air, scream to herald his entrance into the world and finally turn a rosy pink color.

With each breath, the infant's screams kicked up a higher octave. An Amazon shouted above the wailing, "Whew, this one's gonna be a strong one. He's gonna be a fighter. You ready for this, Bird? You got you two little ones now. That's a lot to handle."

"Give him to me. Give him to me, Mama." Birdie's outstretched arms and fingers danced in the air. With his purplish-blue coloring now retreating to a fresh toasty brown, Birdie inspected the little one's fingers and toes. His tiny fists and feet were moving to some rhythm like he was celebrating his freedom. "Yep, I can see already you are going to be like your father, alright," she whispered.

She looked up from her newborn to see a protective circle of women surrounding her. Their arms and hands moved quickly about pressing a warm cloth against her forehead, cheeks, neck and shoulders. They gave her cool water to sip and a fresh gown to wear. The same palms lifted her up to remove towels, stretch clean sheets over the mattress and freshen up the room. Beyond the cluster of women, Jimmy stood, as he had with his firstborn, quietly on the other side of the room, his eyes beaming. He was waiting, she suspected, for the women to leave. He was waiting for the right moment to properly welcome and claim his son.

They had Lil' Jimmy, as everyone had already taken to call him, christened. Chicky told Birdie that Mama said christenings were as good a time as any to strengthen a marriage. They neglected this step when Carmen came into the world, but Birdie prodded until she finally convinced Jimmy to go along with it. Birdie threw herself into planning the event as if it were her wedding or a way to recreate the freshness of their early courtship. She wanted to look fabulous, of course. Chicky made Birdie a classy rose-colored wool suit which she complemented with a fashionable hat Jimmy had brought her from a fancy milliner in Cincinnati. The suit was impeccably cut. The jacket gave the appearance of a tiny waist, and the peplum hid the small lingering bump of her stomach.

When she first tried it on, she posed outrageously in the long mirror. "This ought to do it."

After the ceremony, Mama invited everyone back to her house. It was obvious, by the dizzying array of meats, vegetables and desserts that she wanted to bring the entire family together under one roof for the celebration. And Jimmy, who would generally rail against religious rituals, did not protest when Mama asked him to sign the family bible.

The christening brought a sense of calm. Jimmy went to work and came directly home most days. On the days he was late, he was playing cards with his boys and returned only a few hours into the night. He never left or returned home without kissing his wife and children. Birdie busied herself with caring for an infant and a toddler. In the quiet times, generally a shaded sky past dusk, when the children were bathed and tucked into bed, she'd remember moments when she sat with Jimmy on the balcony at Owl's Nest Park feeling giddy about the possibility of starting an adventure with him. It had been only a few years ago when she thought her life would be anything other than being a housewife and mother living here in Mt. Sterling. She looked down at her children and thought she wouldn't want to be anywhere else.

Birdie was feeling truly at peace on the day Mama came by to visit and ended up taking baby Carmen to stay with her, as she had come to do so often. Carmen, a precocious toddler, was becoming a handful. Surprisingly, Mama didn't mind. Carmen brought out a soft side of Mama that Birdie had never, ever seen before. The Mama she knew would have threatened or just slapped Bessa, Chicky and her for any infraction. When Carmen scrambled up onto Mama's lap and gathered her granny's face in her hands to give her a wet, sloppy kiss, Mama would hold baby Carmen tight and laugh. Laughter was a foreign sound coming from her mother. But it was a relief to have Carmen so close to Mama.

Sticky liquid bubbled up from Birdie's nipples and flowed down over the soft folds of her stomach. It was so much milk. It poured from her as the baby wailed. The windows were thrown open to let the evening air cool the house from the hot day. She was sure everyone in the county could hear Lil' Jimmy screaming.

She stared at her son, a tiny ball of energy. He shook his little red fists like they were rattles punching the air. His eyes were shut tight as he kicked the light blanket as if ready to escape.

"Ooooh, look at you! You are such a demanding little thing...fresh on this earth and insistent that some woman give up her tits to you."

Birdie twisted the buttons of her wet gown to give him what he wanted. She lifted Lil' Jimmy out of the crib, nuzzled his head against her breast and he quickly latched on. She sat on the edge of the bed with him in her arms. The sudden peaceful quiet felt like her first breath since she introduced Lil' Jimmy to the world. After a few deep breaths, and listening to the sound of the baby suckling, the temperature of the air changed. Birdie was suddenly overcome with a strange feeling that she was truly all alone. It was as if someone had thrown a blanket over her head.

Lil' Jimmy was only three months old when Jimmy disappeared again without explanation. He left for work in the morning and never returned. It had been over a month with no word of his whereabouts or if he was even alive. After a week, Birdie asked Jessie who checked the Kentucky jails and hospitals with no news. Birdie checked Wrights and they told her he never returned to work. His supervisor said they hadn't seen him since he went out to a farm in Butler County and they wouldn't hold his job any longer. They gave her his final check of twelve dollars and ten cents for only less than a week of work.

She didn't want to say anything about Jimmy to her family. Every day she checked the mail. She watched the window in hope of seeing a telegram being delivered. She even watched and hoped for a letter to suddenly slide across the floor after being discreetly slipped under her door. Secretly, she posted missing person ads in the *Call and Post*. To distract herself even further, Birdie sent out chain letters hoping the scheme might bless her with untold riches as promised in every note she received and the ten she sent out. She hoped with each batch of envelopes she received there would be one from Jimmy.

Never did she think it would be almost two years before she would see her husband again.

CHAPTER SEVEN

Jimmy's feet rhythmically hit the dirt landing with heavy thuds. Each step got lighter and lighter as he picked up speed and began running on his toes to keep pace with the moving train. He had been riding the rails since he was a boy, first as a means of entertainment then as a necessity to get from job to job. He knew the dangers of hitching a ride on the Pennsylvania, Acheson and B&O passenger lines, or riding some of the single-track freight trains carrying coal or salt from the mines. Too many of his friends had the misfortune of falling among the tracks and losing entire or parts of arms and legs. Although dangerous, it was easier to hitch a ride on an open rail car than trying to board a main line train while passengers got on and off at the depot. There were way too many eyes watching. A black man without a uniform didn't have a chance of sneaking on undetected. Jimmy resorted to waiting until a freight train pulled away from the station to make an attempt.

It was all about timing. He had to keep a safe distance from the rails so as not to trip to his death or dismemberment, then move closer when he was arm's length from the train for a no-second-chance, full grab on the freight car's doors or ladder.

Jimmy flung himself at the rapidly moving train, grabbing a rung of the car's ladder first with one hand then the other to hoist his body up. He could've climbed up and ridden on top for a while, but it was cold, windy and threatening to rain. He hugged his body close to the ladder before inching over to the ladder's edge and extending his leg to place a foot sideways in the open doorway of the boxcar. He grabbed the door's handle with one hand to swing himself into the boxcar. Jimmy landed on his back with an echoing thud as he hit the freight car floor.

Squinting to adjust to the darkness, he saw a dark, jagged outline of folks huddled along the back wall and corners of the car. They were shadows of men, dirty and curled up with knees drawn to their chests. Some were lying flat on their backs or leaning against the walls. Hats way past their glory days were pulled down over their faces; you couldn't tell what color they were. From what Jimmy could make out in the dark, their clothes were filthy. Some wore either thin cloth jackets or shirts covering overalls or dungarees. All had only pieces of shoes covering their feet.

One man looked up when Jimmy entered the boxcar. Immediately Jimmy's skin prickled, a warning sign to stay alert for possible danger. He'd seen it all before. The hobo's piercing gray eyes met his and could mean anything from anger, shame, hunger, or sickness that came with all males drifting from camp to city in search of jobs, redemption or both. Since the Depression, many men went looking for better luck and a new life in the next city, county or state. Many had left mothers, wives and families behind just as Jimmy did for the sake of providing food and shelter.

Jimmy stayed on guard knowing only too well that these men, despite having nothing but the clothes on their backs, saw his black skin as a threat. He knew that even if they only had an ounce of energy left in their bodies it could be dangerous for him as a Negro sharing the same air in this empty freight car. Most of them, unwashed and weak from hunger, were probably stealing away and ducking the law. Still, there was a chance he could hear, *"This ain't for colored...get outta this car, you filthy nigger."*

He had heard it many times before from those with feeble muscles clinging to thin frames and nothing else other than anger. Jimmy knew even these lost men, who he could easily beat in a fistfight, had the power to rally others and bring about a mob that could land him, not only in jail or on a chain gang, but most likely hanging from a limb. He kept his defenses up and his head down. Jimmy jammed his hands in his pockets and moved into the dark recesses of the car, as far away from the others as possible. He kept his sights on the open doors and after a while the sound and movement of the train lulled him into a light sleep. He awoke to see a lilac-colored sky settle among dark green valleys of what he knew were the Blue Mountains. His sides ached from bruises incurred from hitching a ride but also from hunger. He longed for a plate of good food, a smoke and a strong drink or two. He hoped it wouldn't be too long until he would be able to find all those things in New York.

He was sure he would find work in New York. Not farm-hand work he left back in Mt. Sterling, but construction work paying some real money. One of the men at Wrights told him that the NAACP was pressuring the city of New York to give jobs to black men to help build the World's Fair Exhibition and plenty of other WPA projects all over the city.

I can make some real money without having to bow and scrape 'cause right now I'm gonna haf'ta kill the next white man that talks down to me, Jimmy thought.

His anger brought him back to what he just left behind—the experience of his last day working at Wrights and in Mt. Sterling. He had gone out on the truck with the supervisors to check tobacco at a small tenant farm. His supervisors were a father and son duo who must've known Mr. Wright himself in order to land supervisor titles. The father, Beau, was a long-time tobacco farmer and could be respected for his knowledge. His son, Bo, had nothing to contribute but brawn. Bo was only there because of his father. Bo's lack of intellect was the reason Jimmy had been assigned to work with them. Jimmy had worked the farms with them before and never had any trouble when it came to sizing up a crop. In fact, several times they asked his opinion on the quality before talking price.

The ride out to the farm covered three full counties before they reached a forlorn outpost consisting of barely a house and barn in the middle of unending fields of tobacco and alfalfa. Jimmy knew the farmer. Monroe Denton, a black man with eight children, had struggled for years to keep the rent paid on the land. Jimmy could see by the condition of Monroe's house and barn that this might be one of the man's hardest times ever. The land had been farmed by Monroe's family since the first African was bought at a slave auction to toil the earth for a Denton family plantation. At a certain point, Monroe's ancestors made a pact that after being mercilessly parceled out, sold and spread like wild seeds, to never, ever separate again. So when they finally were able to own a piece of the land that had been in their charge for years, generations of Monroe's family stayed right on that exact spot, with no intentions to live beyond the boundaries of their farmland. Jimmy never knew how the Dentons' entire living family tree managed to stay under one dilapidated roof.

They were an enterprising bunch for sure, doing anything they could to make ends meet. Monroe's grandfather, before he passed away earlier in the year at almost one hundred and three years old, smoked meats which were said to be the finest quality and most flavorful around. He sold and gave away pieces to all the colored people in the nearby area.

When Jimmy, Beau and Bo finally arrived at the farm, Beau told Jimmy to stay in the truck while they examined the plants and the farmer's curing process and negotiated a price. Jimmy noted mentally Beau didn't say they'd negotiate a *fair* price. So he played simple, as if he didn't hear their instructions, and jumped down from the back of the truck only after the men walked a good ways ahead. Staying back, Jimmy followed the two men down standing rows of hearty, high tobacco with large puffy green leaves tinged yellow as was usual this time of year. Jimmy could see every leaf had the markings of the Denton family's hands and blood. Every plant was tall, pointing straight upward as if looking to praise God.

They approached a weathered barn where Monroe and a few others were looping limp leaves on poles and hanging them from the rafters. All action stopped when the two white men entered the barn. Monroe walked toward Beau and Bo, catching an unacknowledged glimpse of Jimmy a ways behind. Even from his distance, Jimmy could see the beaten-down look of desperation on Monroe's face and hear Bo's dull, flat voice. Bo, without even a hello, quickly started in by saying he saw hornworms and stilt bugs on the leaves and gnawing at the stems. He folded his arms across his chest and tried to sound knowledgeable when he proceeded to tell the farmer another big lie. He said that Negroes were ordered by the government's Agriculture Act not to grow any more tobacco than necessary because there was a glut of tobacco in the market. He went on to tell Monroe that what he was doing was against the law.

Bo cleared his throat, gearing up to put a final point on his lie. He proclaimed with as much authority as he could muster, "We are the last buyers that Wrights gonna have for a while. We'll fairly take it off your hands, so you won't get in any trouble. You don't want to get fined by the government, do you?"

Beau stayed silent the entire time, letting his son do all the talking for once. On cue, Beau piped in only to offer Monroe a paltry, insulting price at about a penny a bushel.

Jimmy was still far enough behind to go unnoticed by his supervisors, but he could clearly hear everything Bo said. Jimmy knew Bo's role was to set the stage to intimidate and prime Monroe so that Beau could undercut him on the price of this tobacco. Even if he didn't hear exactly what his supervisors were saying, Jimmy knew their drill. Bo, who was greedy and trying to impress his pa, was going to present some fabricated information twisted with only a hint of the truth. His intent was to scare Monroe into selling at even lower than the usual low price they offered black farmers. Jimmy stayed silent until he couldn't take it anymore. He moved in closer and loudly cleared his throat. Startled, Beau and Bo turned around, surprised to see Jimmy standing behind them.

Beau shifted his stance and waved him in. "Oh, here's our boy Jimmy. Jimmy, you tell 'em. Tell these people that Wrights ain't making any more rounds this season and is offering a good price for his tobacco."

Jimmy walked over to a pole of tobacco, folded a wide soft leaf in his hand and told the farmer aloud so the men could hear, "Mister Monroe, if I were you, I wouldn't sell to these boys. You got the best quality tobacco I've seen in these parts. Just hold on. Old man Wright is always buying good quality tobacco. Mr. Wright only wants the best and you got it."

Beau and Bo stared at Jimmy in shock. Jimmy spoke directly to Beau. "You know, Mr. Beau senior, Wright likes to reward all those who bring in the best there is and the best deals. I saw something as I was trying to catch up with you. C'mon, take a look at these leaves on the plants right over here. I believe they're the finest we've seen as of late."

Jimmy walked quickly over to the tall plants right outside the barn and motioned both Beau and Bo to follow. Beau hesitated a moment then walked out to examine the plants. Bo soon followed, glaring directly at Jimmy. As both men huddled around the plants, Jimmy walked back over to Monroe.

"I've talked to Mr. Wright myself. I'll try to get it so they come back and offer what's right. I know how to twist it so these damn crackers think it was their idea."

Monroe pushed back his beaten straw hat and wiped his brow with the back of his hand. "I don't know, Jim. It's not that I don't trust you. I know I ain't getting paid what white farmers get. That's just how it is."

Jimmy didn't know how much time he had to convince Monroe that this was the best course of action but decided to unleash what was on his mind in a last-ditch effort. "Listen to me, Monroe, burn it all if they don't give you what's right! Burn every plant up. Take the government's money and get your family out from under the thumb of these here folks."

Monroe, with watery spotted eyes on the verge of cataracts, looked down at the dirt then back at Jimmy. "Naw, us Dentons is all alive today because of this piece of land. I owe this here dirt that covers my grandfather and all my dead kin to bring it to life every year. Nooo, I cain't leave here, son. I'm sorry, brother, but Im'ma haf'ta sell to these white boys at the price they giving me. I know I'm getting less than half of what they pay them white farmers, but I'll take what I can get and keep going. The missus is gonna be disappointed, but we'll make it work. We've done it before."

Beau and Bo came back, more resolute than ever. Standing shoulder to shoulder, they offered the same price as before. Monroe, without saying another word, walked over to shake Beau's hand to seal the agreement. Bo quickly turned to go back to the truck. When Jimmy got to the truck, he found Beau in the driver seat looking straight ahead and Bo standing outside with a whittled two-by-four nestled in his crossed arms.

"Didn't we tell you to stay in the truck? Nigga, you ain't ever gonna ride with us again. I don't care what you know. You ain't that damn smart, nigga. And you know what else I think? I think a smart-ass nigga like you need to stay out here and study up a bit. I'm sure you smart enough to get home on your own."

With that, Bo walked around to the other side of the truck and hopped inside. Beau started up the truck and peeled off leaving Jimmy behind in a cloud of dust and rubble. At that point, Jimmy knew there was no need to go back to Wrights anymore.

The light through the boxcar doors slowly turned from violet to pink to bright gold signaling the oncoming heat. Chimneys and church steeples began peeking through the treetops. Jimmy knew it wouldn't be long before they were in New York City. The pile of rags that were men rippled around the car without anyone speaking a word. Jimmy knew they were probably, like him, too weak from lack of water and food. To keep his mind off his own whining stomach, he thought about Birdie. She was peacefully sleeping when he left. Curled up, lying on her side, she looked invitingly soft. He envisioned her long dark lashes falling across the faintest freckles on her brown cheeks and her full lips lightly pressed together. It pained him to restrain himself from arousing her.

He recalled the curves of her profile, particularly her angular jawline that showed a bit of the stubborn determination that had first attracted him. She was too young and unaware of it. He could tell by the way her chin retreated into the folds of her neck. It would only be a matter of time before she would raise her chin upward and then, without apology, keep it up there for all to see her full beauty, her majesty, her magnificence. When he first laid eyes on her, he knew that she was the force he needed but wasn't ready for just yet.

He imagined her hands and her long, slender fingers curved with potential. He saw them right away. She held her hands in a way that unknowingly revealed innocence. She hid herself in the knots of folded knuckles and soft fists. When she became a mother, her tapered fingers grew to become ten small whips, prepared to strike out. She held them on guard, resting unconsciously against her throat and chest. He knew they would grow stronger and ultimately become steel bars, pressed against her body to protect her. From him, maybe? He couldn't blame her. Sitting in the rolling train, smelling and feeling like shit, traveling away from her, he deserved to be on the outside of those bars.

The night of the concert back in Mt. Sterling, only a few years ago, he stared at her for a long time before approaching to ask her to dance. When he finally got up the nerve to speak to her over a bottle of Coca-Cola, after their hot steamy dance, he fell hard for her. She was unlike any other woman he had ever known. Since then, he saw her profile emerging lifted, elevated, stronger and defined. She still didn't know, but her time was coming soon.

The train began to slow down. The car swayed and rattled as it rounded a curve in the Kittatinny Mountains. He knew each time he left her he could end up paying the steep price of losing Birdie forever.

But why? Jimmy thought. *Ain't my job as a man to protect his woman and family? That's just what I'm doing. I'm doing what's best for them. It's for them that I'm riding this stinking can of flesh hiding in the shadows.*

He sighed and whispered, "I'll send some money back to you. Then everything will be alright. This is the only way I know how to take care of you, Bird."

After what happened that last day at Wrights, he didn't have the heart to return home to tell her. He didn't say goodbye to her and the children because he didn't even know he was leaving at the time. It wasn't until he spotted the train on the long walk back from Monroe's farm that he knew what his next move would be. If he had gone home to tell her, she would have reached out her hands, with those whips circling, and pulled him back. Her softness would beg him to try again. He would relent knowing full well all would be in vain.

Pangs of guilt ate at him along with the cold, thirst and hunger. His only comfort was that he knew he would eventually return home to be with her.

CHAPTER EIGHT

Without Jimmy, flat and uneventful days stretched outward to three bland months moving into an undiscernible new season. It wasn't until Birdie came home one evening to a pitch-black house that her emotions spiked with panic. Holding the baby in one arm, she flipped the unresponsive entryway light switch on and off. The house remained dark. She looked at the baby, heavy with sleep, then at Carmen, sucking two fingers and clinging to her coat. Carmen's soft round face was gracefully outlined by the shred of light coming in from the street behind them. Birdie stood in the doorway staring into the dark hallway. Her arms strained from carrying the baby and her purse, which dangled at her wrist like an anvil.

She spoke out into the darkness. "Carmen, baby, no point going any further. The gas and electric company is not about to be gracious or charitable today. Without electricity, this hallway ain't going to get any brighter. Damn, I don't even have any candles to burn.

"Now, what reason can I give Mama for coming back home? I can't hear that *I told you so* and I am too tired for a lesson."

She whispered to Carmen. "What to do, baby girl? All we got in my pocketbook is enough for a cab going in one direction."

Reluctantly, Birdie used the money to make her way back to Mama's.

Luckily, Mama gave no lesson, lecture or righteous looks. She opened her arms to Carmen as the toddler ran in for a hug. She took Lil' Jimmy off Birdie's hip and snuggled him until he wailed. She then proceeded to direct her daughter's next move.

"Girl, give those babies a bath while I warm up a little something to eat. Then they need to go straight to bed. Them children been out too long in this chilly night air. We can't have folks catching something because we can't afford to have nobody sick. I'm not feeling too good right now. But I'll make it."

The next morning, unfortunately, it was Mama who coughed and coughed. With each spasm her whole body shook.

Birdie, now rested from her worries, gave her mother a gentle order. "Mama, you rest. I'll take care of everything. Do you have any deliveries today?"

Mama let out a choir of coughs before nodding her head. She wagged her finger in the direction of the little table in the corner of the kitchen where she kept a work schedule and ledger of all her orders. Birdie saw that today she was to make tea sandwiches, salads and luncheon cakes for the Conroys.

Birdie knew the Conroys as she did most folks in the small town. They, like so many other white farmers, had closed down their farm and moved into town where Mr. Conroy had some job at city hall. Birdie had crossed paths with the Conroys' three children on the many occasions she dropped off deliveries for Mama. They were all a little older than her. Two of the boys were sharp and nasty. They always made rude comments when she saw them around town. The youngest, Michael, tagging behind his brothers, always had a smile for her and Mama.

Birdie had practically grown up with Michael Conroy. One of her fondest memories of Michael was when they were both about six or seven years old rolling a small red ball back and forth as they sat on a bench together outside the hardware store one bright summer day. They both giggled wildly each time the ball flew across the wood slats and into each other's hands. When Mama appeared and signaled Birdie to follow her on to their next stop, Michael pushed the ball into Birdie's hand. It was Michael's ball, but when she started to roll it back to him, he said, "No, you keep it. It's yours." With the ball tucked in her palm, Birdie turned to look back at Michael as she tagged behind her mother. His bare feet dangled over the side of the bench. He had such a sweet, gap-toothed smile as he waved back at her.

Mama had prepared food for Conroy events for as long as Birdie could remember. She thought it was odd that Mama would only go there when no one was home and most times she would leave her items on the front porch. The Conroys were the only customers Mama allowed to send their payments in the mail. Most of her other clients paid with cash in hand.

Mama, between coughs, spat out, "Listen to me. Go on over there as soon as you can. Mr. and Mrs. Conroy have gone to her mother's house in Covington and won't be back till late this afternoon. Prepare as much as you can here, pack it up nicely and then take it over. No one should be home for a while, so you'll have time to go in and set everything up nice.

Once you do that, get on out of there and come home directly. I'd ask someone else to do it but I can't trust them to do it right. There's a key under the empty pot in the flower box."

Mama paused a moment to pat her chest. Birdie jumped to fetch a glass of water, but her mother held up her hand signaling her not to move.

"Now promise me, if you hear any of them Conroys pull up, you get out of there that second. Go on out the back door and cut through the wood patch to get back here. Okay? There's no need to say hello or anything. Make sure you do exactly that." Mama pulled her hand up to her mouth. Birdie could hear rumbling in Mama's chest when she coughed, and knew she had to let her mother rest so she could fight off her cold.

Since she had a key and expected the Conroys wouldn't be home, despite what Mama instructed, Birdie thought it would be easier to prepare most of the food in the Conroys' kitchen. That way she wouldn't have to carry food back and forth and would have more time to set up. She'd do it quickly and clean up as if she wasn't even there.

Once inside the Conroys' house, Birdie set the table using the lace tablecloth, china and silverware that were laid out on the breakfront. With the room dressed up, she turned her attention to making tea cakes. The smell of warm baked goods would add a nice touch when the Conroys returned, and their guests arrived. Birdie was so consumed with mixing together butter, sugar and eggs that she didn't hear the footsteps coming up behind her.

Without warning, huge arms snaked their way around her, circling her waist like a noose and jerking her backward. Birdie dropped the bowl. It bounced once then shattered against the floor, barely missing both pairs of feet. The sound of the bowl hitting the floor made Birdie flinch, even though the stranger was holding her so tight she could barely move. She wanted to scream, push and bite, but her arms were locked to her side.

Through short breaths, she mustered, "Please. Stop. Please. Let me go. Get off me!"

The man behind her said nothing. No words at least. Birdie lifted her foot hoping to jam her heel into his foot or leg. Having no effect, she kicked back, landing a hard blow to his shin. She heard only a slight humming sound coming from his throat. Lifting her slightly off the ground, he wedged her tightly against the sink.

He nuzzled his face, rough with stubble, against Birdie's cheek. Each coarse hair of his beard scraped her skin. He was so close his eyelashes fluttered, a racing pulse beat from his temples and the hardness in his pants throbbed and pushed against her. His hands moved quickly upward, cupping then tightening around her breasts. Keeping one arm across her chest, he slapped his other hand over her mouth. Freeing his hand from her breast, he reached down, pulled up a handful of Birdie's dress then yanked down her underwear.

Trapped, Birdie held her breath until she heard a soft ripping sound from behind them. The man suddenly jerked forward grinding her ribs into the sharp metal edge of the sink. He let out a grunt as his arms and hands flew up in the air. Once released, Birdie twisted away and turned around to face her attacker. Mr. Conroy stood facing her, frozen to his spot. Behind him, as still as a statue, was her savior.

Mama's face, bathed in sweat, glistened. A fire burned behind Mama's smooth black skin. Birdie had never seen the traces of yellow, red and orange that appeared beneath her mother's skin. Her lips were bundled together in a deep purple knot, her dark eyes aimed solely on Mr. Conroy's back. She gave no sign that she knew anyone else, let alone her daughter, was in that small kitchen when in one swift movement

Mama twisted the handle of the knife that was now buried deep in Mr. Conroy's back.

Mr. Conroy's eyes suddenly bulged as if they were going to pop from his head. His body arched, convulsed and twisted. His arms swung wildly through the air and with shaking hands he attempted to pull out the knife.

"You mutherfuck'n black nigga bitch!" he seethed through clenched teeth. "I'ma fuck'n kill you and that yellow whore of yours!"

Mama took a few steps back, watching his movements. Her hands were poised with fingers spread wide as if she was going to pull guns from a holster to shoot him and finish the job. However, there was no need. The knife had done its damage. Mr. Conroy clawed at his throat as he struggled to take in air. His legs gave way and he fell backward, gasping. The knife thrust deeper into his flesh when he hit the ground.

Birdie stared at her attacker. Mr. Conroy continued to struggle and writhe on the kitchen floor like a fish out of water in a spreading pool of blood. She watched as he stretched his mouth wide open to capture big gulps of air. She thought if she stared at him long enough, he would become a blur and disappear. As her mind fixed on the ribbons of blood following the dying man's movements, Mama stepped on the man's throat as if she were squashing a bug.

Mr. Conroy made a feeble attempt to grab Mama's leg and push her off, but Mama stood firm, not moving an inch. She simply leaned forward, putting all her weight on him until his face turned deep purple. He gurgled up thick blood until he finally stopped moving. Seconds later, his body twitched and a solitary stream of air escaped from his open mouth. As the life drained from his body, they both, mother and daughter, watched him and remained silent.

Birdie stared, transfixed, not at the misshapen purplish-blue man that had ceased grunting and twisting on the kitchen floor but at her mother. At that moment, it became crystal clear to Birdie that Mama's life was more than she had ever imagined. The strength Mama exhibited while sick and racked with fever revealed that beyond her prim, proper and strait-laced existence was a cavernous well of unpasteurized hatred.

Mama grabbed a cup from the counter and shoved it in Birdie's direction. "Now listen to me, girl. Ain't nothing happened here." Then she sharply added, "Yet. Go on up the block right now to Mrs. Moran's. You know them. They're six, no seven, houses over. I know they ain't home, but their girl is. Ask her for some sugar. Don't act nervous. Be calm. Take your time. Let her know that you making tea cakes in your poor, sick momma place. About now everybody knows I'm under the weather. Some of them probably have me dying.

"Start a conversation. Talk about anything. You know how that girl likes to gossip. Spend a little time. Then come straight back here. Don't run. When you leave her house, walk calmly like you don't have a care in the world."

Mama held her chest to suppress a cough and then pointed a crooked finger at Birdie, "And you don't! *You* don't have a care to worry about, little girl! I ran over here through the wood patch. I don't think anyone saw me. I'm gonna go back that way and get right in the bed. Sister Shirleen should be by to give me some roots. I hope to God I beat her back, because it's important she see me."

With each line of instruction, Mama's knees buckled slightly and she began to sink. She braced herself against the kitchen table. Her arms shook as she tried to hold herself up. It was evident her illness allowed her only so much energy and she used all of that to protect her daughter. *Would Mama be able to make it back home without her help?*

"Now when you get back here, you gonna act like you see'n all this for the very first time."

That would almost be true because Birdie could no longer even turn her head in the direction of Mr. Conroy's distorted body and watch the now-black blood continue to spread across the room.

"Once you get back here, scream as loud as you can. Scream and keep screaming. Then run back to the Morans. They got a phone. Tell their girl to call the police. Do you hear me? Look at me and tell me you understand everything I said. You know what gonna happen if you don't do this, right? Now, step over and see if he's got some money in his pockets. Don't step in any of that mess. He should have some rolled together in his jacket pocket."

"What?" Birdie asked feebly. "You want me to…to touch him?"

Mama cocked her head to the side and shot a glassy-eyed glare at her. Birdie jumped to action, stepping lightly over the blood, stretching her arms out to reach Mr. Conroy's jacket. Just as Mama said there was a roll of dollars wrapped in a rubber band. She eased them out of his pocket and handed it over. Mama immediately tucked it under her breasts.

Mama then reached down, grabbed the handle of the knife and pulled the blade out of the dead man's back in one swift move. She was so fast, not a drop of blood dripped from the blade before she slid it in her pocket. She pointed a finger at Birdie. "Do what I said to the letter, girl." With that she left out the back door and evaporated from sight.

Birdie was left alone with Mr. Conroy. His face, now drained of blood, was turning gray. Birdie took a deep breath and headed straight over to the Morans as instructed.

She was too afraid to be afraid. She fixed her face, stepped squarely through the door without being invited in and asked to borrow sugar in a high-pitched, chirpy, singsong voice. Clara, Mrs. Moran's girl, was happy for company. It was easy to get her to chat but not so easy to get her to stop. Birdie worried that the excess of time would ruin the plan. Finally, she was able to wave Clara off and briskly walk back to the Conroys.

It was easy to start screaming because when Birdie opened the door the acrid smell of blood and death was already strong. After running back to the Morans to get Clara to phone the police, she returned to the Conroys and waited on the porch for the authorities to show up. They arrived along with Mrs. Conroy. Mrs. Conroy walked straight to the kitchen. Without any regard to the blood surrounding her dead husband, she fell to the floor, weeping and pulling at his arms. Two policemen tried to lift her up and away from the crime scene but only succeeded in aggravating her movements. Mrs. Conroy resisted their efforts. The woman screamed and kicked in protest, smearing blood all over her clothes and further across the kitchen floor. Birdie pushed through the policemen to coax Mrs. Conroy up from the floor and lead her into another room. Mrs. Conroy collapsed on the sofa sobbing repeatedly, "What am I going to do now?"

Even before the police showed up at the house, the neighborhood drum beat out the news of the murder. Clara had done her job well. Clara called her own family about the murder the minute the door closed behind Birdie. Then someone told someone who reached out to someone else. When Sister Shirleen showed up to Mama's house with some health roots, Mama's next-door neighbor rushed over to deliver the news that Birdie found Mr. Conroy stabbed to death and she was being questioned by the police.

The gory gossip whet Sister Shirleen's appetite for fresh information. She volunteered to take Mama over to the Conroys to be with her daughter and see if they could be of any help to the family. Mama, leaning heavily on Sister Shirleen's arm, showed up at the Conroys' front door looking frail. With a soft ashen face and moist eyes, Mama offered to go next door to make coffee for the bereaved widow, the detectives, two white policemen and the man with a black truck who came to collect the body.

An officer asked Birdie a few questions and jotted down her answers in a small notebook. Birdie kept her head down, her voice small and said only what Mama instructed. Her answers confirmed what the police observed of the black women on the scene. One was a fragile, sick old black woman who spoke in a weak voice and needed help supporting herself. The other was her prim, colored daughter who was obviously in shock from finding the body of a murdered man. As evidenced by their politeness, the comfort they gave to Mrs. Conroy, and their willingness to prepare and serve food and coffee to them during the investigation, the police concluded that Mama, Birdie and Sister Shirleen were just good neighbors who were not likely to start any trouble. After about an hour, Birdie was dismissed so that the detectives could get on with the work of searching for the culprit in what looked like a robbery gone horribly wrong.

Mama, Sister Shirleen and Birdie walked out of the Conroys' front door and slowly proceeded down the block. They took the long way back to Mama's house so as not to give the police any ideas about looking in the direction of the wood patch that divided and connected the homes. It was obvious that Mama was past being exhausted. As soon as they were a safe sight distance from the Conroys, Mama appeared to be on the verge of collapsing. Both Birdie and Sister Shirleen held Mama up and urged her to take baby steps. Once in the door, Sister Shirleen immediately tucked Mama into bed and instructed her daughter, Gwendolyn, who was there watching the children, to take baby Carmen and Lil' Jimmy home with her for the night. Birdie would stay and look after her mother.

The small lamp by Mama's bed was the only light in the entire house. Darkness and shadows concentrated the nightmare as Birdie came to the realization that only hours ago she'd seen a man violently take his last breath. Birdie sat by her mother's bed shivering in the heat of the room. Mama lay flat on her back with the covers drawn up to her neck. Birdie watched Mama's eyelids flicker wildly as her chest rose and fell. Despite her slight movements, barely perceptible in the bleak light, Mama appeared as though she had passed on to the next life. To make sure she was still alive, Birdie waved her hand in front of her mother's face to check for any signs of warmth.

Birdie didn't want to leave her mother's side, not even to pee. Her mind and body hummed, intensifying the need to relieve herself. Ignoring her bodily needs, she listened to her own breathing to keep images of Mr. Conroy's violet face and bulging eyes at bay. Every time she turned her head, she saw a pool of deep red blood flowing into soft piles of white flour and a wall splattered with yellow batter from a flying bowl. She jumped up, shook her head and scurried to the bathroom to splash cold water on her face.

When she returned, Mama was sitting straight up with her back against the headboard. She stretched out her arm and weakly motioned for her daughter. "Come here, Bird. Come to your Mama, my little bird."

Her voice was soft and low. Mama rarely sounded that sweet, so the gesture made Birdie burst into tears. She ran to hug her mother. Mama patted her daughter on the back and smoothed her hair which was plastered flat and limp against her face.

"Girl, you gotta try hard not to think about what just happened today. And don't worry about me. I've come through the other side of more than you'll ever know."

Mama pulled herself up to sit up taller. Cupping Birdie's face into her hands, Mama looked her daughter straight in the eyes.

"This was pure self-defense. You hear me? It was self-defense, clear and simple. But, of course, ain't no white man gonna see it like that. That devil Conroy and his kind have been doing this for years. Damn devils, always taking what don't belong to them. Listen, girl, that man, he was my demon to kill.

"Look, you need to get out of here for a while. I'll keep baby Carmen and Lil' Jimmy. Don't worry about them. I might not look like much now, but I can take care of those little ones. I got the Spirit behind me. In fact, you go get on the next train or bus right now. Go get you a little place out of this town. Find you some work and live your life out from yo' man's shadow."

Surprised by Mama's reference to her husband, Birdie said defiantly, "Mama, what does Jimmy have to do with this? He ain't even here."

Mama began to cough violently. She spat out between coughs, "Damn right, he ain't even here! But you are. You're right here! Here, in this damn town. Here, with nothing to do but clean up after him, look for him and wait for him. He made a promise to you and to me. Remember? He said he would take care of you...protect you. 'Member that? You haven't seen him or heard from him in a long while...have you? I know you'd like me to believe it only been a short time and he's off somewhere working and sending you money, but I know otherwise. I see you wasting away your young years before you can ever live your own life. Forget about him and move on, girl!"

Mama reached for the cup of now-cold peppermint tea that had been sitting on the nightstand. She took a sip and a long breath to calm her coughs. Birdie remained silent.

Mama leaned closer to her. "I love my pretty little grand-babies with all my heart and, believe it or not, I thank that scoundrel for them. But if you stay around here you ain't going to do nothing but stay underneath him and me. You'll have nothing to show for yourself or be nothing other than this. I know I don't say this to you and your sisters enough, but I love you. I want more for you, baby bird, than what I am and ever could be."

Mama pulled out the roll of dollar bills from under the covers. "Take this and get going." She jammed the money in Birdie's palm. "Take a bus or train, whatever gets you out of Mt. Sterling the fastest. Also, do not—I repeat, do not—tell your sisters anything that happened today. Never! We, you and me, are taking this to the grave."

Birdie sat at Mama's kitchen table, turned away from the window and glanced down at her cold coffee. For the first time in a long time her hands were still. Both were cradled in her lap, palms facing upward with fingers slightly bent and limp. She stared down at her palms filled with the lines of her life and tried to find some strange deviation that suggested her life was going to veer off onto some horrible path. A man had been stabbed to death and now she had to grab her things and run away like a criminal, leaving her children behind.

Mama was right about one thing: Birdie had to leave Mt. Sterling. But Birdie disagreed with forgetting about Jimmy. More than ever, Birdie felt she needed her husband now. She needed the family she and Jimmy created together. She needed the security in the sound of his voice, the safety of his embrace and the warmth of his presence when she watched him rock his children in his arms.

The quiet broke with her heavy sigh. *I don't know where you are, but I know in my heart you're not dead. Where are you, Jimmy? I need you now.*

Birdie drummed her fingernails on the table. With a final thump she decided on a course of action. There was no other choice. Even though she hadn't heard from him, Birdie knew Jimmy was alive somewhere. Deep in her bones she knew blood was pumping through his veins.

"I need to start packing if I'm going to make the next train from Cincinnati to Chicago."

Birdie had to find Jimmy and bring him home. He wasn't in Louisville—she would have heard something from the Amazons. Besides her aunts, she knew too many of his acquaintances that hung around those hole-in-the-wall joints up there. The first logical place to look would be Chicago. Jimmy spoke about Chicago more than any other city he claimed to have visited. In Chicago there would be work, music, books and rebellious black folks who had the same way of thinking he did. Besides, Birdie had family there and could stay with them for a few days.

She had a little money saved from selling sandwiches, boiled eggs and slices of pound cake to hungry workmen at Wrights and other nearby factories. Along with the roll of bills Mama handed over to her, Birdie had a total of ninety-two dollars. It was a large amount for her but with the train ticket, and who knew what other expenses she'd have when she arrived, it wouldn't last too long. Birdie wasn't sure of what she'd find in Chicago. If nothing, there would be no train ride on her return home; she'd have to take a long ride home on the Greyhound bus.

Birdie never dreamed she would be traveling alone. In fact, she had never done it before. She went over to Chicky's house to borrow a suitcase and tell her of the plan to go to Chicago. Chicky had married Clarence shortly after Carmen was born. She and Clarence moved to Clarence's family's old farmhouse a short mile away from Mama. Keeping her promise to Mama, Birdie didn't give her sister any details of what really happened in that kitchen. Birdie said that she was going to visit their cousin's wife. No matter what reasons Birdie gave, Chicky did her best to dissuade her.

"Girl, have you lost your mind? You plan on gallivanting all over God's creation by yourself? For what? You know that ain't right. Anything could happen to you, and we won't know nothing about it...ever. You'd just disappear. You know the world ain't kind to colored folks right now. Maybe they are up north in Chicago but not anywhere in between. Someone might kidnap you or sell your high bright ass into slavery."

Birdie couldn't tell Chicky or anyone that her plan was to look for Jimmy and bring him back home. She was afraid Mama would guess. Then, miraculously, an Amazon or two would know. After that, some version of her plan would get thrown back in her face.

"Chicky, I'll be fine. Cousin Ella is expecting me in a few days' time. It's just a small trip, just a friendly visit. I'll be back before you know it."

Chicky held an old suitcase behind her like it was a county fair gold prize. "You need to be trying to find out where that man of yours has gone. You told me he went down south on some job or something. You think I'm stupid or something? Girl, I know that's a lie. I know this: he ain't sending you no money, is he? I know that 'cause you stayin' over Mama's house and eating up a storm. Now tell me what's the story about you and that man."

Birdie shook off thoughts of family and town gossip while Chicky handed over the battered suitcase. *Someone's bound to realize what I'm up to. I'm sure they'll talk for days about me…sayin' I'm stupid for running after some empty pair of pants. Humph… If I go, they'll talk. If I stay, they'll talk. None of them have anything to do but talk!*

"Girl, Jimmy and I are just fine. He's off working…trying to provide for his family, just like I said. I just got a letter from him the other day." Birdie tried hard to sound convincing, but Chicky only crossed her arms and stared back at her sister with her head cocked to one side.

Not giving in to Chicky's skepticism, Birdie remained upbeat. "I've got to go get ready for my trip or I'm gonna miss that train. Love you, sis!"

Birdie went back to her apartment to gather her things. She recounted the bills in her pocketbook and figured she should send some back to Mama to help with the babies. She knew that any sum she gave her mother wouldn't be enough or last long. She also knew that a lack of money for her two small children wouldn't be the real problem—the real problem would be getting her babies back whenever she returned. Mama was fierce and possessive about everything and everyone she loved. She would grab a hold of her grandbabies and keep them from any perceived harm, even if that meant keeping them from her own daughter. If Birdie came back with Jimmy in tow, she knew Mama wouldn't let Carmen and Lil' Jimmy go without a fight.

But she couldn't think about that now. Time was flying and she had to go. Birdie decided to leave the children with Chicky so they wouldn't catch Mama's cold.

"Hell," she said aloud to an imaginary Jimmy. "You left

me with two babies, no money and promises that disappeared into thin air the moment you spoke."

Birdie snatched up all the clothing she had, not really paying attention to what she grabbed, and threw everything unfolded into the suitcase.

"I fought off everyone telling me otherwise. No, Mr. Walker, you ain't gonna make me the laughingstock of these damn small-town dirt farmers. You are not gonna' make me some old forgotten hag."

Snapping the suitcase shut, Birdie grabbed her coat, gloves and purse, and stormed out the door, slamming it shut without looking back.

PART TWO

Seeking the deepest river...

CHAPTER NINE

Chicago
1940

Birdie took a bus to Union Terminal in Cincinnati to catch the train to Chicago. She had wrangled away a fur coat from Mama. The coat alone, draped over her shoulders, gave the impression that she was a well-to-do colored woman on her way up to see her well-to-do husband. A few tired redcaps winked and nodded in her direction. Birdie knew that if she was going to find Jimmy, she'd need information and getting information would be easier if she looked her absolute best. She knew her looks could get people, mostly men, to talk. She planned to put them to good use in Chicago.

The train ride from Richmond to Muncie, Indiana, was uneventful with nothing to see along the landscape. Birdie was able to move more freely from car to car than she could while restricted to the Negro section on the bus in Kentucky. This gave her plenty of time to think. The last time she saw Jimmy face-to-face, she had been angry. It was just a few days before he disappeared. The argument, on the surface, was about money but it was also about his staying out late again. It was easier to start an argument about money instead of her real reason for being angry. They were doing okay, but it was hard times for just about everyone. If only Jimmy would just go to work and come home regularly like Chicky's husband Clarence. Or go to school and learn a trade, settle down and open a shop of some kind. Anything normal would have helped. Birdie argued they could have everything they ever wanted if Jimmy would focus on getting more out of his job at Wrights. Instead, his dreams and ardent promises to make or have something bigger and better never materialized and the poetry of his new world eventually turned her sour.

Somewhere just a ways past Indianapolis, Birdie asked herself, *What the hell am I doing?*

"Excuse me, miss...are you traveling alone?"

Birdie turned away from the window to see a smiling tan man in a crisp white Pullman porter jacket. He was as clean and sharp as a man could be after toting luggage and fetching food or whatever those folks needed during a long excursion.

Before she could answer, he politely asked, "May I ask your destination?"

When she said she was traveling to Chicago, his smile widened. "Well, alright! That's my town. If there's anything I can do to make your travel and stay pleasant, please don't hesitate to ask." He extended a gloved hand. "My name is Ed. Ed Dixon. If you need anything, please let me know and I will make sure it's at your fingertips."

His voice was soft. Each word he spoke was perfectly pronounced. The syllables dripped over her like a gentle prayer. Blushing shyly, Birdie nodded and thanked him. Ed's light brown eyes and clean-shaven face comforted her.

The rhythmic sway of the train lulled Birdie to sleep. She dreamed of tall blades of dark blue-green grass poking through a blanket as Jimmy's fingertips lightly strolled up her bare arms. She saw Carmen's sticky hands patting her face, leaving traces of sparkling white sugar on her cheeks. She remembered creamy milk bubbles from Lil' Jimmy's soft lips as he fell asleep in her arms. In her deepest sleep, she envisioned a mixing bowl flying through the air—its contents rolling purple, blue and red jagged-veined eyes swirling in pools of blood.

The sound of a bowl shattering on the floor jolted Birdie awake. She was wet with perspiration and her stomach roiled and rocked with the train's stuttered movements. The train car was filled with a heavy smell of garlic, onions and fried chicken. Travelers who couldn't afford the dining car were unpacking homemade meals. Her stomach rumbled. She hadn't eaten anything all day. When she looked down at the empty seat next to hers there was a white cloth napkin neatly tied in a knot. She looked around before cautiously opening it. Tucked inside were a dainty ham sandwich with the crusts removed and two oatmeal cookies.

Cousin Ella met Birdie at the train station in Chicago. Ella was married to an Amazon's eldest son, Joseph, who was in a Chicago jail awaiting trial for murder. Joseph and another man were accused of stabbing a white man in an attempted robbery. From Ella's account, Joseph was nowhere in the vicinity of the robbery. Several people had seen him playing cards that night in the back room of the Key Bar and Grille. The police never bothered asking around for witnesses. They said there was no need to gather information since they had a signed confession from Joseph. Ella said the police beat him pretty badly to get him to confess to something he didn't do.

By the time the news of Joseph's incarceration got back to Kentucky, everyone had already concluded the real reason he was in this predicament: it wasn't because the police wouldn't hear from anyone who could vouch for Joe's whereabouts that night, it was because he owed money to everyone east of the Mississippi River and kept boldly parading his white wife, Ella, around the state of Illinois without a care in the world. Birdie never heard who actually married Joe and Ella, or if anybody witnessed a real ceremony. Birdie didn't even know if the two were legally married, but the Amazons gave Ella the title of Joe's Wife so Birdie followed suit.

Ella was a big-boned country girl and looked like a match on fire. Her wild flaming-red hair—no matter marcelled, finger waved, pinned or rolled and tucked—always found a way to spring loose and go its own separate ways. Birdie could see what attracted her cousin Joe to Ella. She had big breasts, a big ass and big legs. Birdie thought Ella, dressed in a light unbuttoned coat and a dress that draped around her curvy frame, looked like the carvings of bare-breasted women on the front of pirate ships, guiding men to shores.

At the train station, Ella cheerfully bounced up to Birdie as though she didn't have a care in the world and gave her a big hug. "Bird, Big Mama told me you were on your way up here to find your husband. Now you know you shouldn't be up here lookin' for no man from that county pile of sticks. What's wrong with you, girl? You're too pretty to be chasing after nobody." Ella rested a hand on Birdie's shoulder. "They all should be chasing you!"

"Big Mama told you that?" Birdie's eyes were wide. Big Mama was Mama's older sister and Ella's mother-in-law. If Big Mama knew, then Mama probably knew. Hell, the whole town might already know, and it only took the time of a bus and train ride before gossip spread across state lines.

"Listen to me, forget all about him," Ella playfully demanded. "While you're here, we're gonna go out and have some fun. We're going strollin' out in Bronzeville tonight.

I'll show you something or somebody to take your mind off that no good old man of yours."

Birdie thought, *I guess having a husband up for murder shouldn't keep Ella from having a good time.*

The two took a short taxi ride to Ella's place. It was a little kitchenette in an extremely overcrowded building on the South Side. Though downtown Chicago had real glamour, this neighborhood was a fright of rambling wooden row houses that looked as if they were held together by the zigzagging clotheslines filled with dreary worn clothes, diapers, sheets and wind-whipped undergarments. As they climbed the stairs of Ella's building, Birdie saw people crammed around every apartment. The doors were propped open so air could circulate around the crowds inside each unit. Ella's next-door neighbor must have had over twenty people living in their small two-room apartment. They all chatted away, sounding as though they just came off the 'bama trail.

"Don't worry about them, honey," Ella said. "Tonight, we're gonna mix with really nice folks...some men I know who got plenty of money."

After hearing Jimmy's stories about Chicago, a night on the town under any other circumstance would've been a dream. Now Birdie's sole purpose was to find Jimmy and bring him, drag him if she had to, back to Mt. Sterling. She needed him home, at least for now, to make everything right again. She needed him to take care of her, Carmen and Lil' Jimmy. In return, Birdie would take good care of him. She also needed to prove Mama was wrong about Jimmy. Although she was bone-tired, Birdie just knew going to a night club would be the best place to meet someone who might know Jimmy or have seen him recently. Birdie was determined to learn something about her husband tonight.

★ ★ ★

Birdie pulled her hair back into a bun, pinned a silk flower on the side and put on the one nice dress she was able snatch off a hanger and pack in her suitcase. Ella lent her a wrap and a sparkly little clutch. The plan was to stop at a South Side jazz club then head off to the Savoy for dancing. Birdie wondered about the crowd. Would it be black or white? She trusted Ella would know enough not to put her in danger. She also knew the city had been known to produce as much hatred as down south. Race riots had shaken Chicago. The newspapers, both black and white, were covered with headlines and pictures of mobs and the terror they produced.

When Birdie voiced her fears, Ella simply laughed out, "Don't worry, Bird. It's all black and tans where we're goin'. They are just going to love you. We'll be fine. Besides, I got somebody in mind for you anyways. He's not much to look at, but his big pockets should keep you real interested."

They took a short cab ride to Club Delisa where Ella paid the fare with a wink to the driver. Birdie ignored the inter-action knowing that her blood cousin would probably be in jail for quite a while, leaving Ella to fend for herself the best way she could.

Birdie was pleasantly surprised when they entered the club. It was a large, cavernous room with walls tastefully painted from ceiling to floor with modern geometric designs. Tables, covered with white linens, circled an open dance space, and were filled with a few lively parties. The dance floor was prac-tically empty, but it was only nine o'clock, which Ella said was early by Chicago standards.

Eight or so musicians seated on a raised stage banged out some old swing tunes reminiscent of the southern swing Birdie knew so well. The clarinet player, who must have been the band leader, bopped across the stage using his sleek black instrument to squeal out a jazzy snake charm and keep the band in syncopated rhythm. He taunted the red bone drummer who plunged into a solo, stoking the now-rising tide of patrons in the club to attention. The drummer was rewarded with hoots, hollers, claps and stomps encouraging him to sweep across his drums with a range of rhythmic blips, bops and rolling burrs.

Birdie swayed and bounced with each step she took to their table. The music momentarily took her mind off her mission, and she let go of her anxiousness to enjoy the experience. As a delicious smile spread across her face, Birdie thought, *Mama, Chicky and Jimmy would just love this.*

Minutes after they arrived, all the tables filled, and the bar had a double line of people standing shoulder to shoulder. Birdie and Ella were seated a little farther away from the band and the spotlight. Although they were lucky to have seats, it was not the most desirable spot if you wanted to be seen. However, it was the perfect location to watch for Jimmy.

Ella, undeterred by their location, made the best of their vantage point. From the time she walked in the door, Ella glided through the club to their table, swinging her frame as close as she could to tease every man they passed. Once seated, she immediately began making eye contact with those she missed. Most of the men, with or without dates, reciprocated with googly-eyed stares or sly winks and smiles. Ella finally set her sights on two men and waved them over from their prized seats at the bar.

As they walked over with wide grins and bright eyes, Ella said under her own smile, "Birdie, I'm going to introduce you to this gentleman. He and that man with him are pretty high rollers. I bet they just came from downstairs. Be real nice, okay?"

Birdie propped up her face as instructed and squeezed through her own toothy grin, "From downstairs?"

"Yes, baby doll, that's where all the money is."

Birdie had been scanning the club hoping to spot Jimmy. She saw so many familiar strangers. In some ways the big city was just like her hometown back in Kentucky. Many of the faces looked like someone from her neighborhood back in Mt. Sterling. One man looked like Chicky's husband. Another had similar features as the kid down the street who just went off to college. And one was the spitting image of the dentist's son that was about to marry the girl who lived three doors down. They reminded her of every place she'd been and all the brown-skinned people she'd ever seen in her life— the men that frequented Mama's table, the folks who worked at Wrights, members of the families that sat in the pews at church. The familial thread was so strong Birdie felt she already knew them all. Despite the strange comfort of familiarity, she was disheartened that she didn't see the one person she genuinely wanted to see.

A man flopped down in the seat next to Birdie and scooted his chair up close. He wore a well-made, light-colored suit with a white shirt buttoned so tight at the neck his head looked as though it was about to explode. His smooth blue-black skin and slicked-back hair gave off a glossy sheen in the sparse light of the club. The whites of his large round eyes were as bright as the immaculate white teeth that flashed from between thick purple lips.

"Sandy Beamon is my name. But you can just call me Beamon. All my very best friends do." A red tongue rolled out from his mouth as he licked his lips like a thirsty traveler.

Ella yelled out, "Beamon, you old dirty dog, just look at you!" She gave him a wink. "You certainly stay clean. Meet my dear, dear, sweet country cousin, Birdie."

"Well, welcome to the big city, beautiful. Let me get you girls a round of drinks. It's only top-shelf for two of the most beautiful women in the club tonight. What you having, Birdie?"

"A ginger ale, thank you."

"Nooo...we'll have none of that tonight," Beamon protested. "I want to celebrate. Just a few minutes ago, I came into a big fortune, and I want to spread a little of it around." He leaned in close to Birdie. "You know, with that pretty face of yours, I could be encouraged to let go of a little more though. How about some champagne? Let's get that waitress over here pronto!"

Ella turned her attention to the guy who sat down next to her. Within moments, she was practically sitting in his lap. She gave Birdie a wink when the man began nipping at her neck. Birdie thought that, despite this being 1940 and as Ella called it, a "black and tan" club, that the young man must have a death wish. Ella told Birdie the club was owned by some Italian brothers whom she knew personally. She said they were happy healing the racial divide because they were making big money catering to a mixed crowd. The brothers didn't care who came in the doors or what they did, as long as they spent money on drinks, food or a bit of gambling. Birdie only knew—rich or poor, big city or small town—a black man getting chummy with a white woman, no matter how much she participated, could get them all killed. Birdie nervously looked around, searching for reactions. There were quite a few white patrons clustered together casually throughout the now-crowded club, but they didn't seem to notice or care about the interracial couple.

Birdie worked to stifle a yawn. Finding no horrified reaction and no Jimmy, the excitement of her first solo travel adventure was finally catching up with her. The waitress came by with a bucket of ice and set champagne glasses around the table. Beamon produced a roll of bills from his pocket and peeled off a few for the very thankful girl. A shiny brown camera girl popped up at the table and asked if she could take their picture. Ella and her date paused from giggling and locking lips to smile for the snapshot, then went back to holding hands and everything else on each other. Birdie gave the best smile she could muster but knew she probably looked like the saddest woman in the world.

Birdie looked at the toadish man sitting beside her and wanted nothing more than to go back home to Mt. Sterling, Kentucky. She had no real interest in conversing with strange men, partying, drinking or even dancing to the live music. Beamon was making some small talk that she couldn't hear and she didn't care enough to lean in and listen. Birdie forced a smile and nodded when it appeared he said something interesting, but she had no idea what he was talking about. He asked the customary boring questions, and she gave standard responses. *Where are you from? Oh, Mt. Sterling, Kentucky? What you doing up here? Oh, you looking for someone, did'ja say? Like a husband?*

"Yep, that's it," Birdie responded in the most nonchalant tone imaginable.

She knew Beamon took it to mean she was looking to find someone to marry, but she didn't bother to clarify or elaborate. Birdie didn't care what Beamon thought; she was never likely to see this man again. She ignored Beamon and continued sipping her champagne while getting lost in the music.

The piano player's fingers began tripping up and down the keys leading into a fast version of Fats Waller's "Lulu's Back in Town." When the drummer called out "Hey, Lulu," a chorus line of pretty, high-tone, thick-legged girls dressed in shiny white shorts trimmed in black-and-white checkerboard sequins shuffled out onto the dance floor.

Beamon's eyes rolled over watching the dancers shimmy

and shake. Hypnotized by the line of brown thighs, he leaned so far forward into the aisle he almost tipped out of his seat. Several girls were smitten by his ogling as well. They were tap, tap, tapping circles around each other attempting to gain his solo interest. Birdie took Beamon's ridiculous display as an excuse to ignore the froggy-eyed man and continue searching the crowd until Ella pulled at Birdie's shoulder.

"C'mon and go with me to the powder room. I need to fix my face before we go on over to the Savoy." She then turned to Beamon. "You gonna go with us to the Savoy, right, dahling?"

Beamon was mesmerized by the swishing hips of the dancing girls as they exited the floor through the swinging doors on each side of the stage.

"I'll have to see, my belle. I got a little something to take care of..." He looked at Birdie. "It was a pleasure, my dear. Maybe we can have fun some other time. That is if you haven't found a husband yet." He hopped out of his seat and headed toward the swinging doors.

Guess one of those girls was about to get her wish to tap dance for him all night.

"Birdie! You did not tell him you were here looking for that no-good husband of yours, did you?" Ella whispered loudly out the side of her mouth. "I told you to be extra nice to him."

"I told him the truth, Ella. I said I was looking for a husband. He just took that truth a little differently than what I actually meant. I never felt the need to correct him."

"Listen, cousin, there's a whole other club downstairs. It's where the high rollers go when they want to go even higher. That's where we need to be tonight. Sandy is a regular down there and he does pretty good. That's why I wanted you to play nice. You and me, sister, can't just go down there without an invitation. By that I mean we need an arm to hang on. I was hopin', pretty girl, that you could get us down there. I need to make rent and some of those boys get really happy and free with money when they're winning. 'Specially if they think we're their lucky charm."

Birdie rolled her eyes at the thought of Ella's shenanigans. She wasn't interested in finding a date or hanging on someone's arm and partying around some card table. That was not the reason she left her babies at home. But then it hit her: the downstairs club might be just the place to find Jimmy. It would be like him to be somewhere gambling. Anger and opportunity put color on her face at the thought of him having a grand old time.

"Ella, can't your little boyfriend get us in downstairs?"

Ella turned to look over at the bar. "Probably not. That ole 'bama ain't got any more juice and probably less money now. But I think I know someone who could. He can also get us something to eat. I'm hungry."

Birdie was too anxious to sit through a meal or watch Ella cuddle up to some other stranger. "Ella, we'll get a sandwich later. Find one of your bronze lover boys so he can escort us downstairs."

Ella flagged over one of the bouncers and whispered in his ear. Shortly after, a smooth-suited white man showed up at the table. "Ella, you're looking sweet as ever. Where have you been, dollface? And who is this flower you're with?"

Ella introduced him as Anthony Giamatti. He was handsome with an arrogant air about him. He spoke in an overly familiar tone, like most white men did who took to hanging around black folks. He sat down without being asked and leaned in close to Ella. All the while his eyes darted around the club. Ella told him they were trying to get downstairs. He responded with a simple, "Okay, ladies, let's go!"

Anthony guided them to the rear of the club and down a flight of stairs that dead-ended at a pair of double doors. Before they passed through the doors, he said, "Stay close to me. You know it can get pretty rough down here sometimes. Ella, I know you can take care of yourself. Miss Bird, you stay right here on my arm. If we get separated and you need anything, just look for me at one of the tables."

There was nothing remotely familiar like this that she knew of back home. This was a chic and glamorous club within a club. Dark-paneled walls were decorated with large paintings hung between columns topped with sculptures of sleek nude women in various dance poses. Ribbons of smoke rose and curled in the air. Red embers from cigars and cigarettes flashed around the room, glowing on and off and on again like fireflies in the summer night. Each of the dozen or so tables dotting the room was illuminated by a single overhead light that cast the table's occupants in sharply exaggerated shadow. Unlike the frenzy of energy upstairs, a sea of diverging low conversations rose and fell.

The back of the room was lined with what looked like private booths mysteriously hidden by velvet curtains. Handy waiters popped in between the curtains with trays of drinks. Birdie caught a glimpse of men gathered around a pool table behind one of the curtains. Once her eyes adjusted to the darkness, she could see there were people of every hue around the tables and pairs of wide, thick men standing in darkened corners silently watching over the entire scene. But so far, no Jimmy.

Anthony's voice interrupted her thoughts. "You see something you like? You know, I know there might be a few somebodies who'd be very happy to meet you. Have a seat over here, doll."

He led her to the opposite side of the room where a long wood bar lined the entire back wall. Liquor bottles covered the wall from top to bottom. There were only a few women she could see in the entire place and most of them were lined up like the liquor bottles against the bar. Ranging in an assortment of hues from black, tan and white, the women were smartly dressed to match the sleek decor. There was also a sprinkling of women surrounding the tables with arms draped around a man or each other. Only one woman was seated at a table. She was a matronly white woman, dressed to the nines and smoking a cigar. In front of her was a large pile of chips and cash. Close behind her were two finely dressed young black men whom she stroked each time the dealer dealt her a fresh hand.

Anthony scooted close and offered Birdie a cigarette from a silver case. "You look like a cocktail kinda gal. So, how about it?" He signaled to the bartender. "Johnny, bring the lady one of your special *Southside Johnny's*. Put it on my tab."

The light-skinned bartender was an older man that might have had a losing career as a boxer, indicated by the deep vertical lines in his puffy dough-like face. He gave Birdie an obvious once-over, then plopped a small napkin in front of her. He returned shaking a cocktail shaker and poured a frosty yellow drink into a dainty champagne glass, topping it with a piece of mint. Birdie took a sip.

"Oooh, how lovely," she said directly to Johnny. "What's in this *Southside Johnny*? Did you make this up?"

"Nooo, ma'am," Johnny responded with a face full of a crooked smile. He hovered around her even though there were other customers waiting at the other end of the bar. "I didn't make it up. I just refined it a bit. The guys like it and ask for it when they bring ladies down here. So I just keep making it."

"Yes, our Johnny here makes the best drinks around," Anthony crowed.

Simultaneously both Johnny and Birdie said, "Thank you,

Mr. Giamatti," then looked at each other and laughed at the jinx.

Anthony winked at Birdie. "You can call me Tony, doll-face." Turning to the bartender he said, "Keep 'em coming for her, Johnny."

Tony went off toward one of the tables and Johnny zipped off to service other patrons. God knew where Ella went. Birdie looked around but Ella's flaming hair wasn't visible around any of the tables or in the darker corners of the club. Still, there was no Jimmy. Birdie's palms and fingertips itched with a ghost sensation of his skin. His scent surrounded her so intensely she felt she could almost reach out and touch him. She rubbed the sides of her glass hoping the coolness, combined with several sips of her drink would distract her senses. As directed, Southside Johnnys magically appeared before she finished her drink.

Maybe I should peek behind the curtains. Jimmy could be in one of the private rooms.

Birdie slid off her bar stool, a very pretty move until her feet hit the floor. Birdie's knees buckled slightly, and she grabbed the edge of the bar to gain her balance and steady herself.

"Take it easy there, miss."

Birdie heard Johnny's voice as he seemed to materialize directly in front of her from the other side of the bar.

"I wondered how long it would take for you to realize these are some pretty powerful drinks. After a few, you won't know where you gonna end up. That's why them boys ask me to make 'em. Especially that one there." He snapped his head in Tony's direction. Tony was at one of the tables with his back to them. "I watered yours down a bit 'cause I know you're new here. Where's your friend Ella?"

"Ella ain't my friend. She's my cousin. Well, not my blood cousin. She's married to my cousin."

Johnny raised an eyebrow. "Married to your cousin? Really? They legally married? Everybody knows she's Joe's girl and they been shacking up, but when and where'd they get married? Not here in the state of Illinois."

Unleashed by alcohol, Birdie's words ambled out in an unrestrained Kentucky twang. "Not legally I guess, 'cause you know you can't do that kinda thing in Kentucky either. I thought it happened here 'cause I ain't heard nobody say nothing about it since I been here. You know he's in jail right? Yeesss, my blood cousin, Joseph Augustus Spearman, locked up for a murder he didn't commit."

"Yeah, I know." Johnny swiped a look over his shoulder and lowered his voice. "It's a shame what they did to that brother. Those police 'bout split his head wide open right out there on the sidewalk in front of every man, woman and child. I thought I wouldn't see that kinda treatment again since I left Memphis. But it's the same whether you down south or up here. It's a little better here, but not much. Don't step out of Chicago. Those grays will…"

Johnny paused and looked around to make sure no one was listening. "Well enough of that. I hope your cousin can get his self outta that trouble alive. They got an NAACP lawyer speaking on his behalf. But I don't know, ain't no assurances he gonna get a fair trial."

Birdie had pushed her cousin's plight to the back of her mind but Johnny reminded her of Joseph's dire circumstances. She hadn't seen him in a while but remembered her cousin as a joyful young man who always ate the most sweets at the family gatherings. She remembered he was the first one to ask Granny to dance at Cousin Bernice's wedding and got Granny to smile as he gently twirled her around the floor. Joseph fixed Aunt Cecilia's broken pipe and brought Mama fresh catfish along with turnips and tomatoes from Auntie One's garden when they needed it most. It was Joseph who called her "lil' sweet pea" and gave her a bouquet of honeysuckle after church when she was eight years old. He hadn't been around since he went off to the Civilian Conservation Corps camp to make some extra money and ended up here in Chicago.

Birdie knew she would have to carry every word she learned about Joseph back to her Kentucky kindred. From the time Joseph was dragged through his own spilled blood, the connected strings of his life transcended beyond jail cell walls and state boundaries. They didn't do this to just a man in the streets of Chicago but to every human being attached to him. Birdie's family would be depending on her for fresh news, even though she knew it would irritate fresh wounds and old scars of every black person who walked the veins of the migration trail from and to Kentucky.

For those kin who were old enough to know, sadly they already presumed Joseph's fate. Birdie, along with every member of her family, would try to clear away the painful sharp claws scraping the back of their throats as they felt the hands that choked him, stabbed him, beat him, tied him down, dragged him, made his heart race in fear, mashed his face in the dirt, cut off his air supply, broke and crushed bones, blackened his eyes, busted his lips, slashed knives through his skin, slammed him against concrete, unleashed dogs to rip their teeth through his clothes and tear his flesh, and ignore or laugh at his screams.

Birdie suspected Johnny knew what the older men and women back home knew too. That Joseph's pants were soaked with urine and shit ran down his legs over the rusted shackles at his ankles. They knew the odor of the weathered straw of braided rope scouring the skin around Joseph's neck and the sensation of vapid air underneath his kicking feet. They all felt it and rubbed their bodies with the full palms of their hands to blanket the pain. Still Birdie would report back. Churches and prayers would give a kind of hope as they always did during so many times like these. The tribes would have whole towns praying for Joseph's safe return to them or his departure in peace to the King.

The last swallows of her Southside Johnny cocktail went down hard. Birdie quickly changed the subject. "I don't know where Ella is, she's supposed to be helping me find a husband."

Johnny returned to his spot behind the bar and laughed so hard his shoulders shook. "Girl, ain't no husbands to be found in here. You ain't never gonna find no one to marry in here."

Birdie said stiffly, "Not *a* husband...*my* husband!"

Johnny swatted the bar with his towel as he continued to chuckle. "Oooh, *your* husband. You got a husband you looking for? Who in their right mind would leave you?"

The room suddenly started spinning. Birdie tried to adjust to the walls, floors, ceilings and lights floating at odd angles before her eyes. Seconds later, Johnny was at her side again, coaxing her to put one foot in front of the other. She tried to summon enough dignity to walk the few short steps to a booth on the side of the bar.

Johnny said slowly as if he were speaking to a child, "Let me get you some coffee, miss. I mean, ma'am."

Birdie leaned her head on the back of the seat. She wanted to close her eyes, but Johnny came back with a hot cup of black coffee, a glass of warm water and Alka-Seltzer bicarbonate tablets.

"Sip these slowly. Alternate. First sip the coffee, then take this here bicarb. Take one after the other, slowly. It will bring you back quickly so that you get home safe."

"Thank you, Johnny. You're a real lifesaver."

Johnny furtively glanced from one side to the other. "That

ain't my real name by the way. I'll tell you the next time I see you—which I hope ain't here. Who are you looking for?"

"You know a fella named James Walker? He's tall, brown-skinned with slanted eyes?"

"Jimmy? Yeah. Yeah, I know Jimmy." He crooked a thumb over to the wall of alcohol. "He used to bring us some supplies every now and then… Some of the real expensive kind 'cept without the label. I ain't seen him in a while though. You're Jimmy's wife? Man, I didn't think he hit that kinda jackpot."

Birdie perked up. She pulled a picture from her purse. It was the one of him, her and baby Carmen taken last summer in front of Mama's house.

The bartender moved in closer and squinted his eyes to examine the photo. Birdie pointed to Jimmy's wide grin. "This man here… This is the Jimmy I'm talking about."

"Yep, that's him. He's a real smart one," the bartender said pointing a fat finger at the photo. "Every time I see him, he got a book or something with him. Reads everything he can get his hands on. He talked like a preacher sometimes. Man, he can talk his self in or out of any situation. I've seen it with my own eyes."

He then lowered his voice. "Look, ma'am, these Italian boys don't play with their money, liquor or whatever else they got you running. Jimmy's been in the thick of things. He's been having to 'splain every penny or lack thereof. I heard he travels up and down from Cincinnati, even running some things from Detroit. Look, you be careful looking for him. In fact, I wouldn't even look if I were you. I suggest, pretty lady, you go back home and stay put. Jimmy's bound to turn up on his own at some point."

Birdie heard his warning but was determined. "When's the last time you saw him?"

Voices clamored from the bar for service. Johnny, or whatever his name was, jumped to attention and headed over to his patrons. From over his shoulder, he flung a parting glance. "Look, let it alone, little lady. Go home to wherever you came from."

Ella finally wandered out from the dark. Wherever she came from there must have been a few rounds of cocktails because her eyes were glazed, and her body swayed from one side to the other. Birdie pushed the cold coffee and the unfinished bicarbonate over toward her cousin. The bartender was right. Her head cleared almost immediately from his quick remedy. Hopefully, it would work for Ella.

"Ella, I'm ready to go. Let's get out of here. And please do not bring none of those bronze lover boys of yours with us. Do you want to start trouble?"

Ella slid into the booth and threw back both concoctions, wincing at the taste. "Don't worry about that. But someone's got to pay for the cab and for us to get in at the Savoy. Once we're in, I can get us some drinks and maybe a bite to eat. I'm really hungry."

Behind Ella, Birdie could see Tony Giamatti standing behind a man seated at a nearby table where an assortment of card players stared intently at their fanned-out cards. Tony was smiling and joking while jovially patting the man on the shoulders.

"Ella, you think maybe we should tell Mr. Giamatti we're leaving?"

Her voice trailed off as two men approached Tony and stood close to him, positioning themselves on each side. One of the men held his hand to his chin as he leaned in to whisper in Tony's ear. The other nodded to the music. Tony's head whipped between the two men at his side. He reached in his pocket and pulled out something hidden in his fist. In a swift move, Tony raised his arm and sharply struck the man sitting in front of him. The man fell sideways taking his chair with him to the floor. The two men at Tony's side instantly lifted the limp heap of a man and dragged him out of the club. A waiter swiftly whisked away the upended glasses and chair. The dealer swiped away the old cards and dealt a fresh hand to the remaining guests.

"Ella, it's time to go!"

Ella stood up and tugged on the waist of her dress so that her breasts were on the verge of popping out of her bodice.

"Yep, sugar, you got that right. It's time to get outta' here. I got what I wanted anyway," she said under her breath.

CHAPTER TEN

A quick cab ride landed Birdie and Ella at the Savoy dance club. Ella charmed them into the club and got a table close to the band. It was after midnight and the place was packed. Unlike the previous club, which was refined, this spot was a heaving, rolling dance hall. It was loud and raucous. Birdie marveled at how many brown-skinned people were jammed into one big space.

Walter Barnes and his Kings of Swing were righteously living up to their name. The band leader had a clarinet in one hand and a bouncing baton in the other jerking up and down then ricocheting from left to right. Birdie had seen the debonair band leader and his orchestra play before. Their sophisticated swing was known throughout the Chitlin' Circuit, which ran through small towns from the Midwest to the South. Musicians, whether they played in formal orchestras or small-town jug bands with washboards, bottles and spoons, brought their hard-earned reputations in hopes that they could get all the first money in the door. A full house meant full pockets for playing the circuit's juke joints, black hole-in-the-wall spots and social clubs between big-city stops. Mt. Sterling had been one of those stops for Walter and his band along the way too.

Ella waved to several folks in the crowd and drinks magically appeared. Birdie looked down at the brown liquor swirling around a few ice cubes and the smell of alcohol filled her nostrils. After so many Southside Johnnys, her stomach began to do somersaults. She pushed the glass away and pulled out a cigarette. Birdie didn't normally smoke. She only pulled them out on occasion to keep her hands and mind busy when she was out at social events where other people were smoking. She had carried around these cigarettes for a long time and they were probably stale, but this situation called for a cigarette to calm her nerves and keep herself awake. There were only two left. She didn't have any money for frills on this trip, so the fifteen cents for a pack would have to wait until she got home where she could get cigarettes from just about anyone who worked at Wrights for free.

While a singer crooned out suggestive verses of the "Hesitation Blues," Birdie luxuriated a moment with her cigarette. Her conversation with the bartender at Club Delisa left her with a bellyful of conflicting emotions—excitement over learning someone knew Jimmy, and her instincts and dread as to what more she might find out about her missing husband. She needed something to focus on and calm her overactive nerves. The fact that the bartender knew Jimmy confirmed Birdie's loosely made plan to find him was on the right track.

Despite the bull's-eye of information she hit at Delisa, it was going to be hard to find Jimmy or any news about him here at the Savoy. The auditorium was too loud to have a conversation with anybody. Johnny said Jimmy frequently ran liquor from Chicago to Cincinnati. If Birdie didn't find him here, her next stop would be back to Cincinnati. She hesitated at the thought of going to Detroit. Traveling to Michigan was far beyond her comfort zone. Mama said get out of Kentucky so Cincinnati might be the better bet. Birdie would be closer to her babies and could eventually move her family there if things didn't cool down in Mt. Sterling.

Birdie waved away several requests to dance. Ella, once again, had bounced away. Birdie tried to spot Ella's wild red hair above the mostly sepia-toned crowd but there was no trace of her. Birdie was unsure if or when she would see her cousin again. She didn't have a key to the apartment and frankly wasn't quite sure how to get back there. She had no choice but to stay put until Ella surfaced.

Birdie spotted Beamon two tables over with an arm wrapped around the shoulders of one of the young dancers from Club Delisa's chorus line review. They must've been at the Savoy awhile because their table was littered with an assortment of bottles and overflowing ashtrays. The little tap dancer was shimmying in her seat to the music and Beamon was happy to hang on for the ride. Although Birdie couldn't decide who was the cat and who was the mouse, she was glad she hadn't given Beamon any attention earlier.

Birdie yawned. She'd been going straight since she got off the train. It was already two o'clock in the morning and these fools were as fresh as noon. Still no sign of Jimmy and, quite frankly, she held no hope of seeing him. She overheard someone talking about some joint called the Sixty-Five Club, where a crazy trumpet player called King Kolax would be playing and cutting up with his big band until four or five in the morning. It sounded like just the jam session that Jimmy would go to, but Birdie wasn't sure if she'd have enough energy in the tank to tackle another club.

She pulled out the photo of Jimmy and Carmen from her purse. Amid the noise of the crowd, the picture took her back to the exact moment when it was taken. She smiled back at Jimmy and baby Carmen's little chubby face. They both held the same expression. She brushed the photograph with her hand as if she could touch both of them. She laughed softly to herself when she realized Lil' Jimmy was in the picture too. Birdie felt her heart was about to burst, as a cacophony of laughter swirled around her.

"Did you find that husband yet?"

She looked up. Beamon was sitting in the seat next to her wiping sweat off his forehead. Birdie thought, *What is up with these men? Perching themselves next to you without being invited? Don't they teach good manners up north?*

"Well hello again, Mr. Beamon. What happened to your little tapping friend?"

"Oh, she went to do what all y'all ladies do..."

"What, is she looking for a husband too?"

Beamon gave a slow grin. "No, powder her nose. I see you've gotten a bit feisty now that the night's grown young. That's a lot more spirit than I got before."

"Sorry, I'm just a bit tired. That's all. I've been going top speed with my cousin since I got off the train this morning and I haven't had much rest."

"Right, right...you just came in from the bluegrass state of Kentucky, right? Mt. Sterling, Kentucky, did you say? You know, I think I might know exactly who you lookin' for."

Birdie sat up straight. Now Beamon had her full attention. She didn't remember telling him any specifics of her mission.

"Really, how would you know? There are plenty of folks here from Kentucky. Every used-to-be hick that ever pulled tobacco is up there lindy hopping."

"Matt, back at Delisa's, told me you lookin' for some man name Jimmy."

"Matt? Matt, who?" Birdie didn't recall meeting anyone by that name. Then she brightened. "That bartender they call Johnny?"

Beamon nodded.

"Why they call him Johnny?"

Beamon said, "Don't let them slick boys fool you. They ain't catering to no black folks just 'cause they just love being around us. A good few of them don't care about our plight. It's all about the money with them. They just like them country peckerwoods down south. They call all of us who work for them Johnny or Sam. But they call me by the name my mama gave me because I spend lots of cash and help 'em make a whole lot more."

"So do you know Jimmy?"

Beamon rubbed his chin. "Nah, can't say that I rightly do. But I know of him. If I run into him, and I run into everybody in this business eventually, I'll send him your way."

Beamon's little tootsie with a freshly powdered nose slid up next to him. She began rubbing his shoulders to mark her prize, all the while giving Birdie an evil eye.

"If I hear anything, I know how to get in touch with you. I can always find Ella," Beamon said as he followed his girl out onto the dance floor.

Finally Ella's cottony red hair could be seen floating above the rolling sea of brown people. She was wriggling through the crowd and stepping on toes along her way. People moved aside to avoid getting mowed down by Ella. Ella was oblivious to it all and just appeared to be having a gay old time.

"You ready for some more, country cousin? There's one more spot where we can really have fun. Are you up for it?"

Birdie thought, *One more? Oh good Lord no!*

Instead, she lazily repeated, "Sure, cuz. Is it far? My feet are killing me." Although dead tired, Birdie thought she might get lucky and find Jimmy or at least uncover another bit of information about his whereabouts. "I just need another cigarette and I'll be ready to go."

A quick two-block walk in the cool air landed them in front of what looked like a residential building. It was after 3:00 a.m. when they entered a basement door of the brownstone and found a crowded joint filled with low-key conversations and the intense smell of funny cigarettes, fried fish, old alcohol and sweet perfume. Tucked in the corner of the narrow room a quartet played an intoxicating moody jazz composition, "I Got It Bad." A blind-eyed musician propped up by a bass, joined by a sharp, melancholy saxophone player, created an ambiance that Birdie knew would lull her to sleep right where she stood.

"I don't know if I can take this scene, Ella. I need to get some sleep."

Ella said, "Give it a minute, girl. They'll be hoppin' in a sec. You'll see."

Ella acted as though she didn't have any intention of ever going home. She quickly snagged some guy who insisted on buying her and Birdie drinks.

Birdie scanned the room. No Jimmy. However, after three clubs she started to see a few familiar faces. One was the pretty dancer that had been on Beamon's arm at the Savoy. She was now all hugged up on a big, tall red-boned man.

Birdie chuckled to herself. "Well, I guess that big-eyed frog couldn't make it to the final number."

It wasn't long before Birdie felt a tap on her shoulder. She turned and the long-legged dancer was standing behind her.

She wavered back and forth as if her brown legs were tapped out for the evening and ready for a rest.

"I heard you were looking for Jimmy," the little dancer slurred. "You looking for Jimmy from Louisville?"

Birdie stared at the girl as she shifted her weight from one hip to the other. "Well, if he's the one you looking for and you find him, you tell Jimmy Myra's looking to thank him for what he did."

Birdie took a draw on her cigarette. With an eyebrow raised, she said, "And you would be Myra, right?"

"Yes, Myra from Alabama. That's what everybody calls me," she chirped. "Jimmy, well, he got me out of a jam a little ways back. You must be the pretty wife he told me about. You got two little babies, right? What in the world are you doing up here knee-deep in this mess? You know Beamon has an eye for you. Watch out, sister."

Birdie responded coolly, "Beamon? Wasn't he your boyfriend just a few hours back?"

"No, no, no, sugar. It ain't like that at all." Myra from Alabama was slurring her words, making it hard to understand what she was saying.

"I'm Florida Red's girl," she said as she swiveled in the direction of a man seated in the dark corner. "Listen, just tell that man of yours I said thank you."

Birdie raised an eyebrow. "When was the last time you saw Jimmy?"

"About two weeks ago. He saved my life. He told me and Red he was going down to Cincinnati. I ain't seen or heard from him since."

The big man in the corner stood halfway out of his seat and waved for Myra to return. "Girl, I gotta go. Im'ma have Red send over a couple of drinks and some sandwiches for you and Ella. How you know that wild white woman? Oooh, that one... She a real firecracker, that one is."

Myra took a few short steps as if attempting a high wire act then sashayed over to her man.

"Hmmm..." Birdie said aloud to herself. "I guess all signs point back to Cincinnati."

It was after two in the afternoon when Birdie awoke. She would have slept longer if it weren't for the racket around the building. There was shouting, stomping up and down stairs and children fighting and slamming balls against the building. A drum solo from one of the clubs they visited the night before was also ringing in Birdie's head. Ella was still asleep but shifting around in the bed they shared. Birdie looked around the kitchenette for any hope of making coffee and found some grounds in an otherwise empty cupboard.

She went over to the window. In the light of day, the streets were gray and ugly. Ramshackle buildings laced with fragile wooden stairs looked as if they were ready to collapse into splintered dust. The tenements shared a common dirt courtyard filled with debris. A ragtag bunch of children, apparently finding joy among the filth, were laughing and playing. They had found an assortment of things among the garbage for a makeshift ball game. Birdie rubbed her temples. Beyond the tenements she could see something glistening in the distance. The top of the Chicago skyline shimmered like a gleaming oasis radiating from the rays of the sun.

"You about to burn that coffee." Ella was propped up on one elbow. "I need a cigarette. You got any?"

Birdie shook her head. She smoked all she had last night and swore to herself that she wasn't going to buy any more until she got back home.

"I'd go next door, but those wild Geechees are too much

for me to handle right now. I'll get some from Sam—one of the fellas I met last night—when he comes over. Oooh, didn't we have some fun last night? And there were a few out there that were quite smitten with you. That Beamon was askin' me all sorts of questions. You see he was followin' us around. Give him a chance, honey, okay? He got a lot going for him."

"Well, I got a warning from that little performer he was dancing with over at the Savoy," Birdie quipped. "She says he's in some kinda mess."

Rubbing her eyes, Ella responded, "Please, girl, everybody in this town is in some kinda mess nowadays. It's called survival. If you ain't in some kinda mess, you're starvin' or 'bout to die. And, baby, I ain't about to starve and I, for damn sure, ain't dying just yet. Don't pay those folks no mind. They's in a mess too, even if they don't admit it. Yep, they's in it alright."

"Well, the only thing I want to know is where in the world is my husband? Alabama Myra knows something."

"Bird, you need to get out of here, at least for a few hours or so. Go see the city. Take yourself over to the big shopping store or to the Regal to see a movie. I'd go with you but Sam will be by soon."

The apartment was a shabby, messy cluster of grime. Birdie couldn't imagine entertaining anyone here.

"Let me help you tidy up a bit and I'll be out of your way. I'd love to do some window shopping and maybe have a bite to eat at one of those luncheonettes."

Ella looked quizzically at Birdie, stretched out her legs and flopped back down on the bed. "Sure, girl, I'll help you in a minute."

Birdie wandered out to get a glimpse of Chicago. Here she was on a cool, clear day in a big city, alone. She had never been anywhere without family. Even though she had spent countless hours imagining a life of glamour outside of Mt. Sterling, it was never her intention to be too far from her family. Even when Jimmy talked about traveling here or there to see the sights across America, she just thought they were pipe dreams.

Beyond searching for Jimmy, Birdie couldn't decide if she liked Chicago enough to stay for any extended amount of time. She could see why Jimmy talked so much about the town. As soon as she stepped off the train the city pulsated with life right before her eyes. People were everywhere. Cars and buses were everywhere. Trains ran on tracks above her head and the noise never stopped. From corner to corner, blinking theater marquees lined the streets, shouting out movie titles, Hollywood stars, singing sensations, big bands and all-night dancing. Even restaurants and store fronts glittered. It was cluttered, shabby and polished all at the same time. There were plenty of finely dressed black people hopping in and out of shops and tall buildings. Her sleepy little hick town in Kentucky, filled with slow-moving corn-fed people could fit into one minute of Chicago life.

From what Birdie experienced last night, living here with Ella until she got on her feet would be a wild ride. The energy was nothing like she could have ever imagined. So much action packed into endless blocks of clubs, theaters, shopping and services that catered to black people. There were plenty of well-to-do colored people and exclusive black-owned businesses. Money, even in these trying times since the Depression, was flowing and changing hands. Not like back home where so many were struggling and dirt-poor.

Chicago presented itself as such a glamorous option. Birdie could see herself stepping out of a fancy house, with a big car and all the things she dreamed about. But what she couldn't see was Jimmy.

Has that life I originally wanted disappeared? How could my dreams have changed so quickly?

Riding the elevated train and hopping street trolleys, Birdie hoped no one could see how nervous she was or know that she was some hick from out of town, just ripe for the picking. Her heart pounded at each stop. She picked up the *Chicago Defender* from a newspaper boy. The headlines in the black newspaper were the same as back home: "Lynchings and Murders of Black People In Illinois, Michigan and Down South"; "The Fight for Jobs and Fair Pay"; and "The World Fighting Over Seas." The advertising was also the same: Poro School of Beauty products, and those who needed a peek into the future could visit Madame Castle, the gifted palmist and crystal reader.

Birdie slipped into the Regal Theater to catch the latest sepia-toned movie. Like everything else she experienced in Chicago the theater was huge. In the darkness, she felt lonely and small. While the movie—murder mystery with a handsome hero and a beautiful girl as the object of his affection—played out on the screen, her own personal drama played in her head.

Birdie arrived in Chicago on what she thought was a mission to get Jimmy to own up to his responsibilities and do right by their children. In the dark movie house, she admitted she hadn't owned up to her own. She thought, *I've been chasing a pair of pants that walked into my life and then walked out without a care.*

Angry tears flowed down her cheeks and she allowed herself to weep freely as the images flickered on the screen.

Birdie had come to Chicago on a Thursday and was ready to go home on Friday. Reaching into her purse for a handkerchief, her hand caught on a small folded piece of paper. In the light of the movie's rolling credits, Birdie unfolded it. It was the promissory note she had retrieved from Jimmy's pockets before he disappeared. The address of a house in Cincinnati stared back at her. Birdie couldn't remember how the note ended up in her purse. She must've absentmindedly raked it in along with a few other items when she hastily left Mt. Sterling—but it didn't matter. Here it was. She took it as a sign she couldn't neglect.

"Guess I'm on the bus tomorrow for Cincinnati," she decided.

Birdie left the movie theater and stopped into the South Center department store before going back to Ella's place. It was glorious to see so many polished and sophisticated black people working in the large store that offered everything she ever wanted. Back home, preachers, the NAACP and all sorts of leaders like A. Philip Randolph encouraged blacks to use "double duty dollars," which meant spending money where colored folks were employed. She was intent on buying at least a little souvenir for Mama, Chicky and Bessa. She paid twenty-five cents for some Hair-Lay Fine Pomade, some postcards and a few other trinkets.

As Birdie walked up the steps to Ella's apartment, Beamon was walking down. Before she could speak, he dipped his hat down and brushed past without even acknowledging her presence. Stopping on the steps, she leaned over the staircase and watched him scurry down each flight of stairs. He looked up only once but still said nothing.

"Humph, now that was rude!" Birdie shook her head and let herself into the apartment.

It was approaching seven o'clock p.m. and Ella was still in her robe, sitting at the table with a cup of coffee and a cigarette. Birdie was tired from her day in the city but didn't want to wait to inform Ella of her plan to leave Chicago.

"Really? You ready to go already? You just got here," Ella said perching herself on the edge of the chair.

"Yes. My babies are without me and their daddy. I need to make my way back home now."

Smoke curled around Ella as she spoke. Sounding hurt, Ella whispered through the smoke, "I thought maybe we could go to a couple of clubs tonight and have some real fun, even more fun than last night. It's not so hard to live here in this city. These dumbass men... All of them, white, tan or chocolate, will do anything you ask, really. I get by. If you and me stay together, we can get out of this dump and get us a real nice apartment. We could have us a good ole time in this town."

Birdie crossed her arms. "I don't know, Ella."

Ella took a long drag of her cigarette. "You, sweet country cousin, are just what this town needs. A pretty, sweet colored girl with a nice figure and all."

Ella jammed her cigarette into the dirty ashtray and grabbed both of Birdie's hands. She gave them the once-over. "We gotta work on those hands though. They look like they just pulled up potatoes. You need to file and paint those nails bright red, honey."

Birdie looked down at her fingers. "I saw that guy Sandy Beamon going down the stairs as I was coming up. He didn't speak hello or nothing. Does he live in this building too?"

Ella rolled her eyes and waved her hand in front of her face. "Listen, Bird, don't think about leaving just yet. Stay around just a little while longer and I'll make a city girl out of you. Besides with my true love, Joe, in jail, I need the company. I know you pining after that James. But listen to me, James ain't one of those men that can be tied down, sweetheart. He's one that's always gonna have something to prove, not just to him-self, but to everybody in the world. He's gonna keep jumpin' into shit and that shit is gonna get him either put away like my sweet Joe or killed. The world's gonna take him back and bury him, because he is just too much for one person or one place or one anything." She chuckled. "Oooh, ain't I soundin' like one of those beatniks we saw last night."

Ella lit another cigarette. "So let's start off by going to dinner tonight. Okay? How about some steaks? Lobster? Okay, meatloaf it is."

When they stepped out of the building, a man lay facedown on the sidewalk, his arms spread out as if attempting to fly away. His flight was curtailed because he was as dead as could be. People watched from every angle of the buildings as blood continued to travel across the concrete and into the cracks.

Ella stopped short on the top step of the stoop. "Dammit, cousin! Why does this have to keep happening on my block? Can't these brutes go somewhere else to take care of their business?"

Ella's invitation to stay in Chicago evaporated into thin air as Birdie turned around to go back inside the building. The sight of another dead man lying at her feet reminded her of what a mess her life was and the importance of her mission. She had to do everything she could to settle herself and her family. That meant finding Jimmy. Her heart raced and head pounded because now she knew exactly what to do. She packed her clothes and took the next Greyhound bus to Cincinnati.

CHAPTER ELEVEN

Cincinnati, Ohio
1940

The bus ride from Chicago was unremarkable on all counts. Birdie thought since this was a big, modern black and tan city, busses would be integrated, and you would be able to sit wherever you wished. Instead, just as in Kentucky, the bus had seating for whites in the front and a section marked for colored travelers in the back. She sat in the second to the last row. No one sat beside her, and the entire bus was quiet. The bus left Chicago at 7:30 a.m. and throughout the trip everyone seemed tired. Through a drowsy haze, Birdie thought, *They must all be escaping from someone or to something, or in search of a new start in a new place.*

When she stepped off the bus in Cincinnati, a sudden sense of panic washed over her. Back in Chicago, she was so sure about heading to Cincinnati, but now that she was in the Queen City, she realized she had nowhere to go. The motion of the bus and steady buzz of its motor had lured her into a protective sleep which allowed the details of what to do once she arrived at her destination to escape her thoughts. It was a shade past two in the afternoon and she had to quickly find a place to stay. Birdie headed through the "colored only" entrance of the bus station.

The two wooden benches that encompassed the colored waiting room section were occupied by a young man dressed in military uniform with his arm around a young woman. She cradled an infant in one arm and held the hand of a toddler that twisted around the pleats of her dress. The woman's gleaming brown skin was moist with tears as she nuzzled into the neck of her soldier. His duffel bag indicated he was either returning or going. The family tableau favored he was probably leaving for a military camp down south and then set to be shipped overseas which meant he would be away from his young family for quite a while. Birdie's heart ached at the sight of them.

She hated to interrupt the tender moment, but the couple brightened when she asked if they could suggest a rooming house. They seemed to welcome the distraction and were more than happy to give directions to a Miss Purity Ann's Inn and pointed her to a jitney cab which was parked right outside the waiting room.

Birdie took a room at Miss Purity Ann's Inn after passing a bit of scrutiny from the owner which consisted of a series of questions about her faith, social boundaries and ability to pay rent up front. It was a world of difference from Ella's tiny apartment. The inn, located on a quiet gas-lighted street in the Lytle Park district at the edge of downtown, had neat little rooms that did not lack for stark white doilies on every surface. Birdie learned from the jitney driver that the inn was one of the most respectable rooming houses in Cincinnati that offered a few rooms to single colored women. She thought it was funny that the owner and proprietor, Eugenia

Purity McClenden, was far from being a miss and even a further stretch from pure. She was a thick, stern-faced woman who had been married three times over. Her first two husbands went to their graves. The last husband, a sailor, fled his bounds of matrimony by jumping on a ship to New Orleans. He never came back. His flight must have driven her to God because, it was said amongst the other inhabitants of the house that since his departure, she gave up dispensing any sort of kindness along with her sinning to make amends to the Lord.

Miss Purity demanded nothing less than absolute pristine behavior in her rooming house. There were no exceptions to the rules, which stopped short of actual on-your-knees vows of chastity. These rules, along with others, were printed in bold type and posted on the back of the door in each room:

ABSOLUTELY NO MEN ARE ALLOWED IN YOUR ROOM.
- Men are only permitted in the front room during daylight hours.
- No late-night carousing will be tolerated.
- No alcohol or smoking permitted.
- Violators will be tossed into the street immediately!

With the threat of living on the Cincinnati sidewalks at the smallest infraction, Birdie immediately began searching the newspapers for employment. She decided working, while waiting for whatever could possibly happen back in Mt. Sterling and continuing to search for Jimmy, would keep her mind occupied. The *Cincinnati Enquirer* and the *Cincinnati Times Star* newspapers were peppered with "white only" job advertisements, but Birdie easily got a job working as a maid for a wealthy family in Cincinnati. Not exactly what she wanted but the proprietor of her rooming house didn't take any excuses for late rent and Birdie didn't want to solely rely on what was left of the money Mama had given her.

Every day Birdie headed to work with her hair pulled back into a tight bun confined within a starched uniform designed to either make a black woman disappear or stand out as a being of lesser stature than her employers. Donning the pale blue dress with three-quarter-length sleeves and a plain white muslin apron, Birdie walked through the days with her eyes half closed. Mama had said too often, "Idle hands are the devil's workshop." In this case it was true. Birdie occupied herself with mindless domestic tasks to keep her thoughts off her children, her nonexistent efforts to find Jimmy and the occasional vacant pang of loneliness. Flicking a feather duster and polishing tarnished silver occupied her hands while her mind silently protested against not just being a domestic, but also the situation she found herself in.

This is so stupid! Birdie thought. *This is no way to live. I didn't come to Cincinnati to be by myself on my hands and knees scrubbing after folks! I should go back to Kentucky and go to school like Bessa suggested. Maybe become a nurse.*

Echoes of Mama's warnings to stay away from Mt. Sterling, along with reoccurring visions of white flour and purple blood forced Birdie to cook, clean and stay on the job at the cost of her pride. She'd go back to her room at Miss Purity's to wash out her stockings in the sink, wrap herself in the handmade quilt Mama sent to her and rock herself to sleep so she could do it all again the next day.

Birdie spent the first few months in Cincinnati going to work and then straight back to her room. She wrote letters to Mama to let her know that she was safe and to ask about Carmen and Lil' Jimmy. She said nothing about her search for Jimmy. That would be the last thing that Mama would want confirmed. Mama would probably come to Cincinnati just to slap some sense in Birdie's head.

Mama frequently sent reports on Carmen and Lil' Jimmy.

They spent their days scrambling, tumbling and playing in the long grass beyond the house. Lil' Jimmy led the way in mischief. From the time he could walk, there was never a day where there wasn't a scrape or bruise on him—but he never cried once he took a tumble. He was a tough little nut to crack. He took the sting of Mercurochrome on an open cut like a brave little soldier proudly sporting the red stain over his fresh wound. He learned to salute from some young enlisted men who would stop by Mama's. Lil' Jimmy would raise a hand to his forehead and give Mama a kiss every time she bandaged him up from falling or throwing himself down a hill to roll with the older children.

Carmen had become the boss of everyone and had a protective streak when it came to her little brother. She would organize her dolls in a straight line and shake a finger to scold them when they couldn't sit themselves upright. She'd tell Lil' Jimmy that he had to clean his plate at breakfast so that he could grow up to be strong like their daddy.

Mama's reports were daggers to Birdie's heart. Birdie missed her children terribly. Her bones ached at the thought of them. Her goal was to save enough money to bring her children up to Cincinnati and have a decent place for them to live—with or without Jimmy. Having the children attend school in Cincinnati would be better than the starts and stops of a Mt. Sterling education based on farming schedules. She wanted both of her children to have a full education along with college or some sort of specialized training like her sister Bessa.

Bessa stayed diligently on her path of books and studies to become a certified pharmacist. She now taught other black women at Kentucky State College for Negroes. She wasn't married nor did she have any children, but she was well respected and served on every church and civic board imaginable. Birdie envisioned both Carmen and Lil' Jimmy becoming pillars of the community like her sister. And they were, after all, Jimmy's children. She adopted his words of wanting his seeds to be respected within the community.

In all of Mama's letters there was never any mention about the incident. It had been eight months since Mr. Conroy attacked Birdie when she received an envelope from Mama containing newspaper clippings detailing the police investigation and speculation into his murder. Along with the clippings, Mama wrote only a brief note saying, *"The children are fine. Things here are nice and quiet. No one wants to talk to this old lady anymore. Just as well, too many people have been making deals with the devil and doing his work. No one seems surprised when Mr. devil comes along to collect his due."*

The cryptic letter led Birdie to believe that the police hadn't so much as looked in Mama's direction. *Thank goodness!* Up to this point there had been no mention of the police questioning Mama about the murder, Birdie, or anyone she knew. Mama's frail state at the scene of the crime clearly worked. Who would suspect this soft-spoken woman, barely able to stand, of such a gruesome crime?

Knowing the town's penchant for gossip, Birdie guessed the search for Mr. Conroy's murderer might take a different route when news circulated about his gambling, drinking and other women as alluded to in the picturesque stories in the local newspapers. News coverage consisted of sparse facts derived from neighborhood gossip whispered from front porch rocking chairs or in between blowing sheets pinned to clotheslines or across backyard fences. Birdie knew that the rumor mill could be so vibrant that it had the power to shut down any further investigation into Mr. Conroy's murder, at least as far as looking at her or Mama as suspects went. She also suspected that once a bit of insurance money was doled out, his family might lose interest in finding out who killed him. From all accounts, it appeared as though dead Mr. Conroy's wife and sons were satisfied with the money and probably only publicly shed a tear for him when they made an appearance at church or a bar. They moved out of their house and bought a bigger place on the opposite side of town. With this news, Birdie thought she'd only have to wait a while longer before heading home to Kentucky—provided she had the money for another trip. Besides, she didn't want to return home empty-handed, looking like a lost child. She wanted to stride into town looking as though she just stepped off a movie set without a care about money or a lost husband.

In Cincinnati, she ran into people who knew her family and, of course, they knew Jimmy as well. She gave no details when they asked about him. She didn't elaborate on him because she couldn't. She'd simply nod and say that she was here to make a little extra money to send back home to her kids and help Mama out.

Most folks understood because just about every person she knew had a little something going on to make money, no matter how little. There were folks on every block making and selling jams, pickles and bread. They dried and bundled herbs to heal every ailment imaginable. A neighbor suddenly became clairvoyant and sold glimpses into your future for a mere sum that escalated to a few more dollars when she found evil blocking your success. There were land deals for acreage in neighboring states being sold from living rooms. Dresses and suits were made in dining rooms. Hair was straightened, dyed, and styled in kitchens and bottles of sweet wine and alcohol fermented on shelves in the cellar or behind furnaces.

You could walk outside your door and into a neighbor's house to find someone that could provide whatever you needed.

Sometimes you didn't even have to leave your home. A man would knock on your door selling either life insurance to prepare for your ultimate demise or a chance to live life to the fullest by doubling what money you possessed by playing the numbers. If you needed a lawyer there were a few enterprising neighbors who had completed mail order courses certifying them as a legitimate attorney. They were now qualified to act on your behalf for any legal issue from divorce and ownership to murder. Dollars and coins exchanged hands across the sidewalks and floorboards throughout the black neighborhood. It was the only way to survive and thrive particularly when whites wouldn't sell to you, or overcharged you or sold you inferior quality products or services. Black folks knew how to make money or at least make something work on next to nothing.

Despite the struggles of most, there was a growing class of black society that graced the society pages of the *Call and Post* with rituals of balls, galas and induction ceremonies for membership into exclusive orders. The social page featured pictures of complexions fairer than a paper bag, wavy-haired sons and daughters of doctors, attorneys, prominent businessmen and church leaders meeting for teas and luncheons. Birdie scoured the society column religiously while she sat in her room at the boarding house. She pictured herself among those who wore fine clothes, rode around in shiny cars and went to sorority and fraternity balls. They did exactly what white socialites did, which was introduce themselves within closed circles and heap recognition and favor on the next generation of the talented ten percent. Their pride of being such a benefit to the race was also of being the "only one."

The "only one" who was accepted and was the "only one" who crossed the color line, allowed entry into the elevated sphere of white men. It granted them superior status in the black community. They were the degreed graduates of Wilberforce University, or any number of black colleges founded by Baptist Missionary Societies or African Methodist Episcopal churches. They were the firm believers that "by one's own toil, effort and courage" they would prevail over the imbalance of justice between blacks and whites. Nowhere in the pages of social introductions and debutantes was any notation of the grimy business of colored reality—segregation, lynching, chain gangs or low-paying jobs.

It wasn't that they didn't see the need for protests. There were some in society circles who were neatly vocal and active on issues of race. When gathered for tony events, side remarks and discussions about the state of Negroes were held with cautious overtones. There were no vocal revolts or race riots in the streets for those that were light enough to pass black society's paper bag test. They trusted an articulated outcry of dissent by way of suited meetings in court chambers and churches, and behind closed doors of black institutions of higher learning. Civil rights demonstrations for some of the upscale were as proper as a crustless finger sandwich. That was their preferred venue to climb up and over the white walls to be the first or "only ones" to reach manicured lawns of sparkling white houses. And climb they did to a pinnacle of self-sufficiency by way of positions poised for desegregation in jobs that served as a pipeline for the manpower needed to feed a threatening war machine.

It was 1941, a new calendar page and a new year where hard knots formed in the throats of so many black men and women. A peacetime draft had been called in September, but it was easy to see as the year began to unfold that America's frontline involvement in fighting Hitler in a great war in Europe was inevitable. It wasn't unusual to see young brown-skinned men sporting nice crisp uniforms as many began to enlist in the army and get carried off to boot camps. Church announcements included a list of sons who were leaving for foreign shores. Prayers were packed along with pride, masking everyone's fears.

It was Mr. Brown's nephew who came to dinner at Mama's house before going off to a training center. He was the one who showed Carmen and Lil' Jimmy how to salute. They both mimicked him, placing chubby fingers up to their foreheads. Lil' Jimmy saluted everyone he came across to show that he was a soldier too.

In an effort to establish herself in Cincinnati, Birdie temporarily called off her search for Jimmy. She fought to push thoughts of him far into the recesses of her mind. Occasionally, while walking through the streets, she'd catch some sense of him and would start looking through the broken lines of faces that passed by.

She thought finding a room and a job would give her some peace while she waited out the memory of events that took place back in Mt. Sterling. She also thought settling in for a longer period would give her a satisfying taste of independence from Mama. But the truth was she was painfully bored and lonely.

She hadn't been out for fun since she left Ella in Chicago. Birdie was itching for something, anything that would get her to feel something other than a stomach stuffed with the cotton-like anxiousness she constantly felt. She had just turned twenty-two years old and felt one hundred. She told herself it

CHAPTER TWELVE

The midnight blue Mercury Monarch cut through deep puddles of black rainwater and glided up to the curb. The outrageously extravagant vehicle had folks all along Vine Street staring from windows, stoops and street corners hoping to get a closer look at the car and its inhabitants. A nattily dressed, brown-skinned man hopped out and gingerly walked over to the passenger side. He opened the door and, with a flourishing wave of his hand, welcomed his companion out into the evening light. Birdie swiveled off the seat and placed a foot lightly on the wet curb.

Birdie took a deep breath to draw in the cool air. She loved this time in the early night. The deep navy blue sky lined with the lingering pink light of sunset ushered in the evening along with a heightened anticipation of something to come. Everything that ever happened, good and not-so-good, always happened around this time of night. So, Birdie believed when the moon faintly appeared to take the reins from the day, all things were possible. Tonight was a "possible" night. She could feel it. She could just about taste it. From the time Earle asked her to step out with him, she knew this half-moon night would bring something good, something she needed to take her away from her shriveled surroundings.

They arrived when Vine Street was just beginning to hit its stride. Vine Street was a long thoroughfare winding its way down from the top of one of Cincinnati's seven hills, through downtown and ending at the Ohio River. At Vine Street's highest point, all of the Queen City could be seen sparkling at its feet. At its bottom-most curve were three compact blocks where the city's raw energy converged and released itself within one tight, crowded, color-coded neighborhood.

Musicians, nested in the clubs and bars that lined both sides of the street, were just starting to introduce locally composed crazy bebop jazz, sanguine high-steppin' ragtime, smooth crooners or deep-hearted, soulful blues. Music jumped out from every crevice imaginable and hung in the air. From a sooty row house, the Duke's big band swing tune "Cotton Tail" screamed from a radio. A neglected record skipped out "Indian Love Song" from a noisy rent party cranking up from a side alley doorway. From the storefront church, heavy, weary voices from a choir of holy rollers sang songs of hope for washed-away sins. All became intertwined with the syncopated jazz, blues and jump rhythms of the evening.

Earle put a hand to Birdie's waist and guided her toward the swinging doors of Junior's Blue Inn, one of Cincinnati's most popular colored clubs.

"Come on, babe, I wanna make sure Big Junior saved us a booth. I need a strong drink and a big plate of fresh catfish 'bout right now. He knows I'm in town just for a minute and he owes me a favor."

Once inside, they were led to a booth in full view of everyone who came, went, or walked sideways. Birdie flashed Earle a grin. It was the perfect place to see and be seen.

The noise level ebbed and flowed with the growing crowd. A small band, set up in a dim corner of the club, cut away from a bouncy stride piano tune to poorly imitate a Nat King Cole number. Earle whispered in the waitress's ear. She hurried away and quickly returned with an ice bucket filled with bottles of beer and champagne splits.

After a few rounds of cocktails and festive conversation, Birdie buzzed with a feeling of something close to ecstatic. Earle went off to speak with Big Junior. Birdie, feeling slightly uncomfortable sitting alone, took out a cigarette and retreated to her thoughts. Withdrawing into her past was a dangerous exercise because it always led her mind back to the same place—the series of events that brought her to Cincinnati.

The surrounding conversations, spontaneous fits of laughter and the sound of clinking glasses melted into the background. She heard neither the deep vibration of the bass nor stomps and shuffles of the smooth and clumsy dancers braving the small dance floor.

Her past appeared as faded snapshots before her eyes. Each vignette was accompanied by an increasingly cool prickling breath brushing across the back of her neck. The sensation was so consuming that it didn't surprise her at all when her memories suddenly melded into the real-life form of the man she danced with so many years ago. It was as if she mystically conjured up the tall, slender man who stepped through Junior's doors at the precise moment cigarette smoke curled before her eyes.

Jimmy, clean-shaven and dressed in a neatly pressed suit, breezed through Junior's doors. Birdie jolted forward in disbelief, hitting her rib cage on the side of the table. She jammed her cigarette into the ashtray and took a vicious sip of her drink as he stood framed by a crowd of raucous patrons filing in behind him. From that point on she was blown backward into the cracks of her past, back into the messiness she fled, and the anger built up over the past year of searching for him.

She kept a steady bead on her freshly conjured-up husband as he moved through the crowd. When he finally turned in her direction, Birdie produced a wide toothy smile. Once she saw her bright smile had ensnared Jimmy's attention, she swiftly cut her eyes away from him and blew a suggestive kiss to Earle, who was standing behind him. Earle, unaware of the true nature of her unfolding dramatics, took Birdie's act as an invitation to a more amorous evening than he had imagined for their first date. Excited, Earle immediately signaled the waitress to send another round of drinks to the table.

With a quick smile, Jimmy turned to see the recipient of Birdie's fake attention and headed straight for Earle. Surprised, Birdie held her breath. *Damn, I don't need this foolishness tonight.* She reached for her glass and gulped her drink too quickly, which broke her into a fit of coughing. By the time she looked up, Earle and Jimmy were pumping hands and slapping each other on the back. Both were laughing and shouting each other's name as if announcing their presence to potential witnesses. Birdie shifted in her seat as the show of camaraderie played out between the men.

Tingling with excitement, anger and anticipation, Birdie slid off her seat and coolly made her way toward the powder room. She had to fix her face and clear away the alcohol clouding her brain before confronting Jimmy. With his unexpected appearance, and Earle thinking God only knew what, she had to figure out her next move. Junior's was now elbow to elbow at the bar and couples packed the dance floor. As Birdie wound her way through the crowd, she felt a hard tug at her arm and spun around. Jimmy pulled her close to him.

"So you've forgotten all about me?" The smooth sound of his voice hurt; the melody of his words were piercing bullets. The touch of his hand jarred Birdie into reality. Once again, Jimmy Walker had casually trespassed into her life seemingly healthy without a care or concern. Birdie quickly scanned the club then shot a glance over her shoulder to see an empty booth. Finding no sign of Earle, she glared openly at Jimmy.

"What are you doing here, Jimmy?"

Without waiting for a response, Birdie whipped around and headed back to the booth. It took all her strength not to turn back around. If she had, she would have seen him standing as if glued to the spot with a quizzical, yet roguish smile pasted on his face and his arms dangling down at his sides.

Big Junior had sent over to the booth plates of fish, greens, yams, corn bread and a few more cold beers. Earle, having made his way back over from the bar, now sat at the booth with a napkin tucked in his collar. He was about to dive in for a bite when Birdie announced that it was time for her to go. Although several rounds of drinks had softened his features, Earle's face twisted in annoyance. But Birdie was determined. She scooted in next to him, snuggled close and kissed him lightly on the cheek.

"Earle, dear, you've been so wonderful this evening. The Jeffers are having a fancy dinner party tomorrow and I've got to get up early to make rolls and desserts. They're paying me extra."

Earle looked Birdie up and down. He'd seen her talking with Jimmy. He'd known they had history but also heard that it was long over and done. From that kiss she blew his way, Earle was hoping for a little more than a short evening. He wanted to show her off at an after-hour joint in Lincoln Heights where musicians continued weaving the magic of their craft. But *damn*, he had to give in because she was just too pretty to refuse. Sulking, he nodded and went to get their coats.

Earle remained quiet as they drove down Vine and Race Streets, then over to Fifth, passing the outstretched arms of the ever-flowing Tyler Davidson Fountain in the center of the city's downtown. Not a soul could be seen anywhere on the streets.

To avoid evoking the wrath of Miss Purity, Birdie asked Earle to cut off the car's headlights before pulling up to the rooming house. After giving him a peck on the cheek and whispering a few hasty promises to see him later in the week, Birdie slipped out of the car. Earle turned on the car lights and stepped on the gas, spewing gravel across the sidewalk. Birdie cringed as the car peeled away.

She waited a beat before easing her key into the lock and turning the knob of the heavy wooden door. She took great precaution not to make a sound, even watching for the slightest movement in the drawn shades that covered the door's etched glass. She feared the soft flapping sound of the shades against the glass might arouse Miss Purity. She took a half step into the foyer and an arm shot out from the darkness behind her, pulling her back outside. The night air vibrated from the door slamming shut right before her eyes.

"You know, unless you done gon' off and paid for some papers, you're still my wife."

A chilling jolt of anger was all she needed to regain her bearings. Birdie spun around to face Jimmy square on.

"Oh, so now you remember that tiny fact?" She spoke in a venomous low tone through clenched teeth. "That teeny, tiny little fact popped into your head just now? What are you doing here of all places, Jimmy? It can't be that you were look-ing for your wife...not after all this time."

Birdie had expected to feel relieved or triumphant when

she finally found Jimmy, but after all her searching, she was simply exhausted and annoyed.

A light from the first-floor window snapped on followed by a burst of illumination from the porch light. Jimmy grabbed Birdie by the hand and pulled her into the shadows.

"Baby, I want to… I need to… Baby, I really need to talk to you. C'mon with me just for a minute," Jimmy whispered authoritatively.

Birdie gave in to the heat rising from her chest. She wanted to spit in his face, but she was more afraid of being caught out on the lawn in the dead of night by Miss Purity. She couldn't afford to be tossed out in the street. So instead of pushing him away, she allowed him to pull her across the wet grass like an abandoned ship towed by a chugging tugboat.

Silently they tiptoed across the lawn and onto the sidewalk. The sound of shallow breathing and footsteps echoed through the empty street. Jimmy led Birdie by the hand as they walked to a black Oldsmobile parked a block away. He held open the passenger door for her.

"Is this your car?" Birdie asked as she slid into the vehicle.

"Never mind that right now," he said as he closed the door and walked over to the driver's side.

Once inside, Jimmy slid low into the seat and took a few deep breaths. Sweat trickled down from his curly hair and glistened across his forehead. He turned his head and, looking directly at her, shot her a slow smile.

It was the same narrow, deep brown face she had seen covered in morning sunlight as he lay next to her in their feather bed. In the scant light from a gas lamp, she inspected his face for the familiar features—thin lips as they turned upward in a sliver of a smile, thick brows and long eyelashes that framed the dancing dark eyes that had a way of disarming her. Now, just as before, she could never be sure whether that one haunting spark in his eyes signaled an open door to dark thunder or bright sunshine.

Birdie examined Jimmy's every move, registering mannerisms against memories she often revisited. As he had always done, like a maestro, he punctuated the air before curling and uncurling long, slender fingers around the steering wheel. The cool, easy smartness he had about everything, despite the circumstances was still there too. They were all there, sitting beside her in warm, hard flesh.

Jimmy laughed out, "Miss Bird! My Birdie! Whooo, girl, you been so hard to catch up with! You had ta' know I wasn't gonna let you go, at least not that easy. You had ta' know I was gonna find you eventually."

He wiped his forehead with the back of his hand. "Woman, where are my babies? I heard you left Mt. Sterling, but I didn't expect to find you here. Why aren't you with them? Has that evil mama of yours poisoned them against me yet? How my boy doing? He better not be around those shackled-minded farmhands fixing him to be alright with pulling up the fields. My boy got more to do in this world."

Birdie, lips tightly knitted together with emotion, was unable to answer. She caught a bit of sadness and sweetness with a hint of nervousness in his voice making it difficult to carry out her anger. She could only shake her head and stare into the darkness.

She had spent so much time imagining this moment. She fantasized telling him that he left her no choice but to take matters into her own hands. He left her with two babies, no money, no food, and no way out of the hateful talk that went on behind her back. She had planned to say that what everyone said to her from the very beginning was true—he was destined to bring nothing but the police and other white folks to her doorstep. She wanted to say that instead of chasing after him, she should have pursued her education like her sister Bessa. She could have gone away to any of the universities founded by Pennsylvania and Ohio Quakers, Methodists, Episcopalians, Presbyterians and abolitionists who were so haunted by slavery they established Cheyney State Normal School. She could have gone to Lincoln or Wilberforce. She could've become a teacher, a nurse or even a doctor. Instead, she lay down with him on that sunshiny day when she was seventeen years old.

Birdie pushed back and sat stiff against the car seat and finally whispered, "Stop. Don't talk, Jimmy."

She took a long deep breath then repeated it. Only this time louder and clearer. "Stop right now!"

The change in her voice made Jimmy freeze.

"I had nothing, Jimmy! You left me with nothing! No notice and no money. I had to gather up all my pride and crawl back to Mama like a fool with your two babies, an empty purse and runs all up and down my only pair of stockings."

"Wait, please give me a minute, Bird. Just one minute is all I ask. I know you're angry with me. You have a right to be mad, but give me just a second. Just let me tell you what happened."

"Jimmy, do you know how it feels to have absolutely nothing? Do you know how it feels to have to jump through hoops to keep some shred of dignity in that damn town? Every day feeling like I've failed our little ones, our children...their warm little fingers wrapped around mine and those wide brown eyes looking up at me every second reminding me that I have no choice but to do everything, anything I can to keep them safe.

"I know before you met me, you'd been everywhere and were used to clinging to bits and pieces of life, but I can't and won't live like that."

The moon was a moving target as Birdie spoke. It peered

through the car window while skittering across the sky, leaving traces of light across their faces. When Birdie stopped talking, the cool blue moonlight stood still. A deep rhythmic thud pounded between her ears and the hollow sound of her breath rang in her head as she stared at the man who was her husband. Between each breath she thought of one thousand reasons why she should punch him in the face and one thousand more why she couldn't forget what he had been to her.

Exhausted, what remained of Birdie's feelings hung along the roof of her mouth. When she found she couldn't muster up another word, she yanked open the car door and bounded back to Miss Purity's.

Birdie slipped into the house and up to her room unnoticed. She stripped off her clothes in the dark, pulled on a night gown and hopped into bed. The room was stuffy, but she couldn't bring herself to walk over and open the window for some air. If she did, she wouldn't be able to stop herself from peering through the tree branches to see if Jimmy's car was still there or if he had driven off.

She didn't move for fear her mind would tell her heart everything she didn't want to hear. That Jimmy was flesh and blood alive. He was breathing and touched her bare skin. His warm breath had graced her neck. At Junior's, he ran his hand up and down her arm. Once they got into the car, he lightly pinched the folds of her dress.

There was no way she could fall asleep. No matter how hard she tried she saw the smile that stretched across his face, and it snatched away every bad thing she felt about him. *But how can I ever trust that man again?*

An hour passed and the room's stuffiness became unbearable. Birdie was sweating under and over her quilt. She had to open the window to get some air. As expected, from her second-floor window Birdie could see between the full limbs of the oak tree, Jimmy's car was still there.

Hmm... He must not have anywhere to go. I hope he's not thinking about hanging around here. If he's sleeping in his car, the cops will pick him up for sure.

"Damn!" she cursed aloud.

If she went back out in her nightgown at this time of night, Miss Purity would certainly lock her out of the house and throw all her things out the window. Birdie jumped back into her dress, slipped on her shoes and grabbed her coat. Once again, she deftly maneuvered the stairs and heavy door and tiptoed down the sidewalk.

She thought Jimmy might be asleep in the car, but he was smoking a cigarette with his hat tipped low. Cigarette butts littered the front ashtray. She knocked on the driver's side window.

"The cops are gonna take you away if you don't go on somewhere. They don't like nobody sleeping in their cars around here."

He pulled off his hat and his face brightened. She backed away when he opened the door and slid out of the car. They were both in the middle of the street in the middle of the night while every respectable Cincinnatian was asleep.

Jimmy whispered, "C'mon and go with me someplace we can talk."

Birdie held up her hands. "You got five minutes. That's it. I need to hear the words from your mouth telling me why and how you could leave us the way you did."

Jimmy opened the car door for her and as soon as he slid in, he started talking.

"I know I ain't done right by you, but you know that ever since I first saw you, the very first time I laid eyes on you..."

His voice trailed off. After a moment of silence, he started the engine.

"Wait. Hold on, I'll be right back." Birdie ran back to the rooming house to grab her purse.

When she returned, Jimmy stepped on the gas and pulled away from the curb.

Birdie said, "You know the world didn't stop just because you went away."

"I know. You didn't deserve what I've done. You deserved so much more."

Birdie had no idea where they were going, but the one thing she did know was that it was impossible not to forgive him. As the sculpted outline of the moon hung brightly against the black night sky, she did just that. She forgave him for everything that ever happened.

CHAPTER THIRTEEN

Jimmy drove back to Vine Street where they entered a darkened row house that was hugged between a bar and pawn shop. Red and blue neon lights from the bar lit the stairs outside and the hallway inside the house. They climbed up two flights of stairs to Jimmy's small room. It was dark and draped in quiet. The streetlight peeped through holes in the shade, partially revealing dark stains that crawled up from the baseboards and across faded wallpaper. The only furniture in the room, a bed, nightstand and chifforobe, were strewn aimlessly around a threadbare rug. It was one of those rooms probably advertised in the *Cincinnati Enquirer* newspaper classified section as a clean room for "colored" only. Clearly, even in the dim light, it was nowhere close to clean. It most likely cost well over the $1.25 per day whites would pay for a nice well-kept boarding room.

Despite the dreary surroundings, for the first time in a long time Birdie experienced a sense of peace. It was easy. It was easy to let Jimmy gently touch her arm. It was easy for her to let him kiss her and for her to kiss him in the shadowy darkness. It was so easy to feel like he had never left her. Making their way over to his bed and feeling their bodies pull closer together was easy too.

Her head, pressed to his chest, bobbed to the rhythmic sway of their breathing. Jimmy's heart rapped out a steady beat. She held her breath so she could hear and feel the undercurrent of blood rushing through his veins. The sounds of his body, like waves of a river lapping against the shore, soothed her. His chest swelled quietly as he took in the room's stale air, then violently collapsed as his breath frantically ran away from him.

She thought, *It's just like him, always in a rush to go somewhere.*

Birdie lightly traced the lines in Jimmy's face with her finger. His eyelids fluttered, but he did not wake. His skin, almost hot to the touch, invited her closer. She complied and pressed her body into his, wrapping her leg over his thigh and pushing her toes down along his rough heels. It all felt heavenly. His hard body was so soft and so moist. Wrapped and twisted in the sheets, she melted further into him and the bed.

Something within her stirred. It started as a flutter, dancing in her stomach then slowly running up to her chest. The potency of her feelings stung sharply causing her to catch her own long, deep breath. Pressing back heated tears she rolled onto her back and turned her head to admire her husband's dark skin against hers. Birdie ran through the evening from the time they left Miss Purity's rooming house. Between lovemaking, she asked him only once where he'd been all this time. She asked softly, fighting hard not to blurt out even an ounce of her festering anger.

After a moment he said, "I know. I owe you that."

"Yes. Yes, you do," Birdie whispered. "I had nothing. I had nothing to give to our children."

She wouldn't say anything more despite having so much hanging on the tip of her tongue. Birdie wanted to tell him about all the horrid things that happened to her that caused her to leave their children in her mother's care. Instead, she pulled out Mama's latest letter that she had been carrying in her purse. She unfolded the pages and read aloud to him the sweet descriptions of their daughter Carmen's beautiful eyes and her determination to do things on her own. She read about how Lil' Jimmy bounced around on little feet like a rocket taking off. Of course, her mother included a plea for more money. *Your kids are growing like weeds. They don't have any more church clothes or shoes. I've patched them up so many times they're going to start looking like little hobos. Of course, I would never let that happen.*

After reading the letter, she showed him locks of his children's hair that she carried with her to feel close to her babies. Jimmy placed the curly tendrils in the palm of his hand and traced the strands with his fingertips. He then ran his hand gently down Birdie's face, neck, shoulder and hips before burying his head on her stomach as he sobbed for forgiveness and promised he would never abandon them again.

Still and silent, Birdie clung to Jimmy while his body shook. It was then she allowed herself to love him. She initially thought her years of anger had subsided hours ago when they were on Miss Purity's lawn. But she knew reading the letter and showing him the locks of hair would do exactly what she could not. The letter was the dagger she couldn't wave in front of his face. Her babies' tendrils were the knife that painfully carved her questions across his heart. She couldn't bring herself to ask, *Where have you been?* and, even the most important question, *Why did you leave me?*

With his head bobbing in her arms, Birdie suddenly felt ashamed at the cruel way she set out to hurt Jimmy. Her unanswered questions lost their urgency, and she was momentarily satisfied with leaving them in the dark. The curves of his taut muscles graciously dipped and settled against her breasts. With each stroke of her hand along his back, she wanted nothing more than to feel light, airy and loved. She wasn't in the mood to fight anymore. It required too much thinking. Too much thinking and the soft bubble would burst into a million ugly pieces. She had been angry and lonely for so long. She wanted nothing more than to release it and breathe a moment of peace.

It was a few hours past midnight and Jimmy, still wrapped in Birdie's arms, had fallen into a deep sleep. Pieces of drunken conversations floated up from the street below disrupting her thoughts. In the humid darkness, Birdie imagined the green, brown, black and blue of her childhood. She could almost smell the fields, freshly turned earth and musky, sweet odor of manure that permeated the farm town of Mt. Sterling, Kentucky. She turned her head toward Jimmy and the scent of young, dried tobacco radiated from the tight curly hair that drifted from his chest, down his stomach to thickly gather around his privates. She drifted off to sleep.

When the strong bright morning light woke her, Jimmy was gone.

At some point during the night, after a round of sex and promises, he announced he had to be somewhere in the morning. She couldn't recall details or purpose, only that he promised he would be back. Birdie heard him clearly. But the mental calisthenics over the last few hours left her numb and she set the words aside. She placed them so far back in her mind she could barely recall what, where or why he said them. He could've said he was going around the corner for coffee but after the words "I have to go," Birdie tuned him out. In the sunlight, the reality was that he left her again with nothing but his scent.

She brushed her hand across the cold sheets, smoothing out

the wrinkled indentation of his body. In her mind, she kicked and slammed her fists. She gathered up her clothes, quickly dressed and pulled the door closed behind her until she heard the loud click of the lock. She would have taken a taxi home, but she needed the walk. It was a blessing that the streets were empty. There would be no witnesses to notice her party apparel from the previous night.

After a few blocks, aching feet made her toss aside the notion of walking all the way back to Miss Purity's. Several yellow cabs had passed her. They were either racing to start a morning shift or turning in from dropping off night-crawling revelers. Finally, she flagged down a checker cab with a black driver. She instructed him to drop her off a block away from the rooming house to avoid any questions from Miss Purity.

Beyond the sparse trees behind the inn, she could see the shimmering gray waters of the Ohio River moving rapidly along. Even farther was a sliver of the Kentucky shoreline. She passed through the gate on the side of the house and followed a well-traveled dirt path through the backyard which led to the edge of a steep incline. There, hidden from the dark windows of the rooming house, she had a full view of the river. She could hear the distinct sound of the waves slapping against the shore. The river appeared to be moving slowly, but she knew the undercurrent churned fiercely as it threw itself onward to the Mississippi River. In the middle of the water, a speck of something bobbed along on top of a convulsing wave. She followed the object, watching it rise and dip until it was no longer visible. Across the river, an assortment of trees lined the shore. The guardians, still holding on to the last green leaves of summer, stood firm and were either calling her to, or barricading her from, home.

"I should go back now," she said aloud. "I should go back just to lie in the grass and kiss my children's faces." Birdie thought, *Were they still babies...my babies? Do they even remember me?*

Guilt and homesickness swept through her. Every bone in her body ached for her children. Birdie imagined Carmen and Lil' Jimmy in her mother's warm kitchen covered from head to toe in flour while buzzing around their grandmother. She saw her own mother punching down bread dough or creaming butter and sugar for her famous lemon pound cakes.

She missed her mother and craved the rare moments when her mother's hands were comforting. Birdie had only felt her mother tenderly smoothing down her hair or patting her lovingly on her cheek once or twice in her life. Despite yearning for the soft mother-daughter moment, what she missed most was her mother's cold-hearted fierceness. Birdie wished she could summon up Mama's red streak of meanness, an unpredictable occurrence that caught those who did not know her volatile nature by surprise when they stepped over a boundary. Even before Birdie had witnessed the power of her mother's rage, there was no wavering or straying away from Mama's straight and narrow commands. It was by Mama's command that Birdie found herself on this side of the river, far away from her children. As a child, Birdie told herself she would never, ever want to be anything like Mama. But now, all she wanted was to be exactly like her. Mama would know exactly what to do in this situation.

Mama taught her it was useless to dwell on the past. What Mama didn't teach her was just how to go about the actual task of not dwelling on the past. *Was there some trick to it?* Because no matter how hard she tried, Birdie saw her past repeatedly boomerang back. Everything Jimmy ever said or did came back to her over and over again. Even now, his face loomed before her, blocking out the river and the beckoning Kentucky shore. She clearly saw his eyes, teeth and tongue as if he was close enough to suck in all the air that surrounded her.

"Damn!" She closed her eyes tight and shook her head furiously. "I wish that damn river would carry him the hell away!"

Birdie kicked through a swirling pile of dry leaves, then picked up a stick and threw it toward the water. It landed silently in the mud only a short distance away.

"I can't go back home now. Who knows what I'd be facing if I went back? Besides, I don't have enough money saved. I could bring the babies here...but where would we live? I know I can't count on Jimmy. No matter what he said last night, I can't trust that he wouldn't have us scratching in the dirt to survive again."

Defeated from arguing with herself, she thought how silly she must look standing alone on the riverbank so early in the morning. Birdie threw another stick and watched it hit the water with a heavy splash. In defiance, she wheezed out a long stream of breath that had held her captive to the past.

"No, I can't go home. I've come too far to go back. Besides, who knows when or if I'll ever see that man again?"

Pulling up the collar of her coat, Birdie started back toward the house, stepping carefully around the soupy mud. She was so focused on saving her only pair of dress shoes that the crackling sound from a car pulling up to the rooming house blended into the lapping waves of the river behind her.

CHAPTER FOURTEEN

Birdie made her way back to the house from the riverbank. The excitement of seeing Jimmy, falling back into loving him and having him leave her again left her numb. She thought, *Did last night really happen?*

The answer dropped from the sky and stood directly in front of her. As she approached the rooming house, Jimmy was leaning against one of the porch columns as if he were casually waiting for a bus. She blinked to make sure he wasn't a figment of her imagination as it seemed so often happened.

"Where'd you go, Miss Bird?" Jimmy shouted to her as he stepped down from the porch to greet her. Birdie put a finger to her lips and nodded her head toward the front windows. Miss Purity was peering through the curtains.

"This can't be good," Birdie whispered softly to herself. "That damn woman watching me walk up here in yesterday's party dress along with some man will not go well."

Birdie swiftly concocted the story that she would tell Miss

Purity. Jimmy was a cousin from out of town staying at an aunt's house, there was a welcome home party and now she had to hurry and change so that her cousin could drive her to work.

When they entered the rooming house, Miss Purity immediately gave Jimmy the once-over and with skeptical eyes appeared to accept Birdie's story. Jimmy did his part by giving the rotund woman a spectacular smile and a bit of his personal southern charm. Miss Purity blushed and waved him into the living room while Birdie ran upstairs to change into her uniform. She knew she'd have to hurry back downstairs to limit the interrogation Miss Purity would undoubtedly rain down on Jimmy.

When Birdie returned, Miss Purity sat balancing her huge backside on the edge of her chair cushion, girlishly giggling at some story Jimmy was handing her. She glanced over at Birdie and chirped, "Such a nice young man, Birdie. How did you come by such a charming cousin?"

"Just lucky I guess." Birdie turned to politely address Jimmy. She pulled Jimmy by the sleeve to rush him out the door. "We've got to go now, dear cousin, or else I'm gonna be late."

Jimmy flashed a smile in Miss Purity's direction. "I sure hope you have a mighty good day, ma'am."

"Oh no, call me Miss Eugenia," she gushed. Her puffy face was flushed from what Birdie thought was some bronze fantasy floating in her head.

Birdie hated to admit it, but she was grateful Jimmy was there to save her. She was relieved to see him after thinking she'd been duped, once again, by his promises.

Once they were out the door, Birdie teased, "You know, all her husbands, and there were plenty, died or ran off somewhere never to be seen again. So beware."

"Baby, you don't have to worry about me with that one,"

Jimmy laughed. "Listen I just found you. I'm not going anywhere just yet."

Birdie stopped in her tracks. Jimmy, still chuckling and a few steps ahead, whipped around to face her. Birdie stared back at him. She caught his choice of words, *I just found you* tangled up with a *just yet*. She glanced down as if to examine a crack in the sidewalk before looking back up. She took a deep breath and, in her exhale, decided to save the argument for another time.

"Jimmy, I didn't know where you went this morning. I thought…"

His face softened when he saw her struggling. He stepped closer, put his hands lightly on her shoulders and looked at her square on. "Listen, I know I haven't been around, but I'm your husband and I need to take care of you. Believe me, girl, it's hurting me real bad, the thought that you're here and not home with Carmen and Lil' Jim. I never thought in a million years it would come to this. Come on, let's talk. Let me drive you to work."

Reluctantly, Birdie climbed into the car. Maybe it was the bright white morning with the sudden rise of heat, or it could have been the wild swing of emotions over the last few hours, but even with the proximity of their bodies in the closed confines of his car, Jimmy's sentiments lost their luster and power. Birdie took a deep breath and gathered enough steam to unleash the words she had held in for so long.

"Jimmy, you've been gone a long time. I didn't hear one word from you since you disappeared. If I hadn't seen you at Junior's last night, I would have just gone on without knowing if you were dead or alive. Jimmy, so much has happened."

Birdie's throat swelled, causing her voice to tremble and crack. She paused to fight back tears before shaking her head and starting again.

"You know what, Jimmy? Whatever happened to me while you were gone is none of your damn business! It stopped being your business when you didn't return home."

She whipped her hand across her face to wipe away tears now streaming down her cheeks. "At first, I refused to believe you left me. You left us. Just like that, without any warning. Everybody was looking at me like I was a fool! And then I went looking for you! Chicky got married. Bessa got her pharmacy degree. And me? I foolishly went looking for you!

"I left home to find you and bring you back to me, Carmen and Lil' Jimmy. I took my sorry self and went all the way to Chicago, you know that? And all I found was some bartender who knew more about you than I did and... Oh, by the way, some stupid young girl, some little tap dancer, seemed to know you quite well. You know, Myra? Myra from Alabama?"

Jimmy looked at Birdie quizzically. "You went to Chicago? Who went with you? Did your Mama or your sisters go with you? That ain't no town for a young woman to be alone without family. Where did you stay?" Jimmy took his hand off the steering wheel in an attempt to wipe away Birdie's tears. When she leaned away, he dropped his hand close to her lap.

Jimmy continued. "Please, Bird, I tried to get word to you a few months ago. One minute I was working at Wrights, then something happened, and I had to leave. I had to... I can't explain why but I had to get out of there. I got stuck walking for miles on some dirt road somewhere in godforsaken Jackson County and I knew I couldn't go back to Mt. Sterling. My intention was to make some fast cash and bring it home to you. I saw a train that looked like it was headed north, and I hopped it. I ended up in New York City."

Birdie rolled her eyes. She wasn't going to go down without a fight. "Jimmy, I gotta go to work! Regardless of what happened between you and me last night, I don't have time for this foolishness."

"Baby, I know, but listen…a friend of mine told me about some construction jobs building that big World's Fair and a few other skyscrapers up there. But when I got there, it didn't turn out so well. No jobs for us."

Jimmy shook his head. "Why was I not surprised? Them white unions had everything all sewed up and them boys weren't letting any colored men work there. I did get in for a few days though, only because the NAACP started kicking up a fuss. But then I lost my spot because I had to get out of town real fast."

Birdie couldn't look at him for fear she'd get sucked in again. She turned her head toward the window and listened. Her ears perked up again when he mentioned having to leave New York.

"Then I was in Chicago. I thought I could pick up where I left off and make some money. This time, I knew I could make some real big money that I could send to you. I did real good for a while. Matter of fact, I need to run back up there to finish what I started. I promised some people some things. You hear me? I gotta go back, but not today. Today, I want to spend the day with my only girl."

"Jimmy, I'm not that wide-eyed, stupid little girl you left back in Mt. Sterling. I've got to make some money myself and send it back home to my kids."

The car sped up as she spat out her words. Jimmy's face became stoic as they stopped at an intersection. "See that street there? A friend of mine has a house just up that steep hill. He promised to hand it over to me as payment for a debt he owes me, but I ain't seen that man in years. I gotta go check that out."

Birdie had heard enough stories and adventures to last her

a lifetime and didn't want to get entangled in another tiger-by-the-tail pipe dream. "What? A house?" Birdie sniffed. "Somebody just handed a house over to you? Oh, come on, why on earth would anyone just give you a house? Please, I got to get to work or else I won't have a job."

Jimmy frowned and remained silent until they arrived at a gray stone Tudor house at the end of a long driveway. Sheepishly he asked, "Do you have to go?" Before Birdie could open her mouth, he said solemnly, "How long you gonna be? I'm going to wait for you right here to take you home."

Birdie quietly replied. "Jimmy, you don't have to wait. In fact, don't wait for me at all. A black man just sitting in a car all day out here? No, that won't work. The police will be coming around and I'm quite sure they would cause trouble for you. I should be done around three o'clock today."

"Okay. I'll be here at two o'clock, just in case you get done early."

As promised, Jimmy was waiting for Birdie when she walked down the long driveway a little past three o'clock. Throughout the day she thought about nothing else but him, their lovemaking and their argument. As she dusted and cleaned, she was too afraid to get her hopes up that he would be there at the end of her workday. But here he was, and she was now too afraid to think about anything beyond this minute.

Jimmy jumped out of the car and opened the door for Birdie. He was clean-shaven and smartly dressed in a fresh white shirt. He looked so handsome. Birdie had to look away to keep her heart under her control.

"You hungry? I'm starving. Let's go get something to eat. Or do you want to go to a movie or something? We can stop in at Junior's. People gonna be crazy downtown with the

Reds playing the World Series and all. Or we can drive over to Newport and party over there."

He was working overtime to please her, and his efforts were hitting their mark. Birdie was genuinely happy to see Jimmy. "Let me get out of these ugly things, freshen up and we can take it from there."

They ended up at Downbeat, a small corner jazz club that had nonstop music going throughout the night and the best ribs this side of the Mason–Dixon Line. They ordered drinks, reminisced, laughed and ate barbecue, collards and potato salad. The music, from only a piano and a throaty torch singer, was a dreamy complement to the delicious food. Between bites, Jimmy caught sight of an old friend and waved him over to the table. Jimmy, laughing and grinning, greeted his buddy with hard slaps on his back.

"Bird, I'd like you to meet my friend, Chester." A slightly disheveled dark-skinned man with blue eyes wobbled over to the booth. "Me and Ches' go way back to some back woods days in West Virginia."

Everything about Chester sagged. His suit jacket, vest and pants looked as though his wide, squat frame had spent a little too much time in them. The collar of his shirt curled around his tie which was loosely knotted and stuffed haphazardly into his vest. His large head dipped lower than his shoulders at times as if Jimmy's arm around them were weighing him down. His bottom lip flopped open in a weak smile. He had obviously spent a few hours at the bar. After wavering slightly, he poured himself into the seat next to Birdie.

"Ooooh, you so pretty," Chester said as he leaned toward Birdie. Then looking at Jimmy, Chester carried on with a conversation that probably started over at the bar.

"I don't see why any of our boys should go over there to fight. If they make it back, what they got left? Ain't nobody making any money 'cept you, Mr. Walker," Chester said slowly rotating his wide head around to Jimmy.

Loudly, Chester went on. "What they gonna get, man? More of some white cracker with his boot on our necks and kickin' us in the ass? Tellin' me I ain't got no brain...no intelligence..."

His voice trailed off as his head bobbed closer to the table. He tightened his grip around the glass he had been holding steady which, except for a few pieces of ice, was now empty. He suddenly shook it so violently ice flew out of the glass and skittered across the table.

Slamming down the glass, not looking at anyone in particular, Chester continued, "I ain't got no rights to speak my mind to whoever the hell I want or go wherever the hell I want. Hell, I can't even pee where I want."

Jimmy leaned down to pat his friend on the back. "Negro, you done had about enough already."

"Damn straight. I done had enough," Chester snorted. His watery blue eyes shot a glace in Birdie's direction. "Yeah, James, you the only one...seem like you got it all."

Birdie wanted to move on to more pleasant things and for Jimmy to get Chester out of the booth. Chester got a second wind and lifted his hand to motion to the waitress for another drink.

"Hey! Hey, Jimmy! You 'memba Tom Mahan? You know, the youngsta they call Smokey. He got drafted. 'Cept he didn't even get to see no combat. He was gone only but a second. He didn't fight no Germans. He didn't even get out the States, man. The army sent him way down south to some training camp just for colored soldiers. And some redneck white boys caught him walking back from town. They told him he ain't allowed to walk nowhere in these parts. And then, this is what they told me, them white boys...them white devil crackers wasn't even in the army... They ganged up on him. They held him down, beat him. Then one of them boys took one of those big ole 'bama blades and damn near clean hacked off his leg so he wouldn't walk nowhere again. Then they left him on the road to die! To die, like a dog... And he had his uniform on, man."

Although the club was filled with activity, there was a sudden interlude of silence. Birdie glanced up at Jimmy. Jimmy's face was ashen and immobile as old stone. He stood looking down at his friend. As if in a trance, he gave Chester a few slow, deliberate pats on the shoulder acknowledging his pain. Telling the tale took a toll on Chester. He was unable to put on any facade of control. With his face bathed in sweat, Chester flopped back against the booth's high seat. His chest heaved deeply, and his eyes fluttered closed.

Birdie placed her hand lightly on Chester's arm and leaned in closer. "Chester. Chester, are you alright?"

She spoke softly trying not to draw attention if she didn't have to. Birdie knew from her mother's advice and from her own personal dealings with black men, there were some roads a woman should tread lightly or just not cross. Chester's story warned her to choose her actions and words carefully.

At her touch, Chester turned his head slowly and looked at her through narrow slits of his eyes. Suddenly aware of her presence and closeness, he jumped as if stung by a bee. He jammed a hand into his pocket, snatched out a greasy kerchief and quickly wiped his face. He shook off his momentary emotional lapse as if coming back from the count after sustaining a beating from his adversaries—bourbon and whiskey or whatever other demons that haunted him.

A painfully loud rambling riff from the piano sliced through the air. The piano player, providing vocals for this number, was in the middle of his rendition of "Sweet Lorraine." Birdie waved to a bubbly waitress with hard-pressed platinum hair who sold cigarettes and took pictures of club patrons. "Chester, I got someone to take your mind off things."

Soon after, Chester went stumbling off toward the bar with his arm around the waitress's waist, making her dead promises of a good time.

Birdie was deliciously inebriated when they went back to Jimmy's room. In the height of their lovemaking, between the passionate twists and turns, she knew this was the time to ask—no, demand—answers from him. She closed her eyes when she did.

"Jimmy, you've been gone for so long. You must know that I love you. I have always loved you, from that first dance and everything else that has happened since. I wish I didn't. You have to know that or else I wouldn't be here with you now. I love you, Jimmy. There, I've said it twice now and I thought I would never say that again since you left. Now I need to know something. I want you to tell me straight. Why? You say you love me. So, how could you leave? I know things were hard, but how could you leave us like you did?"

Jimmy tightened his grip around Birdie's hand, which he gently laid on his bare chest. "Baby, I love you too. I always have, from the moment I saw you and asked you to dance with me. I knew then… I saw it right before my eyes that you were going to be my wife. I've missed you. You, Carmen and Lil' Jim were the ones that kept me going, no matter where I was or what I was doing. All I thought about was you, our family."

From that point on, the night filled up with Jimmy's stories. Stories he majestically told as if he were Paul Robeson speaking on stage in front of an audience. He finally told Birdie how his supervisors left him in the middle of nowhere after cheating farmer Monroe out of a fair price. He reiterated that he hopped a train to New York hoping to find a job. He spoke about zigzagging all over the country in an effort to find employment and to stay one step ahead so he wouldn't land in jail for vagrancy.

Speaking just above a whisper, deliberate and detailed, Jimmy said, "I've been outside, inside, up and down...just about everywhere. I just grabbed whatever job I saw first."

He traveled through Chicago, parts of Louisiana and all the way out to San Francisco. He found work in construction, factories and fields. He claimed he only made a little bit of money throughout his long absence. He had planned to send it all home to Birdie and the kids, but lost it several times over when a scheme went sour, or the man didn't pay or he got in a fight and had to pay to stay out of jail, or a so-called trustworthy partner turned shady and disappeared. He spoke with great sadness about what he saw too many times down south—men, women and children hanging from trees and the soaked red dirt beneath them.

Looking directly at Birdie as she stared back at him incredulously, Jimmy exclaimed, "Really, that's it, Bird! And after so much time had passed, I couldn't come back to you empty-handed. All I ever wanted to do was to find the best way to feed you and them kids. When I left Mt. Sterling, I set out to make some real money and then come back home to you. That's *all* I wanted to do. I wanted y'all to have a nice house, one where you and even that mean mama of yours could be sitting on the porch without a care in the world. But I couldn't get a hold of it. There ain't no good-paying jobs for us regular Negroes nowhere. Even though there's plenty of factory jobs coming now that them folks over in Europe gonna bring us into war. Still, I done seen too many signs tacked up all over those factories. They even take the time to have them printed up all nice. All of them signs sayin' 'no jobs for colored' or 'whites only.'"

Birdie jumped in. "Well if things are gonna go the way you say, there should be more jobs opening up right here in Cincinnati. There are plenty of factories here. They're always hiring over at Hudepohl, Red Top and Schoenling breweries."

"Oh yeah," Jimmy said sarcastically. "I met some real smart black men, men that are damn geniuses, got degrees and could figure all sorts of things. And you know what they're told? They're told either to go sweep up somewhere, sit in an elevator taking other men up to the top floor or, what them folks consider the pinnacle of success, to be a Pullman porter. Hmph, that's it? You got the brains of a genius and you're told by some white man that you should be grateful to scratch the dirt or work on a train dressed up like some rooster wearing gloves. I'll carry a whole lot for a real purpose, but I ain't carrying nothing for that white man. Smiling like a damn fool. Wearing white gloves so I don't touch damn cracker skin… Nooo, that ain't happening while I'm on this side of the earth."

Jimmy was becoming agitated, and the serene atmosphere began to disintegrate. Birdie stroked his arm and chest as a distraction. She listened as his thoughts leaped to the plight of the Negro in America. He didn't, as usual, speak of his highly regarded Marcus Garvey. This time he spoke about A. Philip Randolph's efforts against unfair labor practices, the NAACP's Walter White's ardent pursuit of desegregating the army and everyone's hope and pride for the 332nd Fighter Group and the 477th Bombardment Group of the United States Army Air Forces, our own Tuskegee Airmen.

He finally slowed down the tempo, ending with his hands in fists. It would be a few beats until he slowly unraveled his fingers.

"I'm sorry, Bird. I'm so sorry. I've been so happy to see

you and so happy that you're here with me now. There was times when I thought I wouldn't ever see you again or that you wouldn't want to see me. Now I'm messing up my good luck, talking about this shit of a world we in."

"Jimmy, I don't know what I can do about all this. It's true what you're saying. In some ways, yes, we're living in hell. It's true and it's not fair. I don't know how to help you, except to say that you've got to see there is so much beauty and things are changing out there too. That's what I see in all the poetry and things you've shown me. Baby, you know life ain't fair for anybody. The only thing I know is that we made a family, and this family needs you."

Jimmy kissed Birdie's hands and then buried his head in her neck. He kissed her forehead, eyes and the tip of her nose before kissing her hard on the lips.

"The only thing I want is my family, Bird. It's truly the only thing I ever wanted. I want you, Carmen and Lil' Jim." He then winced as if in pain. "But I have to go somewhere first. I made a promise and there's no way around it."

"You made a promise—no, many promises—to me first, Jimmy."

"I know, Bird. I am trying to be a better man than I was before."

He told her he had to go back to Chicago and afterward he would have some big money in his hands. He promised, crossing his heart with his finger against his naked chest, that he would be back in a week.

"Once I get back, we're gonna pick up Carmen and Lil' Jim and move somewhere. We'll get a little house with just enough land to grow something."

Birdie threw her head back and rolled her eyes to the ceiling. "Oh please, Negro. You ain't going to do no such thing. If anything, and I mean that with a really big if, we will get a house. We aren't going to do no kind of farming. You are just dreaming."

Jimmy looked hurt so she softened. "Okay, okay," Birdie conceded. "How about a small victory garden so I can have some fresh ripe peppers and tomatoes?"

He responded by giving her a sad puppy dog–eyed expression.

"Okay, a little farm," she laughed. "Close to town. Okay? The children can go to school and move on to college. I don't want them going to one of those one-room schoolhouses that stop every time something shoots out of the ground. Remember how I wanted to have my own restaurant? Maybe we can have a farm stand instead and sell some of the vegetables we grow. I can bake a few things and sell those too. You know those white folks love to travel the countryside looking for fresh farm products."

Jimmy threw his head back and laughed. "Now you got it, girl! Now you're cooking!" He extended his hand. "Deal?"

"Deal," Birdie responded. They sat up and shook hands then fell back into the sheets to make love all over again.

Sometime later, Birdie awoke to find Jimmy's soft eyes staring at her.

"What? What you thinking?"

"I gotta tell you something," he said. Birdie's heart jumped and she turned to look directly at him. "I love you, girl, and I need to tell you what I'm doing from here on in." He paused to give her a long kiss. "'Cause, like I said, I gotta go back to Chicago. I just need one whole week to finish what I started. A week, that's all. I got some people who are depending on me to deliver something."

"You know you got some people here that are depending on you, don't you? You ain't doing nothing dangerous are you?" Birdie regretted asking as soon as the words escaped her mouth. She didn't really want to know the answer.

"Dangerous? Nah, it's just not quite legal that's all." He paused for her reaction. Finding none, he continued. "You know there are a lot of little backwoods bars that need a steady flow of alcohol. I've been working for some people that find a way to keep it flowing. It's been my job to pick up supplies and deliver. My boss can rely on me because I know every curve and bump of those back roads like the back of my hand. I've damn near crawled on my belly for miles at night between here and Fort Wayne, Detroit and back over to Chicago. These hands have felt every rock, pebble and ditch. I know how to duck in and out to stay out of sight."

He paused again, then started up slowly. "I got an agreement with this guy they call Red. He's the boss, the head business-man. He made arrangements with, well I dunno who exactly. He probably made a deal with some devils. It really ain't for me to know. He tells me where to pick up a few cases of gin, bourbon and scotch. I drop it off, get his money from the bar owner and, of course, I keep a little for myself for my troubles. Everybody's happy. It's a supply and demand business, Bird, and there's plenty of demand for supplies. No matter how po' people get in the darkest times, and these are dark times for dark people, they find some quarters to rub together for a drink or two. I'm just the go-between. I'm between some-body feeling happy or staying put in their misery."

"Jimmy, this business you're in doesn't sound right. It sounds dangerous. Why do you have to be involved in this?"

Jimmy pleaded, "That's why I got to make this run. Red's expecting me to come through in a couple of days. He ain't nobody to disappoint. I'll be back. I promise. And when I get back, like I said, we can both go down to Mt. Sterling together and pick up Carmen and Lil' Jimmy. I'll have a bit of cash to give you so we can get this house."

Unconvinced, Birdie replied, "Look, I understand it's hard out there but there's got to be something else. You are one of the smartest men I know. Smarter than those college boys Bessa used to bring around. Let me ask you this...would you want your son, Lil' Jimmy, to be doing this kind of work?"

"Absolutely not," Jimmy said firmly. "Baby, my boy Lil' Jimmy ain't gonna be a baby forever. He's going to do what a strong, righteous man has gotta do. Listen, I know this ain't no traditional job. This ain't the kinda work that a regular person would choose. I tried that kind of work at Wrights. I learned and applied my knowledge in the hopes of getting some fair and respectful pay. But where did it get me? A first-class view of white boys thinking it's their God-given right to cheat and steal from us black folks. That kind of work had me riding in the back of a truck like a dog and gave me a kick in my black ass."

Birdie knew where this was going. She stroked Jimmy's arm to keep him calm. He rolled out of bed, walked over to the chifforobe and pulled out a cloth sack. He thrust the sack toward her. "I bought these for Carmen and Lil' Jimmy."

Birdie carefully opened it to find two books—*Hans Christian Andersen's Fairy Tales* and *Complete Book of Marvels*—a delicate dark-skinned baby doll with curly black hair and a silver cap gun with a red roll of caps. She picked up the doll and watched its big brown eyes open and close as she examined it.

"She's pretty. She looks just like our baby girl. Where did you find her? You can't find a little brown-skinned doll around here, at least not one this pretty."

"I picked them up at a store in Chicago."

"And the books... Thank you."

"Girl, don't thank me like I'm some kind of stranger. These

are for my children. I know I ain't been around but know this, I love them. I got these a while ago and been carrying them around. See, I think of you and them all the time. You all have always been an anchor for me no matter where I am."

Birdie traced the gold-embossed lettering on the cover of the fairytale book with the tip of her finger. She flipped open the book and fanned the pages. Illustrations of swans and little blonde girls in flowing pink dresses with blushing cheeks waiting to be kissed flounced before her eyes. She gently closed the book.

"Anchors? Me, Carmen and Lil' Jimmy are not boats sailing on any seas. I am your wife. We're your family."

He pleaded. "I know. I know. Just hear me out. Give me a few days and I'll make this right for our family. I just got to get a bit above water and then things will be right."

Birdie stopped listening. Her body had run cold. Shivering, she pulled the covers up around her after taking a peek at her naked body to make sure she wasn't turning blue. His words, *I'll be back, I promise*, spun around her head and pounded like drumbeats behind her eyes. At some point Birdie began counting the days until her next menstrual cycle. She said a prayer. *This cannot happen again. Please dear Lord. It just can't.*

Silence followed. The sound of her own deep breaths filled the room. Jimmy fell asleep. Birdie couldn't close her eyes and spent her time in the dark memorizing his profile. She had seen the angles of his face in her dreams every day since he left. It wasn't that the curves of his face were any different than she had always known. She wanted to make sure that everything she remembered was just as it was. She followed the lone sliver of light that outlined Jimmy's features. Each time her eyes swept across his face she found something new. A dimple, a tiny scar, a mole, patches of gray stubble or dots of tightly wound curls dotting his hairline around his ears. The foreign quickly became familiar. She felt his warm skin and the weight of his arm wrapped around her. She couldn't have come this far just to have things slip through her fingers again.

He promised and I have to believe that.

Still, Birdie couldn't fall asleep. All the things she had to do the next day raced through her head. Her list included making a bank deposit into her savings and stopping by Johnnie's corner store for bread. Once Jimmy left, it would be back to daily, dull rituals. *But it's only for a week, right?* The uncertainty finally dragged her into a fitful sleep.

The window had been left open during the night and in the cool morning air the room felt clean and crisp. Jimmy said I love you with goodbye kisses and hugs. It was the only time he had ever said those words together with "goodbye" to Birdie. In some way, Birdie wished he had vanished in the night as he had done so many times before.

Jimmy lingered over her lips whispering, "I promise. I promise to return." He repeated it several times before kissing her on the lips. Just as she was about to cry, he said, "I was just thinking. This, sweet Birdie, is my last drop for Red. When I get back, remember we're gonna get that farm close to the city line like we talked about, okay? I'm going to take care of everything, baby, from here on in."

CHAPTER FIFTEEN

Weeks passed with no word from Jimmy. The lit fuse of slow boiling anger subsided only when Chicky and her husband, Clarence, drove up to Cincinnati to bring Birdie home to Mt. Sterling. Mama had taken to her bed weeks ago and had stopped eating altogether. Both Chicky and Bessa thought Birdie's presence might be able to summon Mama back to herself again. As they drove south, Chicky chatted while Birdie thought about her mother always busy baking and cooking to nourish just about everyone in and around Mt. Sterling. Whenever she thought about home, Mama's hands would fly into view.

Mama would cup her hands to separate eggs or measure ingredients exactly to get cakes and breads baked to perfection. Mama's hands dug deep and raked through flour, lifting, and lightening it with a few shakes before sprinkling it into the bowl. Sugar poured through her fingers until she sensed just the right amount to marry with a slab of softened butter. She pinched seasonings with the tips of her thumb and forefinger then released them gently to heighten flavor.

Birdie tried to use her own hands in the exact same way to bring ingredients together like her mother, but nothing ever came out quite right. Nothing Birdie made was light or fluffy enough. She used the old tin cups and mixing spoons her mother had hanging above the stove. The utensils had been passed down in the family since biblical times. Still, there was always something a little off. People smiled when they ate Birdie's food, but they didn't rave like they did when they ate Mama's.

It wasn't until she was older that Birdie finally made the discovery. The secret was in the size of Mama's hands, which were so unlike Birdie's small palms and slender fingers. One day Birdie playfully coaxed her mother to lay her hands down on a piece of wax paper so she could trace them. She cut around the lines to create two near-perfect images of her mother's hands. Holding her invention up to her mother, Birdie proclaimed she would no longer need any measuring utensils. Instead, the cutouts of Mama's hands would be her guide. That way everything she made would turn out as good as her mother's. It was one of the rare occasions that Mama smiled and laughed with her youngest daughter.

Matching her concern for Mama's health was Birdie's yearning to see her children. Carmen and Lil' Jimmy had been staying over at Chicky's house while Mama recuperated. Birdie's heart raced at the thought of seeing their little round faces and a twinge of sadness poked at her from knowing they had grown in this short time without her. Birdie knew that once she laid eyes on them, she could never leave them again. But even as the desire to see her children churned a burning hole in her stomach, Birdie decided it was best to see Mama first.

It would only take one look upon her mother's face to know what was needed to bring Mama back to them, no matter what the doctors reported. She'd run over to Chicky's to scoop up her babies into her arms once she made sure Mama was on the mend.

Mama was asleep when they walked in the door. Everyone, including Sister Shirleen who was caring for Mama, tip-toed and whispered throughout the house. Birdie opened all the curtains to let sunlight flood the house. In Birdie's mind, all Mama needed was sunlight, some fresh, warm bread and strong dandelion tea. Birdie pulled out yeast and flour. As the dough rose, she wandered outside to find some essential herbs that she would use for a healing tea. As the perfume of fresh bread rose throughout the house, Birdie scrubbed down Mama's room while her mother lay in a deep sleep.

It was nightfall when Mama finally opened her eyes. Her gaze floated over to her daughter and Birdie threw her arms around her mother's frail body to give her a hug. Mama remained silent as Birdie helped her sit up. Mama made no attempts to protest her daughter's authority over her. Birdie took the comb from the bedside table and began to part Mama's hair into sections. She scratched and greased her scalp, then braided Mama's hair. She tenderly patted and smoothed down every wayward strand.

"Baby, my baby bird, listen to me for a minute," Mama said weakly. Birdie, sitting on the side of her mother's bed, stood at attention. Her mother's voice, although frail, still carried the weight of an anvil.

"Don't let your sisters in here for a minute. I need to talk to you, only you, baby."

Mama shut her eyes tight and held them closed for a few beats. She softly pawed at her throat. When she finally spoke, it was through a fog of jumbled words. Setting aside her alarm,

Birdie leaned in closer hoping to make sense of what her mother was trying to say. Finally, she started to piece together the story Mama was telling her.

"When I was about your age, I never minded the long walk and trolley car ride over to the Conroy farm. Back then, they lived right on the outskirts of Mt. Sterling. Mr. and Mrs. Conroy were a joyful couple at first. They had three young sons and another on the way when I first started with them. I cleaned, cooked and watched over them mischievous, hard-headed boys. They needed lots of attention."

"Mama, I know all about them. You told us about…"

"Shhh, baby, listen to me now. Many people said there was something not quite right with them Conroy boys because the elder two always found ways to destroy or terrorize. With slingshots, pellet guns and rocks, they shot at everything. They busted open a neighbor's beehive and fired shots into someone's open window, breaking flowerpots and jelly jars. The youngest, he was a strong-willed little boy. He'd wrap himself in my skirt and when I finally got him pulled away from me, he'd scream to high heavens. I had to pry his little red fists open to free myself from his grip.

"Mr. Conroy was a nice, polite and respectful man. I never heard him raise his voice. So when Mrs. Conroy asked me to take him some lunch while he was working in the barn I was happy to do it."

Mama began to drift off. Her hands, spindly and shaking, pulled at her blanket. Birdie, now on her knees next to Mama's bed, reached over to pull up her covers.

"Mama, you should eat something. Let me go fix you some…"

"Chile, please," Mama breathed out, slightly agitated. "Stop fussin' over me, I'm alright."

She shook her head, took a deep breath, and went on. "Mr.

Conroy turned away from mucking out a stall when I came into that barn. I remember him wiping his brow and smiling at me. He was just staring at me like he wanted to say something to me. I thought he was happy to see I was carrying something for him to eat along with a Mason jar filled with lemonade.

"I handed him a ham sandwich wrapped in a cloth napkin. He quickly flung open the napkin and when he took a bite of the sandwich, his eyes rolled in his head. Then he moved over to a bale of hay and sat down. He was still smiling and looking at me when he took another bite of that sandwich. He must've been real hungry, because he said he ain't never had a sandwich taste so good. Then, and I'll never forget, he stopped his smiling and his eyes shifted to the door then back at me. He said, 'I'll take that lemonade now.'

"I reached out to hand him the lemonade. I was trying to be careful because I had to step over fresh hay to move in closer. The Mason jar was filled almost to the brim, and I didn't want to spill. Soon as I said, 'Here you—'" Mama stopped midsentence for a moment before going on.

"Mama, you need to rest."

"No, Bird, listen." She swatted at Birdie. "Mr. Conroy, instead of taking the lemonade, grabbed my wrists. I was taken off guard and tried to pull back but he yanked me closer to him. When I realized what was happening and turned away, he grabbed my hand and pinned me down over bales of straw. I couldn't move. He had his arm stretched across my neck and I couldn't breathe."

Birdie, horrified at what her mother was saying, spoke between the fingers that covered her mouth. "No, Mama, no… Oh, Mama, you don't have to talk about this. No, not now." Birdie rose up on her knees to hug her mother, but Mama pushed her away.

"He moved his arm away from my neck only when he started yanking up my skirt. At that point I could only catch some air, but I couldn't scream or cough up any words. I just closed my eyes tight, but instead of darkness I saw an explosion of red, yellow and orange light as he pushed his way inside me.

"When he was done, he didn't say a word. He jumped up from behind me and I heard him walk out the barn like nothing ever happened. I still had my eyes closed. I didn't open them until all I heard was the horses shifting their feet. The first thing that came into focus was that Mason jar. For some reason I can't forget that jar. It was laying on its side a few feet away from me as if it rolled to safety. The red-and-white-checked napkin landed even further away. I remember those huge black flies swirling around the pieces of ham, cheese and bread. I jerked myself over and, on all fours, I threw up. I heaved again and again until I felt completely empty. I remember that putrid smell of straw, manure and my own vomit like it was yesterday."

Mama's hands fluttered momentarily over Birdie's arm. Her chest dramatically rose, shuddered and fell. Yet despite her weakened state, Mama sat straight up and suddenly appeared strong. Her eyes, strangely lit, shone brightly in the room's dim light.

"After that, I stood up and smoothed down my skirt and my hair. I ignored the pain between my legs and picked up that jar, the ham and cheese from the sandwich and the napkin. I crammed all the evidence of my misplaced trust into my pockets.

"I started heading back toward the house. All I could hear was my own breathing and the crunching sound of my steps hitting that hard dirt and stone. I still hear that sound now. When I got to the Conroys' back door, I reached for the handle, but couldn't bring myself to go in. I changed direction and started toward the front of the house. I walked down them crooked cement steps that led to the dirt road and kept walking. Before I knew it, I had walked the whole four miles or so back into town. I walked past the stop where I would have caught the trolley car home. Only then did I look down to see the folds of my dress was pressed against my thighs and twisted around my legs. Still, I kept walking.

"All this time, I was clutching that damn empty Mason jar. I held that jar in a tight grip around the neck. It was a miracle it didn't break. If someone I knew had seen me marching through town looking like I did and carrying that dirty jar in my hand I never noticed. Even if they called out my name, I wouldn't have paid them no mind."

Mama reached out for the cup of tea that was sitting at her bedside. Her hands were shaking. Birdie, softly crying, picked up the cup and tilted it up to Mama's lips.

Fat tears rolled down Birdie's cheeks. "Mama, I'm so sorry. I didn't know. But you kept working for the Conroys after that? You sent me over there. I know you warned me, but I didn't… I didn't know why. And when…well, you know happened…"

Mama swallowed hard. "Girl, I told you to forget about that. I meant that. I ain't telling you this for you to carry it with you like some heavy baggage. I been trying to make my peace ever since and I want you to do that too. I ain't finished.

"Now the sky was turning dark by the time I finally got home. When I reached the edge of the walkway, I let go of that Mason jar. I threw it across the street and watched it shatter against the cement. As if I couldn't believe my own eyes, I walked over. I guess to make sure it was really busted into pieces. I pick up the larger pieces and tossed them in the sewer grate. I kicked the little pieces into the grass. Ever since I rounded the last corner, all I was saying to myself was, 'I've got to keep this to myself. Yes, I've got to take what happened in that barn to my grave or someone else is gonna die.'

"I knew only too well the consequences of even whispering it behind locked doors. Back in 1918, this crude town was filled with some truly hateful people. Every now and then they'd show us they really didn't like us. I had no faith that punishment would only fall on the guilty. Lynching was all too frequent and race riots in the big cities ended with little or no change for any of us down here. Somebody was bound to get hurt or even killed no matter what. This would've only stirred a nasty pot for those who demanded righteous justice or those who felt they had a God-given right to protect their own sinful, thieving kin.

"I wasn't going to say anything to Mrs. Conroy, or my mother, sisters, pastor—not even my sweet husband, Octavius. He was overseas fighting for America in the Great War. I wasn't about to write this down in no letter. Besides, I thought his only worry should be staying alive. I promised myself I wouldn't even tell him when he came back home."

Birdie's throat tightened as Mama described her husband so tenderly. Her "sweet husband" was the man Birdie had only seen peering out from the framed picture Mama kept in her drawer. Even though she knew Octavius "Jacques" Jennings was Bessa and Chicky's real father, the man in the faded picture was the only father Birdie had known. She would occasionally sneak into Mama's room to carefully study the picture in hopes of finding anything in him that resembled her. There was something about his straight posture and steely eyes that gave him an aura of nobility. His name, Octavius, confirmed her thinking that he was of regal African descent. Birdie could easily imagine his military garb replaced with glorious robes and a crown of beads, jewels, feathers or beaten gold. She was sure his royal lineage was hidden and confined by his army uniform.

Birdie always wondered why he, an American soldier fighting the war to end all wars on behalf of the United States of America, received his medals of honor from France. It gave her comfort to think that this man whom she only knew from a sepia-colored picture had received comfort, love and devotion from his true tribe. He deserved that and so much more after leading men across a battlefield.

What was hardest to imagine was Mama as this man's loving, doting wife. Birdie had never known her mother to extend much softness to anyone, including her own daughters.

"Girl, are you listening to me? This here is important. Where are your sisters and the children? Don't let them in the room yet. I need you to listen."

Mama paused. Her eyes fluttered as she fell back on her pillow. Birdie jumped but relaxed when Mama, with her eyes closed, continued speaking.

"Now I kept silent when I finally walked through that door that day. Me, Bessa, Chicky and your Aunt Beauty lived right here with your Granny Aurora at the time. I didn't say nothing when my sister asked me why I looked such a mess. Maybe I hugged my little babies a bit too tight when I first saw them. Maybe that's what made your granny look up at me from snapping beans at the kitchen table.

"I remember it as clear as rainwater. God bless your grandma's heart. She said to me, 'Lillian, where you been? Whew, girl, you smell rank. What did them Conroys have you doing over there? No righteous woman should be smellin' like that.'

"I stayed silent like I said I would. I just kept looking down at the floor. Granny stopped her snapping rhythm and held one long string bean, bent almost to the point of breaking, between her hands. Out of the blue, she said she'd heard the sound of crows in a dream last night and saw their black shiny feathers hitting her around her face. Then she asked me if I was okay.

"I stood still as a statue, looking down at my muddy shoes. Then your granny said, 'You go on in there and take a long hot bath. Make it as hot as you can, then put plenty of salt in the water. It's getting cool outside, so I'm going to make us some strong tea. You know something, precious? God gonna take care of everything. He's a mighty God and will make everything right.'

"I stuck to my promise and never uttered a single word about what happened in that barn. Even when Octavius returned home and only months later a pretty little baby girl flew into our lives. We named her Birdie."

Up until that time Birdie, kneeling at her mother's bedside, had been listening to Mama with her head down on the bed. At that moment, she popped her head up and stared wide-eyed at her mother. Sitting back on her knees, she asked, "Mama, me? You talking about me?"

Mama sat straight up and stared directly at her daughter. Her eyes, a bit yellow from sickness, flickered brightly. Their deep brown irises followed Birdie's every move. She then closed her eyes and fell back against her pillow, nodding her head only slightly.

Mama raised her palm and said softly, "And baby, I've never told a soul. But somebody knew something. I guess somebody put two and two together because on the very day my Birdie Autumn Jennings was born, the Conroys' barn mysteriously caught fire and burned to the ground, killing the Conroys' two plow horses and three cows. Nothing was left of that barn 'cept a stain of scorched black earth. Nothing would grow on that spot either. For a long time that black stain remained visible and barren.

"On the same day the barn burned down, the Conroys' hunting dogs went missing. At first it was thought the dogs burnt up in the fire, but their maggot-ridden bodies were found by the reservoir a few days later by children playing along the water. No one knew how the dogs got all the way out there. Some folks said they might have been dragged off and eaten by a black bear, which nobody around here had ever seen."

Mama weakly fanned her face with her hand. She opened her mouth as if she were going to yawn but instead continued as tears trickled down.

"Later that same year, my sweet Octavius Jennings's spirit escaped from the noose that bound his body on a tree by the Kentucky River. Every one of the black churches in Mt. Sterling gave him a courageous homegoing that was attended by just about every black person in town. Windows and doors of every church were flung open wide so the crowds that flowed out on the lawns could hear the preacher's words from the fieriest chapters and verses of the Bible.

"Our own pastor blanketed the congregation with a blazing sermon, all sorts of passages talking about cleansing fires. Shoulders and backs shook, and hands were beating chests. Everyone was rattled with emotion, as the minister trumpeted Octavius's bravery fighting overseas and protecting his family on American soil.

"And even though I lost my beloved husband in such a horrifying way, I kept the promise I made to myself and stayed silent. I cried when I stared into the first candle I lit for him. I watched that flame against the night stars, and it crossed my mind that it didn't really matter whether I bound my words, whispered, or shouted out what that damn Mr. Conroy had done. The results were the same. A black man was dead. Octavius's death was because of me. Baby, I ain't told a single soul till today. I don't know who did though. I'm telling you because I know out of all my daughters you the strongest."

Mama fell into a deep sleep. Birdie watched and waited to see if Mama had more to say. Her snoring signaled there wouldn't be anything more for now. For hours, Birdie sat in the dark by her mother's bed while Mama slept. In the silence, the brutality of her conception swirled around Birdie's brain and the thought of the pain Mama carried all these years stabbed her in the heart. Mr. Conroy now stood front and center in her mind's eye as a blue, dead man lying grotesquely twisted among a pool of light-yellow batter and deep red blood. The image haunted her dreams ever since that day she was in the Conroys' kitchen.

Chicky stepped lightly through the sliver of light that suddenly appeared from the doorway and motioned to Birdie to come out of Mama's dark room. Keeping her voice to a mere whisper Chicky coaxed her sister to get some rest herself. Birdie slowly stood up. Her head pounded and her eyelids felt heavy with worry and the words of Mama's story. She could barely hold her head up. Chicky wrapped her arm around her sister's shoulders and gently led Birdie to their old room down the hall. Exhausted, Birdie followed without a sound of protest.

Once inside, Birdie suddenly clasped her hands to her mouth to suppress a squeal. Carmen and Lil' Jimmy, like two shiny spring peas in a pod, stood before her holding hands, eyes bight and wide with wonder. Chicky held a finger against her lips signaling the children to not yell out so as not to wake Mama. The children bounced on their toes with excitement at the sight of their mother. Birdie rushed over, fell to her knees, and scooped her children into her arms. She pressed her hands against their cheeks, buried her head into their hair and kissed every bit of skin she could reach before tickling their bellies. She was so filled with love she thought her heart would bust out of her chest. Chicky left and returned with a tray of sandwiches, cookies, milk for the children and hot tea for Birdie. Birdie couldn't eat but watched the children gobble down every morsel.

That night, for the first time in what seemed like forever, Birdie fell into a dreamless sleep in her old bed with her arms around Carmen and Lil' Jimmy. When she awoke, every muscle ached as if she had run miles down an unpaved road. She smothered her babies with kisses and the pain from Mama's story lightened.

Over the next few days, Birdie kept her mind occupied, distracting herself with busyness. She gave Carmen and Lil' Jimmy massive hugs, played games and tended to their every need as best she could while caring for Mama. At Mama's, she scrubbed every surface and kept the windows wide open so that fresh cleansing air could sweep away illness and help nurse her mother back to health. The more Birdie did, the less she thought about dead Mr. Conroy. When she couldn't find anything else to clean, she lingered over bundles of ironing Mama had accumulated from her long-standing customers. They had been neglected for weeks. She thought someone must be looking for their starched shirts and undies.

First Birdie carefully pressed and folded the shirts in the wicker basket. She ran her fingers along each of the folds to make sure the corners were crisp and sharp just the way Mama taught her. She heard Mama's voice in every stroke of the iron as she crisscrossed over the stiff cotton. She had to get it exactly right. Cooking and ironing were Mama's pride and joy.

When she was younger, Birdie had been torn between the freshly pressed items, folded and meticulously tied with string like beautiful gifts, and what she also saw as degrading work. She was amazed at the ritualistic practice of the work but also repulsed at what she thought was a demeaning task. Many times, she'd roll her eyes, out of Mama's sight of course, at the thought of taking in other people's laundry despite the food in her belly and the roof over her head. She made a pact with herself that she would never be left with such a miserable option in life. Now she couldn't help but heed every word of advice and apply everything she learned from watching her mother's utmost care and precision.

CHAPTER SIXTEEN

From the start, the liquor run felt wrong. Jimmy knew it was going to be his last run and couldn't wait to get it over with. This wasn't the first time he and his partner, Kelly, attempted to hit their mark. At one point, they discussed calling it quits but the win was too tempting not to keep trying.

They followed the truck all the way from Chicago to a grimy hole-in-the-wall joint outside of Indianapolis. It was known as a spot that stayed open all night for truckers to fill up and grab a bite to eat.

Kelly approached the truck's occupants, two young white men, as they lounged outside the entrance smoking cigarettes. Kelly, with his head down and hat rolling in his hand, kept them busy by cooning his way through a story about looking for work and a ride. Smiling and rolling his eyes, Kelly told them his boss left him here in the middle of nowhere and he needed to get back home to his fine young woman and his big fat old wife.

Kelly added in as slow a drawl possible, "Can you hep' me? I'se so really 'fraid of the dark."

The white men, entertained by Kelly's act, laughed at his slowness, and egged him on by asking questions about fucking his fat old wife.

Kelly laughed big and loud right along with them then begged, "I sho' would like a taste of sum o'dat brown likker juice I know you got so I can be the big man for both my women. Can you hep me out?"

The men got so involved in Kelly's story that they neglected to see Jimmy removing cases of whiskey from the back of their truck. Jimmy didn't think anything was wrong about taking bottles off their hands. He knew these white boys were far from saints because they stole the stuff from someone else.

Jimmy thought, *Ain't no respectable, legitimate merchant traveling these back roads at this time of night. Ain't nobody but thieves stopping at this here truck stop that's known to everyone on the circuit. We all just thieves robbing thieves. Ain't nobody here bothering no good folks, so these cases of liquor is nothing but fair game for all us.*

Jimmy was working on moving the fifth case out of the truck when he heard footsteps hitting the gravel. He ducked deep behind the thick brush that surrounded the parking lot where he had stashed the other four cases he already snatched. He watched a man come around the side of the truck and peek inside. The man stood for a moment, scratching his head. He appeared to be counting. He shrugged then tightened the ropes that secured the tarp covering the back of the truck.

"Damn!" Jimmy whispered. "I just need a few more cases before I can get outta here. Where the hell is Kelly?"

Jimmy waited a few beats after the man disappeared. He'd take the chance to go back out to the truck, knowing it would take some time to untie the tarp and squeeze in and out with more cases of whiskey. Jimmy didn't know where or when

Kelly would show up to help him get the stuff to their truck, which was tucked underneath some trees a short distance away from the lot. It would take a couple of trips and each trip would increase their chances of being seen. The consequence of getting caught wouldn't be jail—none of these guys believed in the police. The consequence would be taking a bullet in the head.

Jimmy untied the tarp again and squeezed through the opening to land inside the truck. He opened his eyes wide to adjust to the dark. Moving as quietly as he could, he listened for Kelly's bird call to let him know he was in place and ready. What he heard instead was the start of an engine. The truck shivered at the start causing Jimmy to lose his balance and fall into the cargo. He needed to get out of there fast before he ended up back in Chicago with his life expectancy at zero.

Jimmy heard the muffled voice of the driver. "C'mon, Sam! Stop shittin' with that nigga. We gotta go! Check the back and make sure everything is nice and tight."

The truck vibrated as the engine revved up then idled. Jimmy, staying low to the floor of the truck, quickly rolled over to the opening to slide feet first out from the covering. As he eased himself out, his leg became entangled in the rope. Jimmy had one foot barely touching the ground and the other trapped in a noose when the white man spotted him dangling from the back of the truck.

"Hey! What the fuck?!" The man charged at Jimmy.

Jimmy shook his leg violently to unravel himself from the rope. He fell to the ground as the man pounced. Jimmy easily shook him off and leaped into the bushes, bounding over his prized cache, the four cases of whiskey. He zigzagged through the trees so as not to give them a straight path to the hidden truck he and Kelly stashed earlier. Kelly was already behind the wheel when Jimmy finally made it to the hiding place.

"Where you been, man? I heard 'em hollering so I knew it was up. I headed back here. Did we get anything?"

Jimmy responded between breaths. "Nah, man. I left it in the ditch. I don't hear anything. Don't think nobody followed me here. Sit low. Maybe they already took off. If that's the case, we can go back."

Kelly said, "Man, I don't like staying here. We're sitting ducks just waitin' to get shot."

Kelly started up the old truck. It started like a whisper. That was the benefit of having Kelly as a partner. He was a mechanic and knew how to make any vehicle purr. The truck may have been silent but the two men charging through the woods were not. Branches and twigs cracked as they closed in. Kelly shifted the gear, and the truck flew into Reverse then lurched forward as he punched his foot on the gas and took off. The truck bounced a few times as Kelly shifted into Drive, weaving through the trees and brush in the dark until they got onto a dirt path. Once on the road Jimmy knew no one could catch them because Kelly was the best driver around.

Jimmy began to breathe easier. There wasn't any point of going back to see if the cases he stashed were still there. Now, without whiskey or anything left to bargain with, he just had to figure out what they were gonna tell Florida Red. He'd have plenty of time to think of a story on the way to Louisville.

He also thought about Birdie. He knew she probably wouldn't speak to him ever again since he had repeated his mistake by being gone way longer than promised. He had to try though. Over the past few weeks, he had heard from his cousin, Jessie, Mama wasn't doing well and probably wasn't going to make it. Jimmy knew Birdie would go home for that, so chances were she'd be back in Mt. Sterling soon, if she wasn't already. Once he got through with Red, he'd head back home and see if he could salvage some kind of kindness from Birdie and see his kids.

Jimmy rubbed his chest. It was either his recent brush with death or guilt that was causing him pain.

CHAPTER SEVENTEEN

When Dr. Wolfgang told the family that Mama was too weak from sickness to possibly turn around, Birdie stubbornly believed Mama would pull through. There was no need for crying. She never allowed herself to imagine a time when Mama wasn't with them. Mama would return reconstituted, healthy and ready to bake a cake. Mama was sick and tired, needing only rest to bring her back to health. God would pull her through this. Bessa was all business, taking care of bills and business arrangements ahead of time. Chicky contacted all kith and kin to deliver updates on Mama's existence and took care of the children. Birdie stood by, watching her mother's every move while ironing shirts, bed linens, tablecloths and hankies. When she wasn't ironing or folding, she sat quietly by Mama's bedside, watching.

Mama continued to weaken. She hardly ate or drank until her thin arms, covered with papery, crepe-like skin stayed pulled up to her chest. Her eyes had sunken in their sockets.

Her muscles fell away revealing a bony outline of the mother Birdie knew. The girls took turns watching their mother. At no time was Mama alone. When it was Birdie's turn, she'd sit close and hold her mother's hand. She sat still with her fingers entwined between her mother's.

She moved in to rub Mama's arm. Mama shifted in the bed twisting the sheets around her. As Birdie leaned over to straighten the covers, Mama opened her eyes and smiled at her daughter. She cleared her throat and in a barely audible voice she said, "My girl, my sweet little bird. When I first saw you, all I saw was the best parts of me and I knew you would always fly. Oh, baby, look who else is here…"

Mama's eyes searched the room. Birdie turned to see who had stepped through the door. When she saw no one, she turned back to see Mama's chest sharply rise and fall. She heard air whoosh through her mouth and nostrils as she took a few short, panting breaths. Then Mama let out one deep exhale. It was her last breath.

Tears rolled down Birdie's face. She made no effort to release Mama's hand to wipe them away. Birdie's mouth shaped her sisters' names. There was no sound. No one came. It was just her and Mama alone. Birdie held Mama's hand with both of hers until only the faintest warmth passed between them. Bessa came quietly into the room and knelt by the side of the bed. Chicky entered moments behind her sister. She covered her mouth, stifling a short wail. She then placed an arm around Bessa's shoulders, a hand on Birdie's knee and wept softly. Together the sisters said the Lord's Prayer.

As Birdie had so often witnessed when life entered, when life exited, an army of women swept in to welcome, comfort, provide safe harbor and bid farewells. They did so for Mama. Once the word went out about Mama's passing, women came in to assemble pieces of an honorable homegoing service.

Food in baskets, platters and jars was brought in and placed on every surface of the home to accommodate the nonstop flow of every branch of the tribe. There were moments when the house shook, and the floors creaked and bent from the weight of visitors. The only moment of silence was in the early morning as the sun began to bless the shadows that graced the ground where the sisters huddled together. Bessa, Chicky and Birdie wiped each other's wet faces, hugged the flesh of her flesh, and whispered their goodbyes. Collectively, they breathed in with the lungs their mother gave them and brought Mama forth through their bones to skin to fingertips.

Mama, organized to the very end, left a neatly handwritten note with instructions for the division of her things. Mama left Birdie her cherished mahogany four-poster bed. It was the largest and heaviest piece of furniture in the house and one of Mama's most prized possessions. Family history said the bed's head and footboard, which were carved like church pews, were stolen from a plantation after a murderous uprising. The dark wood was supposedly hand carved by shackled slaves whose blood seeped deep into the wood grain giving it its deep reddish hue. The slaves finessed the fine mahogany wood into intricate carved designs and polished the wood with their blood. The original plantation owners who slept in the bed would never have a good night's sleep as the captive spirits in the wood would violently disrupt their dreams. Mama would say her ancestors were in the wood and they were at peace protecting her and all that were made or born in that bed.

Birdie would have to figure out how to move the bed to Cincinnati. With Mama gone, Birdie decided she could no longer remain in Mt. Sterling. She also had to figure out how to move Carmen and Lil' Jimmy as well. She couldn't leave them in Kentucky any longer.

Since it had been months since she last heard from Jimmy, it was time for Birdie to take over. She thought bitterly, *Hmph, a week my ass. Jimmy, you were always such a wild dog, good at leaving me to go chase something down a hole.*

Nauseated, she swallowed hard. The sharp, dry crumbs of their lost love scoured her bowels scraping up regret and hate. She was too exhausted to let that pain linger. She heard Mama's voice, "I see you wasting away your young years before you can ever live your own life. Forget about him and move on, girl!"

It was decided that Chicky and her husband would move into Mama's house. They had a whole brood of children now. Bessa, busy with her own life as a teacher, pharmacist and president of all sorts of civic groups, had her own house in town that she shared with her friend, Clara. Bessa announced after Mama's funeral that she had been accepted into the first ever Women's Army Auxiliary Corps. She was one of forty black women from all over the country to be accepted into the Officer Candidate School and would have to go to Fort Des Moines in Iowa for six weeks.

Birdie, Chicky and Bessa sat at Mama's kitchen table sipping coffee as they took turns voicing their pride and concern.

"I'm so proud of you, big sister, but I don't want to think about you going over to Europe and being in harm's way," Birdie said.

Chicky slapped Birdie on the arm. "She'll be alright. She's going to be in the Auxiliary Corps, not going into battle. Are you?"

Bessa replied, "Not sure where I'll be stationed. I really want to do something to help our boys over there. Even though I might have to go overseas, don't worry. Mama will watch over me, I'm sure of that."

"If Mama has her way, which I know she will, you going to

end up not only fixing up those soldiers but also cooking for them," Chicky laughed out as she wiped away a tear. Birdie patted her sister's hand.

"Bessa, you going off overseas just reminds me of Daddy. He went off to war and came back a hero." Chicky scooted from the table and returned with the picture Mama kept in her drawer. "I don't remember much about him. This is all I really know. I've seen this picture a million times, but just look at him. He's something to be proud of. You going to be just like him, Bessa. Maybe you should take this with you so he can look over you too."

Bessa told her sisters that the only memory of their father she had was of being lifted up to the sound of a kind man's voice. She said she remembered when she was small that Mama explained why she lit a candle for him every night. Because in the same year their father died, thousands of black- and brown-skinned women, all dressed in white, and colored men dressed in their finest marched in complete silence down a wide street in New York City to protest the lynching of Negroes throughout the United States.

Chicky, who always boasted that she was Mama's favorite child, was surprised by this new information about her mother. "What a sight that must have been to see row after row of our people marching down those big wide streets of New York. Can you imagine?"

Bessa poetically said the marchers proceeded down the main street shoulder to shoulder without saying a single word. Their presence and the sound of their feet must have shouted out for them. Bessa said, "Without a word they said I am here, alive and American. We are free to call on our American government to bring lynching to a halt. We call, in silence, for justice."

Bessa gently circled the photograph with her finger. "Baby

sisters, our daddy, Mama's beloved, was murdered and hung like a criminal. The pain she must have felt from that experience was the reason Mama acted so cold most times."

Bessa said Mama told her that after Octavius Jennings was killed, she was saddened that the marchers' voices were never heard all the way down here at the footbridge to the South. Maybe she could have done something to prevent another noose from being used anywhere close to Montgomery County.

Uncharacteristically dreamy-eyed, Bessa said, "Mama carried a trunk-load of guilt for our father getting killed. She thought if she could have stopped him from going fishing that day he wouldn't have wound up dead. She felt guilty for not turning her silence to protest with those folks up in New York."

Birdie held on to her big sister's words while in her own thoughts remembered what Mama told her before she died. No matter what, Octavius was who she knew and felt was the guiding patriarch of their family. It made complete sense that the flame of the candle lit for Octavius was Mama's voice shouting as bright as she could and asking for forgiveness. The tiny flickering light for an American soldier of the Great War—a leader decorated with medals, not from his country but from one far away, a man who was then lifted up, stripped, slashed and hung from a tree over the bluegrass in the fifteenth state to join the Union—was a symbol to let everyone know that Octavius did not die in vain. His spirit, love and protection over his family could not be extinguished.

"I'm with Chicky." Birdie stood up from the table. "Bessa, take the picture with you. It will keep you safe."

"Girls, I will be alright. Don't worry about me." She shoved the photograph back at Chicky. "Keep this in Mama's drawer, where it's always been. That way we'll know they are both there watching out for us."

Just a few weeks after Mama passing, Birdie and Chicky had a going-away dinner for their sister. Mama would have wanted it that way.

When she was younger, Birdie thought her sisters lived silly little lives in this hick town and were destined to do nothing but breed and work dull jobs. Now she envied them. The pace of their lives tugged and lured her with an enticing air of family and comfort. Although Mama's death chilled her to the core, Birdie felt a magnetic warmth from being with her family and all those who knew her. The week she planned to stay at home in Kentucky easily stretched into months.

CHAPTER EIGHTEEN

Florida Red sat behind a desk which was cleared of everything except a pistol. He leaned forward placing his elbows on the desk, forming a perfect triangle between him and the gun's barrel which was pointed directly at Jimmy. Jimmy sat facing Florida Red, ready for an inquisition. Red needed to determine what kind of partner Jimmy would continue to be and how much, if any, loyalty could be expected. Red knew Jimmy generally operated as a loner and offered only allegiance out of necessity of the moment. In Red's mind, this meant Jimmy was, more often than not, unreliable. The gun was simply a means to determine which side of the fence Jimmy was on at this moment and reveal if he could be trusted to follow through and deliver money and merchandise as instructed. It might have to serve double duty if he sensed an imbalance in the conversation.

With his hands in a steeple position, Florida Red rubbed his index fingers together.

"You got something for me, brother? You know you owe me a great deal of something."

Jimmy knew he was at a slight disadvantage without his partner, Kelly, by his side. Jimmy and Kelly had just ordered drinks when word came that Red wanted to talk, but only to Jimmy. After being assured that Jimmy could handle Red alone, Kelly agreed to hang back at the bar. Jimmy also knew that if Kelly was smart, he should see Red's request as an opportunity for him to hightail it home, all the way back to Mississippi.

When entering the dark office, Jimmy planted his feet and solidly stood his ground before sitting in the lone chair in front of Red's desk. He had been in worse spots. Besides, he knew Red and where he came from. They both grew up fast. As young boys, each eked out an existence traveling the back woods and dirt roads from the most southern points of Florida to parts far north to avoid the law, a beating from the Klan or a noose. They both had the same instincts for survival.

Red was bred from a mix of Irish, Chickasaw and enslaved Africans. He had a quick, sharp mind, and a cold-blooded, mean and vengeful demeanor. Even though Florida Red was merciless to those who interrupted his business, he was also more of a calculating, greedy son of a bitch that quickly recognized an opportunity to keep his pockets perpetually filled. Since his failed attempt, Jimmy anticipated Red might ask for a bigger cut of his next run, leaving him with less profit and a quick exit from the business. Even though the barrel of Red's gun pointed directly at him, Jimmy thought Red wouldn't kill anybody over this. There was too much money to be made.

Behind Florida Red, partially hidden in shadow, an expressionless big country boy stood silently. He was young and grimy as though he just came in from working the fields and hadn't bathed for a while. Jimmy thought that if the boy was working for Red, he was stupid and desperate, a combination that indicated he would probably do anything for money.

Red placed his hands down on the desk, positioning his fingers spread-eagle with the gun between them. Without waiting for Jimmy's response, Red started in with an unexpected line of questions.

"You think your woman loves you? You think she even gon' miss you if you don't show up tomorrow? Where she think you gonna be?" He chuckled. "Oh right, it wouldn't be just one sweet little woman missing you. You got a few wild ones by the tail. Right?"

Red paused a minute, staring at Jimmy to gauge the effect of the words that rippled out of his mouth. Red bounced back in his chair and pulled his hands away from the desk. Smiling and rubbing his chin he asked, "Hey, how's that bright gal of yours doin'? That real pretty one. If you no longer interested in that one, I know some Cincinnati nigga got a shine on her real bad."

Red paused and posed with a phony look as if he were deep in thought. "You might know 'em, but for the life of me I just can't 'member his name. Damn, it's right on the tip of my tongue."

Jimmy avoided all of Red's traps. He put on his own wide toothy smile to match Red's treacherous grin and responded. "Look, brother, I don't recall the agreement between the two of us getting that specific. You know, there weren't no detail about how much was owed to you if I missed a drop. But now that we've come to this juncture, why don't we spend a little time discussing these new terms. That is if our plan is to remain partners."

The dirty white boy understood the threat embedded in Jimmy's words and took a step from out of the shadows. He stood behind Red with his hands deep in the pockets of his overalls. Except for one raised eyebrow, Red didn't move a muscle. His green eyes suddenly darkened.

"You know the folks that buy that whiskey are my long-standing customers. You knew that, right? They are folks that don't like to be disappointed. You know how this works. They will definitely find someone else to take care of them. I promised them they'd have more in a few days. I don't like breakin' my promises. They could easily go with some other nigga out there. Then I'd be losing money."

Jimmy stood firm and answered calmly. "Look, Red, me and Kelly were so close to lifting that cargo. It just didn't go our way. We'll get them next time. I'm gonna make another run in a few weeks. I got a different plan to hit a different spot. I'll get your money and merchandise then."

"I don't know, James. You done failed me a few times now. I know you're smarter than that. At least that's what everybody says. I'm getting to think that what you really doing is cheating me. This is a small pond here. And once word gets out I can't deliver. Well, once again man, I start losing money."

Red waved the white boy back into the shadows. "My girl, she's done taken a shine to you. Myra always talking about how smart you are and how you can figure out how to do just about everything. So, what's the problem?"

Red leaned forward and knitted his hands together right above the gun handle. "You know what? Never mind all this dancing around talk, Jimmy. This is how it's gonna go. You get back on the road. Watch those Italian boys and get whatever you can. Now I expect twice my usual cut and three times the merchandise, ya hear? Now you go on out front to the bartender and have a few drinks on me."

Jimmy shifted from one foot to the other, took a deep breath and walked up to the desk just inches away from the gun that separated the two men.

"Sure, Red. Like I said, you'll get your money. You know, brother, I ain't got nothing but respect for you, nothing but respect, but I need you to know this, because here is where I don't play—that bright gal you was talking about is my wife. And if you mention my wife again, you and me, we gonna have some problems."

Red threw up his hands. "Got it, brother. As I said, drinks are on me out front. Whatever you want."

Jimmy took Florida Red at his word and drank until he staggered out of the backwoods joint. Kelly had left the bar to head home about five drinks earlier. The lack of a ride really wasn't a concern. It was a warm night and Jimmy thought about finding a safe spot to catch a few winks outside in the fresh air. He wasn't too proud at the moment, and it wouldn't be the first time he just lay down in the grass to sleep the alcohol off. Jimmy shook his head and thought he would see how far he could get before he'd have to give in to his drunkenness. The path was well traveled but also well forgotten. The narrow trail had carried slaves and tobacco, probably stolen from plantations, to Ohio. It was a liberation trail of sorts. Jimmy had been down this road so many times. Many times, crawling in the dark to keep from being seen. He had hauled stolen merchandise and led newfound acquaintances down this road to escape wives, girlfriends, police and people who wanted to kill for money. There would always be a fee of some sort for their escape, like some drinks or a cut of the profit to obtain Jimmy's silence.

Every step Jimmy took fell heavily against the ground making a muffled padding sound. The night was perfectly still. The heat from the day still lingered like a low-hanging cloud. Maybe it wasn't the heat, but the drinks that were making him sweat so profusely. His shirt was soaking wet. He could still smell whatever it was they passed off as whiskey.

"Dammit, Red, you ain't selling nothing but grain alcohol in them fancy top-shelf bottles and charging all them saps plenty. Whew, glad I didn't pay for none of that shit tonight," he said aloud to no one.

Crickets rhythmically chirped in response. Jimmy's drunkenness began to pull him down. He had to lean forward to propel himself to keep walking. Under the cover of the high trees, it was pitch-black with only fragmented spots of moonlight and a small burst of illumination from lightning bugs. It didn't matter. He felt right at home using this path as his own freedom trail.

A sudden burst of red and yellow lights exploded inside Jimmy's head like a strike of lightning. Big beefy fists, from every direction, battered his skull, causing him to fall face-first into the dirt. Someone jerked him up by the back of his collar then slammed him hard onto his knees. His arms snatched behind him, Jimmy felt his wrists being tied with what felt like a wire cutting into his skin. Warm sticky blood poured from his head and ran into his eyes and mouth.

Dammit, that son of a bitch got me! Jimmy thought. He struggled to break free but couldn't move his arms. *If I could just get my gun.*

The man jerked Jimmy upward then knelt behind him, pulling and locking Jimmy's arms tighter. Jimmy now knew it was Red's country boy, breathing hard in short grunts.

"Hey, son…hold on, ain't no need for all this," Jimmy spat out between bloody clenched teeth.

His gun would be of no use as the boy took a sharp blade and in one quick motion, slit Jimmy's throat.

CHAPTER NINETEEN

It was something in the rustle from the canopy of trees that called Birdie to walk the dirt path that led to the church and finally attend Sunday service. It was early. A mist rising from the moist ground was a signal the day was gearing up to be a hot one. Chicky had taken all the children to Sunday school. Birdie knew by the time they left church the ground would be toasted dry. She looked up to see squirrels playing in the trees, leaping from branch to branch, making sudden crackling sounds when they landed on tree limbs.

With a gloved hand Birdie took a hankie out of her pocket. Mama had enforced that her good upstanding daughters always carry a handkerchief, particularly to church, as every proper lady should. One of Mama's customers, Mrs. Louisa Marie Styvesant, had tossed aside a few heavy Irish linen handkerchiefs. The monograms were missing a few stitches, but they were still elegant regardless of the chewed-up letters. Birdie felt she should at least look and act the part of an upstanding

Christian by fanning herself with a proper hankie while giving praise to the Lord. She blotted at the small beads of perspiration dotting her nose and upper lip as a light mist of sweat formed under her arms and breasts.

After being absent for so long, she wasn't exactly excited about entering the church and being assaulted by a flood of sad and pitiful looks. Some were well-meaning and offered condolences and affection for Mama, others were just to verify some false gossip about the state of her "so-called" marriage to a man no one had seen in years.

Birdie waved her hankie across her face, pulled her shoulders back and kept walking, hoping she wouldn't see anyone from Second Christian Church along the way. She was, as she had been since Mama died, too tired for pleasantries. The bubble of emotion rose from her chest at the thought of Mama but immediately burst at the sight of a man walking toward her. The distance and stark white sunlight blurred his features and casted him in shadow. She could tell the man was in pain. He plodded slowly and unevenly as one foot quickly bounced back from the ground like it couldn't take his full weight.

The man, dressed in overalls and heavy boots, was probably coming from the aluminum plant farther down the road. Given the need for war materials, the plant offered overtime by running shifts on Saturday, though it wasn't usually open on a Sunday. Sharp bursts of sunlight reflected off the buckles of his overalls as if sending warning signals of ominous news. The heat was suddenly intense. There was no holding back Birdie's sweat now. The front of her blouse was dotted with expanding drops of perspiration. She held the hankie, twisted in her fist, to her chest.

The man raised his head, paused, and slowed his gait even more. Birdie's chest rose and collapsed once she recognized him. It was Jimmy's cousin, Jessie.

Oh, Lord… Now I really have to pull my thoughts together and prepare for a few mindless pleasantries. I'm not gonna ask about Jimmy. I don't need to find out where he is or who he is with. No matter what I say, I'm sure he will surely carry information back to Jimmy. And I want Jimmy to know that I hoped he dropped dead.

As Jessie came closer, his long face, slanted eyes and thin lips became clearer and the knot in Birdie's chest returned. Except for a broader nose and some amazingly large ears, Jessie bore such a remarkable resemblance to Jimmy. Birdie thought at one time that they were really blood brothers. But when asked about the strong resemblance, Jimmy laughed it off and said, "Who knows what really happened only a few generations ago?" He'd often say "Somewhere deep down, all of us Negroes were more related than we'd ever want or care to admit. You never know where the blood flows, where it stops and where it starts. Every one of us is related. We bleed a family of love, hate and madness."

Jessie saw Birdie too and picked up his pace. His eyes widened as he got closer. Shaking his head, he crowed through a voice cracking with sobs, "Bird! Bird! He's gone, Bird. Somebody beat him real bad."

Although Birdie was still a distance away, every word Jessie said was clear, each syllable distinct. She needed no time to process what he was saying because something inside her knew it was all true. The simple sentence was too much. It was all too much. The bend in the sapless branch finally snapped. Not a clean break but a painfully slow twisting and turning that resulted in each muscle, fiber and tendon finally giving way.

In the middle of the dirt road on her way to church to pray for her mother and ask forgiveness for her sins, Birdie stopped and fell into a heap.

★ ★ ★

The house was still veiled in silence from Mama's passing and now the air was sealed in death's grip. The drapes were drawn but Chicky made sure the back and front doors remained open regardless of the temperature. She said with so much death and sadness, they needed sweeping fresh air throughout the house.

Carmen and Lil' Jimmy wailed for their mother's comfort as they sensed dread and fear. They clung to Birdie's knees and climbed into her arms, placing their heads in her lap or deep in her bosom every chance they could. Birdie watched tears stream down their faces as she herself went in and out of consciousness. She kept thinking, *That's it? It's over?* The ending came too soon. It was too abrupt. *There has to be more.*

A dark chasm opened, and Birdie fell into a well of wails. It wasn't just that her heart was broken, she physically felt as though, from head to toe, she had broken in two. People came out of the woodwork offering more condolences. It was an unending trail of people coming to Mama's house again, dropping off food just as they had done not so long ago.

Chicky, still heavy in her own grief over Mama, never left Birdie's side. No one spoke a word about the details of Jimmy's death, at least not to Birdie's face. Jimmy's sister, Pearline, who was a teacher in Alabama, came up to manage things and help plan the funeral. Bessa, on behalf of her grieving baby sister, tried desperately to take charge as she normally did, but Jimmy's sister proved the stronger of the two and flicked Bessa aside to take over the arrangements. Bessa gave up easily and decided to concentrate her efforts on consoling Birdie. Besides, within days she would be going away to army camp.

Birdie didn't care about anything. Jimmy was gone no matter how his body was going to be placed in the ground. She only knew he wouldn't want anything big and flashy. Just a plain box lowered into Kentucky's richest dirt would do. Scripture wasn't necessary. That, his sister or whoever else who needed it, could have. A Langston Hughes poem and his children placing wildflowers on the grave site would be all that she required at the service. *Save the scripture for those whose feet are planted around this side of the grave,* she thought.

At the church service, Pearline and the stalwart Christians got their moment by giving James Bryant Walker a proper church funeral. Birdie only knew a few of the sparse assortment of folks that were sprinkled throughout the pews. Those that she knew came from either Louisville or Wrights Tobacco Company. She sat quietly, and surprisingly so did Carmen and Lil' Jimmy. When they did begin to squirm, Chicky took them out of the sanctuary. Birdie looked down at her hands cupped in her lap and was thinking about how useless it was to wear white gloves until a pair of wing-tipped shoes appeared in her line of sight. She looked up and was startled to see an impeccably dressed dark-skinned man.

"Sandy? Sandy Beamon? Oh, my goodness, Mr. Beamon. I didn't know you knew Jimmy."

He leaned down and clasped her hands. "I'm so sorry for your loss, Miss Bird. I also heard you lost your mother not too long ago. Let me extend my deepest, heartfelt condolences. I know what it's like to lose a mother. We are never prepared. It's a tragic loss no matter how old we are."

"Thank you. So how do you know Jimmy? I asked you about him in Chicago and you said you didn't know him."

"I'm so sorry, ma'am, I don't remember you asking. Me and James were partners in a little enterprise of mine. He was a good man, a really good man that will be sorely missed. When I heard the news, I wanted to come through to pay my respects." He slipped his hands away from Birdie's. "I've got to go now, miss. But please if you ever need anything—it don't matter if you stay here in Mt. Sterling or go back to Cincinnati—please give me a call."

He looked genuinely sad backing away from her with his hat in his hand. "Everybody knows me as Beamon. Just ask around and I'll get back in touch to provide whatever you need."

People finally left the house and again silence embedded itself among all the little pieces of things that made up Mama's house. Birdie looked around and thought, *She didn't care too much for you, Jimmy. In her eyes, you were always gonna be a lazy liar destined to ramble through life. She did everything she could to protect me from you. She tried, in her own way, to take care of me because she didn't think you could. She loved me. She loved our children. I think in the end she might have softened toward you…a little. So here we are at Mama's house. She's gone and she's still taking care of us.*

PART THREE

Over dry stones in the road...

CHAPTER TWENTY

Cincinnati, Ohio
1943

Birdie shielded her eyes from the glare of the sun. "Look, baby. Look how far that trolley car goes up the hill. It's going up to the sky then back down again," she said pointing at the Mt. Adams incline.

Lil' Jimmy jumped up and down clapping his hands, his eyes wide with amazement. The streetcars, loaded with people, looked as though they were barely holding on to the slender steel tracks as the trolley car was lifted up to the top of the hill. The children had never seen anything like it before and it was a welcome distraction that helped to get them situated in Cincinnati. With both Mama and Jimmy gone, Birdie thought the Queen City would be the best place to take her children and make a new life.

Chicky had protested against Birdie taking the children away from Mt. Sterling. Birdie countered Chicky's arguments, stating Mama had always wanted her to stand on her own two feet and what better place than Cincinnati to do it. Birdie had a little money saved and with the money Mama left her, now was the time to strike out on her own. Chicky begged her to change her mind about going. She pleaded with her baby sister to leave Carmen and Lil' Jimmy with her so they could grow up in the house and surroundings they'd known since they were infants.

"No need to take them babies to live in some sad little nest in Sin-Sin-nati. It's gonna be so pitiful 'cause you ain't got *that* much money and no real job. I know you think you some kind of royalty or something but you won't be living like no queen. That's for damn sure, Missy B. There's no need of you crossing that bridge at all. Just stay right here, baby sister, and find you a good man. That's all you need to do."

With those last few words, Birdie knew it was the right time for her to go—and let go. Besides, Mt. Sterling reminded her too much of Jimmy.

One of her cousins told her about a small kitchenette apartment that was available at DeSales Corner in Cincinnati. The neighborhood was only about three blocks in every direction and contained a few rowdy dents like a pool hall and pawn shop on its main thoroughfare. The apartment building itself was considered safe as it stood in the shadow of a looming Catholic church that lorded over the intersection of two busy streets.

The landlord, Mr. Baumgarten, made it quite clear he wasn't fond of renting to single women, particularly colored women, with children. The old man stared at her and the children from over his glasses as if they were insects.

"I don't like the idea of having to put anyone out, but trust me on this, Mrs. Walker, if you miss paying the full rent by the first of the month, I will turn you and your children out on the street. If it weren't for Miss Eugenia Purity vouching for you, I wouldn't even rent to you at all. Renting to you coloreds is like inviting trouble, but she said you were a good girl."

Birdie pulled Carmen and Lil' Jimmy close to her and buried their ears in her coat so they wouldn't hear the white man belittling her. She stayed silent and simply nodded, as if in pain, agreeing to pay $22.50 a month and knowing that it was much too high a price. She gave him two months in advance.

Mr. Baumgarten pressed the key in her hand all the while dispensing advice dripping with condescension. "Listen, girl, you need to find you a sugar daddy fast. You know what I mean. That shouldn't be a problem for you. But I don't want to see all kinds of men sniffing around here. Get you one of those colored soldier boys. They gonna have some government money when they come home. I live right up the street and come by here every day, so I'll know what's going on. Even if you don't see me often, you'll definitely see me at your door on the first of the month." He pointed a crooked finger at her. "Watch yourself."

Birdie moved in to the gloomy two-room apartment where sunlight fought to enter through two windows facing the gray bricks of the next building a few feet away. The apartment was furnished with a wobbly table, a wooden chair and an ancient dresser with two drawers and an empty space where the third drawer should have been. It didn't matter because her only possessions were Mama's huge bed and mattress, a few pots and pans and two suitcases filled with the only clothing she and her children owned. There was an old ice box, a Frigidaire, and a tiny stove in the narrow kitchen. The exhausted children immediately flopped on the bed and fell fast asleep.

Birdie never felt so alone in her entire life. The loneliness was gripping. When her cousins, who helped her with the move, left to go back to Louisville, it took all her strength not to run after them and beg them to take her back to

Mt. Sterling. She climbed in the bed with Carmen and Lil' Jimmy and pulled the quilt around them. The quilt gave her some comfort. She stroked the patches of fabric with the palm of her hand. Mama had used snips from pants, dresses, blouses, robes and even socks that had made the rounds within the family. Each patch represented Birdie's family and everywhere she touched brought her back to happier times.

"We'll be alright, my babies. I'm going to make sure of that," she said to assure herself in the dark.

After a breakfast of apple butter sandwiches and warm milk, Birdie allowed the children to make tents in their own corners to occupy their time. The children were excited about their new space no matter how dismal it appeared to Birdie. Later, they ventured out for a walk to a store to get a few groceries. They were only two blocks away from the apartment when Birdie spotted a tan Chrysler New Yorker parked at the curb.

"Hellooo, Miss Bird. Welcome back to Cincinnati," shouted a voice from inside.

"Beamon? Hey, what are you doing here?"

"Where are you on your way to this morning? Would you like a ride?"

Before she could answer he leaned over and pushed open the car door. Birdie gathered her children into the back seat then scooted in the front. Beamon turned to get a look at the children in the back seat. With a wide grin revealing his two gold teeth he asked, "Are those little monsters trained?"

"Of course, silly, they're being raised right and know how to act." Then just for added precaution she sternly instructed them to sit still and not touch anything. "This is a really nice car, Sandy."

"Why thank you, pretty lady. Yeah, this is a '41 Chrysler. It was one of the last off the assembly line. I hope after the war they start up making them again. I'd like to get me a new one."

"Well, not that this looks bad at all, but a new one might be in order since you travel a lot. Ever since I first met you in Chicago, I've been running into you all over. Where do you really live and what is it you do anyhow?"

"Yeah, isn't life funny, Miss Bird? I was saying the same thing about you. When I first met you back at Delisa's you just happened to be visiting with your cousin. Now we seem to be always bumping into each other all over the United States. It must be fate. You think? You believe in fate, Miss Bird?"

Birdie shrugged. Believing in fate and dreams had always been Jimmy's department. "I don't know anything about fate, Beamon. But I do find it quite interesting that we've run into each other in three of the forty-eight."

"Well, I do believe it's fate that our paths always seem to cross. I live here in Cincinnati. Been livin' here most of my life. I was born down south and raised in just about every state they consider down south. And what I do is a little of this and little of that. I guess you can say I'm in the entertainment business."

"You sing or in a band or something?"

"Naw, I manage commodities for clubs, lounges and bars. Whatever those venues need to show people a good time, I get it for 'em."

"Oh, so that's how you knew my husband, Jimmy."

Beamon nodded. "Jimmy was a good man, a real smart man. I hope they get whoever did that to him."

Birdie told Beamon they were on their way to pick up groceries. He volunteered to take her downtown to Findley Farmer's Market.

He insisted on paying for the groceries and bought some

candy for Carmen and Lil' Jimmy. He also gave them each a handful of pennies to buy whatever they wanted.

Beamon brought the bags up to the apartment after driving her home. Birdie stopped him at the door.

"Thank you so much for the groceries and your help, Sandy. I'd invite you in but it's not presentable right now. When we get settled, I'll invite you over for coffee, maybe dinner. Nothing fancy these days though. Right now, I'm not even sure how or if the stove works."

"Miss Bird, it's been my pleasure to escort you and your little ones. Listen, I want to take you out, sort of a welcome to the city party. I'll give some time to get settled in. What are you doing week after next? Say you'll go out with me. I know of some clubs that's got music that will knock your socks off."

He had done so much for her today. She felt it was only right to say yes.

Over the next few weeks, Birdie began to piece together a daily routine for herself and her children. Birdie found a job as a cook for the Jeffers, a wealthy family in nearby Hyde Park. Mrs. Lucille, the only other colored woman in the building, agreed to watch the children when Birdie was at work. Birdie still had her moments of sadness though, mainly at night when she dreamed Jimmy would come through the door or she would hear his voice reading to her. Frequently, Beamon would show up out of nowhere. Birdie would see him when she went to the Rexall Drug store, post office or hopping on the bus to get to work. Each time he would offer some diversion that helped to take her mind off things.

They went out to dinner, movies, and once sat in on an after-hour jazz gig until the wee hours of the morning. Whenever Beamon popped up, he was never without a present for Birdie. He told her repeatedly that she was such a fine woman, a beautiful woman that should never be left alone. She let him wrap his arms around her shoulders because he laughed deeply and spoke softly, as if he cherished her every word and action. After their third date, he said he loved being with her and that he'd do anything to have her as his own.

Beamon wasn't a handsome man, but he was a smart man of means. He possessed all the things Birdie was told she should have in life. Yet she was racked with guilt for going out with him, accepting gifts and money from him, for laughing with him and mostly for wishing he was someone other than who he was. Every time Birdie got dressed to go out with him, she felt the heat of oncoming tears and fought to hold them back. Tonight was no different. She patted powder over her cheeks to cover up. They were going out for a good time, and she didn't want to be late.

Chipper's Playhouse was a small joint that did the best it could with one large, long narrow room. The bar took up most of the space leaving only a few tables scattered at each end. The regulars, folks who evidently didn't bother to change from their work clothes, were saddled up to the bar. Based on uniforms, there were a few mail carriers, porters and others dressed in company standards. All were awaiting the night's promised entertainment—a comic with a full floor show in the tiniest of performance space.

Vivian Holmes had secured a place at the bar. Birdie knew Vivian from Mt. Sterling, where the Holmes family was known for making and selling their own brand of whiskey. Vivian, a long, lanky deep-brown-skinned woman, had given up demurely sipping drinks or waiting for someone to buy her one. She could be seen at any local club, sitting close by the bartender belting down top-shelf liquor. She nursed her liquor like the child she never had.

From years of steady practice, Birdie could see that Vivian had honed her craft. She was a champion. With surprising clarity, she would spend the evening teasing and toying with men to keep a steady stream of drinks. She could drink a man under the table and had done so many times. She'd toss them back hard all night and still, with her head held high, walk a straight line out of a bar and into some ferocious back-alley fight. There were ugly arguments with men who wanted more from Vivian than their now depleted pockets. Or there were jealous girlfriends, waiting to teach Vivian a lesson for drinking up their beau's weekly paycheck and leaving nothing for the rent.

A man strode up to Vivian, wrapped an arm around her and signaled the bartender for a refill. From her table, Birdie tilted her head and squinted to get a better look at Vivian's next challenger. It was Jessie. Although he was losing the battle to retain his former slim figure, the extra pounds looked good on him. Life seemed to be treating him well, at least up until this point. Hanging with Vivian meant he was about to have a bad day tomorrow when he woke up without a cent to his name.

Birdie leaned in. "Sandy, I see some friends of mine over at the bar. Let me—"

Beamon rolled his eyes and abruptly cut her off. "That one? Naw, that woman over there will suck a man's pockets dry. You don't need to be anywhere around her. Just leave that woman over there."

Beamon excused himself from the table, stating he had some business to take care of with Chipper, the bar owner. Once he ducked out of sight, Birdie made a beeline over to the bar.

"Hey, old folks," she said cheerfully.

Jessie turned around first and shouted, "Birdie, Birdie, Birdie!" His eyes danced as he moved in for a big bear hug. "Girl, where you been?"

Vivian slowly turned her head and gave Birdie a flat look then returned to her drink. Birdie could tell Vivian was just pretending to ignore her because she caught Vivian watching her every move in the mirror behind the bar. Eventually she must have gotten bored, because she slipped out of sight as Jessie and Birdie caught up.

Jessie took a long head to toe look at Birdie. Birdie thought he was about to cry.

"How's my little baby cousins, huh? You plan on stayin' in the 'nati? You doing okay? I ain't seen you since..."

His voice trailed off. He gave her another big bear hug, rocking her side to side. She laughed and breathed in the air around him. He smelled like a new garden right when the shoots were just making their way up through the dirt. He smelled like cake, pie, stewed meat and fried green tomatoes. She breathed in all the good things she remembered. She closed her eyes and saw Jimmy behind him. She missed him too and was on the verge of tears.

"I'm okay, Jess. Carmen and Lil' Jimmy are strong and healthy. They're getting big so quick and becoming so smart. They're just missing some of that good old country cooking. Lil' Jimmy is looking just like his daddy. You know it ain't ever been the same since he left us. It ain't easy, but what you going to do?"

Birdie's eyes raked across the mirror behind the bar and caught sight of Beamon along with two other men in a doorway at the other end of the club. She overheard one man addressed as Florida Red, and remembered he was the same red bone man from Chicago who had been with Myra from Alabama, the little tap dancer that claimed to know Jimmy.

Hmm, ain't this really a small world, she thought to herself. She heard Jimmy's voice ring in her head. *Red, he ain't one to be disappointed.*

The other man was a huge white man who furtively scanned the club from underneath a fedora. Outside of the police, Birdie had never seen a lone white man in a night club around these parts of town before. Generally, they wouldn't dare come to this part of the city. There was an invisible border separating Cincinnati's black and white neighborhoods. No one crossed unless they wanted to get chased or hit in the head. Most of the bar's patrons were as surprised as she was by the white man's appearance. A noticeable few took a moment from their conversations to eye the white man's every movement as the trio he accompanied slid through the crowd and out the door.

Birdie headed toward the ladies' room and quickly regretted her decision once she opened the door. Vivian was sitting on a chaise.

"You can't speak? So you must think you're better than me, don't you?"

"Hello, Vivian," Birdie said stiffly after rolling her eyes, knowing it was too late to back out.

"*Hello, Vivian?*" Vivian repeated with animated offense. "Birdie! Girl, I know you, your sisters and that whole family of yours and all you can say is a curt little *hello, Vivian*? You treatin' me like I'm the tax collector or something."

"Vivian, you know I didn't mean nothing by that hello... How are you, girl? I haven't seen you since back in the Wrights days. You lookin' good."

She didn't look good at all. Vivian was in a state of drunkenness where all road signs pointed to her crossing the border to disaster. Birdie thought the lie would deflect from Vivian's early declaration to pick a fight. It was best to say anything to avoid Vivian's claws. Birdie had no intentions of rolling around the ladies' room floor fighting off Vivian.

Birdie patted her nose and offered another fake compliment to make sure Vivian heard her. "Yeah, girl, you about to reel 'em in tonight."

"Yes, I am, ain't I? Now when did you and my brother start going out?"

"Your brother? Vivian, I'm not dating your brother. Where did you hear that?"

"Yeah, girl. Yes, you are. Beamon. Beamon is my brother. He didn't tell you?"

Birdie stared quizzically at Vivian's reflection in the mirror. "Beamon? Sandy Beamon is your brother? How come I ain't never seen him around back then?"

"Well, you know how it goes, brother from a different mother. My daddy had plenty of stories to tell and Beamon is just one of them."

"Well, I really didn't know. He didn't say a word."

"Yeah," Vivian said slowly. "We're blood, but he really does think he's the cock on the walk. He gets sometime-y and don't speak. He better watch out or he's gonna take a tumble and then he'll see how the other half lives."

She paused to pull a lipstick from her purse. Waving the brick red lipstick for emphasis Vivian continued, "You're just his type too. Know something? I asked that big shot brother of mine to loan me some money awhile back. He gave some sorry excuse."

Vivian looked Birdie up and down. "Now I see why he didn't give me a god damn dime."

The rocky road through the state of inebriation suddenly got dark and twisted. Vivian paused to give her lips a quick application before unfolding herself from the chaise and stepping closer to Birdie. She leaned down to whisper in her ear.

"You think you better, but sister, you and that brother of mine... Well, you'll see. I've seen this all before. You betta collect all the trinkets and baubles you can before he tosses you aside."

"Excuse me, Viv. I've got to return to my date."

Vivian chuckled. "Right, your date...my brother...my flesh and blood? Yeah, you got to get back to him and all that money he's got. He got more than your husband, excuse me, your dead husband ever had. Now that dead one was a catch..."

Vivian's voice trailed off behind her as Birdie scurried out of the ladies' room and made a beeline back to her table.

Beamon returned to the table in a rather joyous mood a few moments after Birdie sat down. "I see you found that old friend of yours over at the bar," he said through a wide smile. "I thought I told you that woman ain't nothing to be messing with and that gentleman she with..."

Birdie crossed her arms. "He's family. Jimmy's cousin. Speaking of family, why didn't you tell me you were Vivian's brother. I've known Vivian a long time and I never seen or heard of you as family before."

Beamon snarled. "I don't have much to say about her. We weren't raised together. My daddy asked me to watch out for her before he died and I promised him I would. But it's a promise I'm not sure I can keep. That woman is more trouble than you can imagine." He looked over at Vivian, who had returned to her barstool. Jessie seemed to have moved on because Vivian was tickling the chin of some other man that sat down at the next barstool and immediately draped himself over her. Beamon shuddered and flipped open his cigarette case to offer Birdie a cigarette. Once he lit her up, he quietly said, "Nevah mind, babe, forget about that. Let's have some fun tonight."

The rest of the evening progressed as if they were celebrating something. Beamon ordered drink after drink, and the music was nothing short of elevating. Chippers had folks stuffed in like a tin of tuna. Alcohol passed up and down the bar, and over to the crowd lucky enough to get a table. A band squeezed into a small corner space and made a pretty good run of Ellington's swinging hits, "Cotton Tail," "Take the A Train" and "Perdido." Singers royally belted out Nat King Cole's "There Will Never Be Another You" and Kansas Joe McCoy's "Why Don't You Do Right." Couples eked out an area for a dance floor while folks swayed in their seats.

When Beamon went to fetch fresh cigarettes from the bar, Birdie, unable to sit still, stood up to get a better view of the band and let her body move to the music. Jessie walked past her skittering sideways through the packed club. As his shoulder touched hers, he turned and whispered into her ear,

"Take this." He slipped a folded-up piece of paper into her palm. "I see who you're with. Call that number if you need anything. Just ask anyone who answers the phone for me. They'll know how to find me. Call any time of day or night."

Without looking down, she responded with a big laugh while patting the front of his suit jacket. Birdie turned toward the bar to see Beamon glaring directly at her as the cigarette girl flirted and passed him a pack of Lucky Strikes. Jessie kept stepping through the crowd. Birdie clasped the note tightly in her hand. Its pointed corners dug into her palm as if to affirm the immediate importance of the message.

Beamon came back to the table, lit his cigarette and ran his hands over his slick hair. He casually stated they were leaving after the next set because he planned to have a jam session with a few musician friends at his place once the bar closed.

Looking over at Jessie, Birdie asked, "Can I invite my cousin and his date?"

Beamon raised an eyebrow and replied, "Nah, babe. Not

this time. I think it's going to be pretty tight with the fellas and a few of their lady friends. Maybe next time, okay?"

It was nearly 1:00 a.m. when they stepped inside Beamon's apartment. Once the door slammed shut behind them Beamon gripped Birdie's arms and shoved her into the wall. Without saying a word, he kissed her hard, mashing her lips against her teeth. She was so startled that it wasn't until he was moving her over the couch that she started pushing him away. Birdie clumsily tried to step on his feet to get him to stop. Energized by her protests, he reached under her dress.

"Stop it!" Birdie pulled his hand away.

"C'mon, girl. I been thinking about you all day. You know how I feel about you. C'mon. We had fun tonight, didn't we?"

Birdie rubbed her face. Her lip felt as though it was going to swell from Beamon's rough kiss. "Yes, we had fun, but this is not. Take me home."

"Oh, girl, not now," he pleaded. "I'm sorry. Don't give up on me now. The boys are coming over in a bit and we just want to keep the party going. C'mon."

Birdie slid out from her trapped position between Beamon and the wall. He cut in front of her and grabbed her hands, cupping them in his.

"I'm sorry, baby. It's just, you know you're so damn pretty and I—I like you a lot. Listen, I'm gonna make us some drinks. How about I make us some good old spaghetti? You'll like that. Everybody likes my spaghetti."

"Beamon, I really should be getting…"

Beamon let her hands go and danced on his toes over to the stereo.

"Just wait, darlin', I'm going to put on some Nat Cole to set the mood 'til the boys get here and get cookin'."

He placed the needle on the record and once it advanced

beyond the crackle of static, smooth music cut through the tense air. Beamon swirled around the room, took off his jacket and reached out for Birdie.

"Now you can go on in there and freshen up." He pointed her toward the bathroom. "You can even lay down on my bed and relax while I set everything up. Go an' put on a fresh face and kick off your shoes."

Birdie gave in, noting Beamon's mood was lighter than it had been all evening. He seemed genuinely sorry. It was almost comical to see him dance around the room trying to get her to stay. She went to the bathroom to check herself in the mirror. The fluorescent light revealed a blotch of red stretching across her face and a bruise forming on her shoulder. Beamon knocked on the door.

"Hey, babe, I fixed you a nice highball. It will get you all tickled up for the rest of the night."

CHAPTER TWENTY-ONE

Birdie didn't remember removing her clothes but awoke alone and completely naked as the sun began to rise. She didn't remember any musicians stopping by for a late-night jazz set, or enjoying a plate of spaghetti or, most importantly, what happened before she wound up in her current state. The last thing she remembered was lying down on Beamon's bed—fully clothed—to rest before the festivities were to begin.

She lifted herself up and stood on wobbly legs. As if walking a tight rope, she stepped over to the closed bedroom door. She pressed her ear to the door and heard only her own short breaths and the drumbeat thumping in her head. The apartment was dead quiet. There was no rustle of movement and no sign of Beamon on the other side of the door.

Thank God Beamon was gone. Not knowing when he would show up left Birdie teetering between panic, fear and more than enough anger. In the light of day, as the fogginess cleared from her head, she regretted letting him convince her to stay after treating her so roughly. If she found a gun, she'd shoot him dead as he entered the door. Birdie turned around and took a sweeping glance around the bedroom while still listening for any movement from the outside hallway. The sight of the twisted bedsheets made her stomach flip. She had never been with anyone other than Jimmy. She had no time to even imagine being with someone else in that way. She knew someday it would happen, but not like this. Beamon was a little uncouth at times but had always been such a gentleman. She never expected him to be so crude, so uncaring.

Birdie looked around the room for her stockings. One was flung over the chair. She limped over and saw it had a big lattice run up the back. The other was just as bad. Clearly, they would be of no use to her. The satin dress she had proudly worn the night before lay in a pile on the floor.

She glanced over at the clock on the bedside table. It was almost 6:00 a.m. Next to the clock was a neat roll of bills bound together by a rubber band. Birdie pulled on her clothes, her eyes darting back to the door after every move. She grabbed the money with the intent of finding a corner phone booth to call a cab to get home. She knew she might have to walk a ways to find a cab that would pick up a colored fare.

"Shit. I got to get to work this morning. How am I gonna make it through the day without them starin' and askin' me a whole lot of questions?" Once she made it home, she'd take a quick bath and apply a pound or so of makeup. She might be able to get to work by eight. She'd be late, but respectable. The story to her employers would be an unfortunate fall down the stairs. Maybe she could sneak through the back door and slip up the stairs without being noticed. She'd wear a sweater all day to hide the bruises on her arms.

The bath felt good. Birdie wanted to stay in the tub and soak awhile, but she didn't have the luxury of time. Thank goodness, Carmen and Lil' Jimmy were spending time at her friend Ollie's house. Birdie swirled her fingers in the warm soapy water revealing bruised arms and legs through the ripples and foam. She pressed the washcloth to her lips and breathed deeply letting the steam soften her face.

As the water cooled, her anger rose. "Damn him! What the hell was that? Is that what he does for sex?" She slammed her fist down. Water splashed out of the tub and onto the floor. She thought aloud. "That's no way to treat any woman. I should call Jessie. I should call my cousins. They'd ride up here and beat his ass!" She began breathing hard but shook her head.

"I can't have them Negroes ride up here ready to fight. No matter what happened. I can't be the reason for someone going to jail or getting killed over some sick mess like this." She sniffed and said aloud, "And I can't have a trail of tears down my face. Remember, girl, you said you would never cry over another man again. Humph, never again. I'm going to have to handle this myself."

Birdie did the best she could with makeup and quickly dressed. Unfortunately, dark circles around her eyes gave everything away. As she reached for the compact powder in her purse, her fingers landed on the roll of dollars taken from Beamon's bedside table. She whistled softly after counting one hundred thirty-eight dollars.

"He's surely gonna kill me for taking this," Birdie said to herself. "But then again, he ruined my best dress. That was certainly worth the money."

She counted out fifty-eight dollars and wrapped it several times in a piece of newspaper, stuck it in an envelope and wrote out Chicky's name and address. She put the envelope in her purse and promised herself she would mail it as soon as she got off work. She'd put the rest in her Fifth Third Bank savings account.

Birdie rushed to the bus stop. As she passed the church, she caught sight of a dirty gray blanket wrapped around a man sitting in the doorway of an empty storefront. She slowed her pace, trying to ignore the urge to come to a full stop as the church bells rang a quarter hour chime. She had to get to her job, but something wouldn't let her continue. She stared at the man and recognized him instantly. Despite the filth covering his skin and clothes, the light eyes that peered out from the dirty blanket were as clear as her own.

"Michael? Michael Conroy? Is that you? It's me, Birdie… Birdie Jennings from Mt. Sterling. How in the world did you get here? Where is your, your family?"

He looked up at her without a flicker of recognition and lifted his outstretched hand higher, waiting for coins to drop into his open palm. The few passersby took no notice of the black woman reaching down to help the frail white homeless man. These days there were quite a few men hovering around the streets down on their luck. They perched themselves on corners waiting for soup kitchens to open or someone to give them money for coffee or alcohol.

People around Mt. Sterling would say that as a toddler, Michael would sit quietly playing in the dirt then just fall over and lie in the mud wiggling his arms and legs. The saddest thing was his mother would just leave him squirming and giggling on the ground. As he got older, he'd wander around town following behind his mean brothers. Every time Mama saw Michael, she would give him root beer candy wrapped in crinkly clear wrappers, pennies or whatever trinket she had in her pocket or purse. He acted as if he was overwhelmed with joy no matter what she gave him. Mama said she felt sorry that he never got the love and kindness he deserved, so she would always help him when she could.

Most times, he parked himself on a park bench at Mt. Sterling Square. The Square was a small island in the middle of the city's main thoroughfare. Cars circled the meticulously trimmed stamp of green, which was planted with seasonal flowers by the garden society. An air-tarnished statue of some unknown military man entwined with mischievous cherubs riding mythical dolphins stood as sentinel. Small plaques recognizing long-standing wealthy contributors to the city were pinned with bronze nails on park benches where the pebbled cement could probably tell the story of Native Americans who originally owned the land. From each side of the wide street, it appeared as an oasis of greenery that folks would enter to cross over to go to the grocery store, dress shop and pharmacy on one side of the street or to the ice cream parlor and hardware store on the opposite side. Most people paid no attention unless their children chose to cartwheel across the grass or hop from park bench to bench.

Michael was the Square's only consistent visitor. He was there so often he blended in with the scenery. For hours, he'd sit on the farthest bench drawing pictures in a sketch pad, on scraps of paper, a brown bag or whatever he had on hand. He expertly drew whatever or whoever he saw or imagined. There were life-like pictures of curling leaves, full and barren trees, squirrels, and images of people who may have passed through or sat awhile. While in the throes of his art, he'd take a moment to ask all those who smiled back at him if they were his friend. Some would stop to admire his work or return to bring him sandwiches. Kind local shopkeepers gave him food, paper and pencils.

The last time Birdie saw Michael his stringy hair was long even then, and he only had a scant trace of blond stubble along his jawline. It had been one of the many days when she was tired and frustrated from going from store to store trying to get something for dinner while Carmen, a wide-eyed fussy infant dressed in a pink sweater and ruffled dress with a matching bonnet, actively fidgeted in her stroller. Michael was sitting on the patch of lawn in the Square surrounded by a ring of bright green grass that shivered in the breeze, announcing the change of season.

She remembered weathered sketchpads stacked around him; pencils and sticks of charcoal of various sizes were neatly lined up in a narrow box. Another box had an assortment of coins and three pieces of candy wrapped in clear cellophane. As she and Carmen approached, he smiled. Even though his face was pale and streaked with swipes of black charcoal, his gray eyes remained bright and vibrant. He sat up on his knees and stretched up to see into the stroller.

"Hello, little one. You my friend? Oh, she's pretty."

"Hi, Michael. This is my little girl, Carmen. Can I see what you're drawing?"

Michael sat back and flipped over his sketchpad. He had drawn a picture of a woman with full lips and high cheekbones sitting reflectively. Gradient shades gave her skin the illusion of deep color. Her hands, drawn with bold strokes, rested in her lap. The collection of curved lines, soft and delicate, created black and gray spaces that gave a sense of fullness as if the woman could jump off the page. He held one hand against his chest and smiled while showing off his work. He was not only proud of his work but clearly had love for his model. Looking at Michael's drawing, Birdie couldn't help but take a deep breath. A sense of coolness and calm overcame her. Michael was an incredible artist. The image was perfection.

There must have been a complaint or two that Michael's dirty clothes and unkempt hair were too unsightly and marred the picturesque little park in the middle of the street. Maybe someone complained to the police that all his scattered sketching materials were a nuisance, or made a case that he appeared vagrant and should be taken off the street. Whatever happened, Birdie hadn't seen him until this moment on the streets of Cincinnati.

"Michael, remember me? It's Birdie. Remember me and my mama? She would cook for you and your folks sometimes."

As Birdie came closer, the light in Michael's eyes changed. Birdie continued, "Remember those nice buttery tea cakes? I remember you really liked them. You used to kiss each cake before taking your first bite and you kissed a lot of them."

He stared intently at her face just as she was searching his features for anything familiar. He shook off the blanket and let it fall around him in a cloud of dust. He reached up with both arms extended, fingers grasping at the air. He was so filthy. Patches of dried sores dotted his arms. Birdie was beyond his reach but, struck by the clarity in his eyes, moved into his grasp.

Michael pulled at her softly. He whispered, "You my friend?" over and over again.

"Yes, Michael. I'm your friend, Birdie. Remember? You need to get inside, Michael. It's cold out here. There's a church on the corner. Go down there and get some soup."

Michael violently shook his head and moved further back into the doorway drawing his knees closer to his chest. He covered his eyes as if protecting them from the nonexistent glare of the sun.

"Okay, Michael. Stay here. Don't move until I come back."

Birdie walked the half block back to church all the while trying to figure out a new story to tell her employers for her lateness. The soup line had not opened to the public yet, but she convinced a hesitant parishioner to give her something to take to Michael. They handed her two old sandwiches wrapped in wax paper once she promised she would return to attend Sunday services, Sunday school, Bible study and to volunteer when she could.

Michael was right where she left him, only lying straight out on his side, bare feet extending out from under his blanket onto the sidewalk. It broke her heart to see him. She tapped his shoulder and noticed the blanket was damp. He turned and reached for her. She wasn't sure if he wanted to hug her or if needed help standing up. He surprised her when he delicately touched her cheek then jerked his hand away. Shaking, he touched his lips. She stayed still even though every impulse she had wanted to recoil at his touch. He patted her cheek again as softly as before. Closing his eyes, tears rolled down his face.

"Michael, oh sweet Michael, don't cry. Here, I brought you some sandwiches. You need to go inside. Go to the church for shelter. They'll take care of you. Michael. You hear me? C'mon let's go to the church."

Michael wouldn't budge. He pulled his soiled blanket up tightly around him. He was only a few years older than Birdie, but he looked like a very frail old man. He shook his head furiously, pointing a bony finger at her face.

Birdie had forgotten what she must look like since she left Beamon's place. She had forgotten about a bruise that must have blossomed and a swollen lip that left a telltale sign of her exchange with Beamon.

"Michael, are you getting upset about this?" She pointed to her face. "Oh, my sweet, don't. I just had a silly accident. Really."

Michael grunted an objection. She looked around to see if anyone was watching them. "Listen if you don't want to go to the church now, promise me you'll go if it gets any colder. I'm going to pass by here tomorrow and look for you at the church to make sure you're safe. I'll bring you something good to eat, something just for you, from back home. Okay? Promise me, Michael."

Michael nodded, this time looking right into her eyes. "You my friend," he said softly. "Hi, you my friend?" He kept alert, clear gray eyes on hers and repeated it as if he were drifting off to sleep.

"Yes, I'm your friend, Michael. I've got to go now. I'll see you tomorrow."

She set the sandwiches down next to Michael and stepped away slowly before turning to leave. She glanced back. He was still staring at her.

Oh dear, somebody should be helping you take care of you. Birdie shook her head. *Where the hell is your mama?*

She turned back around, shivering at the thought of how he might have ended up in Cincinnati. There was, as before, always something behind his eyes. Hunger? Fear, maybe? She thought, *That cold-hearted family of his must have shipped him away. If Mama were here, she would've done something if she had known.* Birdie made a promise to tuck a little ginger candy in her pocket in case she saw him in the street again.

Suddenly the image of a dead blue man lying in a pool of dark red blood on the linoleum kitchen floor appeared. It had been a long time since she had thought about that day. Birdie had won the battle, burying the memory deep in the back of her mind just as her mama instructed. Now it was back to haunt her.

Damn them Conroys, they don't even take care of their own kind.

CHAPTER TWENTY-TWO

The unexpected knock on the door was followed by the presence of two sweaty men. One was leaning on a shiny new stove that took up the better part of the hallway. The other was wiping his forehead with a greasy rag. Both were huffing and puffing after their trek up three flights of stairs.

"Miss Walker? We have a delivery for you."

Birdie stepped back. Carmen and Lil' Jimmy swarmed around her legs, their eyes wide with curiosity. "For me? You must be mistaken."

"No, ma'am. No mistake. It says here to deliver, install and haul away the old stove."

Birdie squeezed between the two men and stepped into the hallway to examine the porcelain white- and chrome-handled stove. "This is for me?"

"Yes, ma'am. Mr. Beamon paid us already. Now if you don't mind, please, ma'am, we've got to get this installed 'cause we've got more deliveries to make today."

Hesitantly, Birdie stepped aside and let the men jostle themselves and the stove through the door. Once they left, Birdie sat staring at the stove. The old one failed to heat properly, making baking impossible. She had scrapped an idea of baking fruit cakes to sell to restaurants during the holidays to help her make rent but was relieved she could start baking again.

The new gleaming stove looked odd in the dingy old kitchenette. Birdie frowned. It shined like a beacon of caution. Birdie wished she had refused the delivery. Something in her flashed a warning but she shook off the intuitive danger signs in her head and flicked on a burner. The yellow and blue flame popped and flickered over the burners. She watched the fire hiss and dance before placing the old copper tea kettle over it to boil water. She didn't need the water for anything at the moment, but the kettle belonged to Mama and was most appropriate to use to baptize the stove. The fire quickly lapped the sides of the kettle turning the bottom black from the heat of the flames. Birdie, not wanting to damage the kettle, lifted it off the stove to rinse it in the sink and wipe off the soot.

Birdie grabbed her old apron off the hook. It was another item she cherished from home. As she smoothed down the front of her apron, Birdie felt something in the pocket and pulled it out. It was a yellowed, neatly folded piece of paper that read:

PROMISSORY NOTE
April 22, 1939

To my family, I promise to give James Bryant
Walker one hundred dollars and the deed to

```
my house located at 1859 Erkenbrecher Avenue,
Cincinnati, Ohio, should I die.

Signed,
Archibald Inskeep
```

"Jimmy," she whispered. She held the paper as if it were a fragile piece of heirloom china. She reached over to turn the water off, which had been running over the burned kettle as she fought back tears. Birdie looked around to see if her children were watching. She didn't want them to see her crying. She gently placed the paper on the table, not taking her eyes off it, and smoothed out the folds. As she wiped her face with her apron, it dawned on her that there must be a message in finding this note, now of all times. A warm sensation swirled in the pit of her stomach. She felt Jimmy was with her.

On Monday Birdie had to report to work and was again running late. She hoped she hadn't missed the last bus she could take to arrive on time. When she pushed open the door of her apartment building and stepped foot on the sidewalk, she spotted the tan Chrysler idling at the curb. It was too late to turn back inside, so she walked straight toward the vehicle, set on telling that bastard Beamon a thing or two.

"Good morning, Miss Bird. How's the new stove? I hope you like it."

At that point Birdie decided not to stop. She made an abrupt turn and continued walking toward the bus stop. She slowed down only to stare inside the vehicle. "I'm not talking to you," she said. Over her shoulder, she added, "Ever."

She picked up her pace knowing that her chances of catching the bus were a remote fantasy. Beamon drove alongside matching her gait. "Miss Bird. Miss Bird, please stop for a moment. I want to apologize," he shouted from the slowly moving vehicle.

The few people walking along the street slowed down to watch the exchange. Birdie's cheeks flashed hot with embarrassment.

"C'mon, Birdie. Give me a chance to say I'm sorry. Get in the car and talk with me please. I'll take you to work. It'll save you a little money and time."

Now, the curious passengers of passing cars began to stare. To end the public display, despite her better judgment, Birdie pulled the car handle and slid in, sitting as far away from Beamon as possible.

"This doesn't mean I forgive you."

A half empty bottle of bourbon rolled along the car floor. Birdie stared directly at Beamon. He was uncharacteristically disheveled and unshaven. His big round eyes were yellowed and bloodshot. His face was soft and sullen.

It must have been the Four Roses bourbon. It had to be, because never in a million years would she have ever imagined Sandy Beamon breaking down in tears.

"I'm sorry. So sorry, Bird! I never, ever wanted to hurt you. You must know that. I lost my temper thinking about you with that man. You must know how I feel about you. Please say you'll forgive me."

Calmly, Birdie asked, "Did you buy that stove for me because you felt bad about what you did?"

Beamon sat up straight and cleared his throat. "I did feel bad...really bad. When I saw the stove, I thought it was something you might really like and need. I'm sure those children would want a really nice country-cooked meal. I remember you saying you didn't like the one you had." He grinned sheepishly. "Plus, I didn't want anything to interfere with my dinner invitation."

Birdie softened. Ignoring the heavy anger that pulled at the back of her mind, she stared through the windshield. "Lucky for you, the invitation still stands. I'm a woman of my word."

CHAPTER TWENTY-THREE

The cold, hard bench was designed so you could only sit straight-backed, making it extremely difficult to sit for any length of time. It was quite obvious that loitering or slouching was not allowed in the cavernous hallways of the Hamilton County courthouse. Whatever your fate in the courtroom, whether jubilant or sorrowful, lingering in the hallways would not be tolerated. People darted in every direction and the sound of footsteps reverberated off the marble floors and walls. Moments before, Birdie pulled open the etched glass door of the county clerk office and within seconds, left the office with the disappointing sound of the door slamming shut against her back.

The clerk, a weathered elderly woman, read the promissory note Birdie presented, looked down her nose from wire spectacles and spoke to Birdie like she was a simple fool. Not surprised, Birdie expected they were going to be anything but helpful. In frustration, she left after a few versions of "No, there is nothing I can do to help you" from the arrogant clerk. Birdie took a seat on the bench outside the office. She was uncertain of what to do next, but something within her was not going to let this go no matter how rude they were in the courthouse offices.

Birdie looked up from her uncomfortable seat. An alabaster statue of a draped woman with sleek adoring dogs curling around her feet stared back at her. The sculpture's eyes, carved as smooth as her round cheeks, lips and breasts, carried a sense of soft compassion as the woman glanced downward from her perch at Birdie. The stone woman was laden with a bow and arrows and poised with quiet determination intent on hitting her mark. Birdie shifted on her marble seat and leaned forward hoping the sculpted woman would grace her with words of wisdom. Birdie was not ready to leave the courthouse. Leaving without a course of action would be a signal to abandon her plans and admit defeat, something she simply was not ready to do. At least, not yet.

She had confided in Ollie, her closest friend, who advised her to go to court and fight for possible rightful ownership of a house promised to her deceased husband. Ollie was a real firebrand. She was always ready to rally, protest, start a petition or plan a march on Washington.

Ollie lectured, "That's what those white folks want you to do. If they get a whiff of your potential ownership, they will want to keep you in the dark, hoping that you'll get frustrated and give up your rights. You got to stand up for what's fair. But be careful, somebody is going to try to steal that property right from underneath you."

Birdie's determination to get the house satisfied Ollie's need to rail against the system; Ollie said the system was stacked against black folks. She stated in a scholarly fashion, "You got a promissory note, sister. If you look up promissory in the dictionary it means a promise, promises, promising to pay... Hell, that means *give me what you owe me*, if nothing else."

Birdie had to admit, in this case, Ollie had a point. She started thinking, *this little piece of paper might be my ticket to have something of my own*. Birdie not only wanted a place to live, but a place to expand. With the new stove, Birdie had been cooking and baking as much as possible for the soup kitchen at the church. She was itching to do more. She saw plenty of social clubs, night clubs and even the pool hall up the street that might want to offer sandwiches or sweets to their patrons. She, like Mama and all the women in her family, could make something out of just about any situation. But it wasn't until Lil' Jim raced through the tiny kitchen and knocked down several cakes cooling on the rack that she knew that she couldn't think about making extra money under her present living conditions. From time to time, when walking past one empty storefront on her block, she'd press her face close to the glass to try to look through the painted-over windows. From what she could see through the scratched paint, it had the potential of being an ideal location for a workspace or even a restaurant. But having a place like that would take a lot more money than Birdie had in her savings. Each time she'd sigh at the thought of what it could be. It was still a fanciful dream that she shared with Jimmy under a canopy of fragrant yellow honeysuckle so long ago.

"Think, girl," Birdie whispered. She shifted again on the hard bench to give her backside relief. Birdie pulled the promissory note out of her purse. "There must be some reason why this thing shows up now of all times."

Although she memorized every word and could visualize the signatures clearly in her mind, Birdie reread the note several times over hoping it might provide an answer as to what she should do next.

She passed her fingers over the signatures, all three: the Archibald fella, Jimmy's and a witness's signature that Birdie couldn't make out. Jimmy's voice rang in her head, "A friend of mine has a house… He promised to hand it over to me as payment for a debt he owes me…" His voice floated in and out of her brain and swirled around her head.

Birdie looked around the courthouse and shivered. "How can a place that's supposed to make right all our human conditions be so cold and inhuman?"

Wrapped in her own dilemma she heard another voice, this time coming from a slightly older man standing next to her.

"Hello, young lady, I don't mean to be impertinent, but you look awfully familiar. I've been racking my brain for the last fifteen minutes trying to recall where I know you from."

Birdie couldn't place him either. "I'm sorry, I don't think we've met."

"Oh no, ma'am, I'm sure of it," he stubbornly insisted. "Even more now that I've heard your voice. I know we've met before. I never forget a face and particularly one so pretty as yours."

His voice was soft, his smiling tan face even softer. "I just finished some business and I saw you sitting here alone. I'm used to seeing people sit, seeing as I spent many years as a Pullman porter." He chuckled. "Guess I got used to recognizing folks from the waist up."

Birdie stared openly, searching for a spark of recognition, until suddenly she found it. "I remember you! I was on my way to Chicago a few years ago. I think we met then, on the train."

"Yes, that's it! It's Ed. Ed Dixon. You were that gorgeous thing with a fur coat. Me and the other porters were wondering who you were with that big coat on such a warm day. We thought you were one of those ingénues in the movie business."

Birdie smiled and stood up. She was happy for the distraction. "So, Ed, I don't mean to be nosy or impolite, but what brings you here? To Cincinnati I mean, not the courthouse."

"Oh, me and my wife live here, out in Lincoln Heights. My brother died not too long ago and I had to come down here for probate. What about you?"

"Well, Ed, I'm in a little bit of trouble."

Ed's eyes widened. "Not you, pretty lady. Well seeing as you sitting on this side of the courtroom and not in the jail-house on the other side, it can't be that bad."

"It's not bad trouble. It's just that I'm not sure what I can do in my situation, legally. You see my husband left this note saying this other man owed him some property to pay a debt. I came down here to find out if I had any rights and if so, how do I go about claiming it. My husband is dead you see."

She thrust the note in front of Ed. Ed had such a trusting face that she felt no need to hide anything from him. Ed politely pushed it away.

"Do you have an attorney?"

Slightly embarrassed that she didn't, Birdie shook her head. "I'm just exploring the possibility." She couldn't admit she came to the courthouse with only hope and a dream.

"Young lady, before anyone comes down here for anything legal, especially us black folk, you got to have an attorney. Without one, they'll have you running around in circles. I know just the right person who can help you. He's a friend of mine. His name is Walter. Walter Houston, Esquire can help you out of anything."

Birdie double-checked the address Ed had given her and began walking up a spotless walkway to a white Spanish mission-style home. The stucco house with red clay tile roof was out of place on a street lined with traditional Victorian homes. A shiny deep green Cadillac was parked in the driveway. She read the address over and over but wasn't sure she was in the right place. This was a Jewish neighborhood. A huge columned synagogue that wrapped around the corner loomed over the block and signaled the neighborhood's religious leanings.

Ollie verified Ed's legal recommendation, telling Birdie that Walter Houston was top-notch. "Yeah, girl, he is the best black attorney there is, as far as helping folks get what they deserve. He successfully worked on behalf of several community groups to break down color barriers in segregated establishments and get black people hired in places that still trumpeted 'whites only' hiring practices."

Ollie offered to go with her, but Birdie knew that if she brought her dear friend along the meeting would break down into some other protest leaving little room for her to solve her own predicament.

Birdie tapped the brass knocker and immediately a thin dark-skinned woman without an ounce of spark in her eyes opened the door. Birdie said timidly, "I'm here to see Mr. Walter Houston, Esquire?"

The woman motioned for her to come in and led her to a spacious room. Books, trophies and plaques lined the shelves and walls on one side and a fireplace dominated the other side. From what Birdie could see, the house was decorated with heavy, intricately carved mahogany furniture as if the house had been uprooted from an old plantation home in the Deep South. The woman waved her hand signaling Birdie to have a seat on a high-back antique love seat. She then disappeared. Nervously, Birdie folded and unfolded her hands, and crossed and uncrossed her legs. The quiet house and unfamiliar surroundings made her highly suspicious and apprehensive about meeting this strange man. She tapped her feet to tamp down her nervousness. Birdie whistled through her teeth. "Maybe this is just a fool's errand."

The room had a number of doors so she wasn't sure where Mr. Houston would be making his entrance. She jumped at the sudden sound of prancing taps against the floor tile. A large white French poodle danced up to her wagging his tail. He placed a paw on her knee then nuzzled his nose into her lap.

"Pierre! Pierre, get down!" A booming voice came from behind her. The dog popped up and obediently retreated to a pillow by the fireplace.

Walter Houston was a tremendously big man. He was as wide as he was tall. He had to weigh just south of four hundred pounds. He was what they call undertaker sharp, wearing a fresh, crisp white shirt that still had the remainders of fold lines from being sternly washed, starched and ironed. His shirt was neatly tucked into razor-creased black pants. Birdie tried not to stare but was drawn to his belt. She marveled at how much territory it had to cover. Gold cuff links, along with a massive ring, were emblazoned with a "Brotherhood" insignia. His arm reached around from his waist to extend a hand as he wheezed out an introduction in a very noticeable country drawl.

"Miss Birdie Walker? Walter Houston here, how can I help?"

Birdie fished the note from her purse. "Mr. Walter Houston Esquire, Edward Dixon said that you might be able to direct me in possibly obtaining this property."

"Just Walter is fine." He pushed heavy black-rimmed glasses up to the bridge of his nose. For a few minutes all that could be heard was Walter's deep breathing and Pierre's panting. Walter looked at Birdie. "What makes you think you're entitled to this property, miss?"

"Not miss, its missus. Mrs. Birdie Walker. That promissory note is made out to my husband, Mr. James Bryant Walker. As you can see it's witnessed and everything. That makes it official, right? My husband is dead. So as his widow, do I have a right to this property?"

Walter rubbed his chin. He had taken a seat behind an enormous desk. The chair squealed out protests as he leaned back.

"Helen, bring us some coffee and a few cookies," he bellowed.

Birdie surmised that Helen was the woman who showed her in, and she was not a resident of the house but the maid. Birdie knew there were quite a few well-to-do black families in Cincinnati, but she didn't know anyone who had a maid.

Helen placed a tray of butter cookies on the desk and was filling cups with coffee when the wavering high-pitched voice of an elderly woman, dripping with a squealing southern accent, floated down from upstairs.

"Waalltah! Waalltah, are you downstairs?"

Walter shouted back, "Mother, I'm down here with someone. I'll be up in a little while."

"Who you down there with, Waltah?"

Helen froze in her tracks and stared at Walter. Walter, his cheeks flushed, was clearly embarrassed. He looked at Helen and flicked his head toward the stairs. Helen caught the gesture, quickly finished pouring Birdie's coffee and whipped around to leave the room. Birdie assumed Mother was about to get a not-too-happy visitor.

"I am so sorry, Mrs. Walker. My dear mother is not well. Please excuse the interruption. Do you have a signed marriage certificate?"

Birdie pulled out several neatly folded papers from her purse. She handed him her marriage certificate, birth certificate, her children's birth certificates and a Domestic Workers Union card. "Will these do as proof of who I am?"

He spread the papers out before him and pulled out a magnifying glass from a drawer in the desk.

"You know, Mrs. Walker, my family has, for many years, owned and operated a number of funeral homes. You can't bury as many people as I have without learning about the skeletons that hang around above ground. I know of you and your family. My family is from Owensboro, Kentucky."

Birdie stopped midsip of her coffee. She should have guessed from his speech pattern that he was from the corn-cracker state. She thought, *What could he possibly know about me?*

"I know your family. And I know a little bit about your late husband and a few of the men he used to pal around with. It's my job as an undertaker and attorney to know that sort of stuff. You with Sandy Beamon?"

The blood froze in her body at the mention of Beamon. "With Sandy?" She blushed. "No, I am not with him. We've been out a couple of times, but…"

She didn't know the details of Beamon's business and didn't want to know. Despite ominous warnings, it really wasn't until Walter Houston, Esquire looked at her side-eyed that she thought Beamon might be doing something that could drag her into a jail cell. All she knew was it involved night clubs, lounges, bars and other sordid holes where people gathered to forget about their worries. Like any businessman, Beamon was there to take advantage of it all, dollar by dollar.

Walter interjected. "I didn't mean to sound like I'm prying into your personal affairs. It's an occupational hazard. There are some unscrupulous people out there. I try to get to know a little about my clients beyond their initial requests to make sure we both stay on the up-and-up. And I don't want to get thrown by a pretty face."

He held his arm close to his face to look at the watch that was buried into his wrist. "Have you even seen the property?" When Birdie shook her head, he asked brightly, "You want to go for a ride?"

The Cadillac was spacious and luxurious, apparently custom-made to accommodate a man of Walter's size. Birdie stretched her legs out in front of her and couldn't touch the front. Walter, however, still had to squeeze behind the steering wheel.

Within minutes they were parked at the curb outside a vacant duplex on Erkenbrecher Avenue. Three uneven cement stairs led to a cracked walkway which led to three uneven wooden stairs and a porch, which dipped to one side. The house was dark and looked lost in the nest of weeds that made up the lawn.

Walter turned to her. "So this is what you want, Mrs. Walker?"

Looking up at the weary structure, Birdie nodded. She never wanted anything more.

"Well, it doesn't look like anyone has lived here for a while. Do you know this Archibald person or his family? Is he alive or dead? I think if he hung around anyone the likes of your late husband, no disrespect, ma'am, and he took the time to have this notarized with the thought there was a chance of death, then he probably is dead. Frankly, we don't even know if he really owned this house. There would have to be a title search and we'd have to see if there are any heirs who are entitled to the property. And who knows about taxes?" Walter faced Birdie straight on. "Look, Mrs. Walker, this is going to take some time and a good deal of money to sort out."

"I don't have much money, Mr. Houston. I don't have much at all. How much are we talking about?"

"Over one hundred dollars, maybe more, to represent your

interests and do the legwork. That's mostly because there is so much we don't know. And there's no guarantee of you receiving outright ownership, which means money down the drain for you. And one other thing, Mrs. Walker, I know this neighborhood. There is an unspoken line drawn only a few blocks over: blacks on that side, not on this side. This neighborhood ain't ever had black folks living here so I'm sure someone might want to make a fuss and try to block everything we do. They may not burn a cross on your door, but they can do other things just as ugly."

Birdie pursed her lips. She still wanted the house.

Walter sighed. "But I can take care of everything—legally that is. There's standard paperwork we have to submit, and then there's that seething stronghold of segregation we're going to have to break through. If we find ourselves on that battleground, we can bring this up so that it becomes a bit of a political football for the mayor and those sitting on city council. There are a few council members who won't make it to another term without our votes. It doesn't look good if they are seen protesting a hardworking colored woman trying to buy a house and being denied because of her race. I got friends in the pulpits and working at our newspapers that will help with putting on that kind of pressure. Your friend, Olivia, can help rally folks too—I know she's done it before."

Birdie wrinkled her brow. "Do you really think it will come to that? All the political stuff? I just thought—"

Walter interrupted. "As a colored man or woman, this is what it takes to do any kind of business transaction. It's never simple. There are always a few more hoops, more fire or a brick wall we gotta pray though or push through. Going this route, it's going take more savvy and strategy. You know we got to play chess when they think we're playing checkers. But time won't be your friend where the work is concerned,

Mrs. Walker. Time, for me, means hours and services I have to bill you for. Since you're a friend of Ed's, maybe we can work something out."

Walter said all this while licking his lips several times and rubbing his hands along the steering wheel. Birdie suddenly felt a little uneasy. Ed and Ollie both put a lot of faith in the big man's reputation. He couldn't be asking for anything else, could he? Birdie decided to disregard the suspicious voice in her head.

"I can give you twenty dollars. That's all I got right now."

Walter looked at her incredulously, his eyes blinking slowly behind his glasses. "Well, Mrs. Walker, I would love to help a fellow Kentuckian, but I can't possibly do all the work that is required for that amount. Listen, I don't want to take advantage of a pretty young thing such as yourself. I can bring my services down a bit. This is just for my services. There might be additional costs along the way."

He tapped his fingers on the steering wheel while examining the house. "I'll take your twenty dollars as a down payment. Then you can pay monthly on account. Say about ten dollars a month until the debt is satisfied. I can draw up a contract between you and me. But I must tell you if you find that you are unable to pay, I will have to seek transfer of ownership of any property retrieved in this transaction or otherwise to recoup what is due to me."

Birdie looked up at the house. She'd take the chance. Something about it spoke to her and said her efforts wouldn't be in vain. Its deep red bricks stacked one on top of the other, the dusty panes of the windows nestled in the cracked white trim and the lost portion of the worn lattice hiding whatever was under the porch called out to her. Maybe it was that Jimmy had a hand in all this. It could be his way of apologizing to her. She hadn't even seen the inside, but she knew if she had a real kitchen, she could take care of herself and her family. She could even rent out one floor for additional income. The possibilities gave her goose bumps.

"Mr. Walter Houston, Esquire, you've got a deal if you come down to eight dollars a month. If you agree, you will represent me on all legal matters regarding this transaction, right? And, by the way, I want to be in that house as soon as possible." She held out her hand to bind the agreement.

He opened his mouth to say something. Birdie thought he was going to counteroffer. Instead, he laughed and held out his hand to shake on the deal. "I'm a professional. I'll draw up a contract for you and me to both sign. Can you stop by tomorrow afternoon?"

For the first time since Jimmy's death, Birdie felt light and a bit joyful. When she got to her building, she stopped next door to Mrs. Lucille's apartment to pick up Carmen and Lil' Jimmy. They were lying on the floor with their heads deep in a coloring book. Carmen had started school and was happy and content. Of course, they missed Mama terribly and the freedom of running wild outside in the grass as they had done every day in Mt. Sterling, but both adjusted nicely once they were able to meet other children.

Birdie couldn't wait to return to Mr. Houston's to sign the contract. She wanted to bake something and take it with her to show Mr. Houston how much she appreciated his help.

"A big man might enjoy a little something sweet," she thought as she rummaged through her pantry. There was almost nothing left. It was enough to last until the end of the month when she would be eligible for more stamps. Food rations for the war had taken the store pantries down to almost nothing at this time of the month. They wouldn't starve—she had used just about all her red and blue point ration stamps, but

Mama had taught her how to make something out of nothing so Birdie knew she would be put to, and pass, the test.

She was thinking about a cupboard cake, a basic sweet tea cake with raisins, but that wouldn't be special enough.

Birdie was still thinking when Carmen chimed, "Let's make a pie, Mommy." Carmen jumped up and down. "I know how to do it."

"Well, sweet pea, I don't think we have all the ingredients."

But she did have some jars of blackberries that Chicky had sent her way, bread and a tiny amount of sugar. Then she thought she'd make a fruit crumble. The berries were already sweet so she wouldn't have to use that much sugar. Besides, she thought he might like the natural taste of Kentucky's finest berries.

"Thank you, Carmen. You are Mama's sweetest little helper."

Birdie returned to Mr. Houston's house the next day with a dish in hand. Helen let her in and motioned toward the sitting room. Birdie put her dish on the desk. Helen glanced, but said nothing. Walter entered the room dressed as impeccably as he had been the day before. Pierre bounced playfully at Walter's side stretching toward Birdie's lap. Walter pointed to the dog pillow in the corner and Pierre immediately obeyed the command.

"Ah, Mrs. Walker, I'm so happy to see you. What's this?"

Birdie cleared her throat to introduce her pastry. "Since you're from Kentucky, I thought you might enjoy a little something sweet from back home. Those blackberries are from my sister's garden in Mt. Sterling."

Walter smiled. "You are a woman after my heart. Helen! Bring us some coffee, spoons and a couple of plates!"

Walter took one bite and swooned. "You could make a million dollars on this. This is what you do for a living, right? I'm going to tell a few of my lodge brothers and sisters about you. Ain't none of them as big as me but they can put a hurtin' on something like this. We'll keep you working if you cook half as well as you baked this here."

"Thank you. My mama taught me how to coax flavor out of just about anything. I learned well."

"Well, Mrs. Walker, I'm going to have Sister Minnie Cunningham call on you. She does a lot of the catering for our Brotherhood meetings. She could use a hand like yours."

Between extra servings and licking his fingers, Walter took out a folded contract from a desk drawer. With one hand, he shook it out and plopped it on the desk. He pushed a silver pen toward Birdie. Birdie read the contract over and signed.

Walter wiped his mouth, "Now that we are in business together, may I call you Birdie?"

"Like you, sir, I am a professional. Thank you so much. Mrs. Walker will be simply fine."

CHAPTER TWENTY-FOUR

Cincinnati, Ohio

1944

"Where you been hidin', girl? I've been trying to catch up with you for over a week now."

Beamon looked up from tearing up a piece of chicken with both hands. His big frog eyes locked on Birdie's as he threw the ragged bone down on his plate. He wiped a napkin across his mouth and began sucking his teeth. Birdie pretended she didn't hear him and shifted her gaze toward the small group of musicians that were winding down their version of the upbeat "Half Step Down" to a somber melancholy, "Smoke Gets in Your Eyes."

Birdie swayed and swooned to the music, making it easy to avoid Beamon's conversation.

Beamon had invited Birdie to Louisville to party at the Top Diamond Club, a well-known spot where top-notch black entertainers stopped to fill the one-night-only shows and gain publicity between big-city gigs. Tonight, the Top Diamond offered a full show featuring comedians, dancers, singers and a swinging jazz band.

Ordinarily Birdie would've been over the moon about going across the river to Kentucky, but as she was getting dressed a cloud of depression surrounded her. The blue mood overwhelmed her so much that Birdie thought she might back out of the night and tell Beamon she wasn't feeling well. It was at that moment Carmen and Lil' Jimmy started quarreling, snapping her out of her mood. While putting on her makeup she decided she'd have to get over her heartbreak and make the trek back to her home state at some point, so what better time than now.

Birdie relaxed as soon as they drove over the Ohio River and entered Kentucky. She rolled down the window to let the scent of bluegrass fill her up. The cool, fresh fragrance took her to familiar aromas which intensified as they traveled deeper into the state. She fought an urge to ask Beamon to drop her off at her home in Mt. Sterling. Home would always be Mama's house. Even without Mama, it was still home. Though Chicky and Clarence were living there, Birdie knew she could still walk in, kick off her shoes and stretch out on a bed, or start cooking a meal, or pull up a chair at the kitchen table and have a cup of coffee.

"Did you hear me?" Beamon's wide face, all shining white teeth and gold caps, suddenly came into focus. He tossed back his bourbon, circling the drink to cool down the last few drops that swirled and clung to the bottom of the glass.

Birdie's mind said, *I gotta get out of this* but her mouth said, "Sure, honey, you know I've just been going to work that's all. It's been a blessing to have a little something extra these days."

She was referring to her second job working with the Sisters at Walter Houston's Brotherhood Lodge. She neglected to tell Beamon the details of how that came about. The lodge was regularly paying her for pies, cakes and other desserts for monthly meetings and social events.

"You know I made that happen for you, don't you?" His fat hand rubbed her arm up and over her shoulder.

Birdie knew that was a lie, but she coolly responded, "Sure, baby, I'm a lucky girl."

She wished she hadn't agreed to go out with Beamon this evening but, truthfully, she was afraid not to. It wasn't entirely the last episode with him that made her hesitant. It had been months and he had been such a gentleman since then. Beamon had approached her cautiously as if she would break at his touch. He timidly held her hand, asking if he could do so first. He did the same as he softly kissed her on the cheek. This lasted for a while. It was only lately that he had become possessive, starting every conversation with questions about her whereabouts.

Tonight wasn't the first time Birdie had to work to tame and brighten Beamon's mood. More often than not, she had to exert a tremendous amount of effort to do so, particularly around the children. He started dropping by without notice to surprise Carmen and Lil' Jimmy with toys and treats. One time he popped in with a sock full of pennies. He stayed to watch them delightfully count every cent, divide them up equally and drop them in their piggy banks. The children loved when he came by. Birdie cut him short when he asked them to call him Uncle Sandy. She countered by telling them they must always call him Mr. Beamon out of respect for their elders. But Beamon was intent on getting close to them. He frequently twisted his way in the door by pushing stuffed animals, toys or cookies to get their attention and affection. Birdie began to think it was his way of holding her hostage.

At first, she had to admit, she continued to go out with Beamon because of convenience and money. Though she had her regular job cooking and cleaning for the Jeffers family in addition to baking desserts for the lodge every week, she only brought in so much. Her landlord, Mr. Baumgarten, was true to his word and showed up faithfully to pick up his rent. Each time he stressed that if she did not have the full amount, she would quickly have to find another place to live. When Birdie placed the cash in his hand, he would rudely ask where she was getting her money which she would ignore. Beamon gave her a little here and there. That helped a lot, and she was grateful for her stove which made so much possible. She was also trying hard to hold on to her savings in preparation for the Erkenbrecher house. She wasn't sure of the outcome of Mr. Houston's legal findings but thought that if she acted as if it were going to happen, they would more likely have a positive outcome.

Also, Birdie was bored. She loved spending time with her children and Ollie was a great friend, but Beamon was the only option when she needed a little excitement and when she wanted to forget. She needed him when she was lost in sad memories of Mama, Jimmy and the comfort of family. She just wanted to be found in a place with lights, music and a sip or two of something burning cool or bubbly that made her worries disappear. The poetry of the music reminded her of happier days with Jimmy. Most times she enjoyed going out to clubs and parties with Beamon. He was a regular showboat and knew just about everyone. Birdie felt like a movie star when she entered a club on Beamon's arm. Her gut would eventually turn over the truth, that she loved the idea of what he could do for her, even as her genuine dislike for him kept growing.

Birdie searched the Top Diamond Club patrons for a familiar face. If she couldn't get to Mt. Sterling, she'd settle for being around anyone she knew from back then. She searched the crowd half hoping she might see one of the Amazons, a cousin or someone from Wrights. She searched her mind for an image of anyone who might have known Jimmy, thinking they might recognize her and come over to talk. But there was no one she knew sitting around the shiny serpentine bar, or at any of the cloth-covered tables or kicking around the dance floor.

Damn, if I was in Cincinnati, I couldn't walk five minutes without bumping into someone from Kentucky. Where are these folks tonight? Birdie sighed. *Thank goodness the music is good.*

Luke Godman was a local musician that played tenor sax all over town. He was given the nickname "God" because he had a gift for making every note sing whatever sound that made you care deeply about someone or something at that moment. He could manipulate the emotions of anyone who was in range of his music. If God played a happy tune, everyone that heard him bubbled over with joy. If it was mellow, you could bet everyone was crying into their drinks. He was that good. Many said he was too good to be playing small local joints and should have been stroking his horn with any of the well-known jazz artists. Luke Godman was ready for big time but never drifted beyond his circle of stardom in the tristate area. At a very young age, he supposedly left Kentucky to cut a tooth in New Orleans where he studied music under the likes of a spectrum of maestros. He had steady gigs throughout Louisiana playing everything from Basin Street Blues to bebop but eventually he came back to the Queen City.

Between sets, Godman would tell patrons, "That was too much for me. Too many cutthroats in the business. Everybody wants you to play but nobody wants to pay. I'll just stay right here where I can see everybody and count my money."

God always pulled in a crowd, which gave him godlike status with club owners. He was treated like a big celebrity wherever he stepped. Tonight, God had the club in a full range of emotions. Patrons were poised on the edge of their seats as his fingertips said grace over his horn. From deep somber rhythms to poppin' heights of insane craziness, his set reached pure madness. Birdie, sitting down front, loved every moment of it. Birdie's face, beaming with pleasure, caught God's eye. At the end of his set, he sent over a few drinks with a note that said, "With appreciation of such a beautiful aficionado." Birdie was flattered by the attention, waving the note and mouthing "Thank you" in his direction.

It was deep in the early morning hours when Beamon and Birdie left the Top Diamond to head back to Cincinnati. The car was quiet with what Birdie thought was the satisfying sensation from a good time. Tipsy and humming a few notes from a lingering melody, her lit cigarette slipped from her fingers and rolled around the car floor. As she leaned forward to retrieve it Beamon suddenly slammed on the gas pedal, causing the car to lurch forward and speed up. Her head barely missed banging into the dashboard.

"Hey, what's the matter with you? I almost smashed my face in!"

Beamon paid no attention to her as he clutched the wheel and plunged his foot deeper on the accelerator. Picking up speed, he bore down on a man now growing larger in the car's headlights. Birdie clutched the dashboard as she saw Luke Godman scramble to get out of the way.

There was no denying the horror of what was going to happen next. She clawed at Beamon's arm to get him to steer the car away. Unresponsive to her screams, Beamon didn't flinch at her frantic tugs, slaps and punches. She froze the second she clearly saw Godman's face. His features distorted by the light, the realization that the vehicle's driver intended to kill him and the knowledge that there was no way to avoid it flickered across Godman's face. Birdie clutched her mouth to muffle her scream. Godman's eyes were wide with fear and pleading. He twisted his body sideways, holding his saxophone case up as a shield to protect him against the impact, but it was too late. The car jumped the curb and hit him straight on. The saxophone case flew in one direction and God rolled over the hood, sailed up in the air and landed in the street. The impact threw Birdie forward. This time she smashed her face on the dashboard and then was thrown backward into her seat. Beamon turned the wheel to swerve back onto the street. The car hopped and Birdie heard what sounded like the snapping of twigs under the wheels of the car.

Birdie screamed, "Sandy! What the hell have you done?" She twisted and jerked around in her seat to see out the rear window. God's crumpled body, partially hidden in the shadows, lay near the gutter like a pile of discarded rags. His saxophone case on the other side of the street lay open. The bright red velvet interior of the case and instrument shone brightly under the streetlamp. Birdie continued to contort her body around to maintain a vantage point of the scene as Godman's body grew smaller and smaller in the car window. She searched and hoped for signs of movement. There were none.

"That man might be dying! Please, stop! We've got to stop and help him. We've got to call the police!"

Beamon swiveled in his seat. "Shut up, bitch! *We* ain't calling anybody. In fact, I strongly suggest you say nothing to nobody. Do you hear me? Nothing! Ain't nobody gonna ask you nothing anyway. And if they do, you are here with me in this car. What you think the police gonna say about that?" He seethed. "Besides, he had it coming…coming on to my girl right in front of me like that…right in front of everybody."

Beamon said he was going to drop her off at home but instead, once they approached downtown Cincinnati, he drove in the opposite direction of her house. Birdie pleaded for him to take her home. Beamon kept driving and parked in front of his apartment building.

"Get out the car," he said between clenched teeth. "Don't make me say it again."

Birdie was scared out of her wits but did as instructed. She was afraid he would start shouting and wake up the neighbors. She didn't want anyone to see her and thought if she did as she was told, Beamon would calm down.

Birdie was shivering uncontrollably when she heard the click of the lock on the apartment door behind her. Silently Beamon began removing her dress. This time, he kissed her gently. She stood, cold with fear, and let him kiss her while she glanced around the room for another way out. Beamon had just run down a man and left him to die in the middle of the street. She didn't know what more he was capable of or what he was about to do next.

Beamon then stripped down to his shorts and socks. Like a crack of lightning, he whipped out his belt and began beating Birdie. He grunted as the belt made contact with her back, arms and thighs.

"Stay still, bitch, or I swear to God, I'll use this buckle on your face!"

Birdie winced and skidded around the floor trying her best to escape his lashing. She ended up in the corner covering her head with her arms. After several hard whacks, Beamon finally stopped and fixed himself a drink, falling back into a chair. His head dipped and bobbed as he stared at her lying crumpled on the floor. Birdie looked up to see his eyes fluttering. He was falling asleep. It was only a second where she was too afraid to move. When she thought he was out, Birdie quickly recovered and plunged toward the door without her clothes. But that second of fearful hesitation was a mistake.

Beamon jerked awake, caught hold of her ankle and dragged her toward the bed.

Birdie reached for the lamp on the bedside table and ended up with Beamon's fist coming down hard on the side of her face. At once, Birdie saw a rainbow of stars. Through the explosion of blinking dots before her eyes, she caught sight of Mama's face, fire-lit eyes and her hands curled tightly into knotty fists. A roadmap of purple veins appeared underneath Mama's dark skin shining and twisted in sweat. Mama wrenched her way through the excruciating pain Birdie felt all through her body.

Suddenly, the lamp came into focus. It was now teetering close to the edge of the nightstand. Beamon was on top of Birdie, trying to lock her down on the bed. Birdie kept moving her legs and arms trying to wriggle from underneath him. She twisted around and grabbed the lamp cord tipping the lamp enough to get hold of the base. Birdie swung the lamp with all her might to hit Beamon on the side of his head. It was enough to send Beamon rolling off her and onto the floor. Birdie jumped up, spotted an ashtray on the table, and sent it flying, hitting Beamon squarely on his head.

Beamon slumped down on the floor. He was breathing heavily but otherwise not moving. Birdie's head felt heavy and watery. It bobbled around as if it was on its own. Her ears rang. A dull ache radiated from her left temple down to her jaw. Standing over the unconscious man, Birdie lightly touched her cheek. It was slightly swollen and there wasn't any crunchiness under the skin. There was no acrid taste of blood, but she could smell it. She slowly rolled her tongue around the inside of her mouth to check if her teeth were intact. Without looking into a mirror, she knew there must be clusters of purple, blue and red bruises splashed across her face. Simple movements unleashed cascades of pain across her body.

Beamon snorted and blew a stream of hot breath. Birdie jumped back, pausing to see if there might be more movement but what followed was a round of deep snoring. She quickly snatched up her belongings and ran out of the apartment leaving the door wide open. In the stairwell, she pulled her clothes over her wrinkled, sweat-stained slip. Thankfully, no one peeked into the hallway or came up the stairs as she dressed.

The cold air hit Birdie's face as she fled from the apartment building, walking quickly before breaking out in a full-out run. She had to get as far away as she could as fast as she could. Her steps echoed in the empty streets. She stayed off the main street and took side streets and alleys in case Beamon came after her. She had to hurry and get home. It wasn't far between his place and hers, but even running it was a bit of a stretch. Birdie was supposed to be home hours ago; Mrs. Lucille, who was watching the children, would be worried sick.

It was early in the morning but still dark. The air was silent except for an occasional morning cricket. Birdie was grateful for the almost soundless morning; it kept her alert. Her eyes darted in every direction while thoughts whipped around her head. She suddenly heard Mama's voice, "That man has got to go! One way or another!"

Birdie slowed her pace, pulling and patting her hair down, and wiping her face with her hand to get rid of any smeared makeup. Mama's voice rang so strong and clear in her head she turned around to see if someone was behind her. There was no one, but Birdie did notice that the sky was getting light. A few cars appeared on the street and people were making their way to work. A few of the shop owners along the Peebles' Corner shopping district were sweeping away the swirl of trash gathered in their doorways. Birdie kept her head down as she hurriedly walked past the Paramount building, the Woolworth five and dime, and the RKO Orpheum Theater. She remembered a time when men who had stopped by Mama's house for a meal spoke about the old vaudeville shows at the theater. Birdie clutched the collar of her coat, ashamed to be walking the streets in torn stockings and her evening apparel so early in the morning. She knew what she must have looked like, so she searched for either a cab or the first streetcar of the morning to get her the rest of the way home.

A slight rumble underneath her feet alerted her that a street-car was near, and she looked for the nearest stop. Out of a side street appeared a man walking quickly toward her. Although his clothes were clean, his face was smudged with streaks of black dirt as if he had crawled out from a chimney.

"Hey, you my friend?" he shouted. "You my friend?"

He stopped short merely inches from Birdie and hugged her, burying his face in her chest. Birdie took in the acrid smell of urine and other strange scents but remained steadfast until her senses couldn't take it anymore. She wriggled out of his grasp and took a few steps back.

Keeping her tone even in an attempt to sound calm and cheerful, she called out, "Michael! Where have you been? Well, aren't you looking nice this morning, except that face of yours. Have you been going to the shelter, like I suggested?"

She probably looked just as bad as he did, but there was always something about Michael that made Birdie want to take care of him anyway. Since they reunited, she consciously looked for Michael on her way to work and tried to talk him in to going to a nearby shelter. Sometimes he would go but would never stay long. Again, she'd see him wandering the street, in some doorway or tucked in the crevices of St. Steven's Church.

"Come, Michael, come walk with me. I'm going in the direction of the church. You can get a nice, hot breakfast there.

It will be something good to eat. C'mon, we can go there together."

The early morning streetcar roared passed them. Michael made no move in her direction which meant the promise of breakfast fell flat. Birdie reached in her purse, pulled out her handkerchief and passed it to him. Startled by the gesture, Michael leaned away. His smile faded and he stared at her with a quizzical look. He raised his arm and pointing at her face, he slowly reached for the hankie.

"Yeah, you Bird, you my friend, Bird?" He repeated it several times over before flicking the handkerchief softly over his face. The little swipes did absolutely nothing to rid his face of the black stains. He stopped and continued staring at Birdie. His gray eyes clouded over as he dipped a shaky hand into his pocket and slowly brought out a rusty penknife. Michael gritted his teeth as he folded his hand around the knife.

Birdie shrieked. "Michael, no! No, Michael! Put that down."

Michael grunted and released his grip on the knife. The knife hit the cement and bounced a few feet away. Michael fell back onto his knees. Birdie looked around to see if anyone was watching. Her heart pounded and she began breathing hard. She wasn't sure what Michael was going to do, but she couldn't just leave him in the middle of the sidewalk. Forgetting about the pains that plagued her own body, she bent down to pat him on his shoulder. She winced.

Michael wailed loudly and through his tears he asked Birdie, "You hurt? Who hurt you?"

She leaned down and replied softly. "No, Michael, I'm not hurt."

He shook his head. "You my friend?"

Michael lifted his head and peered out with a tear-streaked face. His eyes were clear and focused. He swatted the ground around him until he found the knife and snatched it up. He unfolded himself and teetering to catch his balance as he stood up, ran behind the building.

Someone yelled from behind Birdie. "You okay, miss?" Birdie turned, nodded to the air, and started walking.

By the time she made it home, a sterling-white sun outlined clusters of blue-gray clouds. She was so grateful Mrs. Lucille had opted to stay over to watch the children. Birdie hoped she wouldn't be mad at her for coming back so late. Mrs. Lucille was a matronly woman of undefined age and had a bottomless heart for helping others. From the number of visitors that knocked on her door, everyone in the neighborhood came to her when they were in a fix. Mrs. Lucille was big on the Bible. She always had one on hand but didn't use scripture to lecture anyone. She said God was bigger than she, so she would leave God's plan for others in His hands. She repeated often, "One will come to the Lord when called on in God's time," so Mrs. Lucille felt no need to interfere. She gave food, shelter, a rocking hug in her big bosoms and what little she had whenever someone was in need. Birdie considered Mrs. Lucille a true angel on earth. Birdie pledged she would do anything to repay Mrs. Lucille. If she didn't, Birdie felt she would truly burn in hell.

Mrs. Lucille was awake and reading her Bible when Birdie came in. "Sister, are you alright? What happened to you?"

Birdie began moving quickly to dodge Mrs. Lucille's suspicious glances and hoped she wouldn't take notice of her appearance.

Birdie responded softly, not wanting to wake Carmen and Lil' Jimmy who were curled up like little puppies asleep in her big bed. "I'm fine, Mrs. Lucille. I'm so sorry for being so late. I couldn't call. I—"

Mrs. Lucille raised her hand to cut her off and pulled herself up from the chair. She reached out, gripping Birdie by both arms. "Girl, I don't care what time it is. I know what's going on here. Let me tell you something, that man, any man that hits a woman, needs to be shot in the head. Twice!"

Mrs. Lucille released Birdie with a stern glance and wagging finger to emphasize her point. Birdie fished for a response, but before she could answer, Mrs. Lucille repeated sternly. "Twice! You hear me? Ain't no pair of pants worth that."

Without saying another word, the older woman's eyes traveled over to her Bible. She left it in the chair and walked out the door.

Birdie stood staring at the back of the door then back at the Bible. She was hot and her eyes stung from guilt and shame. Never had she heard anything like that from Mrs. Lucille's mouth. She wiped sweat from her forehead with the back of her shaking hand and began peeling off her clothes revealing the spectrum of bruises from Beamon's anger.

"Did someone hurt you, Mommy? I'm gonna beat them up."

Birdie turned to face Lil' Jimmy in his cowboy pajamas staring up at her back and arms.

"No. No, baby. Mommy just took a little tumble," she lied, jerking her dress back on. "I'm alright. You don't have to beat anyone up for me."

She bent down and cupped his chin in her hand, struggling not to cry. "Oh baby, your sweet face. Mommy loves that little face of yours." She tickled his stomach. "…and your tummy and arms and legs…"

He squirmed and laughed as she scooped him up into a big hug. Birdie looked at her baby boy and saw Jimmy written all over him. Her heart swelled. "You are exactly what your father asked for."

"Mommy, you're what I asked for." He grabbed her face with his chubby hands and gave her a wet kiss. "Can I kiss your boo-boos so you get better?"

CHAPTER TWENTY-FIVE

In the days that followed, all the city's newspapers announced that God was not dead. According to the articles, Luke Godman was a victim of a hit and run that left him in a coma. Police were seeking witnesses and information pertaining to the incident. Birdie didn't see anyone on the street that night, but could someone have seen the car from a window or a side street? It was doubtful anyone was around at that hour since it was a business district made up of darkened store fronts and boarded-up buildings. Birdie didn't dare speak up for fear that Beamon would somehow retaliate. Even if she made an anonymous call, he would know it was her. She didn't doubt for a second if the police called him in for questioning, he would somehow bring her down into the gutter with him. Birdie knew that no number of tears could help her crawl out of this evilness. She couldn't take the chance of leaving Carmen and Lil' Jimmy without a mommy and a daddy if she landed in jail.

For the next few days, while the weather turned cold and

threatened an early snow, Birdie scoured the Cincinnati and neighboring local Kentucky papers looking for more information on God's condition. The *Call and Post* had a photograph of him wrapped up like a mummy in his hospital room. The *Herald*, another black newspaper, had pictures of Godman playing his saxophone and another of the dented-up sax that was left at the scene.

Each photograph unleashed a flurry of fast-moving images of that horrible night. God's rubbery limbs flying through the night and his body landing lifeless at the curb. The glint from his saxophone shining as if lit on fire under the light of a lone streetlamp flickered before her eyes. She couldn't turn away from that night, not from Godman's gruesome fate or her own under Beamon's fists.

Her bruises had begun to change from deep purple and plum red to blue, green and icky yellow splotches. She wrapped her arms around herself knowing that even as the bruises faded from sight, the pain Beamon inflicted seeped well beneath the surface.

Birdie wrestled with what action to take next. She figured if she sat still long enough, the answer would come. However, any sudden clap of sound or escalation of noise—a cup falling into the sink, a sharp blast from the whistling tea kettle, or the children, cranky from being cooped up in the apartment, began fighting—would set her on edge. Finally, Birdie told herself, "I need to go to the police. That would be the right thing to do. Would they even believe me?"

That thought prompted the hair on the back of her neck to rise. Beamon could appear at any given moment. She was sure that with the news about God circulating, Beamon would be wondering what she was going to do. He could be lurking around a corner, on a side street or show up at her door unexpectedly. Birdie agreed to give herself a few more days to see what might happen before going directly to the police.

"I've got to plan this perfectly. Maybe even take the children to Chicky's. I've got to get him in jail before he gets me."

She looked up at the ceiling. Focusing beyond the long trail of cracks and peeling paint, Birdie took a deep breath. *I'm sorry, Mama. You sent me away to learn to be strong on my own. You showed me in every way you possibly could what it was like to be strong and stand on your own two feet. You showed me what the power of family looked like in the clearest light-of-day-blue and gray sky.*

She puffed out a few short breaths before releasing the pent-up tears that rolled freely down her cheeks. *No way will I ever put myself in this position again. Never! I'll walk on broken glass or swallow fire before letting a man lay a hand on me. I swear, he'll be pulling back a stub of a body part if he even tries.*

"Mommy, why are you crying?" Carmen pushed herself into the crook of Birdie's arm, resting a heavy head on her mother's shoulder. "Don't cry or I'm going to cry with you."

Birdie took a swipe at her cheeks. "Baby, no, I'm not crying. It's just a quick way to wash away the blues."

"Mommy, you are not blue."

"No, sweetie, you are so right, I am not. Listen, my sweet little girl, stop fighting with your brother. You two need to love each other and protect each other. We're family and that means we do everything we can for each other. Forever and ever."

Without decisive action, Birdie carried on with her normal routine with one exception. She took great care to move through her days in the shadows. She never walked alone if she could help it. She kept pace with a group of people or walked just off to the side of another person walking in the same direction. She stayed close to buildings and ducked into doorways while waiting for a bus whenever possible. Her desire was not to be seen or noticed by anyone. She even made do with every crumb in the pantry so she would not have to go out for groceries unless it was absolutely necessary.

Still, Birdie worried. When she wasn't worrying about her potential involvement in God's injuries, Birdie was working. And when she wasn't working, she was meeting with Mr. Houston, who was still sorting out the particulars about the Erkenbrecher house. Birdie didn't want to be pessimistic, but things were moving more slowly than she anticipated. Still, focusing on the house kept her mind off the present if only for a little while. She wrote a few letters to her sisters but didn't mention anything about Beamon's rage, Godman's coma or even the house in case she jinxed any luck that was on her side. If she had any spare time at all, which she tried not to have for fear Beamon would find her and figure out some way to keep her busy, Birdie felt compelled to seek out Michael.

As had happened in the past, when things were unsettled, her thoughts and need for family became strong. She needed to feel that something in her life was not unraveling, and the comfort of family and familiarity gave her strength to put one foot in front of the other when she was uncertain about taking the next step. Since she couldn't bring herself to tell the truth to Chicky, Bessa or any of her Amazon aunts, somehow the thought that Michael could be somewhere close helped remind her of the home she knew when she wrapped herself in Mama's quilt. Michael needed her care. If he wouldn't go to the shelter, Birdie could at least keep him company. She would somehow let him know that she was around for him. The thought of connecting with him stirred a warm sensation in her belly. Besides, he could probably be found in the shadows of a side alleyway, doorway or back staircase away from people, which was where Birdie now felt most comfortable when out in the streets.

"Do you draw anymore, Michael?" Birdie asked when she came upon him on a bus stop bench in front of a row of fussy little shops that catered to well-to-do "by appointment only" patrons in O'Bryonville.

He smiled without looking at her and waved away two buses that squealed to a stop and opened their doors thinking they were waiting to get on. He then turned to look at her. Michael's eyes lit up, but he shook his head.

She sat down next to him. "That's okay. Maybe you'll start again someday. It's nice to have something to look forward to, isn't it? Isn't it nice to have a dream?"

Michael kicked at a patch of dirt that separated the curb from the sidewalk. He started drawing something with his toes that looked like a cloud.

"My husband, Jimmy—I don't think you ever met him—he had lots of dreams. He was so full of dreams." Suddenly feeling a wave of sadness, Birdie continued, "And those dreams sent him flying in so many directions. Including right here to Cincinnati."

"You have dreams too, Bird?" Michael's soft voice cracked when he spoke.

Hearing Michael's voice snapped her out of her blue mood. Birdie smiled and nodded. "Yes. I'd like to open my very own restaurant here in town. I'd make my mama's best dishes for everyone to enjoy. Maybe you'd draw up some nice pictures I could put on the menu?"

Michael continued toeing at his cloud. Though he never said much more, Birdie couldn't help but think Michael thought her restaurant dream was a long shot too. She reached in her pocket and pulled out three pieces of peppermint candy and dropped them in Michael's hand. He stuffed them in his shirt pocket and patted his chest as if to assure their safety. Michael waved at a few passersby before sliding off the bench and, without saying goodbye, walked quickly toward the neighborhood park.

Days passed. Birdie was concerned she hadn't seen Michael on her daily routes to and from work. She worried that with every look over her shoulder, Beamon might show up, though she hadn't seen any sign of him lurking anywhere or had even heard from him for that matter. And she continued to be consumed with prickly indecision. Godman remained in a coma. Each day, Birdie told herself she needed another day to think whether or not to tell the police what really happened to God. She also worried that with each passing day her story would be more and more implausible. The longer she waited the less she would be seen as an innocent. Birdie shivered. She couldn't help but think this was the dead quiet before a big, hold-nothing-back storm.

CHAPTER TWENTY-SIX

From the corner of her eye, Birdie saw a flash. A sudden glint of light sparked right at the edge of her line of sight, almost out of view. Birdie snapped her head in its direction and squinted only to see an empty street. She was on her way to Mrs. Jeffers's house to pick up her pay for last night's dinner when the flash of white light prompted her to stay on guard. She couldn't help but sense something was about to go wrong. Beamon hadn't shown himself in over two weeks. So as not to be consumed by the thick air of danger that surrounded her, Birdie mechanically focused on any opportunity to work that came her way. It was the only way she could keep her mind off Godman and Beamon.

Birdie had been cooking, cleaning and ironing for the Jeffers family since the first time she came to Cincinnati. She left their employ once when she had to go back to Mt. Sterling to be with Mama. When Birdie returned, Mrs. Jeffers told her she didn't need "a girl" but asked Birdie to make a few cakes and finger sandwiches for luncheons and cocktail parties. That progressed to preparing and serving, when needed, whole dinners. Birdie had become the Jefferses' caterer although Mrs. Jeffers would never refer to her by that designation. She often heard Mrs. Jeffers refer to her as "my girl, Birdie" or "our Birdie" when guests asked about the food or service.

Mr. Jeffers was a lawyer for a prestigious firm and never had much to say to his wife or his children. On the other hand, Mrs. Jeffers chatted nonstop. She babbled on and on to Birdie about shopping at H.S. Pogue's department store and lunching at the Carew Towers or attending dinner parties at the Indian Hill Country Club. She would mindlessly speak as if Birdie was one of her white socialite friends, insistently repeating, "Oh, Birdie, you must go!"

Birdie thought, *Woman, do you know how much you pay me? That country club won't even let black people on the grounds unless they were cutting the grass or shrubs.* Regardless, Birdie knew to keep her conversation light, devoid of opinion, personal observances, or inflection. She managed to go through her days passing pleasantries, nodding in agreement when it seemed appropriate and wondering how long it would be before she could go home.

It had been almost a month ago when Mrs. Jeffers asked Birdie to prepare a very important upcoming dinner for Mr. Jeffers's law partners. The request for Birdie's help came with a firm warning. "Birdie, I've asked you to do this instead of my other girl because I know you can make food look impressive and these businessmen and their wives must be impressed. I can't have any mistakes. Okay?"

Birdie, elated at the opportunity to take charge, wanted to make sure the meal was spectacular. Whenever she cooked for others, she made a point of never buying anything sight unseen. A phone call for a delivery of meats and produce would not do. Birdie learned from Mama to go directly to the butcher and vegetable markets to pick the freshest by touch and smell. So, she had decided not to use the Jeffers account at their nearby butcher but to use her own account at one of the best butchers in Cincinnati. This way she was assured everything would be premium quality. After buying everything on her own account she would then turn around and pay the butcher and grocer once she got paid. Doing it this way Birdie would be able to make a little profit from her thriftiness and eye for selecting the best cuts of meat. She was lucky to be able to do it. Grocers and butchers all around town had tightened their strings because of shortages. Birdie made sure they knew she was always good for it.

She also learned from Mama that the best way to keep money flowing was to earn your customers' and vendors' trust and then do everything you could to keep it. That way, customers would always come back to you and shopkeepers would be open to giving you a good deal.

Birdie's plan was to present such a sterling meal that she'd be able to pick up new customers from Mr. Jeffers's firm. Like Mrs. Jeffers, Birdie wanted everything to be flawless. In the days leading up to the big dinner and up to the moment the guests arrived, Mrs. Jeffers had been a nervous wreck about all the details. When giving instructions, she shook so much she left a trail of bobby pins that fell from her pin curled head and ashes from her cigarettes went flying everywhere. Birdie took it all in stride and focused on making sure that not only the food would be impeccable but nary a pin or ash would be found anywhere in sight.

Everything about last night's dinner had gone according to plan. Birdie observed guests patting their bellies after each course and even a few ladies tugging at their girdles to make room for dessert. At the end of the evening, Mr. and Mrs. Jeffers thanked Birdie for a successful event and even promised to show their appreciation when they settled-up in the morning. Birdie believed that "appreciation" meant a big, fat tip.

However, today Birdie knew something was wrong the moment Mrs. Jeffers opened her door. Instead of her normal smile and high-pitched ramblings, Mrs. Jeffers was stiff and spoke to Birdie with her nose held high in the air. Without even a hello, she said, "Birdie, you know my husband is an attorney, don't you, girl?"

Birdie thought, *Girl? She never called me that right to my face before.* Birdie replied slowly, "Yes, ma'am. Mr. Jeffers is one of the most distinguished lawyers in the city."

"You know last night's dinner guests were from his law firm, right?"

"Why yes, Mrs. Jeffers. I recognized the judge from his picture in the papers. Was there a problem?"

"Problem? I'll say there was. I heard the food you served us was stolen!"

"What? No. No, ma'am. Where did you get that from? Who told you that?"

"Don't worry about where I heard it. I heard it. I know you didn't go to our butcher. There was nothing on our account. So where did you get it from? Never mind, I don't even want to know. If word got out that I served food that was stolen, my husband could lose his job. I could be named as an accomplice. We'd be ruined, on account of your thievery."

Mrs. Jeffers puffed out her blazing-red cheeks. "How dare you show your face here wanting to get paid. I should call the police and have you arrested right here on my front porch steps. Only that would just draw attention and get our names in the papers. Go away! Don't let me see your face again!"

Birdie jumped back as the door slammed just inches away from her nose. She stood in front of the door for a few moments in utter shock. She had prepared food and taken care of this woman's children for over a year and because Mrs. Jeffers heard some terrible lie, she just believed it? Without question?

Damn! Now how am I going to pay Mr. Green for the meats? Birdie worried.

Birdie rang the doorbell determined to talk with Mrs. Jeffers and insist that what she heard was not true. She could show her the receipts from her butcher to prove it. After waiting a few minutes and getting no response, Birdie banged on the door with the palm of her hand. No answer. She knocked harder, this time with her fist. Minutes passed and still no one came to answer the door.

Determined to state her case, Birdie walked around to the back of the house. She told herself that maybe the woman was out in the back and just didn't hear Birdie knocking. She ignored the warning message in the back of her mind. *Here you are in the thick of this white neighborhood walking around to the back of the house to confront this woman, this white woman, about what is due to you...danger.* Earlier, when Birdie got off the bus, she had been stopped several times by white men in passing cars asking who she worked for or if she was lost. *I guess a black woman without a noticeable uniform or bags in her hands is suspicious.*

Birdie opened the gate and stepped into the Jefferses' expansive, manicured backyard. She followed the brick paved path across the patio to the back door and peeked through the glass. Mrs. Jeffers was sitting at her kitchen table with a pile of envelopes before her. A cigarette balanced between her fingers as she lifted a cup to her lips.

"That bitch!" Birdie whispered to herself. She started to turn away from the window when she saw Vivian, dressed in a service uniform, float into view. "What the hell is Vivian doing here now?"

A week before his attempt to run down God in the street,

Beamon asked Birdie to help him with a personal problem—his sister, Vivian. Her drinking had gotten out of hand. She owed a large sum of money to one person and made promises to pay back smaller amounts to several others. It didn't even matter what she promised because Vivian never made good on anything; she was drinking before, during and after these transactions.

Beamon had pleaded with Birdie to help him get Vivian's behavior under control. "You know Vivian is my blood family. Whatever our history, for the life of me, I can't ignore my promise to look out for her. That girl—and all her shit—is killing me. She's becoming a liability that's starting to hurt my business. Maybe being around a fine woman like yourself will turn her around, so I'm asking you to do me this favor."

The favor was for Birdie to hire Vivian to work with her in the hope of getting her out of the bar and the all too frequent mug shots that found their way into the *Call and Post*. Against her better judgment, Birdie agreed and hired Vivian to help her with the Jefferses' big dinner. She didn't really see how having Vivian work with her would change anything about his sister's character, but she had told Beamon she would do what she could to help. Besides, Vivian would just be serving food. What trouble could she possibly get into?

Vivian showed up to work the Jefferses' party on-time and seemingly sober. She politely greeted Birdie and Mrs. Jeffers. Once Vivian entered, Birdie poked her head outside the door and looked in every direction to see if Beamon was in sight. Although there was no trace of him, Birdie wanted to tell Vivian to turn around and go home, but since Vivian was being so courteous, Birdie thought it might be better to let her stay. Plus, she wanted to avoid the risk of the real Vivian creating an ugly scene in front of the Jeffers. Still, throughout the dinner, Birdie hovered nervously over eggshells, not knowing what Vivian might blurt out at the most inopportune time. Birdie avoided any conversation about Beamon, dismissed Vivian early and thought she had bought her silence by giving Vivian her full pay in cash on the spot. Birdie was grateful the evening came and went without incident and figured she and Beamon were now more than square.

When she agreed, against a mountain of reservation, to hire Vivian, Birdie had hoped Beamon wouldn't ask her to help Vivian ever again. Anything more than this one-time favor wasn't worth the possibility of trouble. *But here we are today in the early light, just a day after I had her work for me. That's what I get for doing a favor for the devil...a damn sneaky woman prancing around the Jefferses' kitchen with her eyes twinkling and that crooked smile of hers, serving Mrs. Jeffers coffee. I gotta give her credit though, Vivian didn't skip a beat.* Birdie was sure that despite the early hour the Jefferses' bottle of Johnnie Walker was probably missing from the bar.

With Vivian in the picture, the little pieces of the nasty rumor started coming together.

Birdie never thought, given Vivian's feelings toward her brother, that she would turn around and stab her so brutally in the back. After all Birdie had risked, for Vivian to whisper an out-and-out lie to an employer about her stealing food was something Birdie could have never imagined.

Again she was startled by small bursts of light flickering behind her like a crystal reflecting the sunlight. Birdie turned again and blinked as she retreated from the window to scan the backyard. She saw nothing out of the ordinary, just the finely tended yard filled with shivering rose bushes waving the last of their faded pink petals back at her with what she thought was distain.

Birdie returned to her extraordinary dilemma. She watched Vivian open the refrigerator and take out a carton of eggs.

Vivian wasn't a cook by any means. Her only talent was sitting at a bar conning people out of their money to buy her drinks. She must have run a pretty convincing game on Mrs. Jeffers. Within a very short time, however, Vivian was bound to misstep. Vivian's ways would soon reveal themselves, but that revelation wouldn't necessarily vindicate Birdie's name and reputation. Mrs. Jeffers would need something for her upcoming bridge game—cakes, finger sandwiches and such. Vivian would need someone to make them for her.

Birdie knew this situation had to be handled quickly, delicately and directly because she not only had bills to pay but a reputation to uphold. She could dig into her savings to scrape together some money to pay the butcher. Birdie knew he would cut her off the moment he heard she couldn't pay despite the fact she had patronized his store for a few years. After paying the butcher, she would barely have any money left for her, Carmen and Lil' Jimmy to survive. It would be red beans, rice and cornbread until money crossed her palms again. She didn't know when that would be because she now didn't have a job. And there was still Mr. Houston and the Erkenbrecher house to consider. Would she have enough money for that too? She left the Jefferses' back window with a headache and the determination to find a way out of everything.

Two days later, Birdie came home to find Mr. Jeffers standing at her apartment door. He was a little man with sandy-brown hair that was slowly retiring to the back of his head. Hat in hand, he looked directly at Birdie.

"Look here, Miss Bird, I never believed a word my wife said about you, never. That other girl is not working out. I knew she wasn't going to because, well, I don't think my wife realizes it, but she always appears to be intoxicated."

Birdie kept her expression neutral as he continued.

"Listen, we need you to come back. The missus has a party this afternoon and another gathering of my colleagues from the firm this weekend. Can you do it? I know this is last-minute. I can pay you up front."

Birdie asked directly, "Does your wife know about this?"

"Well, as of this minute, no. But don't worry. I'll take care of her. She'll listen. She's going crazy right now because that girl, whatever her name is, didn't show up this morning. My wife is driving me crazy now. I had to do something and that's why I'm here."

The dim hallway light hit Mr. Jeffers's bald spot, giving him a small angelic halo. "Please promise me you can take care of this by the afternoon."

Birdie thought for a moment then said, "You know I don't take kindly to being called a thief. If that lie, and it is a big, whopping, bold-faced lie, ever gets out then I'm finished doing business anywhere. What can be done about that? My mama taught me when doing business that my reputation is, well, it's everything, Mr. Jeffers. Your wife has the potential to ruin that."

Mr. Jeffers smiled. "So you want to negotiate. Okay. I get it and that's a good enough point for me. I will pay you for the job you did and…how about two dollars more for this afternoon?"

Birdie smiled. Mama was in her head right now and she could hear her say that she needed more. "The good Lord says to forgive. I was really hurt by the way Mrs. Jeffers spoke to me. I know you and Mrs. Jeffers are my boss and all and sometimes bad things can be said when we're in the heat of it. If I am to do this today, I've got to go to the store and get some things to make it nice for those society ladies. I know you and Mrs. Jeffers have a reputation to uphold too."

Mr. Jeffers chuckled. "Okay, okay. You need to come down

and work for my law firm. I'm sure you'd be really something in court. How about five dollars over your regular rate? I can't go any higher or the missus will get after me."

Birdie nodded knowing that the missus couldn't and wouldn't do anything without her husband's permission. Mr. Jeffers stepped forward with his hand extended. Birdie held out her hand and gave him a quick handshake.

"I've got to get going double time if I'm going to make it to your house by noon."

She went back into her apartment and started writing down everything she would need for the Jefferses' dinner. She had to get a move on to make sure she could get what she needed from the store and make it over to the Jefferses' in time. *Oh, Mr. Jeffers, please have your wife calmed down by the time I get there. I need the money but don't necessarily need that woman getting in my way.*

Birdie was sliding on her coat when there was a scurry of movement and loud whispers outside her door.

"You think she knows already?"

"How could she? It just happened a little while ago. Tsk, that man was nothing but a damn criminal. I never did like the looks of him."

Birdie swung her door wide open to find Mrs. Lucille and two other women parked around the stairs and leaning on the banister. Startled by her presence they immediately stopped talking. Mrs. Lucille started off.

"Birdie, dear, we were wondering if you heard about what happened to that friend of yours. We weren't sure if you knew or not and I—I mean, we were just coming over to break the news and see if you needed help or anything."

"Mrs. Lucille, what are you talking about? What friend? I'm on my way to the store to pick up some things for a dinner tonight out in Amberly Village. Oh, can you watch Carmen and Lil' Jimmy, please? I have to prepare for two social events. I promise I won't be too late."

Mrs. Lucille held up her hands. "Birdie, listen to me, dear, I'm talking about that Beamon fellow. Now you know how I feel about him, but did you know the police found him dead in his car? It was right in front of Junior's. They say he was stabbed several times in the neck. It's a shame he bled all over that pretty car of his. Lord forgive me for saying this...but you see, God don't like ugly."

Mrs. Lucille paused to gauge Birdie's reaction to the news. When she got nothing from Birdie she continued. "And you know them police ain't found anybody who did it just yet. With the way he was living it could have been anybody from anywhere. The police don't care really. He's just another black man dead in the streets."

Birdie stood motionless, looking quizzically at her neighbors who were still waiting for a dramatic reaction from her. Birdie stepped further out into the hallway and closed the door behind her. "Mrs. Lucille, I'll be home as soon as I can. I got a new movie magazine with Lena Horne on the cover. Lord, I never thought I'd see the day when a colored woman would be on the cover. And I made some vegetable soup and cornbread. I also got some canned peaches. Please help yourself."

Birdie ran down the stairs and out the door. *I got too much to do to spend any time feeling sorry about that damn evil frog-eyed man. He got what he deserved.*

Birdie was able to get everything prepared on time for the luncheon and dinner at the Jefferses' house. Both husband and wife were so pleased that they paid her everything as agreed. Standing all day had taken a toll on Birdie's feet. Her feet hurt so badly she could hardly climb the stairs to her apartment. She had to pull herself up by the railing from the second floor on. She caught a second wind when she heard voices above her in the hallway. As she approached the last flight of stairs, two policemen were standing at Birdie's door. Although she knew she shouldn't have had anything to worry about, she couldn't stop shaking as a chill rippled through her body.

Her heart thumped and her scalp tingled as she asked in a squeaky voice, "Good evening, officers. May I help you?"

Mrs. Lucille peeked through the crack of her door and mouthed out the words, "The children are with me." Birdie nodded and opened the door to her apartment.

An officer asked politely, "Are you Mrs. Walker? We have some questions about a Mr. Sandy Beamon."

Birdie knew that innocence didn't always matter when it came to black folks. She nervously asked the policemen to have a seat and even offered them coffee as if they were guests coming for a visit. They started right away asking questions about her work, her relationship with Beamon and the last time she saw him. She had been here before and a voice in her head reminded her to keep it simple and say no more than what was asked. She followed that advice. The officers' monotonous voices spat out question after question.

"When was the last time you saw Mr. Beamon?"

"A few weeks ago, I suppose. At his apartment." Birdie didn't dare mention they had been to see Luke Godman in Louisville that same night.

"And he was your boyfriend, wasn't he?"

"He was just a friend, officer."

"Mrs. Walker, I've already asked a few people who have told me differently."

Birdie swallowed hard before looking the officer directly in the face. "I'm a widow, officer...recently widowed. Being with anyone right now might look some way to outsiders, but I assure you that Mr. Beamon was no boyfriend to me. We were friends." *And even that's being generous,* Birdie added silently.

After jotting down her answers, one officer graciously thanked her but ended with a stern, "We may need you to come downtown for additional questioning."

The moment they left, Birdie exhaled as if she hadn't taken a breath since she caught sight of their blue uniforms. Mrs. Lucille rushed in.

"Are you alright? I didn't want to bring the children in while they were here. I didn't know how this was going to turn out. What happened?"

Birdie started sobbing. She had never been so scared in her entire life. "Oh my God, murder? I'm being questioned by the police about a murder. Please, dear God, I hope no one hears about this back home. How can this be happening to me?" She buried her face in her hands. "That man, that man was evil, Mrs. Lucille. You know that? Did you know what he did to me? I'm glad he's dead. I hate to say it but I'm glad. The last time I saw him, I wished him dead, but I didn't have anything to do with this."

Mrs. Lucille wrapped her arms around Birdie, softly patting her and stroking her arm. "Child, don't worry. This is a test of your faith. You've got to go through it to see and appreciate His work and His love. God has got you in His hands and He loves you. He'll keep you safe from harm. God might want you to get a little help from a good lawyer though. You know of any?"

Birdie sat in front of Walter Houston's big desk patting Pierre's head while he panted and drooled over her knee. Mr. Houston listened and agreed to take her case. Although there wasn't really a case to speak of as of yet, they both agreed it was prudent to be prepared just in case there were charges brought against her. They also knew that in 1944 charges were possible regardless of on which side of the predicament you fell—innocent or guilty.

Mr. Houston wheezed out, "Mrs. Walker, this here situation contains some real salacious material. Many people knew Mr. Beamon and his rather nefarious business. You were seen with him on many occasions, so it is assumed that you were his girlfriend, hence you're a suspect. That's why the police made a beeline to your door. There is so much gossip which means a lot of misinformation about you is floating out in the streets. The police will sniff around trying to tie this up as quickly as possible. They'll take the lies someone spews and run with it to the courthouse. I'll try my best to protect you from that."

Mr. Houston began to breathe hard. His blindingly white shirt heaved up and down with each laborious breath. "Now you know we have to talk about an additional fee."

"I'll give you all I have, Mr. Houston, if that's what it takes."

His breathing turned into a soft rhythmic whistling sound. "And how much might that be?"

"Not much, but you're still working on getting my house, right?"

Mr. Houston pulled a file from a desk drawer. "I was hoping to update you on my progress on that. I guess now is as good a time as any. Mrs. Walker, thus far it looks like there are no encumbrances. No heirs or any other family members to lay claim to that house. I placed an advertisement in the *Enquirer* and the *Post* with no response. You'll be billed for that by the way. We're not free and clear by any means. There's still title work and back taxes to address. I'll let you know once I get more information. Like I said, Mrs. Walker, if you can't pay my fee for any reason, and we succeed in acquiring the property, that house will have to be signed over to me. Again, that is if we can establish your ownership outright and obtain the deed."

Birdie sat with her head and shoulders bent toward the floor. She could see her future slipping away, making it too much of an effort to argue. She nodded and whispered, "I understand, Mr. Houston. If I can't pay the legal fees, you can have the house."

CHAPTER TWENTY-SEVEN

Beamon's murder was on the front page of every black newspaper. The stories were filled with gruesome details, pictures and calls for information, which Birdie knew would probably go unanswered. Every story she read said the murder weapon was a small penknife which had been found on the floor of the car.

Weeks passed without any word or contact from the police. Birdie hadn't slept well since the day she was questioned. She had reoccurring dreams of Carmen and Lil' Jimmy being left alone as she was carted off to jail. She dreamed of Mr. Conroy's contorted body, gray with death. He was lying on the kitchen floor with purplish red blood flowing outward rapidly and seeping between the cracks of the linoleum. The passing days did not provide any solace that she would be in the clear; instead, each day churned up more anxiety.

Though she never told her family about Beamon's murder, they found out anyway. Who knew what version of the story traveled miles over the river to eagerly awaiting ears after being distorted by so many mouths? Out of the blue, Chicky, her husband, Clarence, and all of their children showed up on Birdie's doorstep unannounced in an attempt to convince Birdie to come back with them to Mt. Sterling. Chicky barked and crowed at her sister as soon as the brood walked through the door.

"There is no way you should have been mixed up with some hooligan like that. Children, hold your ears! You weren't raised for that kind of life. I told you about coming to Sin-Sin-nati. Ooooh, girl, if Mama were here, she would've boxed those ears till you saw the next light of day! Girl, you were not thinking straight."

Chicky and Clarence were unsuccessful in their arguments and succeeded only in having the whole family spending the night piled on top of each other all over Birdie's small apartment. The children, of course, had fun sleeping on the floor with their five cousins. The family left the next morning right after attending a service at St. Steven's. They weren't Catholic, but for Chicky church was church, it didn't really matter the denomination. Clarence had his reservations about attending but came along to keep peace, as well as repent a bit since he had slipped out to the pool hall during the night.

On another day, two Amazon aunts showed up unannounced from Louisville. Both brought along sons who were too young to be drafted to serve in the army but old enough to take care of business in the streets. Birdie's aunts threatened to simply snatch her up and take her, Carmen and Lil' Jimmy back to Mt. Sterling.

"Our baby sister, your mother, our China Doll, bless her heart, she would not have wanted her daughter to be living like this. You should be following your sister Bessa's footsteps. She's over there in Europe, bless her, putting all that medical knowledge of hers to the test to help those soldiers over there. You should have gone to school like her. But, no…here you are, with your fast tail, entangled in some mess."

Birdie knew nothing good would come from challenging her aunts, so she listened and let them take swipes at her apartment and her life. The women bustled around the place, rearranging furniture to their liking and commandeering a trip to Findley Farmer's Market to buy food to cook. Birdie, Carmen and Lil' Jimmy, out of respect and fear, fell in line and did as they were instructed. Their obedience calmed the Amazons down enough for Birdie to convince her aunts that she and the children were safe. They left, leaving a few cooked meals in the refrigerator and canned vegetables and jams in the pantry. The Amazons also promised they would be back if they heard Birdie wasn't flying right and next time they offered to take her back to Mt. Sterling they would not take no for an answer.

Almost a month to the day of Beamon's death, the rumor mill began kicking up more fertile tales on his murder. The talk in the street was a homeless man had been arrested and charged with the murder. As Birdie had feared, it was Michael.

The police found Michael curled up behind St. Steven's Church. A blood-stained shirt was found with his belongings. Apparently, he confessed in his own way. He told a parishioner at the church that he hurt a bad man. That, along with the blood-stained shirt, prompted someone to call the police.

Oh, poor baby, I gotta make sure he's alright, Birdie thought. She knew they would probably commit Michael to the state sanatorium. Her heart raced, even her fingertips pulsed at the thought of Michael being tossed in what she envisioned was some dark corner only to be neglected or forgotten.

That can't happen. Not to Michael. He only did it… Birdie

couldn't bring herself to complete the sentence and left the thought hanging around her head. She wasn't sure how to do it, but knew she had to get Michael out of this situation.

Birdie shuffled Lil' Jimmy off to Mrs. Lucille. Mrs. Lucille's greeting, "Bless you, my sister," had given Birdie an idea. With Carmen in tow, Birdie stepped out the door to her apartment and crossed the street to the church. Carmen was attending school at the church, but Birdie had another purpose for being there. She went into the church to speak with the priest.

Birdie had never been one for prayer, never swayed and jumped when ministers rose to deliver even the firiest sermons. She felt her heaven and hell was right in the here and now. Birdie believed there was a God, she just had no need for religion. Growing up, she saw, more likely than not, stalwart so-called Christians as the source of all the nastiest gossip that plagued their town. Maybe this time the church could do its good work. Michael could be found most times around the church. They fed and clothed him and provided him with shelter. Maybe they could help him out of this predicament.

She wasn't sure what she was going to say or ask Father Samuelson, but when Birdie began talking, a confession of sorts flew out of her mouth. She released her words without any control over where they were going. Birdie pleaded with the priest to help Michael.

"He may have done it, Father, but he is innocent. He's always been an innocent. I know him and can't let him... I can't see him..."

It was only then that she came to a complete stop. The words were stuck in her throat as she choked her tears down. Finally, the dam broke. "It's my fault this even happened to him. He was just trying to protect me."

Birdie spun around, shaking with a flood of emotion. She wanted to cling to something, but she backed away when the priest walked toward her and reached out to provide comfort. Instead, he lightly touched her elbow and guided her to a pew.

"Please, Mrs. Walker, please sit," Father Samuelson said calmly. "I know Michael. We've tried for many years to get him help. He has moments when he is very lucid, and in those times, he is very productive. He has helped in the kitchen on those many occasions. There are people here who love and watch over him. I didn't know he was the one who had been arrested. I can't believe that he'd hurt anyone, let alone kill someone. I don't think anyone around here believes he would do such a thing. He has never communicated to us about his family. He just appeared at our doorsteps one day and never really left. Do you know his family?"

Birdie waved a hand in front of her face. "Me and Michael are from the same place. What you'd call his family is back in Mt. Sterling, Kentucky, I guess. But they never cared much. I've known him just about all my life. My mama used to help him sometimes. So I guess I'm as close to family as you can get." She looked up and whispered, "Father, he just can't go to the state sanatorium. I know they won't treat him right. I'm afraid of what they'll do to him. It's my fault really. If he did it, he did it because he probably thought he was protecting me."

Birdie left the church with her face moist from crying. Her hands were still warm from Father Samuelson's grasp. He assured her he would contact the monsignor to find out if anything could be done to help Michael. Birdie hoped that there was some way to keep Michael from being lost in what she saw as a tortured existence in an institution. She'd heard horror stories of people who sent their loved ones off with good intentions, only to learn their family members certainly weren't better for their stay at the sanatorium. Birdie thought at one point they might be able to help Michael, but in her heart she knew otherwise. She envisioned him wasting away without the love and attention he needed.

When she got home, Birdie pulled Lil' Jimmy to her and hugged him extratight as soon as she got in her door. The freshness of his skin and the electricity of his body rejuvenated her. She only wished she could hug Carmen too and couldn't wait until she got home from school. Birdie squeezed Lil' Jimmy so close that he wiggled and giggled to get away. Hugging her son gave her an idea as to what could be done to save Michael. She would press for Father Samuelson's and the church's help. Birdie pulled out two pieces of stationery from her bedside table.

She wrote, "Dear Father Samuelson," and hoped the air would guide her next words. Her letter began to transform into a request and a partnership. She asked if the church could take Michael under their care and give him a place to live and a reliable job, such as working regularly in the soup kitchen on his lucid days—and not just on a volunteer basis. She would provide Michael with anything else he needed. Essentially, as a way to keep him safe and out of the sanatorium, Birdie would become Michael's guardian and the church would become his permanent home. She stated that she wanted to write this in a letter as a signed promise to do what she said she would. Birdie signed her letter, "Respectfully yours in Christ, Birdie Autumn Walker."

She wrote using a pen she inherited from Mama. It was almost out of ink by the time she finished. She bore down on the paper to make sure the last bit of ink ran into the indentations and crevices created by her words and signature. Birdie fanned the paper to make sure the ink wouldn't smear. She read the words again then neatly folded the letter, making three straight creases. After licking the envelope, she walked with a sense of urgency back over to the church.

Surprised to see her so soon again, Father Samuelson read her letter immediately and promised to give the mission his full attention. Birdie left the church praying under her breath and leaving the rest up to God.

During the next few months, Birdie had never known such peace and quiet. While she waited for any news—about Michael, Beamon's murder investigation or the Erkenbrecher house—she baked pies and cakes for the temple, cookies for the church, potato rolls for area beer gardens and the little restaurant on the corner and sandwiches for pool hall patrons. Birdie did everything she could think of to make money. She found a way to put every cent she could aside. Although she hadn't heard from Mr. Houston about the Erkenbrecher house or Father Samuelson about Michael, she held out hope for a positive outcome.

Whenever she thought of Michael, Birdie would be riveted by chills flying up and down her spine. *It's all my fault*, she would repeatedly whisper to herself. *That poor dear is where he is all because of me.* She'd think about Michael and see his familiar eyes peering out from a dirty face. Michael was a piece of home to her, and she felt a tremendous need to take care of him, as Mama would have.

Birdie finally learned from Father Samuelson that Michael had to stay at the institution. Scary stories about the conditions of the sanatorium had swirled around the neighborhood because someone knew somebody who was tucked away there. When Carmen and Lil' Jimmy said their prayers before going to bed, even though they never met him, Birdie made sure they included Michael. Carmen asked once who he was, and Birdie responded that he was someone who needed love and care.

Birdie was allowed to visit Michael at the sanatorium as

often as she wanted. None of the staff asked about her relation to him. She assumed they must have thought she had been his nanny or instructed by his family to see about his care. Nurses told her she was the only one that came to visit him. Most times he would be sitting quietly in a large nondescript room that probably had been painted white but now was yellowed in the corners and tinged with gray where patients must have spent hours leaning against the walls. Michael's hair and beard were cut close. The light from the window revealed only a slight coating of blond stubble surrounding his entire head.

Birdie sneaked him small pieces of candy. He would perk up when he saw the cellophane-wrapped treats and took pleasure in untwisting the paper and listening to the crinkling sound the wrapper made when he unveiled the naked confections. He'd smile and motion her to come closer, which she did. "You my friend," he'd whisper. Birdie nodded and would give him hugs.

She pleaded with the nurses to allow her to give him sketch pads and charcoal. At first, they refused her requests, but she found an ally in a nurse that agreed it wouldn't do any harm. Birdie gave him a sketch pad that had a colorful picture of a bird on the first page that Carmen had drawn with crayon. Lil' Jimmy added a scribbled border of green grass and blue sky. Michael stared at the page before flipping to the next to start a picture of his own. After Michael began drawing, the staff was grateful for Birdie's suggestion. They were not only impressed by his talent, but it became a way he occupied his time and communicated when he didn't feel like speaking.

Each visit thereafter, Michael would have new sketches to show Birdie. The images seemed to illustrate his days at the institution. There were several neatly drawn pictures of Alma, one of the nurses he seemed to like. In every sketch, she gazed at him with a pleasant smile. In some pictures her detailed hands held either a single rose or a bouquet filled with an assortment of flowers. Other sketches were of views of the gardens, an elderly man sadly staring out a window and a little boy running and playing with a red ball.

"Oh, Michael, these are wonderful. You are such a fantastic artist!"

"For the restaurant," Michael said softly.

"The restaurant?"

"Yours," he said even softer.

It was then it struck her that she had mentioned her dream of owning a restaurant what seemed like so long ago. Birdie was touched and surprised that he even remembered it.

"That's so sweet, Michael! Of course, of course. We'll have these masterpieces framed and hung on the walls of my restaurant. You'll have to help me do it!"

Michael looked up. His lips twisted together while his eyes seemed to search the air for words until he blurted out, "I didn't do it. I didn't do what they said."

Stunned by the clarity of his voice and the force of his words, "What did you say, Michael?"

She heard him quite clearly. She needed to hear him say it again to confirm the electric bolt that rode up her spine when he said it the first time.

Michael shook his head. "I didn't, Birdie. I didn't hurt that man. I lost my knife. I lost it."

Birdie froze. Michael's words rang in her ears. She looked around to see if a nurse or attendant was nearby but there was only an assortment of residents sitting at tables or in chairs. The closest nurse busied herself behind a glass-windowed office. In all the times Birdie visited, Michael never uttered a word about Beamon's murder, and Birdie didn't dare ask. She was too afraid to bring it up because she was too afraid of what he would say.

She mouthed the words, "No, Michael. I know you didn't."

It was only a feeling, but she believed him. Or maybe she just wanted to believe. "Did you tell someone, Michael? Did you tell the police you didn't do it?"

Michael turned his attention to his sketch pad and began to dab furiously against the white page.

Michael said softly, "You my friend?"

Birdie leaned in, patted Michael on the shoulder and whispered in his ear, "Always, Michael."

Birdie rubbed her stomach to calm her nerves and then briskly walked out to the hallway in search of someone she could talk to about Michael. It would have to be someone she could trust and who would listen and would take her seriously.

"Alma!" Birdie spotted her at the far end of the long hallway. Her brown skin shone brightly in a corridor filled with pale faces in white uniforms. Birdie waved and Alma flashed the smile that had made its way across Michael's sketch pad.

"Hey, Miss Birdie!" Alma's sunny disposition was immediately apparent. Birdie could see why Michael seemed to be enamored by her. Alma was a pretty girl who looked exactly like the beautiful actress and singer Theresa Harris who appeared in many movies with some of Hollywood's biggest stars. Alma was neatly dressed in a light blue uniform, and a starched-stiff white pinafore, stockings and shoes. Her freshly pressed hair was pulled back in a neat chignon.

"Whew, I was looking for a nurse."

"Well, let me know when you find one," Alma replied. "I'm not a nurse yet. I'm still studying. There aren't many colored nurses around here as you can see, but I plan to be one of the first on this floor."

"Well, I'll be rooting for you. Listen I want to thank you for taking such good care of Michael."

"He is the sweetest. It's so sad that he's here. Never gives anyone any trouble. Oh man, can he draw! He's wasting all that talent. It's nice that you look in on him. Besides an occasional visit from a priest from that big church downtown, you're his only visitor. Well, the only visitor that treats him like you really care, you know, like family. How do you know him?"

Birdie paused. "We are like family. But I need to ask you something. He really likes you—I can tell by his artwork. You know why he's here, right?"

Alma looked over her shoulder then nodded curtly.

"He just told me he didn't do it. I believe him. It's something in my gut. I've known him forever. He couldn't have done it. Has he said anything to you?"

Alma became quiet and leaned in closer. "He has, Miss Birdie, but they all say something like that when something bad has happened to them. I wouldn't take it to heart. At least that's what I told the lady from the police department who came by wanting to talk to Michael a few weeks ago."

"Someone from the police department came here to speak with Michael?"

Alma looked around the wide hallway again and kept her voice low. "I'm not supposed to tell hospital business but yes, some white lady. I never seen a lady police officer. She didn't have a uniform on like those on the street. I think she was a detective or something big. Can you believe that? I've never seen a woman like that at all."

"Well, did she talk to Michael? Did Michael talk to her?"

Alma explained she couldn't offer up much more information because she was not allowed in the room when Michael was interviewed. She did say that, from what she observed passing by the room, the woman seemed kind and calm, and took notes of their conversation in a small notebook. The police hadn't returned since.

Birdie thanked Alma for speaking to her and made a mental note to bring Alma a pound cake on her next visit to show her gratitude. Hopefully, to also celebrate her becoming a full-fledged nurse. Birdie left the hospital praying that something good would come from the detective's visit. Maybe there was a chance that someone would find Michael was innocent and could be released sooner than later.

It would be almost a year before Birdie received word from Father Samuelson that the parish might be able to take Michael into their care to help their live-in caretaker—as long as he completed his stay at the sanatorium, and the police didn't have any further business with him, the monsignor would agree to the plan. Birdie hoped and prayed that this would indeed happen. It would lighten the heaviness in her heart, the guilt she carried because she still felt what happened to Michael was all her fault. She wanted to do all she could to make things right.

CHAPTER TWENTY-EIGHT

Birdie's hands shook as she carefully opened the thick envelope. She wasn't expecting anything from the Hamilton County Courthouse and suspected it was most likely bad news. The first page prominently displayed her full name and address, as well as *Walter S. Houston, Esq., Attorney v. Hamilton County Treasurer.*

"Hmm, so it's us versus them. What else is new? Now who's gonna be Joe Louis in this fight?"

What followed was a confusing jumble of words and paragraphs that blurred together. She could see from the document that the matter of the Erkenbrecher property had been reviewed by a judge, but there wasn't a clear sentence that stated exactly what was decided. Before Birdie could read the court papers more carefully, she saw she had also received a letter from Walter Houston. His letter, typed on his personal stationery, had a simple request:

Dear Mrs. Walker,
Please contact the office of Walter Houston, Esq.
immediately.
Sincerely,
Walter S. Houston, Esq.
Attorney at Law

His signature was an artistic swirl of blue ink that took up most of the page. Since Birdie didn't have a phone, she went over to Mrs. Lucille's apartment to make a phone call.

Mr. Houston's voice boomed through the receiver, "Mrs. Walker, please get a phone. I don't know how you live today without one. I've been trying to reach you to let you know you should expect some papers from the court soon."

"Yes, I've received them, Mr. Houston."

"Good. They outline all my efforts to date to retrieve your property. I'm not going to say anything more until I see you. Let's meet at about two o'clock tomorrow? By the way, would you happen to have any more of that fruit crumble you made before? I have been thinking about it for days now."

Birdie decided, in the absence of fruit in the pantry, she would bake an overly sweet date-nut bread. As the bread rose in the oven so did her hopes that things could be looking up.

"Oh, Jimmy, this certainly is a fool's errand," Birdie whispered through her teeth. She walked up Walter Houston's long walkway not knowing what to expect. The court papers mentioned a hearing but there was no information regarding her outright ownership of the house. Mr. Houston never hesitated to alert Birdie of the mounting costs involved in clearing the way for her to claim the property.

Mr. Houston briskly walked into the room with Pierre bounding behind him. The dog sniffed around the date-nut bread Birdie had wrapped in wax paper and placed on Mr. Houston's desk. Mr. Houston bellowed out to Helen to fetch coffee, plates and butter. He didn't appear too upset about not having his dream crumble.

"Mrs. Walker, we have to make this quick. I have to be downtown in court in a few hours." He licked crumbs from his fingers. "The city owns the property and is eager to get rid of it. Despite their eagerness, the city wasn't too keen about selling to Negroes and was trying to 'redline' the neighborhood. That is, to keep us out of certain areas by denying us mortgage loans so they can keep areas segregated. However, with additional help from the NAACP and letters from my Brotherhood attorneys who have law degrees from Howard University, we prevailed. We, at least, opened the door for not only you to attain your property but for other colored folks who might want to buy in that area as well. I gotta say I'm pretty pleased with the outcome thus far."

He looked at his watch and continued. "Now, I needed to see you because we are at a point where money, real money, needs to be put down on the table. Less your deposit, do you have four hundred and ninety-three dollars? If you can put that amount in my hands, I can hand you the keys."

Birdie took a breath. She needed a moment to take it all in. This was what she wanted, but fear told her this was a lot to take on.

Birdie knitted her brows together. "I don't know, Mr. Houston, that's awful steep. Are you saying that if I give you four hundred and ninety-three dollars cash, the house is mine...all mine? Are you sure that's all you'll need?"

Walter's mother's spindly voice broke her worry. "Waahltah... Waaahltah! Who are you talking to, Waltah?"

Walter sighed and shouted back in a singsong voice,

"Mother, I'm conducting business right now. I'm here with a client." He flipped his head toward the door. "Helen, please."

He looked at Birdie from over his eyeglasses. "Mrs. Walker, I must go. Now don't worry about the papers you received from the court. Simply put, they state that things are progressing the way they should in order to establish ownership. Stop by tomorrow morning with the money so I can continue to work on your behalf."

It was nearly afternoon when Birdie returned and sat down in front of Mr. Houston's big desk. Walter rushed in and quickly pulled keys from his pocket. He dangled them in front of her while Pierre yelped and danced around his feet. Houston smiled broadly as he continued to tease the big dog.

"Mrs. Walker, if you have the money, these beautiful, shiny things are all yours."

CHAPTER TWENTY-NINE

Sugar Bird Bakery
1945

The floorboards groaned as the children ran through the house, dipping in and out of the empty rooms and twisting every knob to peek behind each door. The creaking and popping floor joints under Carmen and Lil' Jimmy's feet, along with their joyful squeals, drowned out the thunderous sound of rain. Despite the downpour, sunlight shone brightly through the windows and painted long images across the dark wood floors in every room.

After handing over four hundred and ninety-three dollars in folded bills to Mr. Houston, the house was all hers.

With her hard-earned savings and the money Mama left greatly diminished, Birdie remained optimistic that she would be able to take care of herself and the children from this point forward. She only had $427.63 left in her bank account. She had worked with much less. However, walking through the house she now owned, her buoyancy came in waves, tossing her between high excitement and even higher anxiety.

Walter said that John Coleman, a friend of his who owned the first black realty company in Cincinnati, would be by with additional paperwork. Birdie was sure that would require more money. Plus, there was no electricity and no water. She'd tackle that tomorrow. That also meant she needed more money. Birdie maintained her job with the Jeffers and had two events coming up at the Brotherhood Lodge. It was August of 1945 and there was a glimmer of hope the war would soon be over. Birdie knew that would mean bringing America's men and women home, which meant welcome home celebrations and new opportunities for her to make money.

Birdie shook out the ring of keys to find the one for the upstairs apartment. Once they climbed up a steep set of stairs, they walked through another door that opened into a good-sized main room. At the other end of the main room was the door to a bright yellow kitchen with a large pantry and a hidden door that held winding steps leading up to an attic space. Birdie held out her hand and slid her fingertips across the kitchen wall. The wallpaper, faded in patches, was printed with pictures of bucolic farms, fields and farmhands gathering wheat.

"Well, Jimmy, here's your farm." Birdie smiled.

Brighter than the lower level, the upper floor apartment swelled with the warm moisture from the rain. Birdie opened the small kitchen window to let the rooms breathe in the fresh air. There were two bedrooms, a bathroom, a living room and, what Birdie found most pleasurable, a little sun porch right off the living room. Birdie placed a foot on the black tar floor of the porch to test its sturdiness. Sensing no give or wiggle in the old structure, she stepped out to a treetop view of at least two or three of the seven hills of Cincinnati. Since the rain had become a light mist, Birdie reached for Lil' Jimmy's hand as he and Carmen followed her out onto the porch. Already so independent, he struggled to pull his hand away. Birdie pointed in the direction of the incline trolley car rails that the family rode when they first arrived in Cincinnati. Birdie told the children that they had to grow just a little bit taller before they would be able to stand on their tippy-toes to see the very tops of the tallest trees in Kentucky where Aunt Chicky, Aunt Bessa and all their cousins lived.

Carmen tugged at Birdie's waist. "Can we go outside to the backyard, Mommy? It's our backyard, isn't it?"

"Yes, baby, it's all ours," she said softly. Birdie wanted to add, *Your father wanted all this for you,* but held it back behind a smile. She shooed her children into the house where, from the sound of their feet pounding the floors, they returned to running through the rooms. Birdie drank in the moment of silence as warm sunshine covered her. She stared out, following the street as it dove down the steep hill and rolled back up again at the end of the block. She couldn't help but think about Jimmy. She remembered that day sitting close to him in the car as he drove her to work on one of the days he came back into her life in Cincinnati. She saw him clearly, telling her about a house someone gave him.

"Oh, Jimmy," she sighed heavily as she looked up into the determined sun. Its warmth felt like a kiss on her cheek.

Carmen came back on the porch and grabbed her mother's hand. "Come look, Mommy. I'm cooking."

Curious to see what her daughter had gotten into in the empty house, Birdie followed Carmen into the kitchen. Carmen had found some ancient mixing bowl under the sink. Dust and dirt from many years hidden in the dark settled in the bottom of the bowl. Carmen sat in the corner and pretended to stir an imaginary mixture. Lil' Jimmy ran into the kitchen clapping dirt from his hands.

"Mommy, I found that bowl for Carmen. It was under

there," Lil' Jimmy said pointing to the cabinets. "There's lots of stuff under there. I can build a fort or something."

Birdie looked around the kitchen. There was more counter space than she thought there'd be and room for a good-sized working table to cool and stretch dough for crusts or rolls. There was a lot of potential here sparking a new thought. The words *Sugar Bird Bakery* popped in Birdie's head. Although there was room to work here, she could open a separate place for all her projects.

Is this possible? I haven't even moved in here and now I'm thinking about opening a bakery or the little restaurant I always wanted?

Her mind turned to the dark storefront on Woodburn Avenue. She had peered into that window so many times she knew the layout would offer an ideal floor plan of her very own restaurant. She would generally dismiss it as a pipe dream. Yet in the bright sunny kitchen, the idea tugged at her, giving weight to her thoughts. Visions of a small neat space with a counter, a few tables and booths, began to flood furiously through her mind. Looking out the kitchen window, Birdie began to speak out loud.

"I'll need help with getting a lease. Houston can help me with that. I'll need some extra hands. Maybe the church can help me there. Maybe, just maybe, I can get Michael to help clean, paint and do other little things when he gets out of the sanatorium. That way I can keep an eye on him like I promised."

Birdie held out hope Michael would eventually be found innocent and released from the sanatorium. Although there were no promises and even less progress, she had seen firsthand the value in never giving up.

"Look, look, Mommy. Look at me, I'm cooking," Carmen chirped to get her mother's attention.

Lil' Jimmy attempted to pull the bowl away from Carmen and chimed in, "Me too."

"Yes, my sweet sugar pies, you both are. You really are. You both are the perfect little helpers."

Birdie realized this place had been the plan all along.

...we all fly home

How long does it take to forget someone? I've been trying and trying, but over the years fragmented memories keep flooding back. It would be so much better if pictures of our past would come when I was sitting quietly alone and attempting to recall a specific incident. But flashbacks of you come at the most inopportune times. While washing a dish, I see your hand reach under the suds to caress mine. I see a child in a plaid shirt playing in the street and my mind suddenly forms a picture of you as a happy boy running through tall grass in the sunshine. And I didn't even know you then! You spoke of your past so often that it is as real to me as if I were there with you. I was there as you played and got whupped for stealing freshly made jars of blackberry jam from Auntie. Now I can't even forget what I don't know, let alone what I do know. I see everything you did and didn't do as clearly as if it were yesterday.

I am mesmerized by the remembrance of a simple brief exchange, the proximity of our fingertips and the rich smell of salty skin. Little by little the door opens to the bright shining glare of need, want and unabashed desire. I step through afraid and terrified but find the warmth intoxicating. Unable to turn back, I see you standing before me defined and golden. I am consumed and blinded. No respite from a nonexistent shadow. No moist, cool grass or luscious shade to refresh me. I fight now to retreat, and failure drips from my lips. I am proud, vindicated and undone by your treachery and inexplicable crimes that chiseled away at my trust.

I remember those boys back in '41. Those poor black boys, and white boys too for that matter, were caught off guard while planes and ships exploded all around them. Those beautiful American boys who melted into water bubbling with fire and heat. We all ran off to war to fight enemies that had no real faces or bodies. You didn't go, but you fought the war around you just the same. Your skin rubbed raw, irritated from a black man's life, only brought out its pearly luster.

Jimmy, you are so strong in our children's faces. Sometimes I wonder, was I even present? Your aura surrounds them and the air around them is scented with you. It is beautiful because my babies are beautiful. They are as incandescently smooth and golden brown as I see you now: beautiful in my memories. Their soft faces, moist and covered with cookie crumbs, are as clear as the image I have of you that appears as I walk to buy groceries at Findley Farmer's Market. Your face jumps before me along the cracked sidewalk, causing me to ignore a greeting from Mrs. Brown and her daughters as they pass by.

The smell of the market, a mixture of rich coffee, pungent cheeses and freshly butchered meats permeates the air. The strong, sweet and biting aroma triggers a scene from our last meeting in Mt. Sterling. The money was gone. The food was gone. And the babies were crying. The lies that passed through my lips to the landlord about your whereabouts and promises that everything would be paid upon your return. You, showing up and smiling as though time stood still and nothing ever happened. You tickled the children. They smiled and giggled despite the many times you left them with nothing to eat. Instead, at that moment colored in my hate and tremendous love for you, I carried your baton and devised another plan.

You dressed me in wildflower honey dripping through my hair and fingers like Langston's rivers and every musical note God played over your back while you danced. With you I flowed, tumbling in the ebullient waves. Yet, slick and sticky, I followed you. You were my sensa-

tion, a sensation evaporating like chemicals underneath my skin. I can't forget your touch. You live over and over and over again in the trees of my valleys whose branches look like you, wrapping their expansive limbs around air. I plucked blossoms and traipsed at your heels through petals gracing my feet and covering sharp stones. It's sweet bitterness I remember still. Your field held a path. With the back of your hand, you pushed aside long fermented grasses. Your open palm welcomes me to my travels. You knew the road I'd take. I did not, until now.

★ ★ ★ ★ ★

ACKNOWLEDGMENTS

So many stories were interwoven unexpectedly into everyday conversation. Evening walks prompted my mother to tell us stories about rowdy young women spontaneously hopping into cars and hitting the road for an adventure at Cowan Lake. Commentary included colorful asides about the men who were hooked on their beauty and magnificent spirit and would do anything for their smile. A word or phrase in a random newspaper article about a city ordinance or even a change in the weather prompted my mother to laughingly share a story about her dear friend, who was a fiercely independent, self-assured woman who always sparkled with drama. Dinner table discussions brought tales of past get-togethers, pool parties, and nightclub dances with my handsome father and their tony acquaintances. When listening to a record spinning out jazz orchestrations, which were the soundtrack to many a Sunday dinner, my mother would casually reminisce about bohemian Chicago days filled with art and artists and nights held together by close encounters with cool modern jazz royalty, and just the plain fabulousness of the late '40s.

Thank you, Olivia (Ollie Mae) Beamon Chenault, for sharing your colorful stories about your talented women friends who, sometimes through shaking hands, brushed back pressed curls with figure-cutting style to live life to the fullest. Also, for showing me what the power of art and passion can do—overcome any obstacle by helping you to see and create beauty in a beautiful world sometimes cloaked in malice.

These stories, along with vibrant memories of growing up in Cincinnati, Ohio, make up this fictional story. People and places that made a mark in my life are incorporated into this coming-of-age narrative of a woman who dreams of and steadfastly pursues the life she wants for herself and her children during a time shaped by palpitating magic, ripe and bursting with social change.

Utmost respect to my grandfather, Sandy Beamon. I knew you only for a little while but remember your wide smile, filled with sparkling white teeth. I remember the socks filled with pennies that you brought me and my brothers. In our eyes we were rich, as we joyfully counted, piled and rolled them up. I knew you were a Pullman porter and happily imagined fantastic faraway destinations you must have encountered while working on the trains that sped across America. You were loved and cherished. It was only the sound of your name that was befitting of the character in this story.

Thank you to my partners in crime, my brothers, Mark and Kevin. Our distinctive experiences growing up together in Evanston and Walnut Hills have given me provisions for a wealth of stories. As mischievous tykes, we'd strategize how to get an early peek at Christmas presents or steal sips of Tom Collins mix or a bit of brown juice from the liquor cabinet. We'd huddle together at the top of the staircase during house parties to spy on the stylish men and pretty, many-hued, brown-skinned women, who swapped saucy stories that sounded like movie-star dreams while cigarettes dangled from the sides of their mouths or from the tips of cigarette holders. Mark "The Colonel," I miss the debates we had around the dinner table, your devotion to art and music and how you were wildly, unabashedly you.

Thank you to the Metuchen-Edison Area Branch of the National Association for the Advancement of Colored People, (NAACP); the Middlesex County Cultural and Heritage Commission, Board of County Commissioners; and the New Jersey Historical Commission for providing me with the opportunity to interview veterans of World War II and the Korean War. Spending time with these true heroes helped me imagine this slice of time when many African American men and women dedicated themselves to fighting for their country and gave their lives on foreign and domestic soil to fight despite the inequities of racial discrimination.

Thank you to my agent, Kevan Lyon, for guiding me through the process and helping me navigate the intricacies of the business. A huge thank-you to my editor, Lynn Raposo, who saw potential in this manuscript and took a chance on bringing this story to light. I am forever grateful for your guidance and the faith you put in this work. Thank you to the entire Graydon House team for bringing this book to life.

Thank you to my dear family of friends who embraced me, encouraged me and kept me going even when I had doubts.

Thank you to those who came before me and persevered with never-faltering arms and locked fingers to keep us joined together as a family.

Most of all, thank you to the loves of my life: John, my husband and steadfast cheerleader since a bag of Doritos was

LONG GONE, COME HOME

MONICA CHENAULT-KILGORE

Reader's Guide

GRAYDON
HOUSE

1. The book opens with Birdie telling the story of not knowing her biological father, though she called her sisters' father—the decorated veteran, Octavius—her father. What significance does Birdie's understanding of Octavius have to the story?

2. What similarities, if any, did you find between the political climates of the 1930s and 1940s and today's political environment?

3. Segregation plays a big part in fostering the spirit of Black entrepreneurship. How do you think the racial climate contributed to Birdie's drive to become a business owner?

4. Jimmy advised Monroe, the black farmer selling his tobacco to Wrights, not to accept the first offer from Beau and Bo. Should Monroe have taken Jimmy's advice in the hope of getting a fair deal? Why or why not?

5. Why do you think Jimmy began to treat Birdie differently after their wedding?

6. Why do you think Birdie decided to search for Jimmy after Mr. Conroy's murder? How do you think her life would have turned out if she had stayed in Mt. Sterling instead?

7. After Jimmy had been gone for so long, do you think Birdie gave in too easily when she saw him at Junior's?

8. Why did Mama tell Birdie about her history with the Conroys after so much time had passed? Do you think she should have kept it a secret?

9. Do you think Beamon had a hand in Jimmy's death? Why?

10. Why do you think Birdie felt the need to seek out and protect Michael?

11. Why do you think Birdie gave Beamon a second chance?

12. Do you believe Michael killed Beamon?

13. Discuss the relationship Mama, Chicky, Bessa and the Amazons have with Birdie. How did they help shape Birdie's decision-making throughout her journey?

14. What similarities can you find between Birdie's family and your own?

15. How did Birdie change from the beginning to the end of the story?

16. Birdie ended up with a house to call her own. What else do you think contributes to the meaning of the title, *Long Gone, Come Home*, and the opening poem woven through the story, *We All Fly Home*?